A DARK AND STORMY NIGHT

A Dorothy Martin Mystery

Jeanne M. Dams

Jeanne M. Dams

This first world edition published 2010
in Great Britain and in 2011 in the USA by
SEVERN HOUSE PUBLISHERS LTD of
9–15 High Street, Sutton, Surrey, England, SM1 1DF.
Trade paperback edition first published
in Great Britain and the USA 2011 by
SEVERN HOUSE PUBLISHERS LTD.

British Library Cataloguing in Publication Data

Dams, Jeanne M.
  A dark and stormy night.
  1. Martin, Dorothy (Fictitious character)–Fiction.
  2. Women private investigators–England–Fiction.
  3. Americans–England–Fiction. 4. Detective and mystery
  stories.
  I. Title
  813.5'4-dc22

ISBN-13: 978-0-7278-6983-8 (cased)
ISBN-13: 978-1-84751-315-1 (trade paper)

All Severn House titles are printed on acid-free paper.

Severn House Publishers support The Forest Stewardship Council [FSC],
the leading international forest certification organisation. All our titles that
are printed on Greenpeace-approved FSC-certified paper carry the FSC logo.

Typeset by Palimpsest Book Production Ltd.,
Falkirk, Stirlingshire, Scotland.
Printed and bound in Great Britain by
MPG Books Ltd., Bodmin, Cornwall.

The photographer in this book, Ed Walinski, walked in more-or-less uninvited when I thought my cast of characters was complete. He quickly took on many of the endearing traits of the real photographer in my life, my husband (also Polish, also, oddly enough, named Ed).

My husband died, most unexpectedly, while this book was being written. I never had the chance to tell him I was 'putting him in it'. I trust he knows now. So – Ed, my dearest love, this one's for you.

CAST OF CHARACTERS

Dorothy Martin, American, sixty-something, once widowed, now living in England and married to:

Alan Nesbit, English, retired chief constable for county of Belleshire

Lynn and Tom Anderson, American expats living in London, good friends of Dorothy and Alan

Jim and Joyce Moynihan, American expats living in converted thirteenth-century abbey, which is still called Branston Abbey

Mr and Mrs Bates, English, servants to the Moynihans

Ed Walinski, American photographer and writer

Julie and Dave Harris, American. Julie is Joyce Moynihan's sister

Michael Leonev (Mike Leonard), English, dancer

Laurence Upshawe, English, former owner of Branston Abbey, retired physician

Paul Leatherbury, English, the vicar of Branston village

Pat Heseltine, English, female, a solicitor from Branston village and the village

ONE

Anyone who has ever read a Traditional English Mystery ought to remember that a country house weekend can be, as Pogo used to say, fraught. I think I've read every TEM ever written, so I should have known better, but obviously my memory was taking a holiday that afternoon when Lynn called. And even weeks later, when we were nearly at our destination, my doubts were of another nature. 'I don't know, Alan. I'm not so sure this was a good idea.'

My husband, fully occupied with negotiating the narrow, winding lanes of rural Kent, quirked an eyebrow without taking his eyes off the road.

'I can't think what possessed me to say we'd go. We don't even *know* these people. And an old house is bound to be freezing cold in this awful weather, and there'll be stairs everywhere, and my knees aren't really healed yet, and anything could happen to the cats while we're gone, and . . .' Running out of objections, I heaved a histrionic sigh.

Alan is used to my moods. 'We're committed now. And you'll enjoy yourself. You know you love old houses. Not to mention the fireworks for Bonfire Night – Guy Fawkes and all that, you know. Lynn wouldn't have wangled the invitation for us if she hadn't thought the people, *and* the house, were reliable.'

Our good friend Lynn Anderson, an American expat like me, had called from London a month or so ago. 'Dorothy, my *dear*! Tom and I have been travelling and just heard about your operation. How *are* you! How are the knees?'

I'd flexed them cautiously, one at a time. 'Better every day, and they'd be better still if the blasted rain would only stop. I wouldn't say I'd want to run a marathon just yet, but then I never did.' My titanium knees were three months old, and functioning better than I'd dared hope. 'You wouldn't believe how spry I am, compared to when you saw me last. Speaking of which, when are we going to see the two of you again?'

'That's why I called, actually. Tom and I have an Idea.'

I could hear the capital letter, even on the phone. 'What sort of idea?' I asked cautiously. The last time I'd involved myself

in one of the Andersons' Ideas, before Alan and I were married,
I'd ended up in Scotland with a lot of quarrelsome people and
a dead body.

'How would you and Alan like to come with us for a country
house weekend?'

I chuckled. 'As in huntin' and shootin' and musical beds? I
thought all that went out with P.G. Wodehouse. And haven't all
the traditional country houses been turned into B-and-Bs these
days, or given to the National Trust, or something?'

'A lot of them have been, what with death duties and the cost
of living and the impossibility of staffing those enormous places.
But a few are still in private hands, mostly rich foreigners, and
one of them happens to belong to some Americans we know,
business associates of Tom's. We ran into them in Antibes last
week. They bought this huge old pile from someone who had
moved to Australia or some place like that, and they invited us
to come for a weekend next month. It's to be over Bonfire Night,
and they'll have fireworks and all. It's a good-sized house party,
I gather, with some other people staying over, so the minute I
heard about your surgery I thought you'd be needing some R
and R and called the Moynihans to ask if I could bring two
more. They said "the more the merrier".'

I'd hemmed and hawed, but after Lynn assured me the
house, Branston Abbey, was old and interesting, and that the
present owners had installed central heating and an elevator,
I'd said that Alan and I would go. But the rain, which had
kept up for a solid month, had kept my knees aching and my
spirits at low ebb.

The road straightened and widened a bit. Alan looked over at
me and grinned. 'This *was* your idea, you know.'

'Actually it was Lynn's. I should have known better. How do
we know we'll even like these people?'

'Knees still hurting?' said Alan, responding to the real cause
of my ill temper.

'Oh, not much, just stiff and a bit cranky. Like me. Sorry,
Alan. I know I pushed you into this, and I expect I'll have a
wonderful time once we— great God in heaven, can that possibly
be the house?' I pushed back the broad brim of my hat so I could
see better.

Through a stand of trees that had lost some of their leaves, I
could see, on a small rise, a remarkable building. From where
we were it looked like a miniature castle combined with the

Houses of Parliament and a touch of Her Majesty's Prison at Wormwood Scrubs.

Alan pulled the car over as far as he could to the side of the narrow lane and leaned over me, knocking my hat off, to look out my window. 'Well,' he said at last. 'Well.'

'Lynn said it was interesting,' I said faintly.

Alan just shook his head and put the car in gear.

There was another fifteen minutes of twisting lane before we turned into the private drive. It wound for about a mile through a lovely autumn-shaded wood and across a pretty stone bridge, and finally ended up on the gravel forecourt of the house. Up close it wasn't quite so intimidating. For one thing, a lot of the details were hidden around the many odd angles.

Alan took our luggage out of the boot and stood frankly staring at the house. 'I would say,' he said, 'that this is a genuine abbey, late 1400s, that has been treated in rather cavalier fashion over the centuries. Looks like an encyclopedia of architectural styles, from the Late Perpendicular of the original abbey, to Tudor, through Georgian to a few bits of Victorian Gothick, with a hint of Brighton Pavilion thrown in for good measure.'

'A bad case of architectural indigestion, in fact,' I replied rather sourly. 'Reminds me of Brocklesby Hall.' The Hall, a big house near Sherebury, was built in early Victorian times in imitation of a number of styles. It is undeniably impressive, in a nightmarish sort of way.

'Oh, no, no comparison at all. That monstrosity was built all of a piece. It was meant to look like that, God help us. This is organic – it grew, as the needs of the owners changed over the centuries. Good taste here, terrible taste there, but it's genuine. Do you know, Dorothy, I think I'm going to enjoy this weekend. If other amusements pall, we can always go on a treasure hunt for the best and worst bits. I'd swear that gargoyle up there is original fourteenth century, for example.'

'You're showing off. Ten to one you looked it up before we started.' I craned my neck, but my interest in gargoyles is limited, and the wind was picking up. 'I'm sure it's everything you say, but I'm cold and my hat's going to blow off. Can we admire the house from inside, do you think?'

At that moment a door opened and Lynn, effervescent as always, burst out with another woman, middle-aged and running a little, comfortably, to fat. She was dressed in a tweed skirt, a cashmere sweater, and pearls, and the fact that they were a little too new and a little too flawless marked her instantly as our American hostess.

Lynn performed introductions. 'Dorothy, this is Joyce Moynihan. Joyce, Dorothy Martin and Alan Nesbitt.'

'*So* glad to meet you,' said Joyce with a warm smile. 'Lynn's told me all about you both. Dorothy, I love your hat. I wish I looked good in them. Now, dear, you mustn't try the front steps. They're one of our big-deal show pieces, but I'll bet this weather is playing hell with your knees. I had one of mine done a while back, so I know. Anyway, you must be freezing in this awful wind, so if you'll just come with me, there's an entrance to what used to be the servants' hall, and an elevator a few steps beyond. Not exactly the most elegant way to enter the house, but once you've had a nice hot bath you'll be better able to tackle stairs and we'll give you the grand tour. OK?'

Her accent was pure Midwest, speech I hadn't heard in quite a while, and her welcome glowed with that all-embracing cordiality that you get from the nicest Americans. 'OK!' I said, my good spirits restored. I followed her and Lynn into the house, Alan bringing up the rear with our suitcases.

Joyce left us at the elevator. 'I've been running around today like the proverbial chicken, and right now there's a crisis in the kitchen I have to deal with, so I hope you don't mind – Lynn knows the way. As soon as you're rested, come down and have some tea. No special time, just whenever you're ready. See you later.' With a cheerful wave, she was off at a trot in the direction of what I supposed was the kitchen.

'OK, Lynn, you've been here a day already. Clue us in to the set-up,' I said the instant the elevator door closed. 'Why is Madame dealing with kitchen crises? Don't tell me the cook has left in some sort of a huff.'

'My dear, you're *still* fixated back in 1930s novels. Cooks don't leave in huffs nowadays. They're paid enormous salaries and demand exactly the equipment they want, and cook exactly what they please. Most of them are caterers, actually, just coming in for special events. This one is a permanent fixture, lives here with her husband, who's a sort of general factotum – butler cum chauffeur cum handyman. And she's not old and fat and comfortable. Quite the contrary, in fact. Young, *très chic*, cooks divine nouvelle cuisine. Her husband is a hunk – tall, fair, great bones, classic good looks.' Lynn rolled her eyes in a mock swoon as the elevator came to a stop on the second floor, or in English terminology the first floor, the one above the ground floor. She led us down the hall, up a step, to the right, then down a step and around a corner.

'We shall need a trail of breadcrumbs,' said Alan mildly. 'Do you mean to tell me one man looks after this entire sprawling house? Because I won't believe you.'

'Mr Bates – note the *Mister*, please, he doesn't like to be called Bates or whatever his first name is. And he doesn't look after the house at all, except for maintenance jobs, plumbing and electric and so on. There's a cleaning service that comes in for the dusting and scrubbing and all that, and a lawn and garden service for the grounds. Mr Bates supervises – in grand fashion, I might add.'

'And voilà, the servant problem is solved,' I commented, slightly out of breath. 'It must cost a small fortune.'

'Probably, but Jim Moynihan still has a biggish fortune, so it's all right. And here we are, finally. I had Joyce put you in one of the Tudor bedrooms. I thought you'd like sleeping where Queen Elizabeth might very well have slept, once upon a very long time ago.' She opened the door.

'QE One, that would be— oh!' My first sight of the room took my breath away.

This wasn't fake Tudor, 'stockbroker Tudor' as the English sneeringly used to call it. This was the real thing, a room created or at least redecorated when the first Elizabeth sat on the throne. The walls were panelled in carved oak, the linenfold panelling so often seen in the stately homes I had visited. Everything else was carved, too – the fireplace in stone, the ceiling in elaborate plasterwork. The casement windows had tiny diamond panes, and the floor was made of wide oak planks darkened to near-black over the centuries.

'Wow!' I said brilliantly.

Lynn grinned. 'There are no words, are there? And this,' she said, opening a concealed door in one corner, 'is not the priest's hole or the powder closet – though it certainly may once have been one or the other – but your very own bathroom. Joyce and Jim remodelled them all – after *months* of delays getting planning permission, I might add – and all done in the very latest American-style plumbing. Yours has a whirlpool bath, *with* steps to get into it.'

I sank into a chair by the fire, which was blazing away. 'I've fallen into a dream of paradise. Don't anybody wake me up.'

'Told you you'd like it,' said Lynn triumphantly, and left us to get settled.

I walked over to the window. Alan came to stand beside me, and we looked out on to one of the most beautiful landscapes I've ever seen. A broad stone terrace next to the house gave way to a sloping lawn, the kind of lawn I'd never seen anywhere but in England – lush, green, and perfectly smooth. I remembered reading, somewhere, someone's recipe for the perfect lawn: You plant grass, and then mow and roll it for four hundred years.

The rain had stopped for a bit, mercifully, and the clouds had thinned enough to let colours assert themselves. To one side, flower gardens were still brilliant with chrysanthemums and asters, though the roses were getting sparse. In the middle distance, perhaps a hundred yards from the house, shrubs and a pond gave way to taller trees, oak and ash and some I didn't recognize. A path wound through the plantings down to a silver river on which a few swans floated, pale and graceful, their feathers ruffled now and then by the rising wind.

'"This scepter'd isle",' my husband quoted softly, '"... this other Eden, demi-paradise . . . this precious stone set in the silver sea . . ."'

'Mmm. Or, as we crass Americans have been known to put it, this is what God would do if He had money. No wonder the Moynihans love it here. The view alone is worth however many million pounds they paid for the place. And Joyce is a perfect dear. You were right, Alan – as is your irritating habit. I'm going to have a good time here.'

I took a long, luxurious bath in the wonderful tub. I hadn't been able to get in and out of a regular tub in ages, what with the bad knees, so I was especially grateful for the steps.

'You're going to turn to a prune, love,' Alan said finally. 'Besides, tea awaits, and I'm feeling rather peckish.'

So I reluctantly got out, dressed, and found my cane, and we set out in search of a staircase to take us down to tea.

Alan has an excellent bump of direction, which is a good thing, because I have virtually none. Give me a map and I can find anything. Without it I'm hopeless. I paused in the hallway. 'This way?' I said tentatively, pointing to the left.

'No, to the right, I'd think. We didn't pass any stairs on our way from the lift, so it must be on down the corridor.' And of course he was right – again. The next little jog brought us to a somewhat more modern part of the house and a grand staircase down to the entrance hall. 'Georgian?' I ventured, looking at pillars and pilasters, marble and polished stone.

'Well done, my dear! Basically Georgian, modified a trifle so as to blend in with the rest of the house. I imagine this part was redone when a particularly prosperous owner began to entertain largely, and wanted to show off. The place must have an interesting history, though the Internet didn't mention much.'

'Aha! You *did* look it up! Well, I'll just bet our hosts are dying to give us all the details. I tell everybody about our house, and it's not at all in the same league.' Monkswell Lodge, the house where Alan and I live in Sherebury, was built in the early 1600s as a gatehouse for the man who bought what used to be Sherebury Abbey before Henry VIII dissolved the monasteries. It's a wonderful house and we love it, but it's always been a modest dwelling. Branston Abbey was a showplace.

The stairs were broad and shallow, easy even for my not-quite-perfect knees. They were feeling better, anyway, after my bath. The house was, true to Lynn's word, filled with a gentle warmth that spoke of efficient central heating, and when we followed the sound of voices to what was probably called the drawing room, we found the fire lit and the temperature almost too warm. Several people were gathered in the room, chatting and drinking various beverages.

'There you are,' called Joyce. 'Found your way, I see. I keep meaning to have maps of the house printed up, but I keep forgetting. It really isn't complicated, anyway, once you figure out the basic plan. So sit and have some tea – or whatever you'd prefer – and let me introduce everybody.'

Evidently the kitchen crisis had been solved. The meal laid out on several trays was an elaborate, Ritz-style spread of the kind I didn't know anyone ever did in private homes these days. Alan and I sat down next to Lynn and Tom, and I looked dubiously at the array of sandwiches and scones and cakes. 'It's all right, D.,' said Tom, *sotto voce*. 'Dinner isn't till eight. Eat all you want.'

Well, I wasn't going to do that. I engage in a perpetual struggle with my love of carbohydrates. Besides, I'd lost some weight after my surgery, and I didn't want to gain it all back. But I accepted a cup of tea from my hostess – 'Yes, milk and two lumps, please' – and took a couple of tiny sandwiches and a scone. Lunch was a distant memory, and I was truly hungry.

'Now, let me introduce you to everyone,' said Joyce, when

we'd eaten and drunk our fill. 'You know Tom and Lynn. And this is my husband, Jim. Jim, this is Dorothy Martin and her husband Alan Nesbitt. We'll all have to behave ourselves this weekend; Alan's a retired police VIP.'

My husband, who was a chief constable for many years, was used to this kind of remark and took it with equanimity. Jim Moynihan smiled and hoisted a teacup in salute, as another, very graceful and good-looking man approached.

'And I, my dear lady, can*not* wait another moment to meet you. Michael Leonev, at your service.' He pronounced it Mee-kha-ail, but his accent reminded me of the Beatles and his hair was blond. I must have looked sceptical, because he took my hand, kissed it, and grinned. 'Between you and me, luv, Mike Leonard from Liverpool, but all the best dancers are Russian, so—'

'Royal Ballet,' I said, a faint memory surfacing. '*Swan Lake*. I saw the reviews, though I didn't get to town to see a performance.'

'Yes, well, next time I hope to do Siegfried, but Von Rothbart isn't a bad role. More acting than dancing, actually, and usually done by someone *much* older.' Mike, or Michael, frowned, which was unwise. Lines appeared that made me wonder if he was really too young to play the evil sorcerer, but then he gave me a winsome smile and looked like a boy again.

Joyce deftly disengaged us and led us to the two men sitting in front of the fire, who rose as we approached. The smaller one extended his hand. 'Ed Walinski. Glad to meet you.'

'You're American!' I said, pleased. He looked the part, too. He was dressed like most of the men in slacks and a sweater, but the clothes looked more Brooks Brothers than Savile Row. Of modest height, he nevertheless looked as if he could hold his own against most challengers. At the moment, though, his round face was creased in a smile.

'Of Polish descent, with a touch of Irish and some German somewhere. And that's about as American as they come!'

'Ed's going to do a book about this house,' said Joyce with obvious pride. 'We're very excited, because no one's ever done a proper history of the place, and certainly not an illustrated one.'

'Oh, how stupid of me!' I slapped my forehead. 'You're *that* Walinski – the photographer! I've admired your work for years, and your narratives are just as good as your pictures. Are you going to take pictures of the fireworks?'

'Sure! Fireworks over that roofline – wow! And I can afford to waste shots – I brought tons of film.'

'You're not a convert to digital, then?'

'Yeah, for some things. Snapshots, Bertha-in-front-of-the-Parthenon, that kind of junk. And I use it for test shots, to make absolutely sure the picture's set up right. I'll use it for the preliminary house shots a lot, because that's going to be tricky, particularly those gargoyles. I may have to spend the whole weekend just figuring out how to get up there for a good shot.'

'No, you won't,' said Joyce firmly. 'Aside from the pyrotechnics, you're going to spend the weekend having a good time and getting to know the house a little. And Mr Upshawe, here, is going to help. Dorothy and Alan, meet Laurence Upshawe, the former owner of Branston Abbey.'

Upshawe, tall, thin, graying at the temples and looking almost too much like an English landowner, gravely shook our hands.

'Oh, my, how could you ever bear to sell such a wonderful place?' I gushed, and then could have kicked myself. If the man had had to part with his ancestral home to pay death duties or something awful like that . . .

But he smiled. 'You mustn't think it was a frightful sacrifice, or anything of that sort. Actually, you know, I didn't grow up here, and I was never terribly fond of the house. Branston Abbey belonged to my father's cousin. My father inherited it because his cousin's son died quite young, and Father was the next in line. The estate was entailed then, you see, and Father was thrilled when it came to him. He had visited the place often as a child, and he loved every gable and gargoyle with quite an unreasonable passion. But entail's been done away with, so when my father left the house to me, I was free to do with it as I liked.'

'And what you liked was to sell it to the Moynihans and go to – Australia, was it?'

'New Zealand,' he said with the patient air of one who grows tired of explaining the differences between two widely separated countries. 'But in point of fact, I sold Branston Abbey—'

He was interrupted when the door to the room was flung open and a couple marched in, puffing and stamping and complaining noisily.

The woman wore several layers of sweaters. The top one looked expensive, as did her wool slacks, but the net effect was lumpy and shapeless. The man was dressed in a red plaid flannel shirt over a rather dirty yellow sweatshirt, over a black turtleneck, with goodness knows what underneath that. His pants were liberally splashed with mud, as were his L.L. Bean boots. He had in one corner of his mouth a large cigar from which issued a cloud of foul smoke.

'Holy shit, tea you're drinking!' he roared, removing the cigar for a moment. 'That stuff's for old grannies and pansies. Gimme some Scotch, Jim. It's cold enough out there to freeze the balls off a brass monkey. Why anybody lives in this godforsaken country's beyond me, let alone in a draughty old wreck like this. Cheers, everybody.' He drank down at a gulp half the stiff drink Jim had silently handed him, while the rest of us sat dumb.

Joyce cleared her throat. 'Dorothy and Alan, my sister Julie Harrison and her husband Dave.'

TWO

The party broke up quickly after that. Alan left with the photographer, after getting my assurance that I'd much rather the two of them toured the house without me. The dancer, whose eyebrows had risen nearly into his hair, did an elaborate stage shrug and performed a neat series of pirouettes out the door. Upshawe murmured something inaudible and drifted away, and I had only a moment to wish I'd gone with Alan and the photographer, after all, when Tom took me on one arm and Lynn by the other. 'The ladies are tired, Joyce. I'm sure you'll excuse us.'

'I'm not in the least tired,' I said when we were out of there. 'But thanks for rescuing me. I couldn't figure out how to escape tactfully.'

Lynn sighed. 'Tact isn't really necessary anymore. Joyce is used to Dave and the effect he has on civilized people.'

'And she's thoroughly fed up with him,' added Tom. 'Are you up to the stairs, D., or do you want to use the lift? I warn you, you have to go back through the drawing room to get there.'

'The stairs, by all means. They're not at all steep, and up is always easier than down, and I wouldn't go back in there if the alternative was climbing to the top of the Statue of Liberty. Is he always like that, or is he drunk?'

'Not drunk yet, probably, but he soon will be,' said Tom. 'And yes, he's always like that, drunk or sober. I met him something over twenty-four hours ago, and the acquaintance has already been about a week too long. And his wife is just as bad.'

'Oh?' I said. 'She didn't say a word in there.'

'She will,' said Lynn, and I had seldom heard her sound so cool. 'She's a whiner, not a blowhard. She'll be launched by now on a steady trickle of complaint about weak tea, dry sandwiches, the wrong kind of jam tarts, and hard chairs. I'm sure she'll throw in a few jabs about the village, too. The essential message will be, if it's English, it's inferior. Dave agrees, but louder.'

'So why did they come to visit, if they hate it so much?' I had reached the top of the stairs and could stop concentrating on making my knees do what they were supposed to.

'We haven't figured that out yet,' said Tom. 'You still need an arm?'

I shook my head.

'We thought at first,' said Lynn, 'that they came to sponge on Joyce and Jim. But Dave keeps telling everyone how rich he is, how he could afford to retire young because he was smarter in business than everybody else. So either he's lying or there's some other reason they're here. I don't know how Joyce and Jim put up with them.'

'Jim isn't going to, much longer,' said Tom. 'I overheard him—' he looked around and lowered his voice, 'talking to Joyce earlier this afternoon, and he's about had it. Says they can stay through the weekend, because of the big doings on the fifth, but after that he's kicking them out. I think he'll do it, too. I got the idea, from the tone of the conversation, that the two sisters have never hit it off, and one reason the Moynihans moved to England was to get away from the Harrisons. So I suspect he'll happily give them their walking papers.'

We had reached our bedroom. 'Let's go in and have some privacy,' I suggested. 'I guess there aren't servants listening in every corner, like in the old books, but I'd feel more comfortable behind a good solid door.'

We settled in front of the fire and Tom found some sherry in a cupboard. 'Good hosts,' he said, pouring us each a glass. 'They think of everything for a guest's comfort.'

'Dorothy, it's pathetic,' said Lynn. 'Joyce and Jim are so proud of their house. They've put so much time and effort into fixing it up – and money, my word, tons of money. Everything was to look authentic, but at the same time be modern and labour-saving.

They went so far as to take out a perfectly good Aga, because it was an old solid-fuel one Joyce wasn't sure she could make work right, and put in a state-of-the-art electric one – but specially designed to look just like the old ones. They wanted this first big party to be perfect. I gather they've been planning every detail for weeks. And then a couple of days ago sister Julie barged in with her impossible husband and went about alienating everybody in the house. Joyce was in a rage this morning over Dave's criticisms of the house. He doesn't know a thing about the subject, but that doesn't keep him from holding forth. And Julie saw Mike yesterday making eyes at Laurence—'

'I forget who Laurence is.'

'Upshawe, who used to own the place. Such a nice, easy-going man, and absolutely brilliant – he's a retired surgeon. And good-looking, even if he's not very young. Anyway, Julie saw them, and made the most awful remarks. I won't even repeat them, they're so foul, but let's just say they represented her views about gays, foreigners, dancers, and the English in general. And Laurence, poor dear, isn't in the least interested, but he's kind, and didn't tell Mike to go peddle his papers. But Julie went straight to Joyce to tell her all about it.'

'I'll bet she just laughed. She looks like the unflappable sort.'

'Well, she didn't take it seriously – not in one sense. But she was upset all the same, because of Julie's sheer malice. Julie actually tried to get Joyce to kick Mike out of the house for "flagrantly immoral behaviour".'

'When all he did was look at the man?'

'That's all. And half of that might have been acting. Mike's a trifle . . . dramatic.'

Some of my sherry went down the wrong way. 'Yes, I'd noticed,' I said when I could speak again. 'A necessity in his profession, I'd have thought. And anyway, who cares, nowadays? Well, it's all going to make for an uncomfortable weekend. I wonder if we—'

'Oh, Dorothy, *don't* think of leaving! For one thing, Tom and I need someone to talk to if everyone else stops speaking to anyone. For another, Joyce is almost at her wits' end, and you and Alan can be counted on to behave yourselves. Besides, everyone is interesting except the Horrible Harrisons.'

'I'd say Dave Harrison was interesting,' said Tom thoughtfully. 'In the sense of the old Chinese curse.'

'It's a strange mixture, certainly,' I said, relaxing as the sherry took hold. 'For an English country-house weekend, there's a remarkable shortage of Brits. Let's see.' I began counting on my fingers 'Two, four, six, seven Americans – no, eight, I forgot Walinski, the famous photographer – and just three Englishmen, the dancer – Mike – and Laurence Upshawe, and Alan. Oh, and the Bateses.'

Alan came in just then. 'Someone taking my name in vain? I'll have one of those, Tom, if you're pouring.'

Tom poured Alan's sherry and then went to put more wood on the fire, and I stretched my legs out to unkink my knees. 'So did you enjoy your tour of the house, love? You weren't very long about it.'

Alan took a sip of his sherry. 'The tour was curtailed by Mr Harrison, whom we encountered in the oldest part of the house, the only remaining part of the original Abbey. He imparted a great deal of misinformation about the building materials, style, and construction methods of the period, contrasting them unfavourably to the . . . er . . . dwellings he was responsible for building before he retired from business. I believe he called them "manufactured homes". It seems an odd term.'

I shook my head in disbelief. 'They're houses built in trailer factories, using many of the same materials and methods. They aren't bad-looking, some of them, but they tend to crumple like paper in bad storms like tornadoes and hurricanes. The mind boggles at the idea of comparing them with a building that's stood for – what? – seven hundred years.'

'That, in rather more colourful language, was what Walinski said. The disagreement became rather heated, whereupon Walinski called Harrison a damned idiot and punched him in the nose.' Alan tossed a handful of cashews into his mouth.

'He *hit* him?' I said in disbelief. 'What did you do?'

'The man didn't seem to be in need of medical attention. So I shook Walinski's hand – gently, in case he had injured it on the idiot's face – and found my way back here.'

Lynn broke into song. '"Hooray and hallelujah, you had it comin' to ya",' she carolled. 'I mean he had it coming, but it doesn't rhyme that way. Anyway –' she raised her glass – 'here's to Ed Walinski and his strong right hand.'

Alan grinned. 'I might have done it myself if Walinski hadn't got his licks in first. More sherry, anyone?'

After Lynn and Tom left, I put my feet up for a few minutes with ice-packs on the knees, which were protesting a little about recent activity. But I was restless, and it still wasn't anywhere near time to get ready for dinner. 'Do you suppose,' I said to Alan, who was absorbed in *The Times* crossword puzzle, 'that it's safe to wander around and explore a little? I really, really don't want to run into either of the Horrible Harrisons.'

'He's probably retired with aspirin and a case of the sulks. That blow to the nose was painful, and when he fell he hit his head against an oak door jamb. As to his wife, I couldn't say.'

'I think I'll chance it. Coming with me?'

'Thanks, I'll finish this, if you can cope on your own. What on earth can they mean by "He touches with a pot, pleadingly"?'

I thought a minute. 'How many letters?'

'Ten, beginning with a P., I think.'

'Eureka! I finally got one. Panhandler.'

'Hmm. It fits, but what's a panhandler when it's at home?'

'A beggar. An American term. Pot equals pan. Touch equals handle, and also ask for money, and the whole thing means pleading. Ta-da!'

I'm no good at the English 'cryptic' crosswords, so I was ridiculously pleased to have solved a clue Alan couldn't. He grinned and saluted as I picked up my cane and left the room.

I walked, carefully, down the beautiful Georgian staircase and turned right, since I had seen nothing of that side of the house, the oldest part, if my vague idea of the layout was correct. Leading out of the entrance hall was a lovely panelled door, with an elaborate cornice over it and a massive bronze door knob. I turned it, pushed the door back, and stepped into a different world.

This had surely been part of the cloister of the old abbey. It was now an enclosed hallway, dimly lit. Arched windows on my left looked out on the gloomy November afternoon. Darkness had fallen early, as it is wont to do in the autumn in these northern latitudes. (The coming of short days still catches me by surprise in my adopted country. Because of England's mild climate, Americans tend to forget that all of the UK lies farther north than any point of the Lower Forty-Eight.)

By the light of a lamp outside, I could see through the diamond panes the shadows of trees and bushes, tossed fitfully back and forth by the increasing wind. Above me, the fan-vaulted roof stretched ahead perhaps forty feet to another doorway, this one pure Gothic, with a pointed arch.

On my right, small but sturdy buttresses supported a wall

pierced by two similar arched doorways. The door in the nearer one was slightly ajar, and through it I heard voices.

The male voice was loud and bombastic. I would have recognized Dave Harrison anywhere. I hadn't heard Julie speak, but I assumed the petulant female voice was hers. Alan had guessed wrong. They were up and about, and in foul moods, and their bitter quarrel was getting closer to the door.

I loathe embarrassing encounters, but all the escape routes were too far away for a person with healing knees, so I took the coward's way out. Sliding behind one of the buttresses to wait in the shadows until they had left, I hoped devoutly that they wouldn't glance my way.

'. . . why we had to come to this pile of garbage in the first place! There isn't even a TV in our room. And the food!'

They were in the doorway now, their shadows bulking large in the light from the room.

'Well, we didn't come to watch TV,' said Dave, 'so just shut up about it. And you could stand to lose a few pounds, babe.'

'Me!' Julie's voice rose to nearly a shriek. 'What about that beer belly of yours? And you put away Jim's Scotch just fine. With no ice, yet. God, I hate this place.'

'Keep your voice down! Do you want your sister to hear? You came, sweet cakes, for a loving family visit, and don't you forget it. And we're staying till we get what we want. And till I get even with that dumb Polack!' The last came out in a vicious whisper, as they moved past me up the hallway toward the main house.

Once I heard the connecting door open and close, I breathed again and moved on down the corridor. But as I explored the old abbey rooms, I wondered mightily. The Harrisons could have bickered and complained anywhere. Why had they chosen Branston Abbey?

THREE

I had been unsure about the clothes I would need for the weekend. 'Are we going to have to dress for dinner?' I had asked Alan, and he'd been mildly amused.

'Only as formally as you'd dress for a meal at a good restaurant. I shall certainly not take my dress suit.'

So it was a 'little black dress' I wore that first night, with a pair of small diamond earrings Alan had given me one Christmas, and a string of pearls. I regretfully left my frivolous black cocktail hat in its box. I may be the last hat wearer in the UK, barring the Queen, but there are limits to what one can get by with in a private house.

We gathered in the drawing room for a pre-dinner drink, and my hopes that the Harrisons would absent themselves were immediately dashed. There they were, standing by the fireplace. Julie's dress was of gorgeous dark green satin, well-cut, but not quite concealing those extra pounds Dave had mentioned. Still, she looked quite nice, and would have looked nicer if her face had not been set in a scowl. Dave, with a large Band-Aid across his nose and two black eyes beginning to develop, was waving a glass of Scotch around as he lectured Jim Moynihan on something or other. Plainly the drink was not his first since he left the cloister. His speech was slurred and his discourse rambling enough to be incomprehensible.

'You said he hit his head,' I said to Alan in an undertone. 'Should he be drinking?'

'Probably not. Are you going to tell him so?'

I rolled my eyes. 'Someone should. But no, I'm not brave enough. Besides, if he passes out he'll be a lot less trouble for everybody.'

'The sentiment does not do you credit, love. I agree with it wholeheartedly.' He handed me a glass of sherry from a tray, and took one himself.

The slurred voice rose higher. 'Be damned if I will! Came to this fuckin' place and I'm not goin' home till I get—'

His wife's shrill voice rose over his. 'Shut up, Dave! You're drunk and sounding like an ass!' She removed the glass from his hand and threw its contents into his face.

He turned to her, his face alarmingly red, his mouth opening and closing rather like a fish. Jim took a large handkerchief from his pocket and handed it to Dave. 'You'd better mop up, pal. Then we'll send a tray up to your room. Julie, you'll look after him, I'm sure.'

Julie looked rebellious for a moment, then shrugged. 'He'll pass out in a minute or two, anyway. And be better company, at that, than this mouldy bunch.' She stalked out of the room.

'Mr Bates, would you help Mr Harrison to his room, please?' Joyce took over smoothly. 'I'm afraid he's not feeling very well. And if Mrs Bates could prepare a dinner tray for them?'

It seemed as if the entire room breathed a collective sigh of relief as the butler seized Dave in a firm grip and 'helped' him out of the room. Certainly Joyce took a deep breath before she smiled and addressed us all.

'Sorry about that,' she said. 'Dave drinks a little more than he should, from time to time, but I'm sure he'll be fine. Now some of you haven't met our other dinner guests. Dorothy, Alan, this is the vicar, Paul Leatherbury. And this lovely lady is, believe it or not, our village solicitor, Pat Heseltine. Pat, meet Dorothy Martin and her husband Alan Nesbitt.'

Pat Heseltine resembled my idea of an English solicitor approximately as a peacock resembles a mouse. Perhaps fifty, she still had a perfect figure and smooth, creamy skin. She was poured into a little gold number that must have set her back hundreds and hundreds of pounds. It set off her flaming red hair beautifully. She wore no jewellery, and didn't need it.

My dear husband's eyes widened. He took her hand and held it, in my opinion, just a moment too long.

'Good evening,' I said, with a smile that, despite my best efforts, was a little stiff. I trust my husband completely, but this woman could tempt a celibate saint.

'Don't worry, luv,' said the vision in a voice of whiskey and honey, winking at me. 'They all do it – doesn't mean a thing.'

I responded with a meaningless smile and turned with some polite remark to the vicar. We were interrupted by a strident, discordant clamour from outside the room. I nearly dropped my sherry glass, and all conversation stopped.

Joyce looked mischievous. 'The dinner gong, ladies and gentlemen. I believe dinner is served!'

There were no empty places at the table. Evidently the efficient Mr Bates had removed those assigned to the Horrible Harrisons. I did a quick count as we walked into the room and nudged Alan. 'Eleven of us at table,' I whispered. 'There would have been thirteen with the Harrisons. Isn't there some kind of English superstition about that?'

'Then it's a good thing they're not here. For more than one reason.' He grinned at me before we were separated by our hostess.

In the old days husbands and wives were never allowed to sit together at table. The Moynihans were sticking to tradition, so I found myself, quite happily, between Ed Walinski and Mr Upshawe, with Lynn, the vicar, and Mike Leonard across from us, and the Andersons, Pat Heseltine, and Alan scattered about on either side. I wasn't altogether happy that Pat and Alan were seated next to each other, but the woman had to sit somewhere, I supposed. Given our uneven numbers, there were too many men sitting next to each other. Jim Moynihan sat at the head of the table and Joyce at the foot.

For a little while I had no attention to spare for anything except my dinner. If I'd thought about it at all, I had expected decent food, but not like this. We started with a consommé julienne, none of whose ingredients had ever seen a tin. The fish was a morsel of perfectly cooked sole Bonne Femme, followed by chicken in some sort of creamy cheese sauce, accompanied by perfectly cooked vegetables. I had got to the salad course before I became interested in any conversation that didn't involve passing the butter or accepting a little more wine.

'I know almost nothing about the history of this amazing house,' I said to Mr Upshawe, 'except that it was obviously once an abbey. Did your family live in it for a long time?'

'Well, my father was the first one in my immediate family to live here,' he said, 'and his cousin's family not for very long, in relative terms. They bought the house in . . . 1843, I think it was – when the Branston line ran out. Now the Branstons *had* lived here for centuries, literally. Henry VIII gave the original Lord Branston the Abbey property, and incidentally the title, for "services rendered to the crown". Nobody knows exactly what those services were, but I gather tradition tended to believe they were of a salacious nature. Old Henry was a bit of a Jack the Lad, as I expect you know.'

'What's a "Jack the Lad"?' asked the photographer.

'Oh, sorry. Let's see . . . a rip, a roué, a rogue.'

'A Royal Rascal,' Ed contributed.

'In short,' I said, 'a man who does exactly as he pleases. Which would fit Henry, all right. Although all I really know about him, come to think of it, is that he had six wives and murdered two of them.'

'Please! Beheaded them. *Judicial* murder.'

'Oh, yes. I stand corrected. It does make a tremendous difference. Especially to the victim.'

'Who should have tried to keep her head,' Ed put in. I was beginning to warm to this man.

Laurence Upshawe laughed and held up his hands. 'I'm not

here to defend Henry. He would need far better counsel for the defence than I. And how did we get started on him anyway?'

'The house,' I prompted. 'He gave it to Lord Branston for services rendered.'

'Oh, yes. In fifteen-something. And it remained in Branston hands for three-hundred-odd years, until there were no Branstons left and my great-great – I forget how many greats – uncle bought it. By that time it was pretty much the hodgepodge you see now, except for the Gothick and Regency touches, which were added by the first couple of Upshawe generations.'

'For which,' put in Joyce Moynihan, 'they are either blessed or cursed, depending on whether you prefer your architecture pure or fun.'

'"Pure" was past praying for at that point,' said Upshawe with a chuckle. 'The old chaps who built the place wouldn't have known it by the time my family took possession.'

'The monks didn't approve of such monk-ey shines?' That was Ed. We all groaned appreciatively.

'The resident ghosts apparently took it in their stride,' said Upshawe amiably. 'If ghosts can be said to have a stride.'

'In their glide,' suggested Ed.

'Exactly. But the County didn't like us, ghosts to the contrary notwithstanding. We were called the "Upstarts" for years, my father told me, and even now I think there's some feeling in the village that we're incomers. In any case, the Vicar could probably tell you a great deal more about the history of the house than I can.'

'Then the vicar's the man I need,' said Ed. He looked across the table, but the vicar was deep in conversation with Jim Moynihan. 'Tomorrow,' said Ed.

'I want to know about the ghosts.' I turned back to Upshawe.

'Well, again, I don't actually know much about them. No one's ever seen them, so far as I know. Certainly I never have. I will admit there's an odd feeling about some of the rooms occasionally, especially in the cloisters and on the second floor. That is, the third floor to you Americans. We never used those bedrooms much, for some reason. And there used to be a story in the village about strange noises, but I don't know that I give much credence to it. I'm something of an agnostic when it comes to ghosts.'

'But surely, in a house this old, where people have given birth, and died, and lived happily and unhappily for centuries, there would be plenty of reasons for restless spirits, or at least an atmosphere,' I argued. 'I'm inclined to believe in ghosts. In England, anyway. Not in America so much. We're too young a country to have really old houses. Partly because we tear them down before they have a chance to turn into something amazing like this place.'

'"Amazing" is the word, certainly. Some would call the whole place a travesty,' said Upshawe apologetically.

'Interesting, though. You gotta admit there's nothing boring about this heap,' said Ed, serious for a change. 'I can't wait to get started with the pictures tomorrow. Something different, everywhere you look.'

Alan left off his conversation with the delectable Pat to say, 'Dorothy and I may go with you, if you've no objection. We thought of going on a sort of treasure hunt for architectural oddities. I agree with you about the house, Ed, but it wouldn't appeal to a purist.'

'Nor,' said Mike, the dancer, with a malicious smile, 'to our American visitors the Hor— the Harrisons. One does hope their views do not prevail. I heard Mr Harrison say, this afternoon, that the entire structure – "the whole damned place" was the charming way he put it – should be levelled, and a modern resort hotel built on the site. The better, one gathers, to attract tourists, despoil the countryside, ruin the village, and make millions.'

'My brother-in-law's opinions,' said Joyce calmly, 'are often somewhat . . . peculiar. Jim and I usually pay no attention. This is, in any case, a listed building, and therefore untouchable. You cannot imagine the hoops we had to jump through just to get planning permission to modernize the bathrooms, and add a few. More wine, anyone?'

We were nearly all suppressing yawns by the time we'd finished an amazing orange soufflé and refused (most of us) Stilton and biscuits. Those who cared for after-dinner coffee had it in front of the drawing room fire, with drinks available for those who wanted a nightcap.

The miserable weather had returned, with rain falling in torrents. I turned to the vicar, who sipped his pale whiskey and soda in the armchair next to me. 'You're going to get terribly wet going home, if this keeps up,'

'I've accepted Mrs Moynihan's kind invitation to stay the night,' he said placidly, 'as, I believe, has Miss Heseltine. In the words of the immortal W.C. Fields, "It ain't a fit night out for man nor beast".' His English-accented version of the famous line set me into such a fit of laughter that I developed hiccups and had to be slapped on the back.

No one lingered long. It was a night for snuggling down under the covers, and besides, 'We're all afraid the Horrible Harrisons will show up again,' said Lynn in an undertone as she and Tom left the drawing room with Alan and me.

I yawned. 'I think Dave's out for the count, but you're right. The mere possibility casts a pall. Let's just hope his hangover is bad enough to keep him in bed late tomorrow.'

'Amen,' said Alan piously, and we trooped upstairs to bed.

FOUR

I woke much later, feeling far too warm. The fire in the fireplace had died out long ago, but the duvet felt stifling.

Drat it all, I hadn't had this bad a hot flash in years! This was unexpected, and unpleasant. I didn't want to freeze Alan, but I had to have some relief. I crept out of bed, went to the window, and pushed it open.

The wind rushed in, billowing the curtains and knocking over a small lamp on the table by the window. No wonder it was hot in the room! It wasn't me – the rain had stopped, and the outside temperature must have risen twenty degrees since we'd gone to bed.

Odd.

I got back into bed, pushed the duvet away, and curled up covered only by the sheet.

Sleep wouldn't come. The wind seemed to strengthen every minute. It howled around the corners of the old house, battered against the walls, flung itself down the chimney. The house creaked and cracked, and so did the trees outside.

I have never liked wind storms. I can enjoy a good thunderstorm, but high winds make me nervous. I put the pillow over my head, but I could still hear the wind, could still feel it, too, blowing against the sheet, chilly, chillier . . .

For heaven's sake! Now it was cold again – and raining again. Impatiently, I got out of bed again and forced the window closed.

'Can't sleep, love?' Alan sounded pretty wide awake, too.

'It's the wind. You know I hate wind. And I was too warm, but now I'm cold. The weather is behaving very oddly. It's . . . unsettling.'

'Put in your ear plugs and come back to bed. This is a strong old house. It can withstand the wind. There, now, isn't that better?' He pulled me close, as if to shut out the wind and the storm. I relaxed and after a time I slept.

'*What* was that?' I sat straight up in bed, my heart pounding furiously. My dream of gunshots was still clinging to my consciousness. The loudest dream-shot had wakened me. In my dream it had been a cannon. But the bangs and booms continued into wakefulness, sounding loudly over the howls of the wind.

I didn't know what time it was, though it felt like the middle of the night. The room was pitch dark, but I could hear that Alan was awake, too, and getting out of bed.

'Alan, what's happening? What's all the noise?'

'It's the wind, blowing things about. Devil of a wind, I've never known one like it. That last crash was something hitting the house, something big. I'm going down to see.'

'Not and leave me here by myself, you're not!' I fumbled for my slippers as I reached for the bedside lamp.

Nothing happened. The switch clicked uselessly.

I have a recurring nightmare about waking in the middle of the night and trying, frantically, to turn on a light. I try every lamp, every wall switch. There is no light.

My nightmare had just come true. 'Alan, wait!' I shouted in panic. 'Alan!'

'I'm here.' His voice, raised over the tumult, was calm, and calming. 'I'm looking for the torch. Do you remember where you put it?'

I tried to remember what I'd done with the flashlight we always take along when we travel. 'I think it's on the table on your side of the bed. Or in the drawer, maybe.'

An interval. The wind howled, and when it let up for a second or two, we could hear voices.

Light, blessed light. Alan pointed the flashlight at me and nearly blinded me. 'Sorry, love. I wasn't sure where you were. Let's go down.'

I put on my robe and followed him out the door.

Other lights were dancing in the corridor. Ed Walinski and

Mike Leonard came out of their rooms. Tom and Lynn followed closely in their wake, with Alan behind them while I brought up the rear.

Our host and hostess, sketchily clothed, were already in the hall. 'It's the oak!' Joyce screamed over the wind. 'We think it fell on the house!'

They rushed to the door into the old abbey, and we followed, while other guests arrived in various states of undress, carrying flashlights or candles.

The Moynihans were having trouble pushing open the door to the old cloister. Tom and Alan helped them shove and kick and shoulder it part-way open, and then shone their lights on what lay beyond.

Branches and leaves. Broken glass, splintered wood, dust, water.

The wind rushed through the open door, bringing rain and debris with it, extinguishing the candles. Jim Moynihan withstood it for a moment, then moved away and let the door slam shut. He took his wife in his arms. Tears were streaming down her face.

'It's OK, sweetie,' Jim said gently. 'Lucky it happened there and not in the main house. Nobody's sleeping in the cloister. Nobody's hurt, just the house, and we want to keep it that way. It's dangerous to go out there until the storm lets up. Come away, hon. Nothing we can do till morning.' He stroked her hair. 'We'll see what the damage is then, and start doing something about it.'

Joyce was still crying. Well, I'd cry, too, if something awful happened to our house. An old house is more than a pile of bricks. It has a soul, a life of its own, echoes of the lives of all the people who have lived there over the centuries, the master craftsmen who built it and put into it their pride of work.

I wished I could say something to make Joyce feel better, but I didn't know her well enough, and all she needed right now was her husband.

Who was treating her with great kindness and understanding. He kept his arm around her shoulder, looked up to the rest of us, and raised his voice. 'Meanwhile, I don't suppose anybody can sleep. How about some coffee?'

The word fell on my ears like a blessing. Coffee! I suddenly realized how cold I was. I took Alan's arm and snuggled close to him for warmth, and we all trooped to the kitchen.

The kitchen walls were thick; the noise of the storm was less terrifying there. A gentle light pervaded the vast room, and warmth, and the heavenly smell of coffee. Mr and Mrs Bates were up, dressed, and busy. A fire blazed away in the fireplace. The Bateses had lit kerosene lamps and set out cups, sugar, cream.

'The Aga is out,' said Mrs Bates, 'but the water was still nearly hot. We boiled it over the fire. There's tea, as well, and toast is coming, and I can make cocoa if anyone wants some.'

The scene took on a festive air, rather like an illicit midnight feast at some boarding school for superannuated children. We chattered eagerly about the storm. 'Well, I couldn't sleep anyway, and when I heard that awful crash . . .', 'I hope the house isn't badly damaged. Irreplaceable . . .', '. . . and I swear to you I positively *leapt* out of bed, a *grand jeté* if you will . . .'

'If the power is out for very long, I'm afraid we'll have to put you all up at the White Horse in the village,' said Jim. 'We have plenty of lamps, but the Aga is electric, and so is the central heating. We wouldn't be able to make you very comfortable.'

'Oh, but this is so exciting!' Now that I was warm and no longer frightened, I was beginning to enjoy myself. The kitchen cat lay purring in my lap, having devoured the saucer of cream I'd slipped her under the table. 'Lynn, you'll laugh at me, but I do feel exactly as if I've walked into an Agatha Christie. Any minute now, we'll find the body.'

'I certainly hope not,' said Jim dryly. 'But that reminds me. Are we sure nobody's been hurt? There's a lot of debris flying out there, and something could have come through a window someplace.'

'Perhaps a head count is in order,' said Alan. He stood. 'Joyce, remind me. There ought to be fifteen of us, am I right?'

'Right. Jim and me, Mr and Mrs Bates, and eleven guests. So let's see – Jim and me and two, four . . . I only find nine more. Am I missing someone in the shadows?'

'No,' said Alan. 'I believe your sister and brother-in-law are missing.'

I could have sworn I heard someone mutter, 'No great loss,' but it might have been only my own uncharitable thoughts. The party atmosphere of a moment before was certainly gone, though, and that *wasn't* my imagination.

There was an uncomfortable pause before Tom Anderson rose from a kitchen chair. 'I'll go and look for them, if you like. They may still be . . . asleep.'

Well, they would have had to be the world's best sleepers to slumber through the uproar of the storm. But Dave had been drinking heavily, and for all I knew Julie might have joined him after they went upstairs. Maybe they had just passed out.

'I'll go with you.' Jim and Laurence spoke at the same time. Each stopped, hesitated. Finally Laurence spread his hands in a deprecating gesture. 'Jim, it's your house, and they're your family. I should—'

'My wife's family,' Jim corrected in a voice with no expression whatever. 'And let's have none of this "After you, my dear Alphonse" stuff. You know the house a whole lot better than I do. If they're not in their rooms, they could be anywhere, and you're qualified to search. You go ahead, and thanks. They're in the back wing, at the end – the Palladian suite overlooking the river.'

'Yes, of course. Shall we, Mr Anderson?'

'If I take my flashlight, I'll leave Lynn without one. Jim, is there another somewhere?'

'Excuse me, sir.' Mr Bates materialized with a lantern. 'This will provide brighter light, and will be more dependable. Mind you carry it by the handle – it can get quite hot.'

'I should go,' murmured Joyce.

'You're not going,' said Jim flatly. 'The storm is getting worse, if anything. This is the solidest part of the house, and the safest. You're staying here, and I strongly suggest the rest of you do the same. The damned wind can't last forever.'

We stayed. Nobody wanted to go back to bed. In moments of stress, humans crave company. But our cozy mood was gone. The cat, sensitive to atmosphere like all her kind, had jumped down and vanished, and my coffee was cold. We sat in silence, watching the flicker of firelight on ancient stone walls and listening to the roar of wind down the chimney.

I was beginning to feel sleepy again by the time the search party returned half an hour later. They were alone.

Joyce, who had been nodding on a bench next to Jim, sprang up. 'You didn't find them?'

'We found them.' It was Tom who spoke. 'They're not hurt, just a little . . . er . . .'

'It seems they've both drunk a bit too much, Mrs Moynihan,' said Laurence, being very formal. 'We found Mrs Harrison asleep in a bathtub three bedrooms away from her own, and Mr Harrison on the floor of the small sitting room next to the

Blue Room. We did attempt to rouse them, but it proved easier to leave them where they were, so we found blankets and covered them. I fear there'll be ... er ... some cleaning up to do in the morning.'

'Oh. Well.' Joyce bit her lip and then visibly pulled herself together. 'Thank you so much for checking on them. In the morning I'll ... do what I can.'

'The morning, hon, is now,' said Jim. It was still dark as the pit outside, but the kitchen clock chimed six. In less than an hour the sun would rise behind those lowering clouds and the day would, officially, have begun.

I was suddenly unutterably weary.

FIVE

'What time is it? Why did I wake up?'

'Getting on toward eleven,' said Alan, 'and I have no idea why you woke. I was trying to be quiet.'

'Quiet. That's it. The quiet woke me. That awful wind has stopped. Well, died down, anyway. How long have you been up?'

We'd all gone back up to bed to get what sleep we could for what little remained of the night, and I'd conked out as though I'd been hit on the head. I still felt muzzy.

'About an hour,' said Alan. 'I went down in search of breakfast, but the pickings are a trifle slim. The electricity is still out, and from the look of things – well, see for yourself.'

He pulled open the draperies, letting in light. The rain had apparently stopped. I staggered to the window.

'Dear God.'

I had seen such devastation before. On television. In the newspapers. The aftermath of tornadoes, floods, hurricanes. Of war. I'd never seen it outside my window.

The little wood we had driven through yesterday when we arrived was gone. Just ... gone. As far as the eye could see, no big trees were left standing. They'd been torn out of the ground, their twisted roots pointing distorted fingers at the sky. Among them, saplings looked forlorn, bereft. Nearer the house, what had been the garden was a sea of mud with a few twigs shivering, naked, in cold, unforgiving sunshine. What must once have been a greenhouse lay in a heap of glass shards, and broken slates and bits of carved stone were strewn everywhere.

'But, Alan, this is . . . what *happened*?'

'Hurricane-force winds. That, coupled with the saturated ground, and the trees went down like so many wisps of straw. I listened to the car radio for a few minutes. A storm the like of which we haven't seen since 1987. And even that one wasn't as bad as this, not in this part of the country at least.' He shook his head and held up his hands in a despondent gesture. 'Joyce and Jim are beyond distraught. The house can be repaired, but the landscaping! The famous Capability Brown landscaping was one of the things they loved best about the house. They keep talking about it. It's a bit depressing.'

'Alan, let's go home! They don't need company at a time like this. And I want to see what's happened to our house, to Sherebury.'

Alan is a lovely man. He was patient with me. 'My dear woman, how precisely do you think we might get home? Remember the drive, that picturesque mile-long drive from the road to the house? With trees on either side?'

'Oh. I suppose they're all down.'

'One good big one would be enough to block the drive. Not to mention the state of the roads once one got to them.'

'Trains?' I asked hopelessly.

'Not running. Nothing's running. The entire south-east of England is shut down.'

'We'll go to the pub, then. The White Horse. We can walk there if we have to. Jim said last night . . .'

Alan just looked at me pityingly. 'It's nearly five miles, and your knees aren't up to that yet awhile. *If* they're open, which I doubt.'

'We could call and find out.'

'Love, get a grip. The phone lines are out of service and the mobile masts are down, which between the two of them also puts paid to the Internet and email. Let's just hope Jim and Joyce laid in plenty of food, because until crews can get the thousands of trees cleared away, we are well and truly isolated.'

I sat down hard on the bed. It was sounding more and more like an old mystery novel, but I wasn't having fun. 'Satellite phone?' I suggested – one last, feeble attempt to pretend there was some kind of normality within our grasp.

Alan smiled wearily. 'Joyce and Jim might have one, I suppose. But not many people do, so whom could we phone?'

'Oh, but . . . other people will be trying to reach us, and when they can't—'

'They'll try to reach the authorities, and be told the situation. It's no use, really, love.'

I gave it up. In this age of instant communication, it was hard to believe we really couldn't communicate with anyone, but I would accept the idea for now. At least Alan was here with me. Isolation from the rest of the world was bad enough, but I didn't think I could manage if I were isolated from him.

When hunger and cold finally drove us downstairs, there was little cheer. Oh, it was warmish. A big fire in the kitchen fireplace heated the place a bit, but not enough. Lynn was the only person there. She came over to us when we entered.

'Fry your face and freeze your backside – or the other way around? Your choice. Have you ever used a toasting fork?'

'Um . . . maybe for marshmallows, a long, long time ago.'

'It works the same way for bread. If you have patience enough, the bread will toast. If not, or if you get too close, it burns.'

'I used to like burnt marshmallows.'

'I *don't* think you'd care for burnt toast. Anyway, it falls in the fire. There's cold ham, or the pot over there' – she pointed to a spot in the corner of the hearth – 'has boiling water for eggs or tea.'

I ladled some of the boiling water into a teapot. 'Where is everybody?'

'The Bateses are helping Jim and Joyce clear away the tree that fell in the cloisters. So is Tom, and I think some of the other men. I don't know where the women are. Joyce said we were just to help ourselves to anything we could find. Dorothy, I'm *so* sorry I let you in for this.'

'You didn't conjure up the storm. And we're lucky, really. We can keep sort of warm, and I'm sure there's plenty to eat – if we can figure out how to cook it. Lord knows there's enough firewood for ten years – and most of it's already in the house.'

'It's green wood, Dorothy,' said Alan, a little grumpy now that I had someone else to help me cope. 'Won't burn for months.'

'You're hungry,' I replied. 'You always get cross when you're hungry. How about a nice ham sandwich? And I just made a pot of tea.'

We both felt slightly better when we had some food inside us, and Lynn came up with an idea. 'Look, Dorothy, why don't we see if we can put together a meal? Everyone will be starved when they come in. Surely we can concoct something besides boiled eggs and ham sandwiches.'

'Do you think Mrs Bates would mind us invading her domain?'

'I doubt it. She seems like a sensible woman. Anyway, she's busy elsewhere, and somebody has to think about food.'

So we foraged. 'Make sure there's an inside latch on that door,' said Alan as Lynn and I walked into the cooler. 'I'm going out to help with the clean-up effort, and I don't want the two of you getting stuck in there and turning into ice sculptures. Yes, I do know the power's out, but it's going to be very cold in there for a long time.' He gave us a dubious look and then left the room.

'There's a lot of round steak we could cut up into stew meat,' said Lynn after a moment or two.

'That might do for supper, if it thaws fast. Can't have it ready in time for lunch. Oh, here's five pounds or so of hamburger!'

'We could make that into a soup with canned vegetables, and heat it in a big pot in the fireplace. I knew all those years in Camp Fire Girls would come in handy some day.'

There were obstacles. We had no way to brown the hamburger, so we just chopped it up into the smallest chunks we could manage and put it into the biggest pot we could find. Then the can opener was electric, but I had my Swiss Army knife with me. Slowly, laboriously, we opened tins of tomatoes and corn and green beans. I chopped onions and found herbs. 'Potatoes, do you think?'

'Not sure they'd cook in time. Better cook some macaroni in the boiling water, if we can find any macaroni, and add it at the last minute.'

The pot had no bail handle, which didn't really matter, because the fireplace hadn't had hanging hooks for generations, probably. We used other pans to improvise a platform for the big pot, thrust it into the fire, and hoped for the best.

'And that's enough of that,' I said, dusting ashes off my fingers. 'I wish we could bake some cornbread, but even if we had the ingredients, I do *not* know how to bake on an open fire, and I don't intend to try to find out. What do we do now?'

'Why don't we see what we can do outside? We might find roof slates that are reusable, and some of the plants might be salvaged.'

I had serious doubts about the plants, but it was worth a try. I'm no gardener, but I do love flowers, and the sight of the ruined garden was painful. 'I didn't bring my wellies. Do you suppose there are some I can borrow?'

'Bound to be. Shall I go ask Jim?'

'No, don't bother him. We'll manage.'

We found our coats and hats and a variety of footwear. Lynn slipped into somebody's garden clogs and I found a pair of wellies so big I could wear them over my shoes, and we went out into the hard, bright sunshine and the devastation.

The wind was still blowing steadily, a cold, insinuating wind, but by comparison to the storm winds it was as a gentle zephyr. We wandered more or less aimlessly, and soon stopped trying to pick up slates. They were heavy, and so many of them were chipped or broken that I doubted they would be of any use. As for the garden, it was heartbreaking.

'Still,' said Lynn after we had looked in silence at the stripped rose bushes and the flattened annuals, 'the perennials will come up again in the spring, and the bulbs. Small plants are sturdier than trees, in a way.'

'The bigger they are, the harder they fall,' I said glumly. 'Look at that oak, with its roots in the air.' I pointed to one on the edge of the wood. 'It's fascinating, in a macabre sort of way. Do you suppose they ever save trees that are uprooted that way?'

'I wouldn't think so.'

We walked in that direction, squishing through the mud. 'Well, but they wouldn't have to dig a new hole,' I argued. 'The hole is there, see? Darn it all, if they could just get to it with a crane or something, before it dries out, I'll bet— *what's that*?'

We were at the edge of the deep cavity left by the fallen giant. Tangled in its roots was . . . something . . .

'Dorothy Martin, if you faint I'll never speak to you again! You've got to stay sensible, because *somebody* has to, and I don't know if I can.'

Lynn's voice seemed to come from far away, but her hand gripped mine painfully.

I cleared my throat and gave my head a shake. 'Tell me that isn't what I think it is.'

'Oh, yes, it is.' Her voice rose higher and higher, and she began to laugh. 'You can't really mistake a skeleton, can you?'

SIX

have seen a few dead bodies in my life. I didn't enjoy it. If I had ever thought about it, I suppose I would have expected a skeleton to be less disturbing. A body, after all, looks like a person. A skeleton is just bones.

Or so I would have thought. It isn't so. There was something so absolutely final about that skeleton, so utterly and irretrievably dead, that it turned my own bones to water.

Once when I was a teenager I went into a 'fun house'. For me it wasn't fun. I've always been claustrophobic and a little afraid of the dark, and I didn't, even at that age, like things that jumped out at me and made loud noises. But the worst thing, the absolutely worst, was the skeleton that dropped down an inch from my nose with a horrific shriek. The word 'blood-curdling' is overused, but I felt exactly as if my blood had turned solid and stopped my heart. I had nightmares for weeks afterwards, that grinning skull looming closer, closer . . .

That skull had been plastic, or something. This one was real. I turned away from it and sank down on the nearest fallen branch.

My friend was still giggling. 'Lynn!' I said sharply. 'Pull yourself together and go get Alan. You can run. I can't. Don't tell him what's happened yet, just bring him out. I'll stay here.'

'Why?' said Lynn, still in that high voice, near hysteria. 'He–she–it isn't going anywhere.'

'I don't want anyone else seeing it yet, if I can prevent them. Lynn, *go!*'

She went. I took a deep breath, and then another, and tried hard to think.

The skeleton was not intact. The ligaments that had held the bones together had gone the way of all flesh. But the smaller roots of the tree had intertwined with the bones, creating a kind of net that held them in some semblance of their original alignment. I shuddered at that thought. Roots, weaving their tough, mindless, inexorable fingers through muscle, through heart and brain and . . .

I shook myself, nearly dislodging my hat, which was being teased by the wind. I replaced it more firmly and gave myself a lecture. Dead tissue feels no pain, knows no indignity. What happens to our bodies after we're dead doesn't matter a hoot. It's what happens when we're alive that counts.

That skeleton had once belonged to a living, breathing human being. If its owner had met a natural death, he or she would have been buried in the usual way in a churchyard. The implication was obvious.

On the whole, I came down on the side of 'she'. The sad fact is that it has never been uncommon for a young lord of the manor – or an old one, for that matter – to seduce a serving maid or village girl. If the girl, discovering herself pregnant, or humiliated past endurance by her 'ruin', killed herself, she might well have been buried to prevent talk. Some story would have been put about that she had left for greener pastures. Or, if the seducer was someone whose reputation would have suffered, he might have killed the girl. Murder in either case, according to my way of thinking.

I wondered how long ago the murder had taken place. I had no idea how long it took for flesh to decay and leave clean bones.

My stomach was getting queasier and queasier. Better stop thinking about that sort of thing. There was no point, anyway. The place would soon be swarming with Scene of Crime Officers, some of them with enough knowledge of forensics to make a very good guess about the age of the skeleton.

And then, with sinking heart, I remembered. No, there would be no SOCOs. There would be no one to help, no one to study the scene and then take away that pathetic evidence of murder, no one to set in motion the efficient machinery of homicide investigation.

We couldn't call the police. We couldn't get to a police station. Or if someone managed to walk to the village, the constable there would have no way to summon the nearest homicide team.

We were cut off, alone here with a group of people who barely knew each other and the skeleton of a murdered person. I wrapped my coat more closely around me and wished Alan would come.

It seemed a long time, but was probably only a few minutes before I saw him striding across the muddy, littered lawn. He was alone. Lynn had undoubtedly sought the comforting presence of her own husband. I could understand that.

When Alan was close enough, I simply pointed.

My husband, bless him, can meet almost any occasion with

aplomb, and he'd seen lots of corpses and probably a few skeletons in his long and distinguished police career. He studied the
bones, then took my hand and grinned. 'I can't take you anyplace,
can I?'

I was able to smile back. 'Now really! I know I've managed
to get involved in a few crimes over the years, but you can't
blame me for a body that's been there for . . . how long, would
you say?'

'Probably years, but I don't know how many. It would take
some time for the roots to entwine themselves around the bones
like that. As for the decay of the body, there are so many variables − type of soil, temperature, whether the body was naked
or clothed, what insects are in the soil − sorry, love. Not pleasant,
I know. But only an expert would be able to say with any certainty,
and even then, it will be an estimate.'

'And we can't get an expert here,' I wailed. 'Alan, what on
earth are we going to do?'

'First we tell our host. It's on his property, after all. Then
we're going to have to try to get through to the authorities.'

'How? Smoke signals?'

'A satellite phone, if someone here has one and I can find
someone at the other end. Or I'll walk to the police station in
the village and see what, if anything, they can do. At the very
least, a constable might be sent to guard the remains, though
given the storm emergency, I'm not sure if that will be possible.
The village probably has only the one constable.'

'Shall I stay here and keep watch?' I asked. 'I don't mind,
now.' Alan has a marvellous gift for steadying me in a crisis.

'That would be a help, love. I'll send someone to relieve you.
I can trust Tom. Then I'll talk to our hosts and see what can be
done, given the circumstances.'

'Jim and Joyce will be shattered.'

'They already are. Blast this storm! There are times when I'm
tempted to move to some place with dependable weather.'

'If there is any such place, which I doubt, you'd be bored to
tears.'

'I've heard parts of Australia— ah.' His voice took on a speculative tone.

'What?' I asked apprehensively.

'I believe I remember someone saying Laurence Upshawe
lives now in Australia.'

'New Zealand,' I murmured, but Alan wasn't listening.

'Do you have any idea when he sold Branston Abbey and moved away?'

'Not a clue.' I was getting impatient. 'Alan, shouldn't we—?'

'Because,' Alan went on with maddening calm, 'depending on how long the body's been there . . .'

'Oh! Oh, obviously. My head's getting soft in my old age. But Alan, I *like* Mr Upshawe!'

'So do I.' But he said it grimly, and strode off toward the house.

I sat back down on the uncomfortable branch, left alone once more to listen to the wind and commune with a pile of bones.

In the few minutes before Tom Anderson came to take over the vigil, I was able to notice a few things in that huge cavity left when the tree toppled. I dared not approach too closely. The ground was soft and unstable, and I shuddered at the thought of falling into the embrace of that grinning horror. But from where I sat I could see some dark fragments of something hanging from the tree roots, moving in the wind as if alive. They could almost have been leaves. Oak leaves are tough, and decay very slowly. But how would leaves have made their way deep into the earth?

No, I was pretty sure they were rags of cloth, the sorry remnants of what the person had been wearing when he, or she, was buried. And if they were identifiable . . .

'What a hell of a thing!'

I jumped. Tom had come up behind me while I was brooding.

'Sorry, D., didn't mean to scare you. Honestly, I don't know how you manage to get into these messes.'

'Alan said something like that, too. I refuse to take any responsibility for this particular mess! That pile of bones has been down there since before I even moved to England, probably. And may I remind you who is responsible for Alan and me being here this weekend? How's Lynn holding up, by the way?'

'She's fine. She's pretty resilient, you know. She was just a little perturbed by the bones. You don't expect to find a skeleton when you're out for a walk in the pleasant English countryside.'

'You don't expect hurricanes in the pleasant English countryside, either. I've never seen destruction like this, and I've lived through a couple of tornadoes, years ago in Indiana. I *wish* I knew what was going on at home. In this age of instant communication, it's incredible that we have none.'

'Well, D., you'll get your wish as soon as Alan manages to get in touch with the outside world.'

'*If* he manages to get in touch with them. Anyway, even if the police get here, they won't be wanting to waste time putting me in touch with our Sherebury neighbours.'

'Not the police, sweetie. The media.' He jerked his head toward our grisly companion. 'This is *news*. As soon as they hear, they'll be here in force, if they have to use a helicopter.'

'Oh, Lord. I hadn't thought of that. Talk about your mixed blessings! They could be a big help – but they'll also be a major nuisance. I've changed my mind. I don't need news from home that badly. I hope the TV crews and all the rest don't learn about this for a while. Especially for the Moynihans' sake.' A thought occurred to me. 'Tom, when you first talked to them about this house, back in Cannes or wherever it was, did they say how long they've owned it?'

'So you've thought about that, too. It was Antibes, and no, I don't believe they said. I got the impression it'd been a couple of years, because they talked about how much work had needed to be done, and their frustration over the usual delays. So . . .' He held up his hands and shrugged.

'So they could maybe be involved. Or some of the workmen could. Tom, we need to get this . . . this thing identified as soon as possible, and find out how long it's been dead. Because until we do . . .'

We didn't need to spell out the unpleasant possibilities.

I was glad to leave Tom on guard duty and get back to the house. I met Alan on the way. He was carrying a tall walking stick.

'What luck?' I thought I knew the answer.

'No satellite phone. Jim and Joyce have been thinking about getting one, but haven't got around to it yet. So it's Branston village and any help I can find there.' He sounded tired.

'Alan, it's five miles! And I hate to mention it, but you're going to be seventy in May. Should you walk all that way?'

His discouraged expression changed to one of amusement. 'My dear pampered American, I'm English. We still remember what feet are for. Five miles is nothing, at least on clear roads. These will be littered with debris, so it may take a bit longer. That's why I borrowed the staff.'

I know a lost battle when I meet one. 'Have you at least had something to eat? And do the others know? Besides the Moynihans, I mean.'

'I told Upshawe. And obviously Tom and Lynn know. I haven't

broadcast it yet. I made a casual remark to the effect that I needed
a stroll, and would come back to report on what damage I found.
And yes, I had some of your excellent soup. Go in and have
some yourself, love. I'll be back well before nightfall.'

'But you have a flashlight, just in case?'

'I do. Stop fretting. A brisk walk will do me good.'

He gave me a peck on the cheek and strode off. I went inside
to fret.

SEVEN

The entire party was gathered in the kitchen. The moment
I opened the door I could hear Julie Harrison, who was,
predictably, taking the disaster as a personal affront.

'. . . slates came right through our window. We could have
been killed!'

Which window, I wondered. The sitting room where she'd
slept it off, or the bathroom her husband stumbled into?

She whined on. 'And I think one of them hit me on the head.
I have the most god-awful headache. I need to get to a doctor!'

Joyce said, 'Sis, I've told you.' She was near tears. 'No one
can go anywhere. All the roads are blocked by fallen trees. And
we can't call a doctor or a pharmacy, or anyone. We're cut off.'

'Yeah, well, I'll tell you right now, I intend to sue.' The other
Horrible Harrison spoke up. 'Bringin' us out here in the middle
of nowhere to a rickety old house that's fallin' apart—'

'I will remind you,' said our host through clenched teeth, 'that
we did not "bring you out here". You came for reasons of your
own, and without invitation. I'm not sure whether you plan to
sue God for the storm, or the long-dead builders of the house
for the flying slates, but I think your lawyers will advise against
either course. And I'm not exactly astonished, Julie, that you
have a headache. You drank enough to fell an ox. As soon as
the roads are clear and the trains are running again, I will escort
you to the station in Shepherdsford.'

The shrill voice and the hoarse one rose in united protest.

'That's enough!' Jim didn't shout, but the Harrisons stopped
in mid-tirade. 'I've put up with a lot, but I'm not going to subject
Joyce, or our guests, to any more. You have a choice. Pack up

now and set out on foot if you think you can get a train quicker that way. It's something like ten miles to the station at Shepherdsford. Or stay in your room until the roads are clear.' He held up a hand as Dave started to bluster. 'There is no third option.'

'Dave! Do something!' shrieked Julie.

'Oh, I'll do somethin', all right,' he growled. 'I'll sue the pants off both of 'em when we get back to civilization. Right now we're getting out of where we're not wanted.'

He grabbed Julie's arm and towed her out of the kitchen.

I was beginning to get used to the sort of silences left behind by the Harrisons. This time it was broken by Mike, the dancer. 'Ooh, do you suppose he *could* have meant what one hopes he meant? That they're actually leaving?'

'I doubt it,' said Lynn. 'He had a bottle under his arm. I saw him filch it from the liquor tray a few minutes ago.'

'Then perhaps they will anaesthetize themselves again,' said the vicar, mildly, 'and we will hear no more from them for a while.'

I sighed and sat down to the bowl of soup Mrs Bates offered me. Conversation resumed, in bits and snatches. The gorgeous Pat was trading witticisms with Ed, but neither was being especially brilliant. Mike and the vicar were discussing emergency steps to secure the house against further damage by rain or wind until a repair crew could get through. Lynn and I tried to find something to say to each other that had nothing to do with storms or skeletons, but without much success.

The Moynihans were huddled in a corner of the vast room with Laurence Upshawe. Their voices were inaudible, but for those three, who knew about the grisly discovery under the tree, there was only one likely topic of conversation.

Mrs Bates was going about preparations for supper, a set look on her face. These were not, her expression said, the conditions under which she was accustomed to working. I didn't know where Mr Bates was. Probably repairing something. There was certainly no shortage of work to be done.

I finished my soup, ate an apple from a bowl on the table, and was trying to decide what to do next when the kitchen door opened and Alan walked in.

I stood, startled, but he ignored me, went straight to Jim Moynihan, and spoke to him in an undertone. Jim grimaced and nodded, and Alan moved to the centre of the room.

'May I have your attention for a moment, please?' He sounded perfectly courteous, perfectly relaxed, but there was something in his manner that stopped all conversation. I drew in a quick breath. This was a man I scarcely knew, the chief constable in person.

'I'm afraid I have two pieces of unpleasant news. The first is that evidence of what appears to be a crime has turned up quite unexpectedly. A human skeleton, apparently buried under one of the oak trees at the edge of the wood, has been unearthed, literally, when the tree was uprooted by the storm. My walk was intended to take me to the village, where I meant to try to find some help in dealing with what will soon become a crime-scene investigation.'

There was a shocked murmur from those in the party who didn't already know about the discovery under the tree. Alan waited for it to subside before he continued. 'And that brings me to my second piece of bad news. I will not be able to walk to the village. Nor can anyone come to us, for quite some time. The river is in flood, and I'm sorry to say that the bridge has been destroyed by falling timber. Until it can be replaced, we are marooned.'

'Oh, no!'

'But, surely—'

'That's impossible! A boat—'

'But I have to be in London—'

Everyone was shouting at once. A resurrected skeleton was distressing, but disruption to one's own schedule was outrageous.

'What's in the other direction?' Ed, the photographer, asked.

It was Laurence Upshawe who answered. 'No joy there, I'm afraid. I don't know how much chance anyone has had to explore the grounds. The river makes a loop around the estate, making us very nearly an island. Branston village is to the north of us, on the other side of the bridge at what one might call the top of the loop. There are no bridges to east or west. To the south lies a particularly deserted stretch of country, without so much as a farmhouse for probably ten miles. In any case, the bottom of the loop, where the river nearly bends back upon itself, is low-lying ground, marshy at the best of times. In flood, it, too, is impassable, making the estate a true island.'

Tom Anderson began to tick items off on his fingers. 'No way to get out. No electricity. No phone. I don't suppose anybody's cell phone works?'

'Almost all the masts in the south-east are down,' said Alan. 'I heard the news on the car radio earlier this morning.'

'No cell phone,' Tom continued. 'Nobody has a satellite phone?' The lack of answer was answer enough. 'What about wireless Internet?'

'The card's on order,' said Jim glumly. 'Should have been here last week.'

This time no one spoke, no one protested. It's sinking in, I thought. They're realizing. We're all stuck here with no communication till heaven knows when. I cleared my throat. 'Alan, how long did it take for everybody to get their power back after the storm in 1987 – and phones, and so on?'

'Two weeks, as I recall, for the most remote areas.'

'And the roads?' Joyce asked tremulously. 'How long before . . .'

'The Army cleared the main roads quite quickly. Secondary roads took longer, and private drives . . .' He shrugged. 'It was a few days before all the railway lines were cleared, as well.'

'Well, then,' said Jim, 'we need to get to work. Thank God the chainsaws don't need electricity, and we've got plenty of gas.

'No, we don't, Jim.' It was Joyce's disconsolate voice. 'We're nearly out. You were going to drive into the village today for that, and some nails and things. Remember?'

'Oh.' Jim looked blank. 'You're right. Still, there's some left. Maybe . . . well, who's game to help me try to cut up some trees and build a bridge?'

The men, and most of the women, rose in a body, but Alan had more to say. 'Is there anyone here who has any medical experience?' Well, at least it wasn't 'Is there a doctor in the house?' but it still sounded ominous.

Surprisingly, Laurence Upshawe spoke. 'I am a doctor. Retired. How can I help?'

I was sure I knew. Upshawe, a very likely suspect in the crime, was not the ideal person to examine the skeleton, but someone had to, and the sooner the better.

Alan hesitated, though, and Joyce saw what he was thinking. She buried her head in her hands and began to sob.

As Alan and Upshawe moved off, I went to Joyce. Whether she was mourning her beautiful house, or worrying about an old crime, or despairing over the now-compulsory continued presence of the Harrisons, she needed comfort.

'It's all a bit much, isn't it?' I murmured. 'One thing on top

of another. Would you like a cup of tea?' Good grief, I thought
with exasperation. I've lived in England too long. A cup of tea,
indeed. 'Or some brandy?'

'I'm sorry,' she said, sniffling and trying to control her sobs.
'I'm just . . . it's just . . .'

'I know. But at least you have lots of workers, and lots of
company. I'll bet the guys will get some kind of a bridge rigged
in no time, even if it's just a tree or two across the river. And
then there'll be professional help. It'll be all right.' I could hear
the false brightness in my voice.

'My trees! My beautiful trees!' she wailed. 'And the gardens!
They won't be all right.'

Lynn joined us and handed Joyce a glass of something amber
that looked a lot more like brandy than tea. 'Drink it,' she said.
'You'll feel better. And no,' she went on, 'the old oaks won't be
all right. They're gone forever. But not the young ones. Just
think what an opportunity you have now to redo the gardens.
You can plant all sorts of interesting trees and shrubs, plants you
really love, and watch them take shape.'

The outcome hung in the balance for a moment, and then
Joyce took a sip of brandy, sniffed, and reached in her pocket
for a tissue. 'It's true there were some changes I wanted to make.
The rhododendrons are terribly overgrown. And I've never much
liked white roses . . . but the trees! The landscaping was by
Capability Brown, you know, and it was famous!' Tears threatened again.

I was nearly in tears myself. If I'd owned one of the famous
gardens of England and seen it destroyed in a night, I would
have been devastated. But Lynn is made of sterner stuff.

'Now, Joyce,' she said bracingly. 'That was two hundred and
fifty years ago. Brown himself would have wanted to get rid of
some of those trees. They were too tall. Out of proportion. The
saplings are OK, a lot of them, and they'll grow much better
without the shade of the old ones. Stop fussing over what you
can't change and start planning what you can.'

Joyce mopped up her eyes, blew her nose, and sipped some
more. 'You're right. I'm in England now. Soldier on, keep a
straight bat, and all that.'

'*And*,' said Lynn practically, 'as soon as the front drive and
the bridge are negotiable, you can get your sister and brother-
in-law out of your hair. I don't mean to be rude about your
family, but surely their absence is something to look forward to.'

'Yes . . . well . . . you've gathered we don't exactly get along. To tell the truth, Julie and I never did.' The brandy, or something, was loosening her tongue. She became confidential. 'I'm the eldest, and Julie was the middle child. We had a kid brother. He died when he was a teenager – hit by a car – but he was the pet child before that. And I was the one who was given responsibility. Julie, the middle kid, had nothing special. I think she thought it would be better after Stevie died, but my parents never got over him. Well, naturally they wouldn't. I mean, you don't get over the death of a child, but somehow they resented Julie for still being alive when Stevie was dead. They had always compared the two of them. You know, "Why can't you do as you're told? Stevie does, and he's only a baby." That sort of thing.' She polished off the brandy.

'Sounds like an unwise way to raise a child,' I commented.

'Oh, it was, but they couldn't see it. Anyway, I didn't mean to tell you my life story. The point is, Julie has always resented me, and when—' She broke off, suddenly cautious. 'Good heavens, I think I've had too much to drink . . . I'd better go see what everyone's doing about the bridge.'

Lynn and I exchanged glances, then followed her out the door.

EIGHT

We could hear the snarl of the chainsaws, even over the rising wind, the minute we stepped outside the house. Jim had two of them, in different sizes, and both were going full blast. It's a sound I've always hated, a sound that nearly always means the destruction of some living thing. In this case the trees were already destroyed. That didn't make the sound any more pleasant.

No progress had yet been made in bridge-building. They had to get to the river first, and the drive was impassable. Everyone was working hard to clear it. Even Pat, to the imminent ruin of her manicure, was helping the vicar tug and roll logs out of the drive as the other men positioned them and cut them apart.

It was a heartbreaking job. The drive was a mile long, and there must have been fifteen or twenty big trees lying across it, in some cases one atop another. Mike, slender though he was,

was working like a lumberjack. I saw him single-handedly nudge one oak tree off another, nimbly skipping aside so as to protect his feet. I must have been staring, because he caught my eye and grinned. 'Nothing at all, compared to lifting a hefty ballerina forty or fifty times a night.'

Well, most of the ballerinas I'd seen were the reverse of hefty – anorexic, one might have said. But I took his point. Dancers were athletes, first of all.

They'd dealt with one tree so far. Jim and Mr Bates had used the chainsaws to cut off the portion actually lying on the drive, while the others used handsaws and loppers and axes to remove protruding branches. At this rate it would take days even to get to the river, much less bridge it. And how long could they work at this pace? Most of them weren't young, and none except Mike had any genuine physical strength.

And how long would the gas hold out?

Lynn and Joyce moved into the work area and picked up tools. I found a pair of loppers and looked half-heartedly for some branches to cut. It all just seemed so pointless – emptying the ocean with a teaspoon.

I had created a small pile of brush and a couple of large blisters when Alan and Laurence hove into sight. I laid down my loppers with relief and went to meet them.

'Well? Have you figured out anything about her?'

Alan looked confused.

'The skeleton,' I said impatiently. 'Weren't you trying to identify her, or at least fix an approximate time and cause of death?'

'Where did you get the idea it was female?' asked Alan. 'The doctor says quite definitely not, and you know that's one of the easiest things to determine.'

'Oh! I thought— but never mind. A man, then. Anything else? Age, maybe?'

'I can't be certain,' said Upshawe. He looked tired and distressed. 'This isn't my field – I'm a surgeon – but one learned a certain amount in anatomy classes. The man was past adolescence and not yet senescent – not yet old. There is no obvious arthritic degeneration. The femurs are relatively long; I think we can assume a man of above average height. Beyond that . . .' He spread his hands. 'An expert in these things would be able to tell you a great deal more.'

'Gideon Oliver,' I murmured. 'Where are you when we need you?'

'Who?' said Upshawe and my husband simultaneously.

'Sorry. A fictional detective. A physical anthropologist. Never mind. Is there any way to tell about how long he'd been there?'

'Not for non-experts like us,' said Alan. 'There were some fragments of cloth, probably clothing, but as I don't know how long it takes clothing to rot, that takes us no forrarder.'

'Nothing else, then? No billfold? Leather surely doesn't rot as soon as cloth.'

'No, it doesn't, usually. We did find bits of his shoes, but nothing that told us much – except that he went to his grave shod. It wasn't easy to look, love. You understand we were actually down in the hole with the tree roots, very insecure footing and none too safe, if the tree had shifted. When we can get the proper equipment and personnel here, we'll institute a search. Until then, we're pretty well stuck.'

Laurence Upshawe was looking a bit green. I glanced at him and said brightly, 'Well, then, we'd better get to work on that drive.' We moved back to join the work party, but before we could even pick up tools, Jim Moynihan stepped up, sounding irritated.

'What did you think? Who died? What's going on?'

'We don't know,' said Alan. 'A man, aged anywhere from the late teens to perhaps the forties. Tallish, probably. No identification.'

Jim rolled his eyes. 'Then what the hell do we do now?'

'If we were in any position to do so, we – you – would call in the police. They would bring equipment to get the skeleton up and out to a forensics laboratory, where every effort would be made to solve a number of questions – how the man died, how long ago, and naturally who he was.'

'Yeah, well, we can't do any of that, can we?' He gazed bitterly down the disaster area that used to be his drive.

'Not at present,' said Alan with a sigh. 'But as this is plainly a crime scene, we must do what we can. I will put a guard on the – one hesitates to call it a body – on the remains, and ask whatever questions I can think of. None of it is likely to be useful, but it has to be done.'

'And by what authority,' asked Laurence, 'do you take it upon yourself to ask these questions?' He tightened his grip on the axe he had picked up.

'No authority at all,' said Alan calmly. 'But as we are isolated on our island, and I am the only representative of the law present, I considered that some questions were in order. Anyone may certainly refuse to answer.'

Upshawe put the axe down, carefully. 'Representative of the law?'

'Perhaps our host didn't mention to you that I am the retired chief constable of Belleshire. I'm off my turf, this being Kent, but once a policeman, always a policeman. If I can gather any facts to lay before the real authorities when they can get here, it may make an investigation a bit easier. Don't you think?'

Upshawe swallowed. 'Yes, you're right. I'm sorry. I didn't mean to be rude. It's just a bit ... difficult ... the idea of a murder here. This was my home for many years, and although ... well, yes, naturally we must all do what we can.'

'Then if you agree, Jim, when we take a break from work here, perhaps we could gather in the house and pool our ideas.'

Jim looked at his small crew, who were beginning to flag. The irritating whine had diminished. I could see only one chainsaw working. Had the other run out of gas?

The vicar stood at one end of a log, arching a back that was obviously hurting him, while Pat had sat down on the other end of it and was rubbing one shoulder. We were all cold. Jim shook his head helplessly. 'We might as well go now. This is getting us nowhere. I was an idiot to suggest it. We can't even get to the river, much less fell a tree to bridge it. It'll take bulldozers to clear away this mess. God, we'll be cut off for weeks!'

'Or until phone service and electricity are restored.' Alan was trying valiantly to look on the bright side. 'That will take days, probably, but not weeks. May I suggest that in the meantime we leave two people to keep watch at the oak tree, and the rest of us go in out of the chill?'

Tom and Lynn volunteered to take the first watch. 'Because,' said Lynn sensibly, 'we never heard of this place until a few weeks ago, so we can't possibly have anything to do with old Boney there.'

'And apart from Dorothy and me,' Alan replied *sotto voce*, 'you are very nearly the only people who can make that claim.'

'Let me make my position quite clear,' said my husband, when he and the others had seated themselves in a group around the cold hearth of the drawing room. The wind was still blowing, not as it had, but steadily, strongly. Now and then the curtains swayed a little. I was glad to be inside, even if the room was cold.

The Harrisons were nowhere to be seen. I thought about asking Alan if someone should look for them, and then thought better of it. If Alan wanted them he was perfectly capable of saying so, and meanwhile this was going to be unpleasant enough without them. I took a chair a little distance away and tried to fade into the woodwork.

'As I said outside,' Alan began, 'I have no authority whatsoever in this matter. No one is under any obligation to answer any of my questions, or even to remain while I ask them. In a certain sense, Mr Moynihan, I am abusing your hospitality if I carry out any investigation. However, having said that, I must also say that in this situation, with all indications that a serious crime has been committed, an investigation *will* have to be launched. We are in the peculiar position of having, for the present, no one to call upon who does have authority. With your permission, then, Mr Moynihan, I'd like to do what I can to get at some of the truth.'

Jim set his chin pugnaciously. 'OK, let's clear the air. In the first place, my name is Jim. Second, this is my house, and it used to be Laurence's here. Now I don't know about you, Laurence, but when a human skeleton's found on my property I want to know how the hell it got there, and I guess you feel pretty much the same way.'

'Certainly. I merely— no matter. Proceed, Mr Nesbitt.'

'Splendid!' Alan sounded composed, as though there were no tension in the air. 'Now I think you'll all agree, our first task is to learn who the unfortunate fellow under the tree is, or rather, was in life. In a week or so, when we can get a forensics team here, we will be in a position to know much more. For now, we simply have to muddle through.'

An English specialty, I thought with a private grin.

'At the moment,' Alan went on, propping one ankle on his knee in an attitude of total relaxation, 'we know two things about the chap. First, that he *is* a chap, not a woman. Even I know enough about skeletal anatomy to make that guess, and Mr Upshawe – Dr Upshawe – confirmed it. Second, that he's been buried there for some time. I wish I could be more definite than that, but it's simply not possible at this stage. Still, I can make an educated guess that the roots of an oak tree grow fairly slowly, as does the part of the tree above ground. And the bones were

well entangled with the roots, so provisionally – *very* provisionally, I must say – I think it's fair to assume the body's spent
several years where we found it.'

Alan reached into his pants pocket, made a grimace, and withdrew his hand. I knew he'd been feeling for the pipe he gave
up some years ago, on doctor's orders. Old habits die hard.

'Now you and your wife, Mr— Jim, took possession of this
house some time ago. When, exactly?'

'Two years ago last May,' said Joyce. 'It was the most beautiful place. The gardens were . . .' Her voice broke.

Alan looked at her with sympathy, but he went on. 'And did
you notice any evidence of digging around that particular oak
tree?'

Jim snorted. 'We didn't do a detailed inspection of each tree,
man!'

'I'm sure. But that one was quite near the house, and an
impressive specimen.'

'The grass ran right up to it, Alan,' said Joyce. 'I did notice
that. It wasn't in the wood, proper – more a part of the lawn.
Sort of reminded me of the old oaks in people's yards back
home.'

'Splendid. That helps. It would surprise me very much to learn
that our friend was put there in the past two years, and you've
strengthened my opinion. Now, Ms Heseltine.'

The femme fatale cocked her head to one side with a half-
smile. 'Yes, luv?'

I refrained from gritting my teeth.

'You have lived in the village for some time?'

'All my life – except for Oxford, and my time at Lincoln's
Inn, eating my dinners.'

Ed Walinski, sitting next to me, looked bewildered, and I whispered, 'Part of getting admitted to the Bar. I'll explain later.' I
hoped I could. The process confused me, too.

Alan went on. 'Under normal circumstances I would never
ask a lady her age, but may I ask just how long "all my life"
implies?'

'You may,' she cooed in that devastating voice of hers. 'But
as you pointed out, I am under no obligation to answer.' She
gave him a brilliant smile.

'Yes, indeed. I will simply ask, then, if in your years in Branston
village – however few or many they may be – you remember
anyone going missing.'

He had put just the slightest stress on 'many', and given me the briefest of sidelong glances. I don't think Miss Glamourpuss of Kent noticed, but I grinned.

'Not a soul. Except for Harry Upshawe, of course.'

NINE

That caused a stir. Everyone looked at Laurence, who held his hands up in a gesture of annoyance.

Alan frowned. 'Can you tell me about that, sir? Harry Upshawe is . . .?'

Upshawe sighed. 'Was. Harry Upshawe was my second cousin. And he died in a plane crash when I was about ten. There was no question of his "going missing".'

'This happened when you were ten, you said. That's rather a long time ago. Can you tell me any of the details?'

'One remembers the pivotal events of one's life, Mr Nesbitt, even the ones that happened fifty years ago. I remember that Harry was going away, going to America. I wasn't sorry, I recall. We were of the same generation, but Harry was too much older than I to have ever been a playmate. In fact he ignored me as much as possible. I was simply the poor relation, the son of his father's no-account cousin.'

'You disliked him?'

'I had no attitude toward him at all, really. We almost never saw each other.'

'But you remember his attitude toward you.'

'No. I'm sorry if I've conveyed the wrong impression. I remember what my father told me, later, about his attitude. About Harry I remember, from my own memory, only an impression of tallness and a hint that I shouldn't cross him.'

'And he was killed in a plane crash,' said Alan. 'You were ten when this happened, you say. That is, when your cousin went away.'

'Just ten. I remember because it was only a few days after my birthday that we heard he was missing in the crash.'

'"Heard he was missing"?' Alan's tone made it a question.

'Yes. It was a private plane, you see, piloted by a friend of Harry's. When it didn't arrive in New York, the authorities

launched an investigation. The last radio contact was a message
to São Miguel, in the Azores, where the pilot had planned to
land for refuelling. He never got there. By the time anyone got
out to search there was no sign of the plane, and as far as I
know, nothing has ever been found of the wreckage.'

'Ah. So no bodies were ever recovered.'

'No, obviously not.' Upshawe sounded impatient.

'So in actual fact you do not know that the plane crashed,
only that it disappeared.'

'The plane disappeared. Neither the pilot nor my cousin has
been heard from in the intervening fifty years. The inference
that the plane crashed would seem to be justified.'

Upshawe sounded very stiff. Jim Moynihan cleared his throat.

'You're thinking me ridiculously precise,' said Alan, smiling.
'I quite agree with your inference – about the plane. Apparently
flight plans were filed, the plane took off with your cousin's
friend piloting it, it never reached São Miguel. It is reasonable
to assume it crashed. My point is that, so far, I can find no justi-
fication for the inference that your cousin was aboard.'

'But . . . he was going! He told everyone. He left the morning
when he said he did, with his luggage.'

'Who saw him leave?'

'His father, naturally. No, I'm wrong. His father was away
at the time. In London, if I remember correctly. But the
servants . . .'

'Are any of the servants still living, sir?'

Upshawe sagged in his chair. 'No. My father kept them on,
after he inherited the place, and after my father died I could hardly
sack them. They'd lived on the estate forever. I pensioned them
off when they got too old for the work, but I didn't replace
them as they left or died. I couldn't afford to run the place on
those lines. That's why I sold it – that, and the fact that I'd never
really liked living here. I prefer a simpler way of life.' He ran
a hand through his hair. 'Look, Nesbitt, I do see what you're
getting at. My cousin "disappears". Years later we find bones
on his property, bones that could, by a wild stretch of one's
imagination, be identified as his. But it's impossible. My cousin's
body, or what little must remain of it, lies under two or three
thousand metres of cold water, somewhere in the Atlantic Ocean.'

A polite cough interrupted what threatened to become an
awkward silence. 'Excuse me, sir. Mrs Bates and I have assembled a rudimentary tea in the kitchen, where it is warmer. It is

ready when any of you care to partake. It is not all I could wish, but under the circumstances, perhaps it will suffice.' Mr Bates bowed and withdrew, and we followed him gratefully to the warm kitchen.

Mrs Bates was a true wonder. She had transformed store-bought petit-beurre biscuits into a treat by dipping them into melted bittersweet chocolate. She had prepared hot buttered toast over the fire, turning some of it into cinnamon toast and leaving the rest to be spread with homemade marmalade or strawberry jam. She had even, somehow, made scones, plump with currants, and brought out clotted cream for them. I bit into one and looked at her with amazement. 'You baked? However did you manage?'

She smiled. 'It's John's doing, really. He's a genius with anything mechanical. He managed to rig a wood fire in the Aga. It isn't terribly reliable, and almost impossible to control, but it made enough heat in the one oven for scones, and I *think* I can brown the steak for supper – and heat some water for washing. There won't be enough for baths, unless he can find time after tea to split a lot more wood.'

Oh, dear. I hadn't thought of that. And we all needed baths, after working outside. Well, we'd just have to make do. Smelling like lumberjacks was going to be the least of our troubles.

'Speaking of troubles,' I said in an undertone to Alan, who could almost always follow my thoughts, 'has anyone checked on the Harrisons? I do hate the idea of those two loose cannons rattling around unsupervised.'

'I don't know, but it's a thought. Jim?'

Our host came over and Alan spoke to him. He nodded and left the room. I'd finished my tea by the time he returned, looking disturbed.

'They're not in their room,' he reported to Alan in a low tone. 'I did a pretty thorough tour of the house, including their . . . um . . . lairs of last night. I can't find them anywhere, and their coats and things are gone.'

'The fools!' Alan smacked the table. 'You don't suppose they've decided to try to get away? It's quite impossible, and they're very likely to come to grief trying. We'd better organize a search party.'

Jim shook his head. 'Not yet. I don't want Joyce to know about this, if she doesn't have to. She and Julie dislike each other heartily, but they are sisters, and I know Joyce would get

upset. Anyway, if I know Harrison, he'll come back the minute
he gets cold, or hungry . . . or thirsty.'

Alan relaxed a little, I saw. 'You may be right. He isn't a
terribly hardy sort, is he? But the thirst could take a while to set
in, if he took that bottle with him.'

'I didn't see it in their room.'

'So,' I put in, 'it'll keep them warm and reasonably content
for a few hours, at least. I'm with Jim, Alan. Let them wear
themselves out. They'll come home like Bo-Peep's sheep,
wagging their tails behind them.'

That, as it turned out, was one of my less fortunate remarks.

There didn't seem much to do the rest of the afternoon. The
vicar half-heartedly suggested work on the drive, but when no
one took him up on it, he seemed relieved and disappeared. Alan
called Tom and Lynn in from their vigil with the skeleton; there
seemed little point, since a guard couldn't very well be kept up
for the next several days. La Heseltine found a copy of *Bleak
House* in the library and sat down in front of the kitchen fire to
read, with every evidence of enjoyment, about greedy Dickensian
lawyers. (I was nastily pleased to see that she required reading
glasses.) The Moynihans, with murmured apologies, went upstairs
for naps, and Tom and Lynn followed suit. Mike Leonard
wandered about restlessly for a while, then disappeared, and Ed
Walinski established himself in a sunny corner of the kitchen
with a book of Steichen photographs.

I was tired, but too keyed up to sleep, or to read. Scrounging
in library drawers, I found a gigantic jigsaw puzzle, one of those
virtually impossible ones with irregular edges and a few extra
pieces. Alan helped me spread it out on a reading table, and we
set to work. I didn't know what had happened to Upshawe and
the vicar, but they were also probably napping.

The wind had died down, gradually, sometime after tea. The
hard, brilliant sunshine of the day faded into an early twilight,
and then quickly to full dark. Mr Bates brought a kerosene lamp
into the library, but we had lost whatever interest we'd ever had
in the puzzle, and were growing increasingly cold.

'Let's give it up, shall we, love?' said Alan, and I gladly
followed him back to the kitchen, where most of the rest had
gathered, and Mrs Bates was trying her best to cook dinner with
house guests under foot. I debated offering my help, but a look
at her face changed my mind. The best thing I could do was try
to stay out of her way.

'It's going to be really cold tonight,' Alan said.

'Mmm. Maybe we'd better find another blanket? I'm not going to bother Joyce about it.'

'That wasn't what I was thinking. The Harrisons haven't come back. Nor does Laurence appear to be around anywhere.'

'Oh. Oh, dear! Dark out, and cold. Do you think . . . ?'

'I do. Reluctantly, but I do. Laurence ought to know his way around, but the storm has changed the landscape so much that even he might have got lost. I think we'd better organize search parties to go and look for them. Bloody idiots!'

My husband seldom swears. He was genuinely worried, then.

Three parties were organized: Alan, Mr Bates and Joyce; Jim, Tom and me; and Mike, Ed, Lynn and Pat. The vicar would have been excused on account of age, but he insisted on being included, so he joined Alan and his party. Only Mrs Bates was persuaded to stay in her kitchen, as we would all need something hot when we came back. Pat admitted openly that she was happy to search for Laurence, but had no real desire to hunt for the Harrisons. 'I hope they got away safely – just so long as they got away,' she remarked, and no one, not even Joyce, could disagree with her.

We all went off with flashlights and lanterns, having set up a communications system by means of the lights and three whistles Mr Bates had produced from somewhere. Alan, who had organized a good many search parties before, handed out ties and scarves and belts and pieces of rope Mr Bates had also found. 'Hold hands as you leave the house, and then form gradually longer chains as you fan out. Those of you who are heading into the wood will have to drop the links to get through the trees, but keep in contact with each other. Shout. Whistle. We don't want to have to search for the searchers.' He indicated directions for each of the three groups, and we set off.

It was like a gruesome children's game. Jim held the lantern and Tom had a flashlight. I, in the middle between the two men, had no hands free to carry a light, but I was grateful for their support as we walked over the debris-littered lawn, making for the wood to the north-east.

'Aren't we headed for the tree?' I asked suddenly. We had been silent until then.

Nobody had to ask which tree. 'We'll need to be careful,' said Jim. 'That's a hell of a big hole, and the ground is muddy and slippery.'

'And everything looks different by lantern-light,' Tom added. I shivered, not entirely from the cold, and moved on.

'I think we'd better spread out now,' said Tom presently. We dropped hands. 'D., if you tie this scarf around your wrist you can hold this flashlight. Just give a shout or a tug when you need me to drop the other end, to get around a tree.'

I did as he suggested. Jim, on my other side, knotted a couple of neckties around his wrist. We moved forward, more slowly now that we were separated.

I moved very slowly indeed. The flashlight Tom had given me was a powerful one, but no flashlight deals well with shadows. We had to drop our tethers almost immediately; the wood was too dense. I was terrified of falling. I was terrified of what I might find – or not find. The downed trees, which had looked unpleasant enough by day, were now monsters, reaching huge gnarled, arthritic fingers up to trap the unwary. As I moved my flashlight the trees seemed to move, shadowy shapes stopping just the instant before I looked directly at them.

It took every bit of self-discipline I possessed to keep moving forward, keep on shining my torch into every gaping hole, under every fallen trunk, around every upright tree – not that there were many of those. Once I stepped on something, a branch or a round stone, that rolled under my foot and nearly brought me down. I stifled my cry, but it brought an immediate response from the men on either side. 'All right, D.?' Tom called, while Jim said, 'Wait there, I'm coming.'

'No, don't. I'm fine. Just . . . banged my elbow.' No need to make them feel they needed to protect me. I'm not a fragile person, and I've never thought of myself as elderly, though I suppose I am. If I fell, I'd do my best to be quiet about it.

I've never known how long we kept on putting one foot in front of the other, flashing our lights here and there, hoping and fearing to find someone – or some*thing*. I had reached the point where almost any discovery would have been welcome, if only to put an end to the nightmare.

It was Alan and his party who found them. We heard shrill whistles blown in the agreed-upon pattern, and when we turned to look, lights were flashing into the air. Jim called to me. 'Dorothy, stand still and shout, and point your light in the direction of my voice. I'll find you.' When he had reached me, and had tied his tether to my wrist, Tom had found both of us, and did the same. In single file, with agonizing slowness now that we longed to rush, we made our way to the designated meeting point at the back of the house.

Alan did a quick head count, and then said soberly, 'There is no easy way to say this. We have found Mr Harrison. I'm afraid he has drowned. Mr Upshawe was nearby, badly hurt. We're rigging up a stretcher for him and will bring him back to the house. He needs medical attention, but as he is the only doctor present . . .' Alan made a helpless gesture.

'And Julie?' asked Joyce in a whisper. 'No one has found Julie?'

'We found no trace of her. I'm sorry.'

TEN

'We'll go out again as soon as it's light,' Alan said to me. 'For now, Upshawe is our chief concern.'

We were all huddled in the library. None of us had had much appetite for Mrs Bates's excellent boeuf bourguignon, a fact she had accepted philosophically. Mr Bates had collected some dry wood and built a big fire, but we couldn't seem to get warm, despite the blankets and afghans that Joyce had dispensed. There was no general conversation. We sat about in groups of two or three, talking quietly. All of us, I think, had the same passionate wish: that somehow we could get out of here and pretend this weekend had never happened.

The vicar, Mr Leatherbury, had remained to pray over the body of Dave Harrison before the men used their makeshift stretcher a second time and brought him back to the stables. They were occupied now only by cars. Joyce and Jim didn't ride, and planned, when they could, to turn part of the building into a workshop, with heat and electricity. For now it was simply a large space. The cars could be turned out, and it was the coldest place on the property that could be properly secured. Harrison was now definitely a secondary concern; there were too many other critical issues to face.

'How is Laurence?' I asked.

Alan shrugged and waggled a hand. 'Holding his own, I presume. Bates has some first-aid training, and naturally I do. Bates was, fortunately, the one who found him, and had the sense to get me there before moving him at all. Then the vicar came, and the three of us we did what we could. We kept Joyce away, though of course we told her a little. The vicar is sitting with him, but he needs a doctor.'

'What actually happened to him?'

'When he comes out of his coma – if he does – we'll know more. From what little we could see at the scene, there had been some kind of a struggle on the riverbank. We found Upshawe lying with his head on a stone; that, presumably, is what knocked him out, although he also has a bad bruise on the left side of his jaw. Harrison's case looks like simple drowning. We could just make out tracks where he apparently lost his footing in the mud and simply slid off. Jim says the bank is undercut just there. You can't see it now, with the river in flood and over its banks, but apparently once Harrison was in the water, he would have had a hard time pulling himself out, even if he was conscious and could swim.'

'He couldn't swim?'

'We don't know, love.'

And if we can't find Julie, we may never know, I thought. 'So Dave and Laurence had a fight.'

'It looks that way, certainly.'

'But *why*? What would those two have to fight about?'

'That's the question, isn't it? But let's defer it till morning, my dear. This day has been a thousand years long, and I'm for my bed.'

One of the supremely competent Bateses had found extra blankets for everyone, so we slept warmly enough. Alan woke once in the middle of the night to go check on Laurence Upshawe, but when I asked him about the man's condition, he just shook his head and went back to sleep.

He was awake at first light. 'Don't get up, love,' he told me. 'It's absolutely freezing in here; you might as well stay in bed where it's warm. I need to get back to searching for Julie.'

But the bed cooled rapidly without Alan's comforting presence, and I couldn't sleep anyway, so I dressed in my warmest clothes and went downstairs in search of coffee.

Mrs Bates, as usual, was efficiency itself. Coffee and tea were standing ready, along with ham (cold) and eggs (boiled), toast, and a steaming pot of oatmeal at one corner of the fireplace.

'I'm sorry I can't give you proper eggs and bacon, Mrs Martin,' she said when I walked in, 'but the fire in the Aga's just about cold, and John's out with the search party. There's porridge if you fancy it, just for something hot.'

'We used to call it oatmeal back where I come from, and it's always been my ultimate comfort food. And I think you're marvellously inventive, coping as you have with a non-functional kitchen.'

'I enjoy a challenge,' she said as she ladled out a generous portion of oatmeal. 'I must thank you, by the way, for dealing with lunch yesterday. John and I were both needed elsewhere, as you could see.'

'Was it only yesterday? It seems like an eternity ago. I hated to invade your kitchen. It's good of you to take it so well.'

Having thus completed the civilities, I asked her to sit and have some coffee with me. 'Is no one else up yet? Except for the searchers, I mean.'

'Joyce went out with them. And the vicar was down a bit ago. He took some coffee and toast back up to Mr Upshawe's room. I think he doesn't like to leave him.'

'Did he say anything about how the poor man's doing?'

'Only that he's still unconscious.'

We sat in companionable silence while I demolished my bowl of oatmeal and poured myself another cup of coffee.

'Mrs Bates – what is your first name, by the way? If you don't mind my asking.'

'Rose. No, I don't mind. It's John who's so stubborn about being called Mister.'

'Well, then, I'm Dorothy. Are you from these parts, Rose?'

'Born in Branston village, but they closed the village school before I was old enough to start, so I had to go to the comprehensive in Shepherdsford. My father had flown the coop by that time, so mum moved us to Shepherdsford to be closer to the school. There were three of us kids. She had to take a job as a cashier at Tesco.'

Rose sipped her coffee.

'Not an easy life,' I said.

'Not easy, no. That's why I worked so hard in school. I was determined I was going to have marketable skills. I got four A-levels – you know what those are?'

I nodded. 'Advanced examinations for the college-bound. University, I mean.'

'Yes, well, I actually won a scholarship to uni, but by that

time I knew I could cook. Really cook, you know. So I went to
the Cordon Bleu school in London instead, and once I got out
I could take my pick of jobs.'

'I admit I was a little surprised to find a cook of your calibre
in a private home. I'd have thought someone with your incredible skills would be at the Ivy or somewhere like that – some
posh London restaurant.'

'I don't care for London. Oh, I could make more money there,
but believe me, I do all right here, and I prefer the country. I
suppose you could say my roots are here.'

'Is your mother still living?'

Rose's face lit up. 'She lives in Branston, in a lovely new
house we bought her, John and I. Fresh as new paint, all the
latest labour-saving devices, and a beautiful garden. Mum always
loved her flowers, but she didn't have time for them when we
lived in Shepherdsford. Nor the space, either. Our front garden
in that nasty little house was about three feet square, and wouldn't
grow anything but weeds.'

'And your husband, is he—'

A commotion at the back kitchen door interrupted me. Rose
ran to see what was the matter, and opened the door to Alan and
the other men, two of them bearing between them a blanket-
wrapped bundle.

'Julie?' I cried.

'Julie,' Alan answered.

'Is she—'

'She's all right, except for being nearly frozen to death. Mrs
Bates, can you heat some water, please? We're going to need
lots of warm compresses.'

The next hour or so passed in a blur. John brought in enough
wood for several fires and kindled one, first, in the Aga, and
then in all the downstairs fireplaces and Julie's bedroom.
Meanwhile Julie was tucked into bed with lots of blankets,
with Rose spooning hot, sweet tea into her a teaspoon at a
time.

When she was finally warm she was left to sleep, with Joyce
at her side, and I was able to question Alan in the privacy of
our room.

'Where was she?'

'In an old shed, or hut of some sort, a couple of miles away.
I suppose it must have belonged to a farm on the estate years
ago, or maybe it was a shepherd's hut, but it's obviously been

derelict for a very long time. There was nothing in it but a few
rusted pieces of iron, bits of ancient tools, probably.'

'So what on earth was she doing *there*?'

'Hiding,' said my husband laconically.

Julie had, he said, been too cold and confused when they
found her to say much. But from the way she had shrunk against
the wall of her shelter when they entered, Alan could tell that
she saw them as pursuers rather than rescuers. She had, in fact,
tried to run from them, but she was too weak to get out of the
hut.

'Does she know about Dave?'

'Nobody's told her.'

The answer was ambiguous. My eyes met Alan's. 'So you
think . . .' I said slowly.

'Love, I don't think anything yet. Too much has happened
too fast. First the body under the tree—'

'Sounds like the title for a mystery novel,' I interrupted, flip-
pantly. 'There was one like that, actually, some years back. *My
Foe Outstretch'd Beneath the Tree*. V. C. Clinton-Baddeley.'

'Yes, dear,' said my husband patiently. 'Stolen from William
Blake, I believe. Then Harrison after the skeleton – and Upshawe
– and now Julie. There has to be a connection, but I'm blest if
I can see it.'

'It was the skeleton that started it all. Finding him, I mean.
Somebody buried that man and never wanted, or expected, him
to be found.'

'And let's face it, Dorothy. The most logical person to be
upset by the man's premature resurrection is Upshawe.'

'But he was attacked himself! He's a victim, not the villain.'

'Yes? Or did he simply slip and fall while fighting with
Harrison?'

'Alan, none of it makes any sense. Why Harrison, of all
people? Just because he's – he was, I mean – a boor and a thug
and all the rest of it? His character, or lack of it, was a good
reason to dislike him, to heartily wish him elsewhere, but surely
it wasn't enough reason to kill him.'

'You'd be surprised at how little motive murder sometimes
requires. But if you don't like that scenario, turn it around.
Harrison started the fight; Upshawe was defending himself.'

'But why, Alan, why? What could Harrison have against a
man he'd barely met?'

'Harrison was drunk, remember. Well, we won't know that

for certain until the autopsy, but it seems a reasonable conclusion, since he was last seen with a full bottle of whiskey in
hand.'

'The bottle, Alan! Jim said it wasn't in their room. You haven't
found it, have you?'

'I've been a bit too busy searching for Julie.'

'Oh, I know, and I didn't mean to sound . . . anyway, if you
could find it, it would tell you something about where Dave
went, and probably Julie, too. It could be a clue!'

'Yes, Nancy.' He grinned at me and ruffled my hair.

'OK, make fun. But I'm far too old for Nancy Drew. Jessica,
if you must. Now look, my dearest love. We're cut off from any
of your normal resources. No medical examiners, pathologists,
crime lab people. All we have to work with is our minds. And—
oh, wait! We do have one essential scene-of-crime man.'

The light dawned for both of us at the same moment. 'Oh,
good grief! Dorothy, I've been an idiot. Why didn't I think sooner
– we have a photographer!'

'Yes, and a really, really good one. I don't suppose he's trained
to do police work, but I'll bet if you tell him exactly what you
want, he'll get great pictures. He brought lots of film; he said
so. And he's got a digital camera, too, if necessary.'

'He could be a godsend,' said Alan fervently. 'As soon as
we've had some lunch, I'm going to sic him on the skeleton.'

'And I,' I said firmly, 'am going out in search of that bottle.'

ELEVEN

Naturally Alan tried to dissuade me. 'There could be
someone very dangerous out there.'

'I thought we agreed it was either Harrison, who is
dead, or Upshawe, who is unconscious. The Gingham Dog and
the Calico Cat, except they didn't quite eat each other up.'

It took him a moment to get that one. 'Ah. The American
version of the Kilkenny cats, I presume.'

'Probably. Anyway, I'm in no danger from either of them at
this point. And if you're still worried about me for some obscure
reason, I'll take someone with me. Lynn, maybe. She got me –
got *us* – into this, she can jolly well help out.'

'Your English is coming along, my dear,' was his only response. I assumed silence meant consent.

I cornered Lynn while we ate our lunch (a chicken curry, which was superb), and she agreed to go for a walk with me in the afternoon. I didn't tell her why until we were on our way. Probably everyone in the house was honest. Probably. But on the off chance, I thought it was better not to broadcast my intentions.

'And what do you think it'll prove if we do find it?' Lynn asked, reasonably enough.

'Well – where one or both of the Harrisons had been yesterday after they left. Maybe no more than that. But at least the bottle is something tangible, and there isn't much else about this thing that is.'

'Yes, well, it's a lovely day for a walk.' She shivered ostentatiously as she spoke. The sun shone brightly, but the wind, which had picked up a bit again, was freezing.

'Pampered American! I thought you'd lived here long enough to become inured.'

'In London, my dear, not in the country. My walks usually consist of the four yards from my front door to a taxi. I don't mind walking a little on a beach in high summer, but this, I remind you, is November.'

I sighed. 'And tomorrow is Bonfire Night. I was so looking forward to the fireworks, but I don't suppose they'll have them now.'

'I don't think they can, even if they wanted to. They were going to have a pyrotechnics expert in, and he'd have brought his own van with a battery and a computer and all, to set off the rockets electronically. No expert, no truck . . . no fireworks.'

'So that's that. Maybe they'll burn the guy, anyway. I suppose they have a guy?'

Lynn laughed. 'You bet they do! Joyce hinted that it's a really funny one. They wouldn't show it to me, though. It's supposed to be a big secret.' She sobered. 'It really is a shame. They invited the whole village to come, you know.'

'The old lord-of-the-manor bit? And would the village have come? If they were stand-offish about the Upshawes, I can't imagine they'd exactly warm to a couple of genuine foreigners in their midst.'

'I get the impression things have changed quite a lot since the middle of the nineteenth century when the Upshawes were the incomers. I believe the village has lots of non-English living there now. A Pakistani couple run the shop-cum-post-office, I know, because I was in there the first day we came. Not a trace of an Asian accent, either, so they're probably second- or third-generation. But I don't think Jim and Joyce are trying to be the village squires. It's just friendliness. But now nobody can get here. Look, where are we going?'

I had led Lynn through the walled kitchen garden and out the gate. We could more easily have stepped over the wall; it had collapsed in several places, and the gate hung crazily from one hinge. But to treat the wall thus cavalierly seemed, somehow, to give in to the devastation. So we had edged through the gateway.

Now we were headed downhill, southward toward the place where Harrison and Upshawe had been found. I shrugged. 'They ended up here. They might have gone this way. It wouldn't have been as dark as heading north, for one thing, or as hazardous. This part is mostly open meadow, with no trees to block the starlight or lie in one's path.'

'I can't figure why they left at all, any of them,' said Lynn. 'The Horrible Harrisons must have understood they couldn't get very far. Jim made it plain enough. And Upshawe didn't seem to have any reason to be out here at all.'

'The Harrisons are, I think – were – I don't know what the right tense is – anyway, I don't think logic is a big part of their make-up. They were furious and wanted to get away; therefore they left. Maybe they thought they could ford the river down that way, or something.' I retied my headscarf; it was much too windy for any hat. 'Upshawe is a harder one to figure out. Alan thinks maybe he went after the Harrisons for some reason, and ended up pushing Dave into the river. But he can't come up with any compelling motive, or any motive at all, really. And neither can I.'

We fought the wind all the way down to the 'bottom of the loop', as Upshawe had described it, and stood, awestruck.

It was impossible here even to guess that there was a separation between the east and west arms of the river. An angry yellow torrent rushed past us, carrying tree limbs with it. As we watched, one limb snagged on something, rotated wildly in the current, and then broke free and sped on downstream. The wind tossed up waves, giving the illusion of rapids.

The river was still rising. Ripples spread closer and closer to us, drowning here a patch of coarse grass, there a clump of dead weeds. 'Those dead branches will have dammed up somewhere downstream,' Lynn said, shouting above the noise of the wind. 'The flood is going to get worse.'

I nodded. 'We'd better get back. I think Alan wanted Ed to take some pictures, and I'll bet the footprints on the riverbank would be something he'd want. And they'll be gone soon.'

We hurried up the hill, moving as fast as my new knees would take me, our quest for the liquor bottle forgotten. It had always been a silly idea, anyway. As Lynn had suggested, finding it wouldn't tell us anything relevant.

But we did find something. As we neared the house, we passed a clump of gorse, that thorny shrub that is so beautifully yellow in an English spring. Low, sturdy and compact, and somewhat protected by a stone bench, it had escaped the devastation of the storm. It wouldn't have many blossoms left now, but—

'Look, there's still one little gold flower clinging here,' I said, charmed. I reached out a hand to it and then pulled back.

'What's the matter, stuck by a thorn?'

'No. Look. It isn't a flower.'

Hanging from an inch of broken chain that had caught on a thorn, a small gold cross shone brightly in the hard wintry sun.

'Alan needs to see this. And look at the way the wind is tugging at it. It could blow away any time. Lynn, could you find him and bring him here? And Ed should come, too, to take pictures.'

I thought I would freeze into an ice statue before Lynn returned with the two men. 'They were taking pictures of the skeleton,' she said, panting. 'I ran all the way. Is it still there?'

I had protected the cross as well as I could without touching it. Alan and Ed approached and looked it over, and Ed pulled out his digital camera. 'Because,' Alan explained to me, 'we'll need to show this around, to see if anyone recognizes it, and we won't be able to get prints from the film shots for a while.'

'Won't be too long,' said Ed, busy all the time shooting. 'I brought chemicals with me; didn't know if the village would have a photo lab. Not many places do, nowadays. And I wanted to see prints of the house pictures before I left, to make sure they turned out.' He guffawed at that, and I joined him. I wondered just how many decades it had been since one of Ed's pictures hadn't 'turned out'.

'Any closet can be a darkroom,' Ed went on. 'I even brought a safelight. Don't know for sure how well that's gonna work, with no electric. These OK, do you think?'

He handed his camera to Alan and showed him how to page through the images.

'Splendid,' said Alan. 'We'll show these to everyone as soon as possible. Meanwhile, though, we'd better go down to the river and see if any of the footprints are still above water. Dorothy, take this up to the house and seal it in an envelope for me, will you?' He pulled the cross free, using his pen, and put it in my gloved hands. 'Handle it as little as possible, and don't touch it with your bare hands. I want to keep this very safe until we can identify it as someone's property.'

'It'll probably turn out to be Joyce's, lost months ago,' I said crossly to Lynn as I walked on up to the house. I was cold, and my knees hurt.

'You don't really think so,' said Lynn calmly. 'It's as shiny as the day it was made. It hasn't been out in the weather for more than a day or two.'

'Gold—' I began.

'Even gold gets dirty.'

It was, thank God, tea time when we got to the house. I would have headed straight for the kitchen, the fire, and some boiling-hot tea, had not Lynn reminded me. 'You need to seal that up, don't forget.'

In martyrly fashion I detoured to the library, where I found an envelope in a drawer, dropped the little gold ornament in, sealed it, and stuffed it in the pocket of my slacks.

Our ranks were sadly depleted around the tea table. With two of our number confined to their beds and two out documenting the scenes of various crimes – and one beyond the need for sustenance – we were only eight. I was glad to see that the vicar had joined us.

'How are your patients, Mr Leatherbury?' I asked when I had one cup of hot tea inside me and had poured myself another.

'Mrs Harrison is feeling much better,' he said. 'There was, I think, nothing much wrong there except exposure, and she was found before any permanent damage had been done. That is, I'm not a doctor, but her skin seems healthy, and she has no fever.'

'Has she said anything about what she was doing out there?'

The vicar looked uncomfortable. 'I don't quite know how much I am at liberty to repeat. She was rambling a bit, but she knows I am a clergyman. She may have felt I would keep her remarks confidential. In any case,' he hastened to add, 'much of what she said was unintelligible.'

Pat Heseltine, gorgeous Pat, was listening closely to this. 'I'm not at all sure the confidentiality privilege applies in this case,' she said thoughtfully. 'You're not her priest, nor were you attending her qua clergyman. If she was rambling, she might not even have known who she was talking to. In which case . . .'

'My dear Pat,' said the vicar with unusual firmness, 'the question is not a legal, but a moral one. It is up to me to make the decision to reveal or not to reveal her . . . conversation is hardly the word . . . her comments.'

'You could be required to, you know, in court. Or I think you could. It's an interesting point. I must look it up when I get back to my books.'

'The matter will scarcely arise. In any case, no one can force me to speak if my conscience forbids it. And the point is moot. I'm sure nothing she said has the slightest bearing on . . . on any of our worries.'

Pat looked stubborn. As she opened her mouth to continue the argument, I hastily spoke again. 'And Mr Upshawe? I gather his condition is much more serious.'

'Yes,' said the vicar. 'Excuse me, please.'

And he left the room.

'*Well!*' said Mike, who had been silently watching the action, his eyes avid. 'The good father has more nerve than one would have expected from that placid exterior.'

'The good father, as you put it, is a man of courage and integrity,' said Pat fiercely, 'and don't you ever forget it.'

'My dear!' Mike looked startled. 'I never doubted it, I do assure you.'

'Then stop sneering at him! We're in enough trouble here without your attitudes to contend with.'

Jim and Joyce started to speak at the same time, thus cancelling each other's good intentions. It was Tom who poured oil on the increasingly troubled waters. 'I'm sure Mike was just saying what we were all thinking, that Mr Leatherbury is handling a difficult situation with grace and kindness. I know we're all grateful he's here, though the poor man must be worried about his duties.'

I looked a question.

'Sunday. Tomorrow's Sunday. Who's going to take the service at St Michael's?'

Speculations about that occupied them for a few minutes, while I consumed tea and various improvised biscuits, and wished Alan would come back.

He wasn't long after that. He and Ed came in looking cold and famished, and proceeded to remedy their condition before they did anything else. The others finished their food and drink and began to push back their chairs. Alan stopped them.

'Ed took a picture I'd like you all to see. Tell me if you recognize the object.'

Ed fussed a bit with the camera until he had the best image of the cross on the small screen. He handed it around. Heads were shaken until the camera came to Pat.

'But that's the cross from Paul's prayer book! I'd recognize it anywhere – see the carving on it? At least, it's scarcely carving, just tracery, but very nice, I've always thought. He's had it for years. His daughter gave it to him, and he always uses it as a bookmark. However did it come to be caught in gorse?'

'That,' said Alan mildly, 'is what I need to find out.'

TWELVE

Alan asked me to come with him, and bring the cross. 'I'd like a witness to what he says, Dorothy, and you're the only one I can trust completely.'

'But you surely don't think he had anything to do with Dave Harrison's death!'

'Caused it, no. Had something to do with it – that's what I want to find out.'

So he tapped on Upshawe's door and went in. We found the vicar sitting at Laurence Upshawe's bedside, his prayer book open on his knee.

'Mr Leatherbury, I need to talk to you for a moment. Will we disturb Mr Upshawe if we do it here, do you think, or would another room be better?'

The priest looked up, his face unreadable. 'Some say the unconscious can hear, even when they can't respond. Perhaps it would be better to move into the corridor. I need to be within earshot, you understand, in case he speaks, or . . .' a helpless little shake of head '. . . or makes any sign of returning to consciousness.'

'It isn't good that he hasn't come out of it yet, is it?' I asked.

'Not as I understand it. No.'

We pulled chairs into the hallway and sat clustered around

the door of the sick man's room. The vicar sat quietly, asking no questions. He looked unutterably weary, and far older than I had earlier judged him to be.

Alan held out his hand and I gave him the envelope containing the cross. Alan pulled a clean handkerchief out of his pocket, spread it on his hand, and tipped the cross out onto it.

'Oh, you've found it! I treasure that little cross and wondered what had become of it.' The vicar reached for it, but Alan moved his hand away.

'I'd rather you didn't touch it just yet, sir, if you don't mind. You recognize it, then?'

'How could I not? My daughter gave it to me when I offici-ated at her wedding. I've always used it as a bookmark.' He held up his prayer book. 'The chain has worn very thin over the years, and I noticed only last week that one of the links was weak. I should have had it repaired then. It was in its proper place last evening, but when I opened the book this morning to read the office, I saw that it was missing and was greatly distressed. May I ask where you found it?'

Alan nodded to me and I answered. 'It was caught on a gorse bush, Mr Leatherbury, just by that bench at the bottom of the garden.'

'Oh! But that was where—' He broke off, glanced through the open doorway, and sighed. 'I have been somewhat unclear in my mind, Mr Nesbitt, about what I should do. But I believe it is time for me to speak. I should not do so, please understand, if there were any question of clerical privilege.'

'No, of course not,' Alan murmured. Folding the cross in the handkerchief and putting it safely in his pocket, he looked as bewildered as I felt. Was Mr Leatherbury about, after all, to tell us what Julie Harrison had said to him? But what could that have to do with a cross missing since, presumably, before the vicar left his room this morning? I was bursting with questions, but Alan gave me an unmistakable *keep still* look, so I waited for what the vicar had to say.

'I went out just after tea yesterday to read the evening office. I was disturbed in my mind by the events of the day and needed a quiet place to pray. It was cold outside, certainly, but the wind had dropped and the sun was still shining a bit. I found the bench, the one by the gorse bush, Mrs Martin. It was far enough removed from the house that I thought I should have some privacy.

'However, I had barely begun the first psalm when Mr Upshawe approached me. It was apparent from his demeanour that he was troubled, so I asked him if I could be of help. He told me a remarkable story.'

Alan took his pen from a pocket, folded the envelope that had held the cross into a more-or-less rigid surface, and waited.

'It seems that when Mr Upshawe assisted you to examine the . . . er . . . remains under the tree, he found something which he concealed from you. I have it here.' From the pocket of his clerical gray shirt, he took a gold ring with a carved black stone. 'This ring, or I should say copies of this ring, have been worn by the Upshawes for generations. Mr Upshawe's father had one. So did his father's cousin, one-time owner of this estate, and so did that cousin's son, Harry.'

'Ah.' Alan pondered the implications of that for what seemed like a long time. 'And why did Laurence Upshawe not tell us about the ring?'

'For the same reason that people often lie, or conceal the truth. He was confused and afraid. The ring, you see, has an inscription inside.' The vicar turned the ring to the light and showed us. 'HU. And the date is, according to Laurence, the date of Harry's coming of age. So he realized, when he found it down there under the tree, that there could be little doubt the ring was Harry's. But how could it be? Harry died in a plane crash over the Atlantic. So Laurence took it, resolving to think out the problem before he said anything to you or anyone else.

'But when Pat brought up the story of Harry's "disappearance", and you pointed out that the fact of the crash did not necessarily prove Harry's death, Laurence was forced to acknowledge that the skeleton could very well be Harry's. And that, in turn, raised the question of who murdered him. For with the best will in the world, Laurence could not make himself believe that a man dead by natural causes would be interred secretly beneath an oak tree.'

'And of the people who stood to gain by Harry's death, one stood out,' Alan pointed out with calm logic. 'Laurence's father, who coveted the house and the estate.'

'That, obviously, was what caused Laurence such distress. He said his father loved the house with a quite unreasonable passion, and was infuriated when he learned that Harry was moving to America and leaving it behind.'

'The plane trip wasn't to be just a holiday, then?'

'Not according to Laurence's memory. He was young, but he remembers the tirade his father went into, talking about a worthless young man who didn't even care about his priceless inheritance – and so on. One gathers he tackled Harry about it, and the young man laughed at him, saying he, Harry, was going to sell "the old relic" as soon as he inherited, and that he, Laurence's father, could buy it then if it suited him. That would have meant breaking the entail, but even in those days it wasn't impossible. What was impossible was the notion of Laurence's father buying the place. That branch of the family never had much money. And Harry knew it.'

'He sounds like a really nasty person,' I put in with a shiver. 'Not a great loss to the world, however he died.'

The vicar looked at me sadly, but said nothing. I knew what he was thinking. "Any man's death diminishes me . . ." et cetera. And John Donne was right, and so was Mr Leatherbury, and I was wrong. But . . . it all happened a long time ago. 'Suppose, for the sake of the argument, that Laurence's father – what was his name, anyway?'

'Laurence, I believe. Confusing, I agree.'

'Oh. Well, supposing he did kill Harry in a fit of temper. He's dead now. Why is the present Upshawe so worried about it? I know, it isn't pleasant to think your father might have murdered someone, but after all these years . . .' I shrugged.

'You haven't thought about the question of inheritance, my dear,' said Alan. 'If Laurence senior killed Harry, the law would not allow him to profit from his crime. He could not have inherited Branston Manor, nor passed it on to Laurence junior. And if Laurence junior didn't own it, he had no right to sell it to the Moynihans.'

'Quite,' said the vicar, and we sat in a melancholy little silence for a moment. 'Laurence first asked me if my predecessor in the parish had told me anything that would clear up the matter. I suppose he thought that his father might have confessed his crime; that family was always rather High Church. I told him that if such a confession had taken place my predecessor would have been most wrong to tell me anything about it, and that in fact he had not so much as implied such a thing. So then Laurence asked if I had any advice about what he should do, and I told him he needed to make a clean breast of the whole thing to you, Mr Nesbitt. Only then can the matter be investigated properly, and the truth known. I firmly believe he intended to take my advice, and that is why I have confided his story to you.'

'Oh, but—' I stopped. It was no use pointing out that the Moynihans would be devastated if it turned out they had no legal claim to their wonderful house. Both men fully realized that. I tried to find a ray of hope somewhere. 'Isn't there some provision for a good-faith transaction?'

Alan and the vicar both nodded. 'Some,' said Alan. 'The law is complicated on the subject. Ms Heseltine could probably brief us, but I suspect what she would say is that the matter would have to go to court and could take a long time to settle.'

'And meanwhile Jim and Joyce couldn't spend money on repairs to the house or the garden, couldn't do a thing, in fact, except sit and worry.'

'Dorothy, do please remember that this is all speculation,' said Alan gently. 'It's now pretty obvious that the skeleton is what remains of Harry Upshawe, but the rest of the story stems from Laurence's fears, and is based on no evidence whatsoever. Furthermore, it does nothing to explain the rest of the things that have happened here.'

'One thing, perhaps,' said the vicar mildly. 'When Upshawe left me, he left in such a state of perturbation that I nearly went after him. I got up to do so, in fact, but I tripped over the leg of the bench, and by the time I had recovered myself he was far away. I suspect that was when I lost my cross.'

'Very likely,' said Alan, handing it back to him. 'Let me restore your property, sir. I doubt it has much more to tell us. I very much wish, however, that you had followed Upshawe. To think that we're so close to knowing what happened down at the river!'

'You can't possibly wish it more than I. I had some feeling that he was upset enough to . . . to do something foolish, but I am not a young man, and he was walking too fast for me. I had planned to talk more with him as soon as he returned. That is why I went with you to search for him. I was most perturbed that he had not returned. I fear now that he went down to the river with some thought of jumping in, but Harrison tried to stop him and perished in the attempt. If Laurence doesn't recover, I shall feel I have two deaths on my conscience.'

And on that unhappy note we let him go back to praying over his patient.

THIRTEEN

Alan went back out with Ed to take some more pictures of anything they could think of that might be useful, and I wandered without direction, exploring the house more than I had taken time to do earlier.

The inside of the house was relatively undamaged. Some ominous patches of damp were beginning to appear on some of the third-floor walls where, I assumed, roof slates were missing, and water was leaking down from the attics. Here and there Mr Bates had neatly boarded up a broken window or two, but by and large the rooms were intact. The Moynihans' excellent taste showed everywhere. I assumed that some of the furnishings were original to the house, but the rest had been found or commissioned to suit the various styles of the house perfectly. Here Jacobean windows were draped in colourful brocades; there a Georgian bedroom reflected that period's interest in *Chinoiserie*. Many of the rooms reminded me, in fact, of the exquisite miniature rooms assembled by Mrs James Ward Thorne of Chicago and on display at the Art Institute there. The same care and expertise had gone into these full-scale rooms.

It broke my heart to think Jim and Joyce might have to leave this house. They had plenty of money. They could buy another fine home. But no amount of money could make up for the lavishly expended love.

I couldn't think about it. I made my way, getting lost a couple of times, down to the kitchen, where Rose was busy with preparations for tea.

'Goodness, you must get tired of the endless succession of meals to cook and clean up after,' I commented, watching her assemble jam tarts.

She laughed. 'I told you I enjoy a challenge, and cooking for a crowd without electricity is certainly a challenge. I don't enjoy the washing-up part so much, I admit. That's not usually part of my job here; the dailies do that. But needs must.'

'Look here, can't we all help? It's ridiculous—'

She stopped me, looking positively alarmed. 'Oh, no, that would never do! You're guests.'

'But the circumstances are unusual, for Pete's sake. You can't be expected to slave away all by yourself. I know Jim and Joyce wouldn't want you—'

She interrupted me again. 'No, really. I imagine you're right about Mr and Mrs Moynihan, but John wouldn't have it. He has very high standards about service in this house – and before you say what you're thinking, yes, he does help a great deal. It isn't easy keeping this stove stoked with wood, not to mention all the repairs he's been trying to do as time permits. Don't think he's a slave driver, for he's not. He just feels strongly about this house and its traditions.'

Well, I had my own ideas about the slave-driving. It was absurd to expect Rose to do all the work that was usually done by a small army of daily workers, and under emergency conditions, at that. Bates seemed happy enough to let the men plan and probably help with repairs, after all. But it was plainly time to change the subject.

'Is Mr Bates from these parts, then?'

She smiled at that, and relaxed a little. 'You Americans do have such interesting ways of expressing yourself. "From these parts." I'll have to remember that. Yes, John was born and bred in the village. His people have always lived here, many of them actually on the estate, in the old days.'

'That would be . . . when?'

'Seventeenth, eighteenth centuries. By the nineteenth the land was giving out, and agriculture didn't pay as it used to, so the Bates family mostly got work in the village. But they never lost their feeling for the estate. John's always felt it belongs to him and his kin, in a way.'

'That's why he works so hard, then. Keeping up tradition, keeping the place up to snuff.'

She smiled again at my odd English, and I went away feeling hopelessly inadequate, involved with people to whom 'the old days' meant three or four hundred years ago. The English and the Americans are two peoples divided not only by a common language, as Churchill or somebody put it, but by a completely different understanding of the words 'history' and 'tradition'.

'His people have always lived here.' I wondered sadly what would happen to the Bateses if the ownership of the house were called into question. What would happen to anyone connected with the estate?

What a royal mess, I thought in another burst of pure American.

I shook myself, mentally, like a dog shaking itself free of water. This mood was non-productive. What I needed was someone to talk to, and my choices were limited. I couldn't say anything to Tom and Lynn about what Alan and I had just heard. They're my best friends in England, but Lynn, bless her, is incapable of keeping a secret. Obviously Jim and Joyce shouldn't know the latest developments until a good many maybes were settled into definites. Ed was with Alan, and Mike was an interesting person, but I couldn't see him being of much help in the present situation.

That left Pat. Plainly one of us needed to talk to her, in hypothetical terms, about the inheritance question. Plainly I would prefer doing it myself; I wasn't wild about the idea of my husband closeted with that undeniably gorgeous – and perhaps predatory – woman.

I went off in search of Pat.

She was in the library, a Dorothy Sayers novel in her hands, its garish yellow and red dust jacket looking out of place in that oak-panelled repository of wisdom. She looked up as I entered.

'Dickens palled?' I asked, pointing to where *Bleak House* lay discarded on the table by her chair.

She grinned. 'I know it by heart. A gross libel on the legal profession.'

'I thought a written work had to be untrue to be libellous.'

She laughed out loud at that. 'Touché. Not that I admit a thing, mind you.'

'I prefer Sayers, whatever the truth about Dickens. Which one is that?' I peered at the title. 'Ah, *Gaudy Night*. My favourite.'

'Mine, too. But I presume you didn't come in here to discuss literature. Looking for something to pass the time?'

'No, I was looking for you, actually.'

'Ah. There have been developments. Or are you going to warn me off your very appealing husband?'

'I might do that, if I thought there was the slightest chance he might respond to your—'

'Charms? Blandishments? It's a reflex, you know. Or protective coloration, if you will.'

I cocked my head to one side.

'You see, Dorothy – you don't mind if I call you Dorothy? You see, in my youth I had to fight off men. Literally, sometimes. It grows tiresome. I pondered my alternatives. I could, certainly, make myself as unattractive as possible, but I was too vain to do that. Quite frankly, I enjoy the way I look.'

'Yes, I can see how you might.' My tone was as dry and chill as the wind outside.

Pat only nodded. 'Yes. So I simply could not wear baggy clothes from Oxfam, eschew make-up, and take to wearing sensible shoes. My alternative was to go on the offensive.'

'Meaning?'

'Take the initiative. Most men, you know, are afraid of a woman who pursues them. The little dears want to "make the running", as my great-grandmother would have put it. So I started to flirt outrageously, and most of the time it scares them off.'

'And when it doesn't?'

'I have a mean left hook.'

I broke up at that. I couldn't help it. I didn't want to like this woman, but she had a sense of humour. And she liked Dorothy Sayers.

'OK, truce,' I said when we had both stopped laughing. 'I didn't come in to fight over Alan, anyway. I want to ask your legal opinion. Hypothetically. What if—'

'Wait.' She held up a hand. 'Do you have any money with you?'

'I might have a few pence in my pocket – yes, here's ten pence.'

'Hand it over.'

'Wha–at?'

She held out her hand and I put the coin in it.

'Now you have paid me a fee, and I am officially engaged as your solicitor. That makes anything you say a privileged communication. Go ahead.'

'Solicitors cost a lot less here than lawyers do in America,' I said, shaking my head. 'I'll have to remember that. Anyway, what if—'

'Purely hypothetically, right?'

'Right. What if the heir to a large estate were murdered, but no one knew about it at the time. And later the murderer inherited said estate, and in due time passed it on to *his* heir, his son. Time elapses – many years. The owner of the estate, the entail having been broken or dissolved or whatever, sells the place. What is the legal position of the new owners?'

'Do you read crime novels a lot?'

'Yes, as a matter of fact. Sayers is my favourite.'

'Yes, well, this *hypothetical* case you've just posed is worthy of the Golden Age – Agatha Christie at her most convoluted. Coils within coils. Are you sure there isn't going to be a long lost heir in there somewhere?'

'Not that I know of. I mean, not in this hypothesis.'

'Well, the short answer to your question is, I haven't the slightest idea how the present owners of this fictional property would stand, legally. There are too many variables. For one, how certain is the identity of the murderer?'

'Not certain at all. It isn't even certain that murder was done, though the evidence makes it extremely likely.'

'Ah. Then plainly, until murder is proven against an individual, the question of the legal ownership of the property doesn't arise, assuming all the documents related to the inheritance and the transfer of property are in order.'

'I think we can assume that.'

'Well, then, what are you worried about? This could take as long as Jarndyce vs Jarndyce, and Jim and Joyce could be dead before it all came to a head.'

'Wait a minute – we were speaking hypothetically,' I objected.

'Sure. And "Love is a thing that can never go wrong, and I am Marie of Romania". Don't fret, luv. My lips are sealed with that ten pence piece.'

I grimaced. 'How am I going to go on resenting you when you read Sayers and quote Dorothy Parker? You are a woman of parts, Patricia Heseltine.'

'Pat. My given name, believe it or not, is Patience.'

'Oh, dear. I can see why . . .'

'Yes. Especially as the aforementioned virtue is not prominent in my character. I suppose my mother lived in hope, but she hoped in vain. Now look, Dorothy. Let's take the gloves off. What reason do you have for believing Laurence Upshawe's father murdered Harry? I take it there's good reason to believe it really is Harry under that tree?'

'Very good reason. Laurence found—'

Again she held up her hand. 'I don't want to know. I'll take your word for it. But what makes Alan think the senior Upshawe killed the little rotter?'

'Was he?' I asked. 'A rotter, I mean? I got the impression he wasn't a very likeable person, certainly, but that bad?'

'From what I hear. And I hear most things that circulate in the village. I never knew him, obviously. He was gone – gone away, everyone thought – before I was born. But his memory lingers on – rather like the faint aroma of skunk long after the animal has vanished. If the truth were known, I understand, there are a good many folks in the village who should rightly be named Upshawe. He wasn't liked, you know. Back in that era, a small place like this still expected a certain acknowledgement of noblesse oblige. His father had been good to his tenants and the villagers, but Harry never bothered. There were only two things about the village that interested him; the other was drinking at the White Horse.'

'A wastrel, then, as the Victorians would have called him.'

'Good word, that. Yes, he wasted his substance, like the original prodigal son. Unlike him, he never came back.'

FOURTEEN

I felt a little better after talking with Pat. It seemed that, unless or until Laurence's father was proved to be Harry's murderer, there was no question about the ownership of Branston Abbey. That was pretty much what we had thought, but it was nice to have it confirmed by an attorney.

I wasn't sure Alan would be comfortable with my telling Pat as much as I had. This business of working with Alan was tricky. He wasn't official anymore, and I'd never had any standing, but his policeman's conscience was acute. When it seemed that he needed to know all I'd said to Pat, then I'd spill the beans, but until then I was working on the assumption that I was old enough to use my own judgment. One thing I would report, though. It seemed there had been a good many people with reason to dislike Harry Upshawe, perhaps to hate him. And where there is hatred, there is motive for murder. The father, perhaps, of one of the village maidens he had seduced? Or perhaps they hadn't all been maidens. A husband or fiancé would have an equally powerful reason to wish Harry ill. Motive is the least important of the three prongs upon which criminal investigations rest. Means and opportunity are much more important, evidentially. But working in the dark of non-communication as we were, and fifty years after the fact, motive loomed larger than usual. And it was certainly good to know that others besides Upshawe senior had a motive for getting dear little Harry out of the way.

The vicar came down for tea, briefly. He asked Rose to prepare a tray for Julie, who was, he said, now fully conscious, but prostrated by the news of her husband's death. 'I had to tell her,' he said. 'She kept on asking me where he was. She is grieving, as one would expect, but she also seems afraid, terrified, even. She refuses to tell me who or what she's afraid of, but she keeps her door locked and won't allow anyone but me to come near her.'

'Not even Alan?' I asked incredulously. 'Surely a policeman . . .'

'Especially not Alan,' said the vicar with a sigh. 'She grew nearly hysterical when I suggested she let him know what had happened.'

'Will she tell you, then?' asked Alan.

'Not a word. I asked if I could pass on even what little she said yesterday, but she was adamant.' He sighed again. 'I have hopes that perhaps her sister might win her confidence in time.'

'I wonder,' I said. 'They're not on good terms. Never have been, I gather. Ah, well. When we have proper policemen here – saving your presence, my dear – maybe she can be persuaded to talk. Meanwhile, how is Laurence?'

'No change.'

Well, that was as expected, but unwelcome news anyway.

The sky had grown overcast, then cloudy, then dark and heavy with impending rain. I had planned to go for a walk, there being nothing very useful for me to do in the house, but the lowering sky discouraged me. Alan suggested a nap, but I was too restless. 'Later, maybe, love. I'm getting stir-crazy. I need to get out of the house, but it's going to pour.'

Without much enthusiasm I began another tour of the house; my knees needed the exercise. I found a long gallery that occupied much of the top floor. It had few pictures in it, but a number of mirrors, and there I encountered Mike. Clad in a sweater, tights and leg warmers, and ballet slippers, he was positioned in front of a mirror, holding the back of a chair and doing *pliés*.

'Practising?'

He nodded. 'One has to, you know. Every day. The muscles have to be worked constantly.'

'Do you know what Arthur Rubinstein said about practising? "If I miss one day, I know it. If I miss two, my wife knows it. If I miss three, the audience knows it." Do you have a show coming up?'

'Alas, no. But one must keep in shape. Hope on, hope ever. And besides.' He left his improvised barre and began doing various steps in front of the mirror. 'I have had an idea.' A *grand jeté* down the long room, then another, then one of those spinning leaps that look so utterly impossible, then a *tour jeté en l'aire* and several *fouettés* brought him back at my side. 'I have been thinking, you see,' he went on, his breathing not even slightly laboured, 'about how to get out of here.'

'Not you, too. There *is* no way out of here, at least not until we get the phone and electricity service back. Then we might be able to get rescued by helicopter, or something, but until then, no. Be reasonable, Mike. Trying to get out of here cost Dave Harrison his life.'

'Dave Harrison, besides being a thoroughly objectionable git, was a lump. I am not a lump. I am a *danseur*, not quite yet *premier*, but not at all bad. Did you see those *jetés*?'

'I did. Very impressive, but what's your point? Are you proposing to entertain us while we're stuck here?'

'I am proposing to go for help. I have been to the river, not to the south where it is wide and flooded, but to the north. It is very high, deep and swift and dangerous, *but* . . . it is narrow, and has not yet breached its banks. I believe I can jump it.'

I goggled for a moment, then began to rant. 'Are you out of your everlovin'? You just said yourself that the river's dangerous right now. If you missed the bank and fell in, you'd be dead in seconds. I've seen it to the south, where it's wider and slower, and it's terrifying even there. Nobody could get out of that torrent alive. If you're grandstanding, Mike, cut it out. I'm not impressed.'

'My dear lady, I am unsure what "grandstanding" means, but I presume you imply that I am seeking attention. I do assure you, nothing could be further from the truth.'

'Oh, for Pete's sake, come off it. Sure you're looking for attention, and at this point, I have to tell you it's not becoming.'

'Dorothy.' He dropped the pose. 'Do you really think I'd risk my life – or worse, my career, if I broke a leg or something frightful like that – for a publicity stunt? I'm the only one who could possibly go for help, and I mean to try it.'

'But why? We'll get out of here eventually, with no death-defying heroics.'

'Laurence Upshawe could die without medical attention. He's a nice chap. I'm the only one who might be able to help.'

I simply could not speak. I had thought Mike a facile, shallow, if amusing, poseur. Now he was prepared to risk everything for someone he barely knew.

I moistened my lips. 'You're not planning on doing it now, are you? We're going to have a storm.'

'That is precisely why I need to do it now. If we get more rain, the river will rise still more and might flood to the north, too. It's very near it now. I was just warming up a bit when you came in, but I fear, dear lady, I must bid you adieu. There is no time like the present. If it were done when 'tis done, then 'twere well it were done quickly. And other assorted clichés. Unfortunately I fear I shall have to wear shoes. Clumsy, but necessary. Where did I . . . ah, yes. You will excuse me, won't you?'

He was out of the room before I could recover. 'Mike, wait! You can't . . . Mike! . . . I'm coming with you!'

But an ageing woman with artificial knees is no match for a young man, fit and trained as a dancer. By the time I found my way to the stairs and reached the front door, Mike was already loping across the front lawn toward the wood. I saw him leap several downed trees with careless grace before I turned drearily back to the house. I couldn't catch up with him. I couldn't deter him. That beautiful man was running with foolish gallantry to his death, and there wasn't a thing I could do about it. I went upstairs to find Alan.

He was asleep, but he woke instantly at the sound of my voice. 'Dorothy! You're crying! What's happened?'

I hadn't known I was crying. I mopped up with the handkerchief he gave me, and said, 'It's Mike. He's gone on a fool's errand, thinking he can save the world – or us, at least. Alan, he's going to drown, and I couldn't lift a finger to save him!'

Long before I finished Alan had swung his feet off the bed and slipped into his shoes, and was looking for his overcoat. 'Where has he gone?' he asked crisply.

'To the river. Near the bridge, I suppose. He was taking off through the wood, the last I saw him. I couldn't catch him, Alan! He can run like a deer.'

'If he thinks he can swim that river, he is indeed going to drown, the bloody fool.'

'He isn't going to swim it. He's going to jump it.'

Alan turned on me a look of sheer astonishment, and then was out the door and racing down the stairs, calling for help as he went.

The sky grew darker still, and I heard a distant menacing

rumble of thunder like the tympani in the Brahms Requiem, low, inexorable, ominous. I looked out the window to watch the storm come, the tears again running unheeded down my cheeks.

The men were all back in less than half an hour, drenched to the skin and shivering with cold – and without Mike. I went downstairs to meet them.

The admirable Mr Bates had prepared a large pitcher of hot toddies, while upstairs Mrs Bates was lighting bedroom fires and slipping hot-water bottles into beds. Hot baths were still impossible to organize, and I worried about Alan catching cold.

They all changed as quickly as they could. Everyone was running out of clean, dry clothes, but I had no doubt the Bateses would somehow manage to wash – and dry – whatever was needed. Downstairs again, in front of the roaring kitchen fire with hot cups in their hands, they told the story.

'We never saw him,' said Jim. 'It had started to rain by the time we got to the river, and the visibility was pretty bad. We found the place where he jumped, though.'

I tried to speak, to ask the question, but found I could make no sound.

Alan took up the narrative. 'It was only the place where the marks of his shoes were pressed deeply into the bank on this side. Or the mark of one shoe, rather. He tried a broad jump, evidently.'

'A *grand jeté*,' I murmured. 'And . . . on the other side?'

There was a silence. Then . . . 'Nothing,' said Alan.

No one had any appetite for dinner. Rose had somehow contrived a pot roast. Under normal circumstances it would have smelled delicious. Now I found it nauseating.

The rain kept up all night, drumming on the roof, as menacing as the tympani/thunder. I suppose in the end I slept.

FIFTEEN

'This is beginning,' I said to my husband in the morning, 'to remind me of *And Then There Were None*. Only they were ten, to start with, and we were thirteen. Now two of us are gone, two are in bed, one is keeping a deathbed watch. Who's next, I wonder?'

'You're getting morbid, and your arithmetic is at fault. We started fifteen, if you count in the Bateses.'

'Oh, they certainly count,' I agreed reluctantly. 'But I was thinking of the . . . the above-stairs crowd, if that archaic term can be allowed.'

Alan just grunted. He hates unresolved problems, and the weekend had produced nothing but. Coils within coils, as Pat had said. No wonder he was a bit testy.

The vicar conducted a simple church service that morning for anyone who wanted to attend. It would have been nice to do it in the old cloisters, but they were unsafe, as well as freezingly cold and wet. The rain had stopped, or had paused, rather. More was certainly to come. We gathered in the library instead, for Matins and an abbreviated Eucharist.

Sunday, November 5. The day I had been so looking forward to, with fireworks and all the trimmings. No mention had been made, naturally, of the aborted festivities, but they were on everyone's mind, I was sure. When one is enmeshed in crises, the mind hunts, almost frantically, for trivialities to fret about instead. I tried to pray for a resolution to all our disastrous difficulties, but found myself wondering wistfully if the display would have been truly spectacular.

After church Jim went to the cloisters with his tools. If escape was impossible, at least he, with the other men, could keep on with repairs to the house. Alan told me to stay away. He almost never issues a command, but this time he had sense on his side. 'The roof could cave in, Dorothy. It's extremely touchy work, and I don't want you and your dodgy knees anywhere near it. See if you can keep the other women in the house, as well.'

I argued that if it was all that dangerous, he and the others shouldn't try it either, but I knew it was a lost cause. The gentleman's code of honour, the laws of hospitality, centuries of unwritten rules about the way an Englishman should behave – I could never win against those odds. So I left him to it and, in the perverse spirit of biting down on the aching tooth, started off on a walk through the wood to the river.

It was a thoroughly unpleasant day, not actually raining but threatening to at any moment. All the colours of the world seemed to have faded to gray and brown, and the most depressing shades of both. The floor of the wood was sodden and slippery with fallen leaves, which made the footing uncertain. More than once I wished I had brought my cane, but I was too stubborn to go back for it. I kept seeing Mike, yesterday, leaping through the wood like a fawn – or a faun. After one nasty near-fall, I picked up a fallen branch to use as a stick, but it was rotten and crumbled the first time I leaned on it. After that I went more carefully, picking my way and testing each step. I should have followed the drive instead. At least my knees hurt hardly at all; there was that to be thankful for.

I smelled the river before I saw it, and when I came upon it I gasped. The placid stream of three days ago was an angry, pulsing, living thing, boiling and foaming, terrifying in its mindless intensity. It had not yet risen above its banks, but it was visibly rising and would surely breach soon.

Walking toward the drive, I tried to find the place where Mike had attempted his crazy, quixotic leap, but it was hopeless. I should have realized that the rain would have washed away every trace. I had hoped, foolishly, that I might be able by daylight to see what the men last night had not, some sign that he had, however improbably, reached the far bank. There was nothing.

I said a little prayer for a lost dancer. Maybe someday someone would compose a ballet for him, along the lines of Debussy's Drowned Cathedral – *Le Danseur Englouti*. But someone else would dance the role.

There was something hypnotizing about the angry, ceaseless, rushing water. I couldn't take my eyes off it, and I could feel myself drawn to the brink. If I watched it much longer, I knew, I would go mad, or jump in, or . . . something. My mind and senses numbed, I fled back to the house.

The men were still at it in the cloisters, cutting up the tree that had fallen through, clearing away broken glass, shoring up the roof where it threatened to fall in. I went close enough to take a look, though I knew I mustn't get in the way. The destruction was pitiful to behold, but I could see signs of progress. John Bates was working like a demon, everywhere at once, giving precise orders which everyone seemed to obey. I didn't know what his work had been before he came to the Moynihans, but he clearly knew what he was doing.

I went to seek out a like expert.

I found her, as usual, in the library, this time absorbed in a bound volume of *Punch*. 'Your tastes are catholic, I see.'

'"Age cannot wither her, nor custom stale the humour in these pages"', said Pat. 'Are you seeking company or reading material?'

'Neither. Pat, something has to be done. This can't go on.'

She put down her book and gave me her full attention. 'I agree, in principal. The men are working it out in sweat or prayer. What do you suggest we do?'

'I want you to do what you do best. You're a solicitor. Are you also a . . . is it a barrister, someone who goes to court?'

'Yes, barrister, and yes, I am. In a village there isn't a lot of scope for that sort of thing, but in London, before I moved back here, I was a pretty good trial lawyer, as I believe the term is in America.'

'I thought so. Now, look. There is only one person who knows anything at all about what went on the night Dave Harrison died, and she's locked up in her room upstairs refusing to talk to anyone. I want you to make her talk.'

Pat said nothing for a full minute. Then she rose, removed her reading glasses, and said simply, 'Yes. I think I might be able to do that.'

I followed her into the kitchen.

'Rose,' she said, 'I thought I'd take a cup of tea up to Mrs Harrison. Please don't bother about it – I'll make it – but I'll need your passkey for her door. Let's see – third on the left after the small landing, isn't it?'

Now if I'd made that request, Rose would probably have insisted on taking the tray up herself. Pat, with her inborn self-assurance, got her own way. In a few minutes we were heading up the stairs to Julie's room.

Pat handed me the tray while she unlocked the door. She didn't bother to knock.

Julie was not in bed, as I had expected, but was sitting slumped in an armchair in the bay window. They had moved her from the isolated suite she had occupied with Dave to one nearly at the west end of the house. It faced the front, so she had a good view from the bay window of the cloister and the work going on there. She didn't look up as we entered, but pointed and said in her whiny voice, 'Look at that, Reverend. It'll cost a fortune to fix that part of the house, let alone the rest. Why, there won't be anything left by the time they get done—'

At that point she looked up and saw us, and screamed. 'What the hell are you doing in here? Out! Get out!'

'I don't think so, Mrs Harrison,' said Pat calmly. 'I've brought you some tea. We need to talk.'

'I don't want any tea! I don't want to talk to you! You had no right to come bustin' in here. I – I'll sue.'

'Well, there you are, then. You *are* talking to the right person. I'm a lawyer, and I never lose my cases.' She had moved a little table closer to the chair, and I set the tray down on it. Pat poured out the tea, then took a small flask from the pocket of her slacks. 'This is good for shock,' she said gravely. 'I think you'd better have a little. You've been through a lot these past few days.'

Julie's eyes lit up at the sight of the amber liquid Pat poured into the teacup, and she offered no more protest. I've never been sure if it was the drink or Pat's air of intelligent sympathy that opened Julie's previously sealed lips. Or maybe she was just tired of her own company. At any rate, once she started talking, the torrent flowed like the river in spate.

'Lady, you ain't just whistlin' Dixie. Let's go visit your sister, he says. Have a nice European vacation, he says. And it's turned out to be nothin' but trouble, right from the get-go. My snooty sister and her snooty husband and their run-down old house, and all too good for the likes of us.' She took a healthy swig of the heavily laced tea. 'Dave, he says we can talk 'em around. Money talks, he says, and when they find out how much money they could make, they'll be draggin' us to the lawyers for the papers. Hah!' Another swig, and the cup was empty. 'Treated us like dirt, tried to throw us out, and then changed their minds and said we had to stay here. We don't gotta put up with this, I told him. I don't care what they say, they're up to something. Stands to reason there's a way out of here, storm or not. They just don't want us to find it, damned if I know why. Dave, he says they're tryin' to put us off the place, makin' out like it's a dangerous place to live and that. So we took off, lookin' for the secret way out. Thanks very much, don't mind if I do.'

The fluid in the cup this time was neat whiskey. If this was Pat's usual technique with reluctant witnesses, I could believe her claim of never losing a case.

'So anyway, we start to look. Kinda sneaky-like, y'know? Dave, he figures there might be a tunnel or somethin' under the river, like they used for smugglers way back when.'

Way back where, too, I thought. Branston was in the heart of Kent and miles from any coast. Smugglers would have had to build an awfully long tunnel. But Julie's geography was apparently a trifle vague.

'So we figured, if the tunnel came out in the house, it'd be in the basement somewheres, so we went down to poke around. But there was nothin' much down there but a lot of wine in one part, and the furnace in the other. Nice and clean, it was, I'll have to say that for 'em. Course, if you've got tons of money like them, you can get somebody else to do all the work. Must cost a fortune to run this house. I wouldn' mind a li'l bit o' that money, myself.'

Julie held out her cup for another round. Pat and I exchanged glances. At this rate, she'd pass out before she told us anything useful. This time Pat made the mixture mostly tea. Julie didn't appear to notice.

'So where was I? Oh, yeah, we're tryin' to find the way out, but there wasn't nothin' in the house, not that we could find, anyways. So Dave says, maybe it came out in one of those other buildings, the garage or somethin'. Well, I told him, I says, dummy, I says, they didn't have garages back then. But he says, hey, brain, they had horses, didn't they? And where they kept the horses, now they keep cars. Dave could be smart sometimes, when he wasn't being dumb.' She sniffed. 'Maybe he wasn't the best husband in the world, but he had ideas, all right.' She sniffed again, and I feared she had reached the weepy stage of her rake's progress, but she took another drink, and it seemed to buck her up.

'So we headed for the garage, and when we was almost there, Dave stopped so sudden I ran into him, and he says, there's somebody out here. Then I heard 'em, too, a couple of guys talkin'. So Dave tells me to keep still.' Julie put her finger to her lips in exaggerated pantomime. 'Ooh! He told me to keep on keepin' my trap shut, and here I've been shootin' my mouth off to you.' She opened her mouth again to finish off the contents of her tea cup, and then shut it firmly, an owlish look in her somewhat bleary eyes.

Oops. Was this all we were going to get?

I had reckoned without Pat. 'Quite right,' she said, putting the flask back in her pocket with a gesture that could have been seen from the third balcony. I wondered if she had ever acted when she was at Oxford, in OUDS, perhaps? 'You wouldn't want to say anything foolish. Dave knew best, I'm sure, so if he told you to shut up, you'd better not say anything he wouldn't like.'

'Whaddya mean, Dave knew best? I'm the brains of this

operation! *I* was the one told *him* he'd better do somethin' quick
when that Upshawe guy was gonna blab about— never mind what.
I was the one told *him* to follow Upshawe and tell him he'd better
keep his lip buttoned, or else. *I* was the one had the sense not to
go with him, in case there was trouble.' She paused and hiccuped.
'And there was!' she said with a wail, and began to sob.

'That's all she wrote,' I whispered, and Pat nodded. She got
out the flask and put it on the table, and we went downstairs,
leaving Julie to her alcoholic blues.

SIXTEEN

'Frustrating,' was my comment when we were back down
in the library. 'We're no closer to knowing what happened
in the encounter between the two men. And I was so sure
she could tell us!'

'It's still possible that she could, if she would. I think we've
got all we can out of her for the moment, but I wonder if she's
the sort to respond to a séance. Do you think, if the egregious
Dave came back and told her to tell all, she's credulous enough
to believe, and talk?' asked Pat thoughtfully.

'Hmm. She's not the brightest bulb in the chandelier, but she's
shrewd in her own way. I suppose, perhaps, if we could work
it out so that she could see some self-interest in the proceedings
– but we're talking nonsense. I wouldn't have the slightest idea
how to stage a séance, and anyway that sort of thing went out
with the thirties, surely.'

'We're trapped in the thirties, hadn't you noticed? That wasn't
just a storm we experienced, it was a time warp. I expect at any
moment to hear someone cranking up a gramophone to play
Rudy Vallee records.'

'You've been reading too much, is what's the matter with you.
What did you make of her ramblings, though? Was there anything
of use?'

'Well, we know she and Dave overheard Upshawe's confession, and that it upset them. I couldn't quite follow why.'

'I think I know. When we first got here— goodness, was it only
three days ago? Feels like several lifetimes. Anyway, the Andersons
had been here a day or two already and had had far too much

time to get acquainted with Dave and Julie. They told us, Alan and me, that Dave had some scheme to tear this house down—'

Pat uttered a horrified shriek.

'—and build some sort of resort. He seemed to want to go into partnership with Jim. Yes, I know, it was an obscene idea, and impossible with a listed building, anyway. But that would explain why Dave went off after Laurence.'

'It would? Oh, sure! What a ninny I am. Your hypothetical situation. If Laurence's father killed the heir, then he couldn't inherit, et cetera, et cetera. And if Jim didn't own the house, he couldn't sell it to Dave, and all the scheming was for naught.'

'Exactly. So Dave had a motive for silencing Laurence.'

'Not a very strong one, though.' Pat frowned. 'You and I talked this out. There are so many ifs, the threat to Jim and Joyce's claim is practically non-existent.'

'Yes, but would a Dave Harrison realize that? I would say that logical thinking was never his strong point, and he was not only drunk at the time, but in the grip of a monomania. He had convinced himself that Jim was going to buy into his plan, that this house was as good as his— oh!'

'Sudden pain?'

'Sudden idea, and . . . rats! It's gone again. Something I said triggered . . . it was right on the tip of my mind . . .'

'Stop thinking about it. Those things are like cats. They only run away and hide if you chase them, but if you ignore them, they come out and beg for attention. So you think Dave followed Laurence and tried to push him in the river, but ended up getting pushed in himself.'

'Or falling in, more likely. He was bound to have been pretty unsteady on his feet at that point.'

'I don't know. Julie was still conscious and more or less coherent when we left her, and I'd poured the best part of a pint of whiskey into her. I think Dave must have had a formidable capacity.'

'Years of practice, probably.' I shook my head. 'How on earth did a sister of Joyce's find such a useless specimen to marry?'

'Just lucky, I guess.'

The vicar surprised us by coming down to lunch. He had retired to Laurence's room as soon as the church service was over, and we hadn't expected to see him the rest of the day, except perhaps to fetch a tray. We all wanted to know about his patient.

'He seems to me to be quite a bit better. He's breathing more easily and looks as if he's sleeping, rather than unconscious. At least his eyes move now and then, beneath the lids.'

'REM sleep,' someone said. 'They say that means he's dreaming.'

'I shouldn't think the dreams would be pleasant,' said Alan.

'He has made little noises today,' the vicar acknowledged. 'Sounds of discomfort, as I interpret them. Moans, I suppose one could call them if they were better defined. Actually, they sound like nothing so much as the little whines produced by a dreaming dog.'

'He hasn't tried to speak? Or open his eyes?' Alan tried to sound casual, but I could hear the sharpened awareness in his voice.

'His eyelids fluttered once, but never opened. And there's been nothing that sounded like words. Still, I am encouraged by his progress, and thought I might venture to take a few minutes away from him.'

'I should think so,' I said warmly. 'You've done nothing but look after him for days.'

'Less than two days, Mrs Martin. We found him Friday evening, remember. It seems longer, I agree. Many things have happened in those two days.'

I think we all tried not to think about Mike.

'Look here, sir,' said Alan. 'Suppose I take the duty for a few hours, and let you get some rest. I have a bit of basic medical training. I think I could serve.'

Mr Leatherbury smiled a little. 'I'm sure you know more than I about nursing. My concern is the cure of souls, not bodies. As I could be of next to no help anywhere else, I chose to sit with poor Laurence in case he took a turn for the worse and needed a priest. But I admit I'm not as young as I used to be, and trying to keep alert all this time has been a bit exhausting. If you truly don't mind . . .'

'Not a bit.'

Pat spoke up at that moment. 'Paul, Alan. I'm of no earthly use to anybody, just sitting around. I don't know a thing about medicine, but I know how to keep my eyes and ears open. Let me take the next shift.'

I was gaining more respect for Pat with each passing hour. It was agreed: Pat went off to sit with the victim, or the chief suspect, depending on how you looked at it, and Alan returned to his work in the cloister.

'I expect you're badly in need of a nap,' I commented to the vicar.

'No, I need fresh air more than anything, I believe. I intend to take a walk.'

'It isn't very nice out there,' I said. 'I went out this morning, to look at the river, and . . .' The lump in my throat stopped me.

'Yes. That poor young man. It was a gallant gesture, no matter how ill-advised. Perhaps, Mrs Martin, you would care to walk a little way with me? The rain will keep away for another hour or so, I believe, and you can wrap up well. I'd be grateful for the company.'

What he meant, I suspected, was that he thought I needed some comfort. He was right about that, certainly. I found my coat and hat and borrowed some wellies, and we set out.

Mr Leatherbury was silent, a companionable silence, waiting for me to choose a topic. I didn't want to talk about tragedy. I was weary of disaster, frustrated by our inability to do anything about – anything. At least Jim and Alan and the other men were doing something constructive, clearing away the worst of the messes and beginning repairs. I could find nothing useful to do or say.

But the thought of repairs reminded me of what, centuries ago, I had wanted to ask the vicar. 'Mr Leatherbury, Joyce or Laurence or somebody told me you knew a lot about the history of this house. All I know is the brief outline Laurence gave us at dinner that first night. Can you tell me more?'

His face lit up. 'Ah. You've hit on my passion. I warn you, I can talk about this house until you're begging for mercy. What specifically did you want to know?'

I laughed. 'I know too little even to ask. But I suppose I'm most interested in the ghosts – if you as a clergyman concede their existence.'

He chuckled. 'Not officially, but I'll tell you some of the stories, and you can judge for yourself. The oldest ghost who is purported to haunt these premises is, as one might expect, a monk who resented being turned out. The story has it that he fought King Henry's men, against the express orders of his abbot, who had commanded them all to go peacefully. So not only was he – Brother David – killed in the scuffle, but his abbot refused him absolution.'

'So he has no home in heaven and must walk the earth,' I finished. 'That's rather a creepy story. Would an abbot actually do such a thing?'

'That's hard to tell. It was a long time ago, and such stories are notoriously unreliable. On the other hand, Abbot Benedict – it was a Benedictine house, and he had chosen the name of the founder – was by all contemporary accounts a tough old bird, harsh with the men under his jurisdiction. And Brother David, as one would expect, was a Welshman, with the fiery temper of his race.'

'What was a Welshman doing way over here in Kent?'

'That,' said the vicar, negotiating a stretch of lawn that was especially littered with storm debris, and giving me his arm for support, 'is one of the details that make the story somewhat suspect.'

'Have you ever seen him? Brother David, I mean?'

'Certainly not.' It was said with a twinkle that left me unsure of whether he was speaking the literal truth or taking the official line that ghosts didn't exist.

'So you said he's the oldest of them. There are more, then?'

'Legions. The usual spurned lovers and bereft maidens. An early Branston, around 1650, who was said to have drowned in one of the garden ponds, is reputed to go about with a fish in his pocket, slapping it in one's face.'

'Ugh!' I shuddered. 'A real goldfish in the face would be bad enough, but a long-dead one – no, thank you! Are there no really romantic legends about the house? Alan had a temporary appointment at Bramshill once, and they had a marvellous ghost story, about a bride who was, with her guests, playing hide and seek on her wedding night. I'd have thought she'd have had better things to do, but anyway, she hid in a chest, it locked itself, and she wasn't found for years.'

The vicar laughed. 'Oh, that one's been around for a long time, at various locations. Hiding on one's wedding night appears to have been a popular pastime. But no, there aren't any like that here. The house has seen its usual share of tragedy, as one might imagine. From the time the monastery was established in 1042, people have lived here. That's a long time. Wars have taken their toll, as have diseases. The household was not immune to the Black Plague, nor to the influenza epidemic in the early twentieth century. Several of the Upshawes fell to the flu, which explains why there was no closer heir than a cousin when old Charles died.'

I sighed. There we were, back at the problem. The elephant in the room. 'Mr Leatherbury, do you think Laurence . . . had anything to do with Dave Harrison's death?'

'I should think that was obvious,' he said, with a touch more acid in his voice than I expected. 'Plainly he was on the scene. However, if you're asking me if I believe he pushed the man in the river, I do not. I've been a clergyman for a good long time, Mrs Martin. One comes to know something about people. Laurence Upshawe is not a killer.'

He had a point. Still . . . 'You knew him before he went to New Zealand?'

'No. I've been incumbent here for only twenty years, and Laurence left in . . . 1982, I believe it was. I know his family's history because I'm fanatically interested in old houses and have read everything I could about this one, but I met the man for the first time on Thursday night – when you did. You're perfectly justified in doubting my judgment.'

'It isn't that so much. As a matter of fact I agree with you, and I think Alan does, too. But the police have to go by evidence – and Laurence was the only other one on the scene.'

'That,' he said with finality, 'is their problem, not mine. It's getting rather chilly. Shall we go in?'

SEVENTEEN

'Wait. Please.' I put my hand on his arm. 'I didn't mean to offend you. It's just that this horrible business is the only thing I can think about. I wish to goodness I'd never seen that miserable skeleton. That's what started everything!'

'No, my dear. And it is I who should apologize. I should not have been so snappish with you. But your discovery did not begin this matter. It began long ago, with whoever buried the poor man under the tree. And if you had not found the evidence, someone else would have.'

'Yes, well, that would have suited me better,' I retorted. 'I was so looking forward to seeing a proper Guy Fawkes celebration. I love fireworks. I'm being childish; sorry.'

'It is a great pity, all round. Have you never celebrated the Fifth of November?'

'No. I've lived in England only a few years, and somehow Alan and I have never been in the right place on that day. He's told me all about it, of course, the Catholic plot to blow up Parliament. I'm still not quite sure why the Gunpowder Plot should be a cause for celebration.'

'But we celebrate not the plot, but the fact that it was foiled.'

'Isn't it just a little . . . well, politically incorrect? Burning an effigy of Guy Fawkes, a Catholic? It seems a bit grisly.'

'You may not know that a celebration of the saving of the King and the House of Lords was mandated by Parliament shortly after the event. Bonfires and the ringing of church bells became traditional. The fireworks and the burning of the guy came later, having little to do with the historical occasion – any more than parades and baseball games have to do with your American Independence Day.'

'Well, it's not quite the same – but I see your point. At any rate, I'm sorry to miss all the fun, though fireworks aren't at all important compared to the issues we're dealing with here.'

'True. Whoops, here it comes!' The rain came as suddenly, and as copiously, as turning on a faucet. We were soaked to the skin in seconds.

At this rate, I thought bitterly as I squelched up to my room to change clothes yet again, I might as well just walk around all weekend in my underwear and have done with trying to keep clean and dry.

The rain also put a stop to the restoration work in the cloister. Alan came upstairs shortly after I did, nearly as wet as I and a whole lot grubbier. He washed as best he could in the limited hot water available, and grumbled. Alan isn't a grumbler, by nature, but this endless 'holiday' was trying even his patience. 'And what am I meant to wear?' he asked, standing in his shorts and undershirt when he had removed as much grime as possible. 'Everything I have here is either wet or dirty or both.'

I paused a moment to admire the view. My husband is a large man, not fat but tall and, even at his age, powerfully built. His gray hair adds authority to his commanding presence. He is, in short, a hunk.

And one of the dearest people on the planet – even when he's grumpy. I smiled at him. 'Aha! You reckoned without your brilliant wife. I thought ahead, and borrowed some clothes from Mr Bates. He's just about the same size, and he was happy to oblige. They're not quite your style, but in the circumstances, I didn't think you'd mind too much. They are at any rate both clean and dry.'

He actually looked quite nice in them, if somewhat more casual than he usually appears. I hadn't fared so well. No one in the house was my size, which rather runs to the dumpling configuration. But one of Joyce's sweaters fit not too badly with my cleanest pair of slacks. Beggars, as I carefully had not said to Alan, can't be choosers.

We went down to a badly needed cup of tea. The rain slashed at the window panes and dripped down the chimney, hissing in the kitchen fire. Nobody had much to say.

'We wouldn't have been able to do the fireworks anyway.' That was Joyce.

'No,' Jim responded listlessly. 'And we can't work on the house until this lets up.'

'But we're coming along on the ark.' Ed tried to lighten the atmosphere. He didn't succeed. I missed Mike, who would have made everyone laugh with some drawling, bitchy remark. Astonishingly, I missed Pat, who had come down when the vicar relieved her, downed a cup of tea and a biscuit or two, muttered an excuse, and gone off, presumably to the library to read something classic. She could strike sparks, but apparently wasn't in the mood. Tom and Lynn hadn't come down at all.

The house party was utterly demoralized, and Jim and Joyce didn't even seem to notice.

'Somebody has to do something,' I whispered to Alan, 'or we'll all go stir crazy.'

'You're right about that.' He rose, stretched, and addressed our host. 'Jim, I have a proposal to make. I know Mr Bates has been trying to assess the damage to the house, but he has a great many other responsibilities. Suppose you and I take a complete tour of the house and see what we can from the inside. An outside inspection is needed, too, but with this kind of rain, we'll be able to tell a good deal from where damp spots appear, where the rain is actually coming in walls and windows – that kind of thing. And anyone else who would like to come along can get the house tour we were promised and never had time for. What do you think?'

There was no wild upsurge of enthusiasm. Everyone was too dispirited for that. But eventually we recruited Ed, who hadn't yet been able to see the house thoroughly, and dragged Tom and Lynn out of their lair. Pat, who was in a strange mood, growled that she already knew as much about the house as she cared to, thank you very much. Mr Bates found several lanterns, since the rain made the house dim as well as gloomy, and we assembled what flashlights we had.

'Should have waited until morning,' Ed complained. 'Can't see worth a damn this afternoon.'

'If we had waited,' I said, *sotto voce,* 'there would have been more murders done. And I might have been one of the villains.'

In truth it was a somewhat futile exercise, but it gave us something to do besides sitting around wishing we were anywhere else on the planet. And though we couldn't see much in the way of storm damage, from the standpoint of a house tour it was perfect. Those rooms hadn't been designed for harsh electric lighting. Daylight, candles and, later, lamps would have provided the illumination for the first many hundred years that the house had been standing. Our lanterns restored the lovely proportions of the rooms, softened and mellowed the old panelling, showed the carving at its best.

They also, less fortunately, made the uneven floors and odd corners that much more hazardous. The first time I tripped on a raised floorboard I nearly fell. After that I kept my hand tucked securely in Alan's arm.

I had wandered a good bit of the house by myself, or so I thought. I soon realized I had only scratched the surface. Mr Bates, who knew the house intimately and soon became our guide, knew the history of every room, every piece of furniture, every painting. This bit of panelling was reputed to have been removed from one of Thomas More's rooms after More fell out of favour with the king. This was an Adam fireplace, this a Gainsborough painting. Here was the bed Queen Anne had slept in, bought for the purpose, her visit nearly bankrupting the family. And so on.

'Mr Bates,' I said when we were climbing to the third floor and I could get a word in edgewise, 'the Harrisons apparently had some idea there were tunnels leading from the house. I thought it unlikely, myself, because those were mostly used for smuggling, and we're too far from the sea. Right?'

'Indeed, madam. To my knowledge there is no history of smuggling or piracy connected with the house, but during the civil wars various hiding places were devised, because the Branstons were royalist, and there were pockets of Parliamentarians out to do mischief wherever they could. The family plate was locked up on several occasions, and once, if the stories are true, the family themselves had to go into hiding. Most of the secret rooms have been converted over the years into bathrooms and closets, but I can show you one of them, or I hope I can. I came across it the other day when I was repairing a bit of the panelling.'

We were in one of the unused third-floor bedrooms. He stepped to the wall near the fireplace and, carefully moving aside a chair, pushed on a piece of moulding. It moved aside to reveal a keyhole, surrounded by old brass, black as iron. Bates took from his pocket a huge old key, the kind I associated with castles and dungeons. 'I don't know that this will fit, but it's the right size and age. It was in a drawer in one of the attics, with a lot of other old keys, and I've found the locks that match most of them. Even if it fits, the lock's apt to be a bit stiff,' he said, man-oeuvring the key into the lock. 'I don't imagine this has been opened for a hundred years or more.'

We were very still. The rain pounded against the house; the lanterns flickered. Our modern clothes were hidden in the gloom; only our white faces could be seen. I felt suddenly oppressed, as if back in that time of terror when King James's loyalists were hunted down by Cromwell's men, Christian against Christian, Englishman against Englishman.

And I suddenly did not, very much did not, want to see that door opened. If I had followed my instincts, I would have fled that room, run down to warmth and light and normality. But I suppose my manners were overdeveloped, so I gripped Alan's arm and waited.

The lock was indeed stiff, but Bates persevered, and suddenly, with a harsh grating sound like the gnashing of teeth, the lock gave. Bates pushed, shoved, then tugged at the door, which finally, with an eldritch shriek of hinges, opened outward. Bates took the lantern he had asked Jim to hold, held it high, and illuminated the interior of the dark hole in the wall.

And crashed to the floor in a dead faint.

EIGHTEEN

Somebody screamed. Maybe it was I. I don't know. I vaguely remember Alan pulling me close, burying my face in his shoulder so I couldn't see. Tom and Ed hustled Lynn away, while Jim tried to deal with the inert form of the butler. When

I could think again, I said shakily, 'Love, you'd better see to Mr Bates. You know CPR and all that. I'll take Lynn to the next room and wait for you. Just – just be as quick as you can.'

'Sure you'll be all right?'

'Sure. But give me the flashlight. Come, Lynn.'

The flashlight didn't give us as much light as a lantern, but it was modern. It didn't flicker evocatively, didn't conjure up images of past dreadfulness.

Lynn and I just sat for a few minutes, our hands clasped together tightly, trying to stop shaking. When I thought I could speak without chattering teeth, I said feebly, 'Was that thing real?'

'I don't know.' Lynn's voice was no steadier than mine. 'I thought it was maybe a ghost. Dorothy, it moved! I swear it moved!'

'I think it just fell forward. I – at first I thought it was the guy. You know, for the bonfire. But it wasn't, was it?'

'It was a woman. I think. There was a dress . . .'

'It looked like . . . Lynn, do you know what it reminded me of? You remember that terrifying scene in *Psycho* when they go into the room where the mother is, and she's in that rocking chair, and—'

'Don't! She looked like that, exactly like that, all dead and dried up and horrible . . .'

Lynn's voice was rising higher and higher, and I wasn't feeling steady enough myself to calm her down, so I was most relieved when Tom and Alan walked in. No two men ever looked more like white knights. I could feel my blood pressure drop about thirty points just at the sight of him. Lynn started to sob on Tom's shoulder.

It took me differently. I had to know. 'Alan, what *was* that thing?' I didn't at the moment even remember to be concerned about Bates.

'A body, my dear. Long dead, mummified by being in there close to the fireplace for so long.'

'A woman?'

'From the clothes, yes. They're remarkably well-preserved.'

'And . . . how old? How long was that poor thing walled up in there?' I was starting to shake again, to gasp. The space was so small, so airless, so dark . . .

'Easy, love. She was dead when she went in. Even a quick glance told me that. No abrasions to the hands. And the clothes are modern. Long hair, held back with a ribbon. It's pretty easy to guess that she was killed sometime in the middle of the twentieth century.'

'When Harry Upshawe died, in other words.'

'About then, yes.'

'It can't be a coincidence.'

'One wouldn't think so.'

Belatedly, I remembered Mr Bates and asked Alan about him. 'Is he all right, Alan?'

'He will be. It was just a faint. Jim and Ed got him down to the kitchen, where it's warm. I'm sure his wife will look after him. He'll be all right,' Alan repeated.

I sighed, a long, shuddering sigh. 'What are we going to do, Alan? Just this morning I said to Pat, this can't go on. But what options do we have?'

'Very few, but you're right, it can't go on. Somehow we must get in touch with the outside world. I have a ghost of— I have a faint idea. It may work, and it may not, but it's worth a try.'

'Anything's worth a try. You're surely not thinking of a boat, though, are you? Because the river's way too dangerous until it calms down.'

'No, not a boat. Fireworks.'

I thought I'd heard him wrong, or had gone crazy from shock. I looked at him dumbly.

'Fireworks and flares are very much the same thing, you know, and flares are always a danger signal. If we can somehow touch them off, it might attract some attention.'

'But . . . the rain. And it's Guy Fawkes Night. Even if you can get them to fire, won't people just think they're part of the celebration?'

'I don't know, love. We have to try. It's the only chance we have. I cannot deal with multiple murders on my own, even with you to help.'

'Two of them are old. And Dave might not have been murdered.'

I was grasping at straws, and we both knew it. We had landed squarely in the middle of a horrible situation, a nightmare, and I wasn't sure how – or if – we were ever going to get out.

'What have you done with . . . her . . . it?'

Alan looked at me, considering. 'I'm not sure you want to know.'

'Oh. Walled it up again?' I gulped and pushed the picture firmly out of my head.

Alan nodded. 'It seemed the most sensible thing to do, until we can get help. I made sure the door was firmly locked, and I have the key.' He patted his pocket and turned to Tom and Lynn. 'Shall we go down? I for one could use a good stiff drink.'

That seemed to be the general feeling. We assembled as usual in the kitchen, where Joyce was holding forth, for once.

'I'm not quite sure what we'll have for dinner, folks. Mr Bates is still feeling unwell, and Mrs Bates is, naturally, looking after him. So I'm mistress of my own kitchen again! There will be plenty to eat, but it may be rather . . . peculiar. Certainly not what Mrs Bates has accustomed us to.

'Now there's something I want to say to you all. I've been a terrible hostess all weekend. OK, OK.' She held up her hand at the protests that arose. 'I'm not going to apologize for anything, because you're all friends and you all make allowances for . . . um . . . circumstances beyond our control. Including what the insurance companies call an Act of God. But here we are, and here we stay, perforce, until the army or somebody rescues us, or the river goes down.

'I won't suggest that we forget all that has happened in the past several days. We wouldn't be human if we could do that. But Jim and I moved here because we love England and the English, and one of their traits we admire most is the stiff upper lip. So I intend to emulate them and suggest that we try to relegate all the unpleasantness – how's that for fine British understatement? – to the back of our minds, and spend the rest of our time here like civilized people. Shipwrecked on an island, if you will, but civilized. And to that end, Jim has opened the bar.'

She made a grand gesture, a sort of visual 'ta-da!' Jim, his face fixed in a determined smile, stood in front of a grand array of bottles, including a couple of rare and expensive small-batch bourbons that I had never before seen in England. I gave Alan a startled glance. He smiled and went to get some for both of us.

My mother had a philosophy that guided her through many a rough time. 'Only worry when you can do something about it – whatever it is. Then it's not worry, it's thinking things through, trying to decide what's best. When there's nothing you can do, it's just plain worry, and it's pointless and self-destructive.'

There was certainly nothing I could do about our present predicament, and I've always enjoyed bourbon. Alan learned to like it years before I met him, when he was on an assignment in Washington, DC. It's still a fairly unusual taste in England, where scotch (called just whisky, with no *e*) or gin is the preferred spiritous liquor. I like them all, but when I need a stiffener, bourbon is my choice.

And so we sat and drank and talked. In the interests of acting 'civilized', we avoided all talk of corpses, skeletons, mummies and assorted horrors. We felt free to talk of storms; surely the weather was a staple of drawing-room conversation. The English talked about the 1987 hurricane, a storm of epic proportions that paled, however, by comparison with the one we had just suffered. The Americans chimed in with 'can-you-top-this' stories, a competition I felt I won with the famous Blizzard of '78 that buried parts of Indiana with over three feet of snow in a single night – though some of the tornado tales came close.

I fear we all drank a bit more than we should. Perhaps it was inevitable, given the strain we'd been living under. It wasn't gone, either. We had chosen to ignore our problems for a little while, but they'd be back in the morning, in full force. So it wasn't surprising that we grew a little too loud, a little frenzied, a little too like Blitz parties or dancing on the deck of the *Titanic*. Ed started coming up with more and more outrageous puns, with Pat topping them. I found myself laughing so hard at one of Ed's groaners that I realized it was well past the time I should have switched to soda water.

I don't remember who first noticed that the rain had stopped, or who broached the idea that we should build a bonfire and burn the guy, but once suggested, the scheme caught hold and spread, if the simile can be forgiven, like wildfire. If we had all been entirely sober, cooler heads might have pointed out that our supply of dry wood was limited, and it might be better to save it to keep us warm until power was restored.

Or then again, they might not. We had been making do, camping out (if in luxurious surroundings) for what seemed like months. We were all in a mood to cut loose, and what better excuse than Guy Fawkes Night?

So the men broke into agitated discussion of the best site for the fire, and exactly how to build it, and whether to use any of the newly-fallen wood ('. . . but some of it was dead anyway – that'll be dry enough to burn . . .'). They finally decided on a hilltop overlooking the river, on the far west side of the property, and trooped to the outbuildings to find wood.

The women, meanwhile, flocked like homing pigeons to the kitchen to make piles of sandwiches with whatever we could find. The Aga was nearly cold, so there was no hope of cooking anything, but there was plenty of cheese and ham and cold roast beef, and if bread was in short supply, crackers (in the American sense) and biscuits (in the English sense) would do. I managed to find some popcorn tucked away in a pantry and popped it, sort of, over the dying kitchen fire as my contribution to the decidedly unconventional supper. Some of it burned and quite a lot didn't pop – I'd never have succeeded as a pioneer woman – but with lots of butter melted over the top it smelled great and would taste OK.

Joyce asked Pat to 'help her find' the guy. 'My dear woman, if you've forgotten where you put it, how can I help?'

'Well, I think I know where it is, but . . .'

Pat uttered something between a laugh and a snort. 'Ah. I see. Yes, I'll come and help keep the vampires at bay.'

Well, I would have been afraid myself to tramp through that dark house alone.

As we packed up everything to take out to the bonfire, I ate a few crackers, on the principle that starch soaks up alcohol. I don't know if the theory worked, since the stuff was obviously in my blood stream already, but my head did feel a little clearer as Lynn and I tramped up the hill together, baskets in hand.

'If anyplace is dry enough for a fire, that hilltop should be,' I commented, somewhat breathlessly. The hill was steep.

'Mmm. Did anyone tell the rest where we were going? The vicar, and the Bateses?'

'I heard Jim say he was going to. I wish the vicar had been able to come. I think he might be rather fun in other circumstances. But obviously he couldn't leave Laurence for so long.'

Lynn, who was leading the way with a lantern, stopped so suddenly that I stepped on her heel.

I stopped too, perforce, and put down my heavy basket. 'Sorry! What's the matter?'

'Nothing. I mean, *everything*, but nothing new. Dorothy, what's going *on* here? Why are all these awful things *happening*? I tried to cooperate with Joyce, poor thing, and pretend this was still a party, but you mentioned Laurence and it all came crashing back down on us. I don't understand anything about it, but I thought *you* would have figured it out by now.'

'Hey, have a heart! I've been here . . . what, three days?'

'Or a century.'

'I know, but things just keep on happening, like . . . like that popcorn. I barely thought I had a handle on the skeleton – so to speak – when up popped more awfulness. Dave Harrison died, and Julie hid in that shack . . . and Mike . . . and Laurence – poor man, I hope he'll make it.'

'He'd stand a lot better chance if he could get some medical care.'

'He's at the heart of this, Lynn. That's the only thing I'm sure of. He and the house are the centre of the whole mess.'

'How do you work that out?'

I thought about that. 'I'm not sure, actually. I hadn't stopped to follow my train of thought. You know how your mind jumps around, relating things that don't seem to have anything to do with each other?'

'I know *your* mind does.'

'That,' I said with dignity, 'was uncalled for.'

Lynn giggled.

'Anyway, I haven't thought it all out, but I know – I feel in my bones, Lynn – that this house is at root of everything.'

'You,' said Lynn, picking up her basket and continuing up the hill, 'are getting as bad as Ed. Bones and roots, indeed.'

That didn't deserve a reply. Lynn was back to pretending it was a party. I saved my breath for the climb.

NINETEEN

The men were just lighting the bonfire when we got to the top of the hill. They had somehow contrived a huge pile of wood, and they must have doused it with kerosene, because when they tossed in a couple of matches, the flames leapt up immediately.

It was beautiful, and warm – hot, in fact. I hadn't been truly warm for days, but after a few moments I had to move away from the fire. It was also more than a little frightening. The ancients thought of fire as one of the four elements, and there was certainly something elemental about this fire, something alive and menacing, as it devoured its fodder, roaring, crackling, almost smacking its lips. Tongues of fire, the Bible called them, and certainly one thought of tongues as the fire licked out to find something new to consume.

'A good fire,' said Alan, by my side.

'Yes,' I said a little doubtfully. 'But is it a good idea?'

He looked at me enquiringly.

'I mean – it's Guy Fawkes. Bonfire Night. If anyone sees this, will it make them think everything is normal over here? Just the folks at the big house having a good time?'

'Might do. On the other hand, bonfires aren't as common as they used to be. And they were once signals, you know.'

'I do know. But they could stand for either good or ill, if I remember. Come, all is well, or stay away – danger.'

'Remember your mother, love. We can't do anything about the way the message is taken, so enjoy the fire. I believe Lynn brought some marshmallows to toast. You Americans do eat the oddest things.'

So we had our picnic and ate our marshmallows (at least the Americans did), and tried not to think about bodies piling up back at the house, about our continued isolation, about Mike and his grand, doomed gesture.

We tried not to think about those things. I, for one, wasn't successful.

Neither was Alan. For when we had eaten what we wanted of the not very wonderful food, and the guy had been dutifully admired (it was an effigy of a former, not very popular prime minister) and burned, and the bonfire was beginning to die down, Alan went quietly to Jim's side and spoke briefly to him. Jim looked slightly startled, then nodded and took off down the hill, almost at a run, Alan right behind him.

Lynn, who was sitting on the ground close to the fire, got up with one of the lithe, graceful movements I envied, and came over to me. 'What are they up to?' she asked bluntly.

'I don't know for sure, but . . . well, Alan had an idea this afternoon. I'm not going to tell you about it, in case it doesn't come off. If it does, you won't need to ask.'

And that was all I would say.

In a few minutes Jim and Alan trudged back up the hill, carrying between them a large box, which they carried near the fire and set down.

Jim then climbed up on top of the box and said, 'Ladies and gentlemen!' in a voice I'd never heard before from him, a voice that reminded me he was a highly paid, valued executive of something-or-other.

'Ladies and gentlemen,' he repeated, a little more quietly now that he had everyone's attention. 'We were to have had a fireworks display tonight. Unfortunately, those plans were cancelled by the storm and . . . other events. However, Alan has reminded me that fireworks and flares are essentially the same – pyrotechnics, both, one simply more spectacular than the other.

'We need, pretty badly, some communication with the outside world, and there seems to be only one way to, possibly, attract the attention of someone in Branston Village. Alan and I propose to set off some rockets, the least flamboyant of my collection, in an SOS pattern. If someone sees and understands, our isolation may be nearly at an end.'

'If,' said Pat with unusual sombreness.

'Yes, if. We can but try. So I'll ask you all, please, to step back at least thirty feet. That's ten metres to you politically correct Brits,' he added with a ghost of a grin. 'Neither of us is an expert at this, and we don't want to set anybody on fire or put any eyes out.'

So we moved back obediently, the six of us. Pat and Ed stood together, while Tom and Lynn and I kept Joyce company. Six of us. There should have been a crowd there, the other five of our house party, and the Bateses, and however many came from the village. And the display should have been beautiful, fabulous, not a few puny rockets for a puny few people.

We watched in silence as Jim picked out nine smallish rockets and lined them up in groups of three. Then Alan, using a long match, touched flame to the fuses of the first three, allowing a second or two between.

Ffft. Ffft. Ffft. The first three went off in rapid succession and exploded, with loud reports, in showers of red sparks.

The next three, lit at longer intervals. Ffft. Silence. Ffft. Silence. Ffft. Explosions. Sparks.

Then the final volley.

'We'll do another set,' said Jim. 'Stay where you are until we're done.'

After all the sparks had died away and the smell of gunpowder had dissipated, we waited on the hill. Waited for what? I wasn't sure. For some response, I suppose, some sign that our message had been seen and understood.

There was nothing. No answering flare, no gunshots, no – what – smoke signals?

After a while we drifted back to the house and went to bed.

'He's awake!'

'Mmm.' I turned over and pulled a pillow over my head to shut out the unbearable light. Alan pulled it off.

'He's awake, love.'

'I'm not,' I mumbled. 'And I have a headache.'

'Then have some coffee and a painkiller. I'm going to talk to Laurence.'

He didn't slam the door. Alan doesn't slam doors. But he closed it with a definitive click that penetrated my consciousness. I sat up, squinting against the light, hands to my throbbing temples. Ooooh! How much had I had to drink last night, anyway?

Then, finally, his words reached my brain.

Laurence. He was going to talk to Laurence. It was Laurence who was awake!

I fell back on to the pillows. I was in no shape to cope with the implications.

Furthermore, I didn't have to. I was supposed to be having a nice holiday. Let somebody else deal with Laurence, somebody who didn't have a hangover. And what an undignified condition for a respectable woman my age! It had been years since I'd got myself in this state. I certainly knew better, but . . . well, put it down to stress. In any case, I needed coffee. I needed ibuprofen. Then I was going back to bed to nurse my aching head. I groped for my bathrobe and made my cautious way down to the kitchen.

No one was there, thank heaven. I didn't want to talk. I wasn't sure I could. There was, however, a large Thermos on the table. As I hoped, it contained good strong coffee.

After three ibuprofen and two cups of coffee, I acknowledged the fact that I couldn't just go back to bed. I was not only, I hoped, a respectable woman but a responsible one, and hangover or not, I had obligations. Several people were depending, at least in part, on me to help ferret out the truth.

Ferrets were rat-catchers. Well, there was at least one rat i' this particular arras, and he needed to be caught.

What, I wondered with gross irrelevance, was an arras?

I hoped not a hidden room. I did not intend to think about hidden rooms.

Enough! I told my wandering mind. Get dressed, madam, and then be up and doing, with a heart for any fate.

Eventually, and most unwillingly, I took myself to Laurence's room, where I found almost the entire household gathered to hear what the poor man had to say. Only Julie was absent. She was probably still huddled in her room, stuck fast in whatever terror, or just confusion, held her there.

Someone had made Laurence a pot of tea, and Joyce was making sure he drank it. It was doubtless loaded with enough sugar to loosen every tooth in his head, but he needed sustenance, after nearly three days without eating.

'So, go on,' said Alan. 'You talked to the vicar and then went for a walk.'

'Yes. I needed to think. I . . . well, there was a decision I needed to make, whether—'

'Yes,' Alan interrupted. 'I know about that. Then what happened?'

'I don't remember very well. I think I walked toward the river . . . the river to the south, I mean. The water meadows. It was . . . the destruction was . . . may I have a little more tea, please?'

'I'll make fresh,' said Joyce, putting her hand to the pot's cheek. 'This is cold.' Rose Bates moved to take it from her, but Laurence shook his head.

'That'll do just as well. My mouth is a bit dry. Cold is fine.'

I gave Alan a worried look. He shook his head, ever so slightly. 'You must be hungry, as well,' he said gently. 'Shall I have Mrs Bates boil an egg or two for you?'

'I'm not very hungry. My head aches a bit.'

'Well, she'll boil the eggs, and if you don't want them, I'm sure someone else will. Now, sir, can you tell me anything at all that happened as you walked toward the river?'

He shook his head, winced, and closed his eyes. 'I remember seeing the ruined gardens, and Mr Bates getting fresh wood for the fires. And there's something . . . I heard something . . . but I can't remember.'

'Alan, don't you think—' I said at the same time that the vicar said, 'Really, Mr Nesbitt—'

We cancelled each other out, but Alan nodded. 'Yes. It's time he rested. Mr Upshawe, we're all very glad you're feeling better. Now . . . oh, yes, here are some ibuprofen tablets to wash down with some of that cold tea. We'll talk again after you've had a nice sleep.'

He shooed us all out, all but the vicar. I saw the two of them hold a brief conversation, but I couldn't hear what they said. Then Alan closed the door – and to my astonishment, locked it behind him.

'The vicar has the other key,' he said. 'He can get out if he needs to, but I've told him to stay until he's relieved. By me. And to wedge the door and respond only to a coded knock.'

And then I saw, and smacked my forehead, and immediately regretted it. 'What he heard,' I said, when the waves of pain receded. 'You don't want anyone to get to him before he's had a chance to finish about what he heard.'

'Yes. And anything else he might have seen. Anything, in short, that he hasn't yet told us.'

'So that's why you had everyone else in the room. And I noticed you didn't let him talk about his conversation with the vicar.'

'He did try, before you came in, but the vicar and I managed between us to suggest that the conversation dealt with private spiritual matters.'

'Which, in a way, it did.'

'Yes, but I didn't want the details revealed at this point. I did want to make the point, very publicly, that he had told us all he knew. Unfortunately, it didn't work out quite that way. So until he can talk to us again, I want him guarded. I wish I had several stout constables to take the duty, instead of one elderly vicar and one elderly retiree, but I must make do as best I can.'

I sighed. 'No reply from the mainland, then?'

He snorted. 'You're in your Agatha Christie mode again, aren't you? No, they've all been told to ignore any signals from— what was the name of the island?'

'Indian Island. *Ten Little Indians*, remember – the other title.'

'Yes. Well, to answer your question properly, no, we've heard nothing. Though how could we hear anything? The village is too far away for a loud-hailer, even if they possess such a thing. No phone, no email—' He held up his hands in frustration. '*If* anyone saw, *if* anyone understood, we'll know only when they come to us, and that can't be until the roads are clear. Hence the melodramatics with locked doors and so on. And Dorothy –' he turned a very serious look on me – 'I want you to be very, very careful. Don't go anywhere alone. Everyone knows you're trying to puzzle this thing out. You're in danger, my girl, or you could be.'

'That's the trouble!' I said fiercely. 'Everything is . . . is misty,
amorphous. I could be in danger. Or maybe not. Maybe Dave
Harrison was murdered. Or maybe not. And if he was, maybe
it was Laurence who did it. Or maybe the other way around.
And there's the skeleton and the mummy and Mike – and Julie
– and I did want to see the fireworks!'

And I burst into tears.

Alan gathered me into his warm, safe arms and let me cry.
When I had reached the stage of hiccuping little sobs, he pulled
out his handkerchief, mopped my face, and said 'Blow.'

'That was really a big help, wasn't it?' I said mournfully. 'All
you need on your plate right now is a weepy woman.'

'All I ever need is this particular woman,' he said, which
nearly sent me over the edge again. 'You're still feeling a bit
fragile, I suspect.' He pronounced the last syllable to rhyme with
mile, and it summed up exactly how I felt. 'Suppose you go
back to that bed I dragged you out of, and sleep it off. Don't
forget to lock the door, though. I'll knock like this.' He tapped
a pattern on my sleeve. 'And, Dorothy, if you feel afraid or
worried about anything – no matter if you think it's foolish –
scream like the devil's after you, and I'll be there. Promise?'

I nodded, feeling foolish already, and trudged back to our
room.

TWENTY

I woke from one of those dreams, the complicated kind that
go on and on and plunge one deeper and deeper into the
labyrinth. I was just about to find the way out, nearly there,
but someone kept hitting croquet balls into my path. Tock. Tock.
Tock-tock. I wished whoever it was would stop, but they kept
coming. Tock. Tock. Tock-tock.

'Dorothy. Dorothy, are you awake?'

'I am now,' I said, and got up to let Alan in. 'I thought you
were playing croquet. But I was just about to figure it all out.'

He grinned. 'Have a nice nap?'

'I feel better, anyway. Alan, if I'm ever tempted to drink that
much again, stop me. I had dreams . . . well, nightmares, really.'

'Where did the croquet come in?'

I yawned. 'I can't remember anymore. But it was all very vivid at the time. And speaking of remembering . . .'

Alan shook his head. 'Nothing very useful. He thought he heard something – perhaps a footstep – behind him as he walked down to the river. But it was still windy, as you recall, not a gale but a steady wind, and between the whistle of the wind itself and the sound of debris being blown about, he can't be sure what he heard. And of the scene at the river he remembers nothing.'

I gave a great sigh. 'Is he telling the truth?'

'I think so, and I've had some opportunity of judging. You know a head injury often wipes out the memory of preceding events.'

'Sometimes the memories come back.'

'But not always, by any means.'

'Have you told him Harrison is dead?'

'No,' said Alan, 'and I've told the vicar not to say anything. At this point that's my one hope of triggering his memory. If I tell him the right way, it might be enough of a shock to bring back . . . whatever happened.'

I began to pace. 'Another maybe. Another misty thing. Alan, I think I'm going to go talk to Julie again.'

'Not alone.'

'No. Anyway, I don't think I'd get anything out of her by myself. And she's afraid of you, for some reason. Oh!'

'Yes, I thought about that myself, but I never pursued it. Why is she afraid of me? I've never harmed the woman; I scarcely know her.'

'She's afraid,' I said slowly, 'because you're a policeman.'

'I was a policeman.'

'Yes, but she may not know the difference. I hate to say it of Joyce's sister, but Julie's none too bright. Probably comes of living with Dave all those years. And I'm sure she's heard stories about the omniscience of the English police.'

'All true,' said Alan smugly.

'Right. But if she believes that you know everything, and she's afraid of you, that means she has something to hide.'

Alan gave me that grave look again. 'I'm not sure I want you to talk to her.'

For once I didn't give him a flippant answer. 'I know. And I agree, in principle. If Julie Harrison has done something criminal, I want nothing to do with her, to be honest. But if she *has*, somebody has to talk to her. Somebody has to worm it out of her. We've agreed you can't be the one. Who else, besides me and Pat?'

'She talked before to the vicar.'

'She was in a state of hypothermia and exhaustion. Now she's fine, except she's terrified of something – or someone. It isn't just you, but she hasn't given me the slightest clue about who or what it might be. No, it's probably not the vicar, but would he know the right questions to ask? And would he pass along the answers? You know that tender conscience of his. And you have to remember, too, that she talked pretty freely to Pat. Which seems to exonerate Pat of . . . whatever it is that worries Julie so.'

'I'm not sure your logic holds up there. I wish I could do it myself.'

'So do I. But you can't. So it has to be Pat and me.'

'All right, I suppose. But I intend to be right outside the door. And it can wait until after lunch. I assume you can eat something now?'

'So long as it doesn't have much taste, or any smell at all.'

I stayed out of the kitchen. Alan brought me some very mild cheese and rather tasteless crackers, and had thoughtfully made a glass of iced tea for my strange American tastes (apparently the freezer was still cold), and reported as I nibbled that the Bateses were back at work and apparently feeling quite normal, except that Mr Bates wasn't quite as urbanely courteous as usual, and his wife was rather quiet.

'Embarrassed, I suspect,' he concluded. 'A big man like that doesn't care to remember that he fainted at the sight of . . . that he fainted, and in front of a lot of people.'

'I would have, too, only I couldn't see very clearly. He was right in front of that . . . thing.' I shuddered and put down my glass. 'I really think that's all I can manage for now. And if I don't go talk to Julie soon, I'll lose my nerve. I don't think I can face kitchen smells, though. Could you find Pat for me and ask if she's willing to act as prosecuting attorney again?'

'Counsel for the Crown,' he murmured, and left the room.

Pat was more than willing. She was, in fact, hovering in that uncertain state between boredom and nervous excitement that makes it impossible to settle to anything. 'I feel like Kipling's rhinoceros,' she said as she walked in the door, giving an impatient wriggle of that magnificent body.

'Cake crumbs under your skin?'

'Exactly. I want something to happen, but I'm afraid of what it might be. I understand you want me to tackle Jovial Julie again.'

'I'm hoping that she may be chafing enough under her self-imposed restraints to open up a little more. Especially if you provide some further . . . um . . . lubrication.'

Pat held up the bottle she had thoughtfully brought along, an unopened litre of a premium bourbon. 'Will this do the trick, do you suppose?'

'Yipes! That's way too good for the purpose. I do hate to see that stuff poured down an unappreciative gullet.'

'Perhaps you'd like a taste first?' asked Pat with a wicked smile.

'Ouch! No, I won't have a hair of the dog, thank you very much. If somebody's going to get a splitting head from that stuff, better her than me. Excelsior.'

We headed down to the far end of the wing, Alan right behind us. He had obtained the key from Rose, assuming that Julie was still barricading herself. I couldn't say I blamed her. If I hadn't had Alan to sustain me, I would have locked myself up, too.

'Dorothy, look.' Pat pointed with the bottle.

Near the end of the long corridor, a lighter area showed, as if a door was open, letting in, not direct sunlight, since that side of the house faced north, but the glow of reflected light.

Julie's door was open, and a glance told us she wasn't in the room.

'Bathroom, probably,' said Pat.

'There's an en suite bath for every bedroom, remember? Every one that's in regular use, anyway.'

'Then she's gone in search of something to eat.'

'I'm sure Mrs Bates brings her food. Something to drink, more likely,' I said, by way of calling the kettle black.

'She'll be back soon, anyway. Should we close the door so she won't know she has a reception committee?'

'Not when she left it open,' Alan put in sensibly. 'Leave every-thing as it was, but stay out of sight of the doorway.'

Feeling as if I'd walked into an Inspector Clouseau movie, I took a position against the wall beside the hinge side of the door (hoping Julie wouldn't bang it into my nose when she returned). Pat stepped into a corner, easily visible but not until one was in the room. And Alan, who was there simply as guard dog, stepped into the unoccupied room across the hall.

We waited, scarcely daring to breath. The hall was carpeted with heavy Oriental runners and the floors, though very old, were very solid. Julie's footfalls wouldn't make much noise, and we didn't want to be caught off guard.

I began to get a cramp in the calf of my left leg. I tried to wiggle it out, but it only got worse. In agony, I had to walk it out. 'Cramp,' I mouthed, pointing to my leg, when Pat glared at me. I walked as quietly as I could and returned to my post as soon as the cramp eased itself.

Pat's nose began to twitch. At first I thought she smelled something peculiar, so I sniffed myself, but could detect nothing but the slightly stale aroma of a room that had been shut up for too long with someone who hadn't bathed for a while. Then Pat sneezed, a sneeze that was all the more explosive for being suppressed.

We both waited anxiously for the sound of footsteps running the other way. Nothing.

I sighed, inaudibly I hoped, and settled down in silence again, changing feet now and then to avoid cramp.

I don't know how long we stood there before it dawned on us that Julie had gone farther afield than the kitchen or the library liquor cabinet. At any rate, I was the first to give it up.

'This is pure farce,' I said aloud, slumping away from my rigid pose beside the wall. 'Julie's up to something, and I think we'd do better trying to find her and figure out what it is.'

Pat agreed. 'My skin was beginning to crawl in earnest. I don't think of myself as a fidget, but when one can't move, one instantly wants to.'

'Well, let's get Alan and decide what to do.'

Alan, hearing us talking, left his lair and joined us. 'The bird has flown?'

'Hopped away, more likely,' I replied. 'I doubt she's gone far, but we'd better find her.'

'Yes. Why don't I take up my surveillance from across the way again, and you two check the rest of the bedrooms. And bathrooms. Because on past form . . .'

He didn't need to finish the thought. If Julie had managed to get hold of another bottle, she might well have found another comfortable bathtub.

It would be tedious to detail our search. It was slow and thorough. We looked in every bedroom, occupied or not (in a couple of cases waking nappers), and their adjacent bathrooms and sitting rooms. We checked two linen closets and found nothing but sheets and towels. We even peered down the shaft of the dumbwaiter.

No Julie.

'She could be keeping one step ahead of us, you know,' said Pat as we sank down on the canopy bed in the last vacant bedroom. 'One could play that game forever in a house this size.'

'Yes, but why? I can't think why she'd want to hide, not from us. In fact, I can't think why she'd leave her bedroom at all, not for any length of time. She only had to ring for anything she wanted, and she's been so scared of whatever-it-is.'

'Cabin fever. She got fed up with being by herself.'

'Maybe,' I said dubiously. 'Or else . . .'

Pat sighed. 'Yes. I was hoping we could avoid that speculation. Or else, you're thinking, she didn't leave her room willingly.'

'I think Alan's had that idea for some time.'

So we trooped back to where Alan was keeping his futile watch. 'No luck?' he asked. But he knew the answer.

'What now, boss?' That was Pat. I was rapidly becoming too worried to be cheeky.

'Where have you looked?'

We told him. Pat summarized, 'She isn't anywhere on this floor. We've exhausted all the possibilities. And ourselves,' she added.

'Did you study her room at all?'

I took that question to myself. 'No. I thought you'd rather do that. At a quick glance, I didn't see anything to show whether she left of her own accord or . . . not. But you'll know better than I what to look for.'

'First,' said Alan, 'we need to determine that she is not still somewhere in the house.'

'Yes, we'll—'

I never got to finish the sentence. 'I hope that you, my dear, will have nothing to do with this search. You've done your part. Please, I want you to go to our room, lock yourself in and stay there. Do I need to spell out why?'

No, he didn't. Nor was I, for once, disposed to argue. With Julie's disappearance the nightmare had overshadowed us completely. There was no more question of pushing it out of our minds, pretending that all the horrors were in and of the past.

We were now living in fear, genuine, unadulterated fear.

'Alan . . . you won't do anything silly?'

'By which I assume you mean heroics. No, love, I won't. I'll be with other people – more than one other person – the whole time. Now Pat and I will see you back to the room. I don't like the idea of her being alone, either. Then she and I will go downstairs, tell the others, and organize search teams.'

I didn't learn until later that Alan had excluded the Bateses from the search, even though their knowledge of the house probably surpassed anyone else's. His stated reason was that someone needed to be available in case, by a miracle, some outside help arrived. His real reason, I knew, was that they were not entirely above suspicion. Neither were Jim and Joyce, but Alan had to have someone who knew the house reasonably well. So Jim had gone with Allen, along with Lynn, and Joyce led Mike, Pat and Tom.

Neither of the Moynihans knew as much about the hidden parts of the house as John Bates, but they knew what one might term the surface very well. Both groups searched the same areas at different times, in case someone spotted a trace – a tissue, a bit of cigarette ash, a thread – that the others had missed. They searched all the living areas, the cellars, the outbuildings. They ranged over the devastated gardens, peering under promising bushes and into the pits left by upturned shrubs and trees. They looked in and under everyone's cars, including the trunks/boots and under the hoods/bonnets, and made sure that all the cars were where they should be.

They found neither Julie nor any trace of her.

TWENTY-ONE

Alan knocked on the door. This time I was wide awake and recognized his code. I knew as soon as I saw his face that the news was not good.

'You didn't find her.'

'No, but that's not the worst of it.' And he related to me the scene when the searchers returned and told Rose Bates that Julie had now to be counted as missing. 'It seems Rose has been busy conducting a search of her own. She said that food was missing from the kitchen – portable food, cheese and biscuits and apples, that sort of thing – and that Mr Bates had reported that two bottles of whisky were gone. Well, Pat confessed that she had taken one of them, and put it back on the kitchen table. But Rose said bourbon wasn't whisky, so there were still two bottles unaccounted for.' Alan heaved a sigh. 'Which would have been the end of it, except then Pat commented that it was apparent Julie was gone, and the only question remaining was whether she had gone of her own free will or been spirited away. And at that Rose flew into a kind of hysterics. Jim and Joyce are still trying to calm her down, so far as I know.'

'But why should that have touched her off? It's no more than we've all been thinking ever since we found her room empty.'

'"Spirited",' said Alan with another sigh. 'Pat meant nothing in particular by the word, but it seems there's a streak of good old country superstition in the competent and efficient Mrs Bates. All the unfortunate things that have happened in recent days have worked on her fears, and the mention – as she thought – of spirits was the crowning touch. She has decided, from what little sense I could make of her ravings, that the house is cursed, or possessed, or something of the kind. God only knows what's going to happen without her in the kitchen. She has been the glue that kept the household together, and now . . .' He raised his hands in a helpless gesture and sat down heavily on the bed.

'There's no chance she'll come to her senses?'

'Oh, eventually, I suppose. I wish we could give her a sedative. When she does come out of it, she could be in a bad way. I'm no doctor, but I've seen full-blown hysteria before, and it's not easy on anybody.'

'Poor Joyce.' I sat down beside him.

'Why Joyce, more than any of the rest of us?'

'Because she's the hostess. She'll feel it her job to try to keep things going, and it's hopeless. I wish—'

'No.' Alan said it with a finality that cut me off in mid-sentence. 'You will not attempt to cook for this crowd. You will not organize a rota for the household chores. You will stay in this room until help arrives.'

'Her master's voice,' I said with a lightness I did not feel. His face didn't change. I studied it for a moment and said, 'You're really worried, aren't you?'

He sighed. 'I am. I didn't mean to shout at you, Dorothy. But I have *no* idea what's going on here, and until I do, I'm genuinely frightened. For everyone, not just you. Until someone responds to our calls for help . . .'

'That could be a long time,' I said meekly. 'What are we going to do about food?'

'I'm going back down in a moment. Tom and I will pack boxes of non-perishables for everyone. Fortunately there's plenty of food, though the variety may leave something to be desired. We will distribute them to everyone, and then my recommendation is that everyone keep to his or her or their own room – with the door locked. I do not intend this to turn into that novel you keep citing, with all of us being picked off one by one.'

'Your recommendation.'

'Well, love, I can't give orders to any of these people, much as I'd like to.'

Only to me, I thought but didn't say.

'I can only advise them, strongly, that there is someone very dangerous among us, and we need to take sensible steps for self-protection.'

Thus began our siege. I wondered what the single people in our party would do, and then decided not to wonder. Laurence Upshawe was still under the care – or guardianship – of the vicar, Paul Leatherbury. Jim and Joyce had each other, Tom and Lynn, the Bateses. And if Pat Heseltine and Ed Walinski decided that sharing a room was less lonely and frightening, good luck to them. I certainly didn't intend to poke my nose into their activities. I had Alan, after all.

Or I would have, when he returned from his commissary duties. I wished, the minute he had left, that I had remembered to ask him for some books. I can endure almost any period of enforced inactivity if I have enough to read. There were books in the room. Joyce was too good a hostess not to see to that. But the ones I hadn't already read didn't interest me. I thought about taking a nap, but I was too tense to sleep. I wanted to *do* something, find some way out of this nightmare.

I started counting casualties. Two recent deaths, three if Julie had met the fate we all suspected. Two much older deaths, the skeleton and the mummy. (I shuddered at the thought of her and forced my mind to move on quickly.) Laurence injured. Mr Bates shocked into a faint.

Seven. Seven human beings killed or injured in this house. *By* this house?

No. That was too fanciful, too much like Rose Bates's terrors.

This wasn't Hill House, with its evil, ghostly inhabitants. But there seemed to be an evil, malevolent presence here, all the same. Only it was human.

Which one? Which of the inhabitants of this house had killed, and killed again, and again?

I went to the lovely little writing desk in the corner and opened the top drawer. Sure enough, there was a small cache of stationery, paper, envelopes, even stamps. The paper was thick and lovely, meant for invitations, thank-yous, gracious correspondence. I had nothing else to use for a list. I pulled out several sheets and the pen, also thoughtfully provided, and headed the top one 'Events'.

The first listing there was obviously the skeleton. I was about to write it in when I had another thought. Really the first odd thing to happen was Dave Harrison's conversation with Julie, that first night, and then his drunken outburst just before dinner.

Julie had shut him up on that occasion. Why? What had he said, exactly, that she wanted to cut off?

I headed a second sheet 'Queries' and wrote that one in, and then went back to the skeleton.

There were plenty of questions about him. It seemed likely that the first question, his identity, had been answered. But assuming he was Harry Upshawe, who killed him? Why? When? And another one that just occurred to me: why had the pilot of that aircraft not tried to contact Harry when he didn't show up for the planned trip?

Maybe someone had called the pilot, someone pretending to be Harry, saying he couldn't make it after all. That could be important, a lead . . .

And then I realized it was only another dead end. We couldn't question the pilot; he had gone down somewhere near São Miguel.

Nevertheless, I wrote the question down. There might be some way to check fifty-year-old flight plans. I doubted it, but Alan might know.

Lots of questions. No answers. I went back to my Events page.

The next things, in the order they had happened, not when I learned about them, were the complicated series of events involving Laurence, the vicar and the Harrisons. I began to note them down with some care.

The first was Laurence's conversation with the vicar. I wrote down the gist of it, as best I remembered. Alan, who had a policeman's memory for detail, could correct me. Then Laurence had started on his walk.

Meanwhile, Dave and Julie, in their irrational state, had decided
to try to get away. They heard Laurence's – confession was too
strong a word – his narrative. Julie, somewhat surprisingly, was
bright enough to realize the implications and warn Dave – who
then went off after Laurence.

And then what? Julie could have told us. Julie had disappeared.
Laurence could have told us. Laurence had received a blow to
the head that wiped out his memory.

At this stage of my unproductive exercise, Alan rapped on
the door, and I let him in. He carried not only a large crate of
food, but – bless him – a canvas bag full of books.

'Sorry I was so long, love. Tom and I delivered everyone
else's first.'

'How are they all holding up?'

'As one might expect. The Bateses are inclined to be a bit
resentful; I am abrogating their responsibilities, after all. Mr
Bates is testy; his wife is defensive but more inclined to cooperate.' He took a box of cereal out of his crate, and a couple
of cans of peaches.

'I suspect Mr Bates is still feeling a bit poorly, after that faint.
It was only yesterday, wasn't it? Time is behaving very oddly.'

'It does. Yes, it was yesterday, and Mr Bates is obviously
feeling "poorly", as you put it. The rest are bearing up, though
Jim and Joyce are desperately worried, and feeling guilty.'

'That's ridiculous. Nothing they did caused any of the
awfulness.'

'They assembled the house party. And of course we're just
assuming that—'

'Alan!'

'I like them, too, but I think like a policeman, love. I can't
help it. Where were Jim and Joyce when Harrison met his death?'

I tried to think back through the eternity that had passed since
last Friday. 'Napping! A bunch of people did that afternoon,
remember? None of us had had much sleep.'

'Exactly. And presumably they'll vouch for each other. As
evidence, it's useless.'

'Well, but what about . . .' I paused to think about the other
victims. Laurence's story was allied with Dave's. Julie had run
off to hide, the first time and possibly this time, too. Mike, poor
idiot, had gone his own ill-advised way. But . . .

'The skeleton! And the mummy! Jim and Joyce couldn't have
had anything to do with them.'

'Probably not. But we're assuming that both old deaths took place longer than two years ago. Until we get a forensics expert in here, that's not a proven fact.'

'Harry Upshawe died fifty years ago!'

'Probably, but we have not yet proven – *prove*n, I said – that the skeleton belonged to Harry, nor indeed that Harry is dead, rather than living in happy senility in America somewhere. I have to put Jim and Joyce in the category of suspects. Unlikely, I agree, but not impossible.'

'We've eaten their salt!' I was beginning to be very angry indeed at my husband's stubbornness.

'Nevertheless.'

Ever since I was a child, I've wept when I was furious. I hated it then; I appeared to be full of misery when I was in fact full of rage. And I hated it now. I felt the tears start and turned my head so Alan wouldn't see. We almost never quarrelled, and maybe there was some misery involved with my tears, after all. I fumbled blindly for a book and took it to the farthest corner of the room.

He knows me rather well. He said nothing, but continued unpacking the groceries and stowing them away as best he could.

'Sandwich?' he offered when he had put all the food away.

'Thank you, no.' I was starving, but unwilling to let go of my anger. I turned another page I hadn't read. In sudden dismay, I glanced at the book to make sure I wasn't holding it upside down. It was right side up, but it was a book of Victorian sermons. Probably Alan had brought it so we could laugh over it together.

Another tear squeezed out and rolled down my cheek.

It was Alan who patched it up. He must have heard my stomach growl; I was really very hungry. He came over to me, gently took my book away, and said, 'I imagine your head and stomach would be happier with tea than a glass of wine, my dear. Darjeeling, perhaps? And a chocolate biscuit or two?'

My stomach spoke again. I swallowed. 'Yes, please.' There were still tears in my voice.

Alan sat down next to me. 'Dorothy. I'm exceedingly sorry. You married a stubborn man, my dear.'

'And you a stubborn woman.'

'And we're both still convinced we're right, but we can't . . . Dorothy, I never want anything that trivial to come between us again.'

'Trivial? A question of murder?'

'A difference of opinion. I fully concede that I've been wrong before, particularly when it came to my opinion about a suspect versus yours, and I may be wrong this time. Now, may I make you some tea?'

I took his hand. 'And several sandwiches. I was ready to eat those sermons.'

TWENTY-TWO

It had grown dark by the time we finished our tea/supper. Alan lit the lantern and a soft glow permeated the room. If I sat close to the light, I thought I might be able to read, for a while, at least.

'I'll trade you the sermons for something a little more frivolous,' I said.

'Agatha Christie?'

I shuddered. 'No. Too topical. There wouldn't be any P.G. Wodehouse?'

He rooted in the box and handed me a large volume of Jeeves stories.

'Perfect. I can't read more than one or two at a sitting – it's like consuming too many desserts – but one will certainly lighten the gloom. Where are you going?'

For Alan had put on his coat and hat.

'To fetch some wood, for a start. The fire's nearly dead, and it's getting distinctly chilly now that the sun's gone down. We'll need more tea presently, and I don't think I could boil water over those embers. Then I thought I'd get Jim to help, and try again.'

'Flares?'

He nodded. 'Maybe three volleys, if the supply will hold up. Most of Jim's stash is more spectacular stuff, not terribly suitable for the purpose, but we'll try.'

I could have made a remark about collaborating with a murder suspect. I didn't. The sore spot was still tender. Leave it alone. I contented myself with a caution. 'Be careful with those things. I'd simply hate to have you blinded, or worse. And come back soon, love. It's . . . creepy in here without you.'

And cold. When I had locked the door behind him, I put on

my coat and hat, moved the lantern to a table near the dying fire, and settled back close to both, trying to pretend I was warm.

I found I couldn't concentrate on 'Jeeves Takes Charge' with much more success than I'd had with the Reverend Entwhistle's sermons. I knew the Wodehouse text almost by heart; perhaps that had something to do with it. I did wish Alan would come back with the wood. Arthritic hands never turn pages easily. Cold arthritic hands have a really hard time. I dropped the book twice, the second time on my foot. Thirty-four stories in one book pack a punch. I gave it up, carried the lantern over to the bedside table, and climbed in, clothes and all, bringing my earlier lists with me.

Studying them by the soft lantern-light, I saw that they weren't very useful. The questions had no answers, or none that I could find. The events made no sense, individually or collectively. I picked up a third sheet of expensive stationery and headed it 'People'.

Begin with Jim and Joyce. What did I know about them? *Know* – not surmise.

I thought about ruling some columns and decided the paper wasn't big enough for that, and anyway, my mind doesn't work that neatly. I think in narrative.

So I wrote down their ages: fifty or so, both of them, at a guess. Americans. Lived at Branston Abbey for about two-and-a-half years. Extremely wealthy. Jim was retired – no, I was assuming that, I didn't know for sure. Tom and Lynn would know. They would also know where he had worked, or was still working, and where they had lived before coming here. Not in America for quite a while, I was guessing. Or . . . wait. Had Tom or Lynn said something about the Moynihans moving here to get away from the Harrisons? I couldn't remember for sure.

I needed to talk to them. Surely Alan would rule *them* out as suspects? Well, whether he did or not, I was going to invite them to come share our food and our fire, and pick their brains.

What else did I know about Jim and Joyce? They loved England. They loved trees and beautiful gardens and old houses. They had excellent taste in furniture and food, and enjoyed tradition – witness the planned Guy Fawkes celebration. They were cordial and thoughtful hosts, trying to make the best of a well-nigh unbearable situation.

They were childless. Did I know that, for sure? I wracked my brains, but couldn't remember being told that. Maybe I only surmised it; I had seen no family photos. I added another query to the list I needed to ask Tom and Lynn and lay back, dissatisfied.

So far there wasn't a thing known about the Moynihans that could clearly exonerate them from any except the oldest deaths, and those did not, necessarily, have anything to do with the modern ones.

'Bosh!' I said out loud. My instincts were usually reliable about this sort of thing. The house and its troubled history was at the root of the whole conundrum. I was as sure of that as . . . well, I was sure.

Tom and Lynn, Alan and I. Well, I knew I hadn't murdered anybody, and I would go to my death swearing Alan hadn't. And Tom and Lynn didn't know the Moynihans well, or the house at all. They were in their early sixties, and hadn't moved to England until about thirty years ago. So even if they'd had motive, which was a ludicrous idea, they couldn't have disposed of the skeleton. For I was utterly convinced that the skeleton was Harry Upshawe's, and that meant it had been under that oak tree for fifty years.

Scratch Tom and Lynn. Not that I'd ever had the slightest notion they'd done any of these things, but I was trying to adopt Alan's skepticism. Without a great deal of success, I realized. My partiality was not to be squelched.

All right. Let's list the rest, just for something to do. Mike Leonard, alias Michael Leonev. Dancer extraordinaire. Gay or giving an excellent impersonation. Funny, quirky. Had reason to be angry with Julie, and maybe with Dave by extension. Older than he tried to appear – nearing forty, at a guess – but still far too young to have been responsible for the skeleton. No known motive for attacking Laurence, with whom, indeed, he was reported to have been flirting. But – any possible suspicion attaching to him (and there wasn't much, in my opinion) was destroyed by his own actions. He had given his life in an effort to bring us help.

Or . . . oh, for heaven's sake! Had he committed suicide because he had killed Harrison?

I had to admit that if Mike had planned suicide, he would have wanted to do it in some highly spectacular fashion. It could be. It just could be. He could have killed Harrison. He was strong and fit, and Dave had been flabby and, moreover, probably drunk at the time.

A variation: he killed Harrison and was trying to escape, but drowned in the attempt.

But for what possible reason? Julie had grossly affronted him, and he would have had every right to be angry. But angry enough to kill? That seemed out of character. I thought Mike might have been capable of deep feeling. If he had fallen in love, he would have fallen hard, and he might have done almost anything to protect someone he loved. If he had loved Laurence, he might have been incensed enough to attack Laurence's attacker – if that was the way the riverbank scene had played out. But I didn't think, from his actions in the very few hours I had known him, that he had been in love with Laurence. That left pique with Julie as a motive, and it just wasn't enough.

People have been known to kill for what seem to reasonable people to be woefully inadequate motives, said Alan's voice in my head.

Still – it was possible. Not probable, but possible. I left Mike's name on the list, reluctantly, and somewhat pointlessly. There is little satisfaction in discovering that a recently dead man is a murderer. Except that it exonerates others. With a sigh, I pressed on.

Ed Walinski. I knew almost nothing about him, really, except that he was a great artist, a hard worker – I'd watched him working with the others at repairs to the house and grounds – and an inveterate punster. Oh, and he had punched Dave Harrison in the nose. That, I suspect, simply proved that he was a sensible human being. If I'd been of an age and physique to do any punching, I might well have done the same thing. Really, John Donne to the contrary notwithstanding, Harrison's death seemed to be a blessing to mankind.

Except for the destruction that followed in its wake, I reminded myself.

Anyway, I'd not known Ed to lose his temper on any other occasion. And was he a sly enough character to shove Dave in the river and then spend the rest of the weekend cheerfully turning his hand to whatever might help?

Boom! Boom! Boom! The reports startled me considerably. I had forgotten about the flares. And hadn't Alan planned to bring firewood in first? I looked out the window in time to see the second volley, spaced a few seconds apart, and then the third one in rapid fire. They let about a minute elapse, and then did it again. And yet again.

The booms died away, and though I opened the window and strained my ears, I could hear no answering thunder.

I closed the window with cold, stiff fingers, and hurried back into bed. I wouldn't do any more with my lists until Alan brought the firewood. I was too cold, and I wasn't getting anywhere anyway.

It was only a few minutes before Alan's knock came at the door. I opened it wide, and he came in – empty-handed.

'Jim is bringing the wood?' I said, shivering and hurrying back under the covers.

'There is no more dry wood.' Alan divested himself of his outer clothing and his shoes. 'It's all been burnt. Tomorrow when it's light Jim's going to investigate the attics and see if there's any valueless old furniture up there that can be cut up and burned. Meanwhile, bed is going to be the only warm place.' He turned the lantern down until the flame wavered and died. 'Move over, love.'

TWENTY-THREE

We found an agreeable way to keep warm and at the same time patch up the last shreds of our quarrel. I fell asleep in his arms.

We had gone to bed very early, so I woke long before the chill November dawn. My arm had fallen asleep; I pulled it out from under Alan to shake it into feeling again, and then got up to go to the bathroom.

Something about the house was odd. I couldn't put my finger on it until my stocking-clad feet hit the bathroom tiles.

I wasn't cold.

I used the toilet and then turned on the hot water tap. It wasn't too long before the stream became warm, and then hot.

I hightailed it back into the bedroom. 'Alan! Someone's found a way to get the Aga going, and I think even the furnace! There's hot water, and the house is warm!'

Alan wakes all of a piece, the result, I suppose, of years of irregular hours as a policeman. He threw back the covers and raised his head, rather like a cat sniffing the air before venturing forth. He cocked his head to one side. 'The central heating is certainly on. I wonder . . .' He put out a hand to the bedside lamp and turned the switch.

'Light!' I'm not sure God on that first day found the light any more wonderful than I did at that moment. 'Alan, that means we have power again! And oh, dear heaven, you don't suppose – a telephone?'

I picked up the one on the bedside table while Alan found his mobile.

'Nothing here,' I said. 'Yours?'

He shook his head and began pulling off the remainder of the clothes we'd worn to bed. 'I,' he said, 'am going to take a bath.'

I let him go first, and then I basked in a hot tub. What bliss to be clean and warm again! One doesn't fully appreciate the benefits of civilization until they're missing for a while.

We had to put on clothes that were considerably less than fresh, but we could soon wash everything. Calloo, callay – electricity!

We forgot that we were supposed to be isolating ourselves. We forgot, for a little while, that there was a murderer among us. I collected all our dirty clothes except for the ones we had on and headed downstairs, recklessly turning on lights as I went, in search of Joyce's washing machine. Alan was right behind me, singing a little tune in which the word 'coffee' featured largely.

The kitchen was brightly lit when we got there, and savory smells filled the air. I didn't know what Rose Bates was preparing for breakfast, but my mouth watered. She beamed at us. 'Isn't it wonderful? You're the first ones down, but I know all the rest will be here soon. Breakfast is nearly ready. I'll serve it up in a minute – in the dining room – but first, shall I take those things to the laundry for you, Mrs Martin?'

'Just point me in the right direction. I'd hate to take you away from whatever concoctions you have brewing.'

'Through that door. I washed towels the minute I got up, so the machine is ready for you. I knew all the guests would be dying to use it.' Then she heard what she'd said, and her smile wavered a little.

I hurried to the laundry and tried to ignore the thoughts she'd conjured up.

We did full justice to that wonderful breakfast. Rose had created a sort of breakfast pudding, an airy combination of eggs and ground ham and I don't know what else that tasted like food for angels. There were sausages, not the bland, cereal-filled ones that desecrate so many English breakfast tables, but real bangers, browned to a turn and bursting merrily when pierced by a fork. There was bacon, both the English and the American variety, perfectly cooked. There were grilled mushrooms, and some sort of fish soufflé, and baked apples with cream, and toast and marmalade and coffee and tea and orange juice. I ate as much as I could hold and wished I could eat more.

A bright blue sky contributed to the holiday mood. There was literally not a cloud in sight, and though the air was cold, it was still. Our dark and stormy weather appeared to be at an end.

It was Alan who, regretfully, reminded us that the situational climate was not so serene. When we had all eaten our fill, and Rose had come in to clear, he stood and tapped in his coffee cup.

'That was a magnificent meal, Mrs Bates, and we all owe you our most hearty thanks.' There were cries of 'Hear, hear!' and a little round of applause. 'I'm all the more sorry, then, to introduce a discordant note, but I must remind you that the restoration of electricity, though welcome, hasn't materially changed our circumstances. A number of serious incidents remain unexplained, and until we can sort them out, I must urge you, once more, to be on your guard. We hope that help may arrive soon, but there's no guarantee of when that might happen.'

'You're not going to confine us to quarters again, are you, darling?'

That was Pat, naturally. I was growing used to her style and tried to take the 'darling' in my stride.

'I have no authority to do that, and I doubt you'd pay attention to me even if I tried to 'confine' you. I will ask – I will plead – that none of you go wandering off by yourself. I've no desire at all to cope with yet another disappearance, or worse.'

That sobered even Pat. 'Well, Ed,' she said with a grimace, 'do you want to read in the library, or shall I follow you about as you take some pictures? It's a fine day, at last.'

I didn't wait to see which alternative they chose. The sparkle had gone out of the day. Rather drearily, I followed Alan to the lovely little panelled den where the Moynihans had installed an anachronistic television set. 'Will anything be on the air?' I asked, without much hope.

'We can but try. I should think it's quite possible. Auntie is quite a power in the land, you know.'

'Auntie' being a quasi-affectionate term for the BBC, I had to agree.

Alan unearthed the remote, turned on the set, and found the news – '. . . power restored to much of the south-east this morning. Work continues on the mobile transmission masts and it is expected that most, if not all, will be back on service by this afternoon. Fixed lines will create more difficulties, since it takes time to determine the exact location of downed wires.

'In other news, looting in outlying areas of London has been largely contained, as the restoration of electricity has reinforced police efforts. The Metropolitan Police say that there are still some isolated problems in parts of Brixton and Lambeth, but police response has been restrained and little violence has ensued.'

The announcer went on talking, but I had stopped paying attention. 'Phones, Alan! Communication!'

'And not a moment too soon,' he said heavily. He turned off the TV and stared into space.

'Dorothy,' he said at last, 'when the police do get here, I'm going to feel like the world's prize ass. Bodies to the left of me, bodies to the right of me, and I haven't a clue who's responsible for any of them. Not to mention two persons missing, presumed dead. If I hadn't already retired, I'd probably be sacked.'

'Well, you're not alone,' I retorted. 'I haven't figured anything out, either. I've been making lists, but . . .' I raised my eyes to the ceiling.

Unexpectedly, Alan laughed. 'Lists, eh? Then I know you're functioning normally. I'd like to take a look at those lists of yours, but first, how would you like to go for a walk? Knees up to a longish stroll around the grounds?'

'Pining for the exercise,' I said gratefully. 'And if I get tired I can always turn back.'

'Not without an escort, my girl. Don't forget—'

'Yes, I know. There's a murderer walking around loose some-where. Do you have any idea how tired I am of remembering that?'

'No more than I am of saying it.'

'I suppose that's why we're going for our nice little stroll. To try to find Julie, right?'

'I didn't marry a dunce, did I? But keep quiet about it when anyone else is around, just in case.'

'Aye, aye, sir. Fire when ready, Gridley.'

It was actually a beautiful day, the first we'd had in a long,

long time. The air was very mild for early November, the sky
that shade of pale aquamarine that I associate with Paris, almost
never seen in America and seldom in England. When it's punc-
tuated with a few fluffy clouds Alan and I call it a 'French
Impressionist' sky – life imitating art again. There was no wind
at all.

We did not, however, have a pleasant walk. I had to lean on
my cane and on Alan's arm much more heavily than I would
have liked, because the ground was still spongy from more than
a month of solid rain. It was also littered with obstacles. Leaves
and twigs, larger branches, bushes torn out by their roots covered
what had once been the beautifully smooth lawn. Near the house
there were slates, broken glass, unidentifiable bits of masonry.
I soldiered on, unwilling to let my slight disability force Alan
to turn back.

'Where are we going?' I asked. For we were not wandering
aimlessly; Alan, though moving slowly in consideration of my
knees, was clearly making for some destination. 'Where do you
think she might be?'

'She *might* be anywhere, dead or alive. I've given some thought
to the question however, and my idea is that she's alive and
hiding.'

'That was exactly my conclusion!' I said triumphantly.

'I would be interested to hear your reasoning.'

'That door was locked, always. She was scared to death of
someone. She wouldn't have just taken a fancy to leave her
room, not when she could ring for anything she needed and be
sure who was at the door before she opened it.

'Now. There is another key to her room, the one kept in the
kitchen for the Bateses to use. Suppose she realized that anyone
could take that key and get into her room. She's not a terribly
intelligent woman, but she has a certain amount of cunning, and
even if she's been drinking, she could have worked that one out.'

'That could be what happened. Someone took the key and
dragged her away.'

'It could. But I can't see it. For one thing, she would have
screamed the house down.'

'Not if she was drugged,' Alan pointed out. 'Someone could
have slipped something into her glass.'

'But then they would have had to drag her, literally, and as
you're in a good position to know, she's not a light weight. No,
if I were someone who had wanted to get Julie out of her room,

to . . . to kill her, or do her harm, I would have tried to entice her out. But she wouldn't have enticed all that easily – or at all, if the person she was afraid of were trying it. I think she decided in that muddled mind of hers that she was more vulnerable in the house than out of it, and left for another hiding place. But where that place might be, I have no idea at all.'

'I agree with your reasoning. That's the way I worked it out, too, except I do have a little idea about her hiding place.' He tapped his temple.

'Little grey cells functioning, are they? OK, tell me.'

'I have an unfair advantage, you see. I've covered more of the estate than you, most of it searching for someone. I seem, indeed to have spent most of the weekend searching for someone!'

'You poor dear. And this was supposed to be fun.'

'Yes, well. I began to ponder the Harrisons' idea of tunnels.'

'But Alan, we're much too far from the sea for smuggling to have been practical.'

'That isn't the only use to which tunnels were put, you know. Think about it, Dorothy. The house is, according to Jim and Mr Bates, riddled with secret rooms and so on . . .' He paused suggestively.

'Priest's holes – oh, how utterly stupid of me! Escape tunnels!'

'Or passageways to a church. Remember Mr Leatherbury commented about the High Church tendencies of the Upshawes? I asked him, while you were off somewhere the other day, whether there was a good deal of Anglo-Catholic sentiment in the parish. He said it had died out a bit now, but that according to parish records most of the communicants were, in the seventeenth and eighteenth centuries, very Catholic-minded. And that implies to me —'

'That they were actually Roman Catholic!'

'Or had been at one time. They – the brave souls who professed that faith – would have had to hide it, naturally. Hence the priest's holes. Now, often a Catholic household would have, somewhere in the house, a chapel, or at least a place where Mass could be said. But the vicar said he had never heard of a chapel here at the Abbey.'

I giggled. 'A secular bunch of monks, they must have been.'

'Now, now. Obviously there was a church here when the Abbey was functioning as such. But it was apparently destroyed when Henry shut the place down, leaving only the cloisters of the old religious establishment.'

'And the papists, later on, wouldn't have dared use any place that was so obvious for their clandestine Masses.'

'Naturally not. So the vicar's best guess is that they used the parish church itself, but approached secretly by dark of night. Hence a tunnel.'

TWENTY-FOUR

'Oof.' I tripped over a root and grabbed Alan's arm. 'Could we slow down a little? I'm fine, really, but I wouldn't mind sitting for a bit. If there's any place to sit.'

'Sorry, love. You should have said something.'

'I was perfectly all right until that last root. It reached up and grabbed my ankle. Reminded me of those trees in *The Wizard of Oz*. Remember? They struck out at Dorothy and Toto.'

'Downright malevolent, some trees are.'

We sat on a felled trunk while I caught my breath. 'So where do you think this tunnel is?'

'Well, it would have come out in the parish church, which is just across the river. The vicar says that end has apparently been blocked up; at least he's never been able to find it. And the entry, in the house, has kept its secret all these years, according to both the vicar and Jim. *But*.' He tented his hands and went into his lecturing mode. 'A long tunnel like that would have had air vents built in, and very likely an escape hatch.'

'Sure! Rather like an animal's burrow. Various ways in and out so that, if an enemy was at one hole, the badger or whatever could get out the other.'

'Exactly. And on one recent foray I found what looked very much like one of those emergency exits. It's not much farther now; do you think you can make it?'

'I told you I'm fine. But Alan – you're not going to make me go into a tunnel, or a cave, or anything like that?'

'Would I do that to you? No, I just thought I'd rather have you along. I hated the idea of leaving you back at the house all by yourself.'

He sounded apologetic. We've worked hard to keep a decent balance between his desire to protect me and my need for independence. Every now and then I get testy about his hovering, but on the whole I find it rather endearing – when not carried to extremes. I patted his arm and we continued amicably.

We were nearing the river now. I could hear the rush of water and smell the freshness. 'It sounds not quite so . . . fierce, I guess is the word.'

'It's gone down a bit,' Alan agreed. 'Now watch your step here.' He guided me around a fallen tree, to the edge of what seemed to be a grassy cliff, if there is such a thing.

'Erosion of some kind?' I asked, dubious.

'I don't think so. I think it's a kind of ha-ha.'

A ha-ha, as I learned on a trip to Bath some years ago, is a landscaping device serving the purpose of a fence without creating a barrier to the view. Imagine a lawn sloping away from the manor house towards a meadow where sheep or cows are grazing. It's a lovely, pastoral scene, but plainly you don't want the animals coming up and eating all your flowers and shrubs. Nor do you want to see an ugly affair of posts and rails in the middle distance. So you have your army of gardeners (we're in the eighteenth century at this point, and you're rich as Croesus) – you have your gardeners terrace the slope so that rather than a smooth incline, the lawn levels off for a few yards and then drops off suddenly, forming something very like a cliff perhaps six feet high. The vertical wall is reinforced with brick or stone, and there you have it. From the house the difference in level is invisible, but the beasts on the other side can't get to your garden. Somewhere you build a flight of steps so people can get down, if they want to.

'This is the wrong sort of place for a ha-ha,' I objected. 'No lawn, no vista, no livestock.'

'That's why I think it's what we're looking for. I think they – whoever "they" were, back during the Civil War perhaps – they built this to make possible a concealed door into the tunnel. Or rather out of the tunnel; it would have been used as an exit rather than an entrance.'

'And you've found the door?' This was getting exciting.

'I think so. There aren't any steps left, if there ever were any. I'll have to lift you down.'

'Don't be silly. Help me sit.'

Sitting on the ground isn't easy when you have titanium knees. They don't flex as readily as your original equipment. And getting up is even worse. You have to kneel, and that can be very painful. However, I wasn't going to give in. With Alan's help I sat,

awkwardly, on the muddy, leafy ground and scooted to the edge.
Then, using my cane as a prop, I slid down on my bottom.

My slacks would never be the same again, but I made it.

I insisted on getting up without Alan's help. That required a
good deal of manoeuvring, grunting, and at least one yelp, but
I was at last standing upright. 'OK,' I said, still panting, 'Show
me.' I brushed some leaves off various bits of clothing.

'You see that bit of stone? It looked odd to me when I first
saw it. Not a match to the rest of the rock nearby.'

I moved closer and scrutinized it. 'Well – maybe not exactly
the same colour. But different rocks are different colours. Aren't
there different sorts of rocks, most places? I never studied
geology.'

Alan grinned. 'It is refreshing, if I may say so, my dear, to
discover something you don't know. In many parts of the country
you get a mix of sedimentary and igneous rocks. Those are—'

'I know what they are. I'm not quite a dunce. Rocks
compressed from silt, and rocks created by fire.'

'Roughly, yes. Well, the fact is, here it's all sandstone. But
this is a piece of much harder stone, and it looks as if it was
once part of a building. It doesn't belong here. So when I discov-
ered it, I tried to work out what it was doing here, and when I
came up with the idea of a door, I came back to try to find some
way to shift it. I couldn't, but if I'm right about this, Julie may
well have wedged it somehow to elude pursuit. So a spot of
force seemed indicated.' He pulled out of an inner jacket pocket
a small but efficient-looking crowbar, and from another pocket
a piece of what looked like old lead pipe, and flourished them.
'Now, if you will hold the pipe a moment while I position the
lever . . . good. And I wedge the pipe over the end, thus—'

'Yes, to extend the crowbar and give yourself more leverage.
That much science I know.'

'Keep your hair on, woman – I wasn't showing off my male
superiority. At least I don't think I was. You'd best stand back
a bit; if Julie mucked about with the hinge points, I may well
pull some of the bank down on us.'

He braced himself as well as he could in the mud, took hold
of the pipe with both hands, and pushed hard toward the wall
to force the business end of the lever outwards.

It was as well I obeyed his injunction to step back. He did
bring down part of the bank, but that wasn't the real surprise. It
was the torrent of water that gushed out, shoving the heavy piece

of granite aside like a falling domino, and knocking Alan off his feet.

He wasn't hurt. That was the first thing I checked, the only thing I cared about. Sopping wet, muddy, and smelling like a swamp – an *old* swamp – he got to his feet with difficulty only because the footing was so slippery.

When I was sure he was intact, I studied him as he looked at me. We both burst into somewhat hysterical laughter. 'You look like the Tar-Baby,' I said when I could speak.

'And you like a most disreputable bag lady. We shall have to creep into the house by a back way.'

'What I'd like to do is get to the laundry room, strip, and wash all our clothes on the spot. But getting up to our room—'

'—stark naked, through several acres of stately home—'

That set us off again, but we sobered as we clambered up the bank and squelched off toward the house.

'You were wrong,' I said to Alan.

'I was,' he admitted.

'It was a great idea, though.'

'It never occurred to me that the tunnel would have flooded, though I should have thought of it, given the rains we've had.'

'And the tunnel runs under the river, and might have developed a leak or two in the past several hundred years.'

'Yes. In any case, Julie could certainly not have hidden in there. I was wrong.'

'Or,' I said grimly, 'if she did, and the flood came later . . .' I didn't need to finish the thought. I went on, hurriedly. 'But assuming she *is* alive and hiding – or being hidden – somewhere, the question is, where?'

And to that question, neither of us could come up with an answer.

When we got back to the house, we managed to sneak up to our bedroom without seeing anyone. I was tired, and nearly as wet and dirty as Alan, but when I had shed my impossible clothes and cleaned up a bit, I wanted some tea.

'Alan,' I called into the bathroom, where he was relishing a hot bath – his second, the first having removed only the top layer of grime. 'Alan, we're out of tea. Will you disown me if I go down to the kitchen?'

'You could ring.'

'I'm not very good at that, and besides, I want to talk to Rose. She seemed, this morning, thoroughly recovered from whatever

fit of superstition assailed her last night, but I'd like to make
sure she's OK. I promise I won't let anyone lure me into a closet,
and if I'm not back soon, you can come looking for me.'

'And don't think I won't!' he growled.

I headed for the kitchen.

'Mrs Martin, what can I do for you?' Rose Bates was once
again her cool, efficient self, disposed to resent my presence in
her kitchen.

'I'm pining for some tea, and I'm sorry, Rose, but I'm just
not used to asking someone else to do what I can perfectly well
do for myself. It seems really rude to ring a bell and summon
you to my side when you're busy doing something else. Is the
kettle hot?'

She pursed her lips. 'It will be in a moment. I'll get a tray.'

I had thought we had established friendly relations, and
wondered why she was now snubbing me. Maybe now that she
had her electricity back and could cook properly, she didn't want
help or companionship. In any case, I'd been put firmly in my
place. I sat on a kitchen chair, feeling foolish, while she prepared
a tray: cloth, cups and saucers, spoons, sugar, lemon and a plate
of biscuits. I didn't dare protest that after that breakfast I wouldn't
need food for a week. Nor did I comment on the lemon, assuming
that the milk was used up, or sour. Electricity or not, it would
be some little time before the household routine was back to
normal.

When Rose had poured the boiling water and put the pot on
the tray, I murmured my thanks and escaped to our bedroom,
where Alan was pacing, in his dressing gown.

'Safely returned from my dangerous mission,' I said, and put
the tray down. 'My love, I really am sorry to worry you, but
you know me.'

'For my sins,' he said, but with a smile. 'You can't have had
much of a talk with Mrs Bates. I've only just got out of the tub.'

'She wouldn't talk at all – back on her high horse. I don't
think I'll ever be an Englishwoman, Alan. I just can't get the
hang of "dealing with the servants".'

'Good job we don't have any, then. I gather she was so annoyed
with you she forgot the milk?'

'I didn't dare ask, but I imagine we've run out, or else it's
turned. And I didn't really want the biscuits, but I didn't want
to offend her. I'm sure they're homemade, and they look
delicious.'

'They are,' said Alan, popping a second one into his mouth.
'Go ahead. You walked off your breakfast.'

'I'd have to walk home and back to walk off *that* breakfast,'
I retorted, taking a biscuit. 'And speaking of home . . .'

'Yes. I tried once while you were downstairs. No signal. But
I'll try again.' He found the cell phone, pushed the button for
Jane Langland's number, listened, and shook his head. 'A signal,
but full of noise,' he said, closing the phone. 'It's progress of a
sort. Now, are you ready for a nap, or do you want to do some
more exploring with me?'

'Not outside! I just got clean. I have to start our clothes
washing, but after that – what did you have in mind?'

He leered at me and twirled an imaginary moustache. 'What
I often have in mind – but later, m'dear, later. For now, how
about the case of the hidden mummy?'

TWENTY-FIVE

'It's not so bad with lots of light,' I said in some surprise. We
were in the bedroom with the hidden room, and Alan had
opened the concealed door – carefully, so the grisly contents
wouldn't fall out again. Alan had invited Tom and Lynn along,
so he would have some help moving the mummy, and Ed, to
take pictures of all the stages, and of course Pat came along with
Ed. Jim and Joyce were there, too – it was, after all, their house,
and their mummy, so to speak. So we were quite a little party,
missing out only Laurence, who was still keeping to his bed,
and the vicar, keeping watch over him.

The room was very cold. Either the central heating hadn't yet
extended to this room, or it hadn't been turned on here. I shivered, not only from the cold.

Lynn wasn't terribly thrilled about seeing the horrid thing
again, but neither Alan nor Tom would allow her to stay alone
in her room, so she and I stayed in a corner of the room, looking
the other way, while the men very carefully moved the body out
of its prison and placed it on a writing table, Ed documenting
every step of the way. Jim and Joyce watched with, I thought,
great distaste, while Pat was frankly enjoying the proceedings.

'I don't *quite* understand about the preservation of the body,' said Lynn. 'I thought mummification was a complicated process, embalming and wrapping and all sorts of gruesome proceedings.'

'I don't know a lot about it either, but I'm sure I read in some book or other that natural mummification can take place when the conditions are right. It would be very dry in there, next to the fireplace, and surely hot when there were fires. The dryness would help, but I would have thought the heat would cause decay, rather than preservation.'

'But there would have been very little heat, actually,' said Joyce, who had drifted over to join us. 'This was one of the rooms that was apparently never used, or not for the past many years, anyway. No one ever told us why not. I suppose I thought it was simply a matter of too many rooms to look after, and never having enough guests to need the space. I know when we first looked at the house, this room and several of the others in this wing looked like Miss Havisham's parlour, right down to the spider webs. Ugh!' She shuddered. 'It almost put me off the place for good.'

'It's a pity,' said Lynn. 'It's a lovely room, and once you get the grounds cleaned up, the view will be spectacular.'

'Yes, but don't you see?' I was getting excited. 'There might have been a very good reason why this room, and the adjacent ones, were shut up and never used. If someone in the family knew—'

There was a subdued commotion in the other corner of the room. 'Eureka!' said Pat softly, and Ed chimed in 'Gloriosky!'

We looked over to see Alan looking gratified. He held in his hands a small dark object, while from his fingers dangled a black chain.

'We've covered her face, ladies, so you can come and see without becoming unduly distressed.' Alan talks that way when he's reverted to policeman mode. We moved nearer. I sniffed cautiously, not sure how much of this my stomach could take, but to my surprise the only smell was a faint mustiness, so I got close enough to see properly.

'This,' said Alan, holding up the chain, 'has been blackened by soot, but it will clean up nicely, I think, as I believe it's gold. I don't know if you can tell, in its piteous state, but it seems to be a locket. If there are pictures inside, and if they are well-preserved, it may be of great help in identifying our young lady here. However, we may not need it for purposes of identification.'

With the air of a conjuror producing the rabbit, he held out Exhibit B. 'We found this wallet in her pocket. It contains money, in the old currency. We haven't counted it, but I saw a pound note and a half-crown. Those haven't been around for a while, which will help us date the corpse. Most important, however, is this.' He showed us, in a cracked vinyl window pocket, what was unmistakably a driving licence. 'Issued in 1958 to one Annie Watkins, born 1940, address Branston Abbey, Branston, Kent.'

There was a quick intake of breath from someone in the room. I couldn't tell who, and neither, from the look on his face, could Alan. In that moment he might have been a hound who had caught a faint whiff of fox. His head came up and I could almost see his nose twitch. 'Did that ring a bell with someone?' he asked, calmly enough.

Pat. It had to be Pat. She was the only one whose history in the village went back far enough. She would hardly have been born in 1958, I thought, but she might have heard something, might know the family name. She said nothing, however, and her face was utterly bland – which in itself was enough to tell me she was hiding something.

'Very well. If you think of something, any of you, come and tell me at once, please. I ask this for your own protection. Knowledge of a crime—' He was interrupted by a loud noise out on the lawn, loud and getting louder. 'Is that what I hope it is?' he asked, and strode to the window.

Just settling on the lawn, with that gentle lightness that always seems so inappropriate for something its size, was a small blue-and-white helicopter marked POLICE.

Alan sprang into instant action. 'Tom, I'll ask you and Jim to stay here with our poor Annie. Dorothy, I'd like you with me, if you will.'

Leaving the rest to do as they liked, which was to trail after us, Alan sprinted out of the room at a much faster pace than I could manage. 'I'll catch up,' I called to him. He said something and disappeared around a corner. It was left to Joyce to guide us through the maze of corridors and staircases and out the terrace doors.

Alan was shaking hands with the two people who had climbed out of the helicopter. The rotors had, mercifully, been turned off and were slowing to a stop. I panted up to Alan, and he turned to me. 'Dorothy, these are Detective Constables Price –' he nodded to the attractive woman – 'and Norris. My wife, Dorothy

Martin.' We shook hands all round, and Alan went on. 'The constable in Branston saw our signals and sent for help, and this is the handsome response.'

'I can't possibly tell you how glad we are to see you,' I said, nearly in tears from the relief. 'I don't know what Alan has told you, but we've been having a pretty bad time here.'

'I've not said anything beyond that. Miss Price, Mr Norris, if you will come into the house— oh, this is our hostess, Mrs Moynihan – perhaps we can take a few minutes to put you in the picture.'

The detectives followed us back to the house, and I heard Miss Norris say, 'Retired CC – watch your step.' I think Alan heard, too, but he made no sign.

Once we were settled in the drawing room, Alan kept his attitude of command. He had no intention, I knew, of stepping on the Kent Constabulary toes. On the other hand, he wasn't going to cede entire control of the case to a couple of young constables who knew nothing of the nightmare we'd been through.

'With your permission, officers, I think it might be wise to assemble the entire household to hear the story. I may forget something, and it will give you the opportunity to decide what's best to be done. Agreed?'

DC Norris was inclined to resent being told what to do. 'With respect, sir, we have no idea why we've been called here, or what your wife means by "a bad time". As I'm sure you must know, there are more emergencies out there than we can cope with, and we're all very tired. We're merely responding to an SOS.'

'I do appreciate that, Mr Norris, and I sympathize. That's why I want to save as much of your time as possible.'

Norris gave a brief nod, and Alan touched the bell. We sat in uncomfortable silence until Mrs Bates appeared. Alan explained the situation to her and said, 'If you will, I'd like you to bring everyone else in the house in here, including you and Mr Bates.'

'Mr Upshawe, sir? And the vicar?' She sounded disapproving.

'If Mr Upshawe is well enough, yes. This shouldn't be too taxing for him, I hope. And please take DC Price, here, to the ... I don't know what it's called, the bedroom where we found the mummified body—'

There was a stifled exclamation from both the constables.

'—and tell Mr Moynihan and Mr Anderson to come down, too. Miss Price, here's the key to that room; you'd best lock it behind you.'

I was hard put not to giggle. The release from the strain of the past several days was part of my light-headedness, but I was getting a real kick out of watching Alan bossing around two police officers over whom he had no authority whatever. 'I'll bet you were a holy terror to your own troops,' I whispered to him. He merely lifted an eyebrow.

It took a little time, but we were finally assembled, all of us. All of us who were still among the living and could be found, that is. That was the first point Alan addressed.

'Now, I'm sure you'll want to begin this interview in your own way, Mr Norris, but you should know that three of our original party are not here. One is dead and two are missing, one at least of those presumed dead.'

DC Norris seemed about to strangle. 'Mr Nesbitt! There is a body upstairs, apparently long dead. Now you're telling me there's another body around here somewhere, and two more possible deaths? What the bl— what on earth has been going on here?'

'Oh, and there's the skeleton under the tree,' Alan went on, blandly, 'but we'll come to that in due course. As to what's been going on, that's what I hope you can help us determine.'

Slowly and carefully, with occasional prompting from one or another of the assembly, Alan detailed all that he knew about the eventful weekend. He kept strictly to what was known, leaving out any speculation. Beginning with the storm and the discovery of the skeleton, he led the rapt constables through the death of Harrison and the injury to Upshawe, the disappearance and re-appearance of Julie, Mike's presumed drowning, Julie's second disappearance, and the discovery of the mummy.

'So you see,' he said finally, 'why we were rather desperate to get help. I do apologize for usurping your job, but I thought it would be easiest to explain the complicated business all of a piece, as it were. Now I'm sure you have questions for all of us.'

There was a strained silence. Finally DC Norris cleared his throat.

'As I'm sure you'll know, sir, we were detailed to respond to a distress call, not to investigate a multiple homicide. If that's what this can be called.' He sounded uncertain about the number of actual homicides involved. As well he might.

'We need to check in with our commander for orders. If the mobiles are working, we can call. Otherwise, I'm afraid one of us, at least, will have to return to Shepherdsford. We're going

to need the full SOCO team, and with everything else that's
going on . . .' He shrugged helplessly.

'Yes, I understand. There couldn't be a worse time for you to
find this mess in your laps, could there? Your commander would
be—'

'Superintendent Westley, sir.'

'Ah, yes. And your CC is Sir Robert Bunyard, if I remember
correctly.'

'Yes, sir.' He swallowed and tried to turn it into a cough.

'Well, you might just tell one or the other of them that I'd be
most grateful for any help they can supply. We're not in danger
of life or limb here – at least I don't think so – but we *are* badly
in need of technical expertise. I've done what I could, but with
no forensics team – and no authority – I haven't accomplished
a great deal.'

For the first time since the police had arrived he sounded
tired, and worried. He ran his hand down the back of his neck
in a familiar gesture and then smiled at me in reassurance. I was
not greatly reassured.

TWENTY-SIX

Mobile service still being unavailable, DC Norris decided
to stay with us while DC Price returned with the helicopter to get more help. Norris had, then, a nice decision
to make. Should he stay with one of the bodies (recent, mummified, or skeletal), guard the living victim/suspect (Laurence
Upshawe), or keep an eye on all the rest of us (potential
victims/suspects)?

In the end he opted to guard Dave's body, I suppose on the
principle that a recent murder, even if not proven, was of more
interest than two very old ones, even though they were almost
certainly the results of foul play. What forensic evidence there
was should be protected. Besides that, Laurence was already
being guarded, and there were far too many of the rest of us for
one man to make any difference.

I suspected, too, that the poor constable had decided we were
all a pack of lunatics, and the corpse in the garage was more
congenial company.

So the pack of lunatics dispersed, each of us left to our own devices. Rose Bates returned to her kitchen, undoubtedly offended by the disturbance to her routine. Her husband went about whatever mysterious tasks he chose to undertake. Pat wandered off toward the library and Ed, camera in hand, to find some good shots while the sun still shone. Laurence went straight back to bed, this time with Jim to keep him company, while Mr Leatherbury took a well-deserved nap and Joyce tried hard to think of some way to keep her imprisoned guests amused and happy. Tom and Lynn went for a walk.

In short, we were back to where we were, almost, except that the presence of one young constable had, perhaps irrationally, eased our fears and our cabin fever. Soon, now, we were going to know what had happened. Soon we would be able to go home. Soon our lives would be back to normal.

Except for Dave Harrison's. And Julie's. And Mike's.

With a heartfelt, Scarlett-like vow not to think about them, I proposed to Alan that we revisit the mummy.

'I thought you found her pretty grim, darling.'

'I do. But I have a theory about her, and I'd like to know if there's anything to be seen that justifies my idea.'

Alan shook his head. 'Unsound practice. You don't formulate a theory and then look for facts to justify it; you collect facts and then—'

I made a rude noise. 'Don't be stuffy. You know perfectly well every policeman in the world forms theories ahead of the facts. You'd never get anywhere with tough cases if you didn't. Anyway, you're going to do the looking, not me. Nothing in the world would get me to look at that grinning skull again.'

John Bates was in the hall outside the drawing room door, hammer raised, preparing to board up one of the broken windows. 'Oh, J— Mr Bates,' I said. 'Is Mrs Bates feeling well? I thought she seemed a bit . . . distressed, earlier.' *Testy* was what I really meant, but it didn't seem politic to say so.

'She is quite well, thank you, madam, but a bit upset, owing to her work having got so far behind.'

'Well, you tell her for me that we all certainly understand, and she's not to worry.'

He gave a little bow. 'Thank you, madam. I will give her your good wishes.'

'He is so exactly like Jeeves, I sometimes thinks it's

Wodehouse I've walked into, rather than Christie. I didn't think they came like that anymore.'

'A *rara avis*, certainly,' Alan agreed.

We took the lift to the third floor. That fruitless little expedition this morning had been harder on my knees than I cared to admit; Alan could tell, though. He unlocked the door to the forsaken bedroom – I had begun thinking of it in those terms – and turned on the lights.

I avoided looking at the table where the mummy lay. 'Alan, I was serious when I said I didn't want to look at her unless I absolutely have to. But you're trained to observe. I want you to describe for me, in detail, exactly what her hair looks like, and what she's wearing.'

'She's rather nicely dressed, or would be if her clothes weren't covered in dust. Everything is black. Her jumper – sorry, sweater to you – is knit in some very fine-gauge yarn, not wool but a synthetic, I think. No moth holes, at any rate. It fits well and has a little lacy-looking collar, removable. It has yellowed over the years, though, and cracked a bit. Starched, I suppose.'

I cheered inwardly, but made no comment.

'You understand I'm describing the way I imagine her clothes would have looked when she was put in here. Her body has shrunk, so the fit isn't good now – but I think it was. Her skirt is of a different fabric, rather thin, and is – I don't know the word – it flares out from the waist.'

I risked a look. 'Unpressed pleats,' I said. 'Quite full, and hemmed just about at the knee. They don't make clothes like that anymore. And black stockings. Alan, I can't make myself touch her. Could you check to see if they're pantyhose – tights?'

I couldn't watch, either. It seemed like such a violation, an invasion of her privacy. Which was foolish. She was dead, had been dead for a long time. Still – she'd taken the trouble to dress nicely. She wouldn't have wanted some strange man pulling up her skirt.

'Tights,' Alan reported. 'Black, fairly coarse – dancers' tights, I'd say, not regular street wear.'

'Yes,' I said absently to myself. 'That would fit. I wore those about then, I remember.' Aloud, I asked one more thing.

'And her hair, Alan?'

'It's gone brittle over the years, and lost its colour. Some of it has probably broken off – the forensics team will be able to tell us more. But it was long, and she wore it pulled back, with a black ribbon, Alice-style. If I had to guess, I'd say she was a blond. All that black would be attractive on a blond. Oh, and she's wearing earrings, small gold hoops – at least I think they're gold.'

'Pierced ears?'

'No. Clip-ons.'

I hated to ask the last question, but I thought I knew the answer, anyway. 'Wedding ring?'

'No. No rings at all. Her fingers are shrivelled, though. It's possible any rings might have fallen off. I'll check.'

He had brought a powerful flashlight. He shone it around every crevice of the poor girl's tomb.

'I don't see anything, and I can't grub around in there without incurring the ire of the SOCOs. I shouldn't have removed her, by rights, but I had no way of knowing the cavalry was on its way, and I didn't like the idea of leaving her to the mercy of anyone who might think it a good idea to do a little cover-up. Now, what does all that tell you, my dear Miss Marple?'

'It tells me when she died, and tends to confirm my theory about why.'

'Ah.' Alan looked at me with that mixture of admiration and indulgence he uses when I'm being sleuthly. 'And are you going to share your insights with a poor dogsbody of an ageing detective?'

'Yes, let's – Alan, do cover her up. It's obscene, somehow, sitting here talking about her in front of her.'

To his credit, Alan did not smile, simply unfolded the sheet he'd used to cover her face and laid it gently over her. We went to a settee that gave off clouds of dust when we sat on it, and I explained my conclusions.

'We know the mummy – Annie, poor girl – we know she was still alive in 1958, because her driver's licence was issued then. Now. The other death, the skeleton – Harry – almost certainly took place in 1960. I thought it would be really strange if they were not somehow connected, so I thought about how to tell when she died.'

'The clothes,' said Alan, enlightened.

'The clothes. They are the fashions of the late fifties into about 1961. After that Mary Quant reigned supreme among the young Englishwoman who cared at all about clothes, so Annie here would have been wearing a miniskirt.'

'How do you know all this? I never thought of you as a fashionista.'

'I'm not now, but I was young then, just a little younger than Annie, if I'm right. We were a bit behind England in catching up with Carnaby Street, but I read the magazines and wished those styles would come to southern Indiana. Anyway, this girl was plainly young, nineteen or twenty, I'd guess.'

'Clothes again?'

'Partly, but mostly her hair. No one wore an Alice band much after twenty, even in Indiana. I never did, in fact. My hair was always thick and wavy, and not even ironing it could give it that lovely straight, shiny fall. I remember – but that's beside the point, which is that Annie was young, and tried to look her best, even though she didn't have much money.'

Alan was stymied by that one.

'The collar, Alan. That detachable collar. I'm betting it's plastic, yes?'

'*Plastic?*' He went back to Annie, turned back the sheet, and gingerly touched the collar. 'Well, I suppose it's possible.'

'Aha! I do know more than you about some things, even English things. When Mary Quant was first starting out, she opened a little shop in London, and one of her special things was little white plastic collars. You could take a plain black sweater and turn it into something chic, just by fastening on the collar. Easy and cheap.'

'And she started selling them – when?'

'The mid-fifties, I think, but they died out around 1960 or '61, when the mini was about to become all the rage. You'll note that Annie's skirt is much shorter than the calf-length that prevailed during the fifties, but not yet above the knee. Also, she wore dancer's tights, because she wanted black, and what we Americans call pantyhose – street tights – didn't come into use until miniskirts made them a necessity. *Et voilà!* She was twenty or so and dressed conservatively, but definitely fashionably, on a tiny income. The sweater, by the way, is probably Dacron. It was really popular for a while, knitted up very fine-grained, and was very inexpensive.'

'So she died at about the same time as Harry. Is that what you're saying?'

I had been a trifle elated by my discoveries, but I came back to earth with a thump. 'Yes, poor thing.'

'And – the wedding ring? Or the lack thereof?'

'This is the hard part, Alan. She doesn't show any obvious injuries, does she? I mean, she wasn't shot, or hit over the head, or whatever?'

He already knew where I was going. 'There are lots of ways to kill a person and leave few traces. Poison, for one.'

'Yes, I know. And the forensics people will have to take everything into account. But I'm betting, Alan – I'm betting she was one of Harry's victims. I'm betting she either killed herself, or died in childbirth. Harry's child.'

TWENTY-SEVEN

'It's the wildest speculation,' said Alan after a long silence.

'But based on a good many facts. Her age. I know that from the way she's dressed and the way she did her hair. Or, OK, Mr Policeman, I surmise that. One is allowed reasonable deductions from the evidence.'

Alan made one of those see-saw, yes-no-maybe gestures.

'And given her age, we know when she died. And it was about the same time that Harry died. Isn't it really hard to believe that the two events were simply coincidental?'

'It's a house of cards – but you know that. Go on building it.'

'I think I'm done,' I said, deflated now. 'But it isn't quite a house of cards. Is it?'

He was quiet for a long time, making little puffing motions with his mouth, as if he still had his pipe. Finally he said, 'You're suggesting that Harry seduced this girl, she bore his child and died in her travail, or killed herself for shame, and Harry decided to flee the country – but someone killed him before he could get away.'

'More or less, yes. I know it's awfully thin, but—'

'Thin! It's tissue paper! We don't know for sure that the skeleton is Harry's. We know nothing about this girl but her name. We don't even know how she met her death. We can't—'

'Alan.' I put out my hand. 'Stop thinking like a policeman for a minute. What if my hypothesis – OK, my wild guess – is true? What if Harry did make this girl pregnant? And just suppose, just for one moment, that she had been your daughter. What if he'd done that to Elizabeth? And she'd died of it. What would you have done?'

Another silence. Then Alan said, softly, 'I'd have beaten him within an inch of his life.'

I held up my hands in the universal 'There you have it' gesture.

'All right,' he conceded. 'It's still thin as skim milk, but I'm beginning to believe it might be possible. We'll have to get—'

'—the forensic evidence. I know. If Annie, here, turns out to be *virgo intacta*, we drop the theory. But she won't. Poor Annie. No baby, no lover, no life left.'

But there, as it happened, I was wildly, seriously, wrong.

It was nearly lunchtime. I didn't know if Rose was up to cooking us anything, but she produced a masterpiece of a meal, as usual. I couldn't imagine how she kept on feeding us with no fresh groceries, but she managed to come up with a salad of canned and frozen vegetables, a pasta dish fit for the gods, and a chocolate mousse that I would have sworn had a dozen eggs in it. I raised my eyebrows at Joyce, who simply shrugged in helpless wonder.

'I don't know how she does it,' she said, shaking her head. 'Like Peter Wimsey with respect to Bunter's coffee, I don't want to know. If it's witchcraft, I'd rather remain ignorant.'

'If it's witchcraft, she's a white witch,' I replied. 'And in any case, a treasure.'

'And Mr Bates – he's just as wonderful. There is nothing he won't turn his hand to, and do it well. He doesn't even need to be told; he just sees what needs doing and does it. Jim and I couldn't possibly keep this place going without him.'

After lunch what I wanted more than anything else was a nap, but I resisted and went to the library to hunt down Pat. For once she wasn't there. A volume of Thackeray lay book-marked on a table, which, given her taste in literature, told me she had probably been there, but she had fled. I noted with approval that she didn't leave books face down, and went to hunt for her.

It took me a while, and the siren song of that nap was sounding ever more clear and appealing, when I finally tracked her down, of all places, in Laurence's room.

Ed had taken Jim's place, and for a moment I wondered if I was interrupting something. Pat and Ed were definitely hitting it off well together; perhaps they had found a cozy place to . . . but Laurence was up, sitting in a chair and wide awake, and Ed was on the other side of the room. Pat sat by Laurence's chair with a small notebook in her hand.

'I'm sorry, all,' I said, hesitating at the doorway. 'I was actually looking for you, Pat, but you're obviously busy.'

'Yes, but come in, Dorothy. I have a feeling you'll want to hear this. Laurence's memory's come back.'

She was right. I did definitely want to hear, and I thought Alan should, too. For once I remembered that there were servants in the house, and rang for Mrs Bates. John answered, though, and fetched Alan with his usual efficiency.

'Now, then, ducks, where were we?' said Pat.

Laurence smiled a little. He was plainly still in pain, and still in need of the long-delayed medical attention – good grief, we should have sent him back with the helicopter! – but he was ready and eager to talk.

'I've told you the first part of it,' he said. 'I talked to Mr Leatherbury, and was still very perturbed in my mind as to what I should do. You know about that part, sir,' he said to Alan, 'and Miss Heseltine has suggested that perhaps I shouldn't talk about it freely.'

'Quite right,' said Alan, nodding approvingly at Pat. 'Go on, please.'

'I told you, I think, that I walked toward the river, to the south, and was appalled at the destruction everywhere. I was never very fond of this house, but the gardens and meadows were lovely, lovely. They will never be the same.' His voice broke, and I was glad neither Jim nor Joyce was there.

'Well. The next part is very clear in my mind now, very. I became aware, gradually, that someone was walking behind me. I don't think I consciously thought "following" me, simply that someone was walking the same way I was. I turned around, and to my surprise it was Mr Harrison. I had not put him down as a nature lover, and I wondered what he was up to.'

He cleared his throat. 'I don't know why that attitude occurred to me – that he was "up to" something, except that he was walking in what I could only think was a furtive manner. I had turned around rather suddenly, I suppose, and he darted behind a tree, only just too late. He saw that I had seen him, or he must have done, because he came out and walked toward me, quite fast. His gait was unsteady, and I thought he had been drinking.'

'He usually was,' Pat put in, *sotto voce*.

'He came up to me and – really, accosted is the only word. He took hold of the front of my jacket and nearly spat in my face. He reeked of whisky. He was so drunk, and speaking so fast, that I could barely understand him, but he seemed to be threatening me. "You'd better not," he said, again and again, but I couldn't make out what it was that he didn't want me to do.

All this time – well, I suppose it was only a minute or two, but it seemed a long time – he was holding me close to him and breathing whisky fumes into my face.

'I had finally had enough. I was not in a happy frame of mind to begin with, and it was just all a bit too much. I pushed him away, or tried to, but he had a strong grip, and though he stumbled – we both did, I think – he didn't loose his hold. And if he was angry before, now he was in a fury. He unleashed a stream of profanity and struck me, hard, on the jaw.' Laurence put a hand up to explore the bruise, now brilliantly coloured and swollen. 'Not broken, luckily, but it was a narrow escape. I saw the blow coming, but couldn't twist free to avoid it. And that's the last I remember until I woke here, in this room.'

'And where were you when this confrontation took place?' Alan asked.

'Fairly near the river, we must have been, because I remember seeing that the water meadows were flooded, and the water was running fast.'

'Were you able to strike back, at all, or defend yourself?'

'I made a pretty poor show, didn't I? Tussling with a drunken man, and laid out with one fist, like a baby in her cradle. No, I wasn't prepared for what he did, and after that one blow – well, as I say, I remember nothing more. I believe the Americans have an expression about a glass jaw?' He looked at me with the ghost of a grin.

'So, Laurence.' Pat leaned forward, her chin on her knuckles, her eyes intent. 'This is really important. Did you get any hint – noise, movement, anything – that anyone else was present at the time Harrison confronted you?'

He thought hard. 'It's possible, I suppose. There was a lot of noise from the wind in the trees. There were sounds, but I was a trifle too preoccupied to analyse them.'

'The wind in the trees?' asked Pat.

'Well – the rustle of leaves and so on.'

I looked at Alan. Pat looked at both of us and then back at Laurence. 'I believe,' she said gently, 'that the wind had died down that afternoon. You went out after tea, right?'

'Yes, I— by Jove, I think you're right! I do remember thinking that the floods would recede when they were no longer driven by the wind. So the rustle I heard . . .'

'Could have been an animal, a twig falling, almost anything,' said Alan. 'But it could also have been a third person.'

'Who didn't come to Laurence's rescue,' I pointed out.

'Well,' said Laurence, 'but there's no need to rely on my memory. If Harrison wasn't too drunk to remember anything, you can ask him.'

Oh. Oh, dear. Nobody'd told him.

Alan took a deep breath. 'I'm so sorry. There hasn't seemed to be a good time to tell you. Harrison is dead. He drowned that afternoon, near where you . . . were.'

I knew he'd started to say 'fought'. But fought wasn't exactly the word, when the fight had consisted of one blow from one of the men.

If Laurence was telling the truth. But I thought he was.

He frowned. 'He fell in the river? He could have lost his footing, I suppose, but we weren't very near the edge. Unless perhaps the bank gave way – waterlogged – the water was running fast—'

'We don't know exactly how he died,' said Alan, 'only that he was found in the river. We won't even know for certain that he drowned, actually, until the medical examiner can have a look at him.'

'You don't know how he died,' Laurence repeated in a flat voice. 'And I've just told you that he struck me. I claim to remember nothing after that, but . . .' He looked hard at Alan. 'You have had someone in this room with me ever since I woke up. And before that?'

'You were never alone, from the time we found you and brought you in. The vicar kept watch most of the time, but he's taking a break, poor fellow.' He returned Laurence's gaze. 'And yes, your companion was there as much for our sakes as for yours. You were very badly hurt. We weren't sure, at first, that you would live. Your skull wasn't fractured, so far as I could tell, but there could have been a subdural haemorrhage. I wanted you watched very closely for any change.'

'But you also thought I might be involved in Harrison's death.' Still those flat tones. 'But— just a moment!' He sounded suddenly livelier. 'A fractured skull? Subdural bleeding? Harrison struck me on the jaw, not the head, and as flabby as he is – was – surely a blow from a fist couldn't cause any serious skull injury.'

'You were found, you see, very nearly at the edge of the swollen river, with your head on a large rock. Which was quite sufficient to cause serious head injuries.' Alan sat back to watch his reaction to that.

'Good Lord! No wonder I've been having God-awful headaches. Concussion, almost certainly, and you're very lucky I didn't have that bleeding, or you'd have yourself another dead villain.'

TWENTY-EIGHT

'**B**ut I don't think he did anything,' I said to Alan as we went back downstairs – using the elevator; my knees were getting very tired of all those stairs.

'Except, of course, to lie to us all about recognizing the skeleton.'

'Well – yes. There is that. But I can see why he did that. He knew that Harry had left the country in 1960. Had died in a plane crash. He'd known those things all his life. To be confronted, suddenly, with evidence to the contrary – it was too much to assimilate all at once. He told you, told us all, the story he'd been told as a boy.'

'Dorothy, that's what I'd like to think, too.' He ran his hand down the back of his neck. 'Damn it, I like the man as much as you do. But he could also have been telling the story because he'd already worked out the implications and didn't want anyone to know.'

'In that case – thank you, that elevator door is hard to manage – in that case, why did he go tell the vicar the whole thing later? No, I'm sorry, Alan. Laurence lied to us, yes, but I find it absolutely impossible that he had any reason to kill Dave Harrison. I believe he tried to push Dave off because he was getting impossibly belligerent, and got himself pasted, but I don't think he ever struck Dave again. I think all that with Dave going into the river, and the rock, and so on, happened later, after Laurence was knocked out, and I think it was that other person who did it.'

'The rustle that might have been a squirrel? House of cards again, Dorothy?'

I stuck my tongue out at him, and would have said more, but we had reached the drawing room, and Mr Bates materialized at our side in his disconcertingly silent way. 'The authorities have arrived, sir, madam. They await you in the library.'

'They want facts, don't forget, Dorothy,' said my loving husband in an undertone as we went through to the library. 'No castles in the air.'

'But where else is one to build card houses?' I whispered.

The police had sent a large detail, in two large helicopters. Evidently the 'old pal of the CC' routine had accomplished exactly what Alan had intended, and got us the cream of the crop. I forget who all showed up, but beside the forensics people (complaining about working away from their lovely labs, but getting right down to it, anyway), there were at least two Detective Inspectors, several Detective Constables, and other lesser lights: sufficient force, one would have thought, to patrol the City of London after a terrorist threat. They were sufficient, at least, to make me feel more secure than I had since the moment I found the skeleton.

It would be tedious to relate the questioning and cross-questioning that went on for the next few hours. Everyone was interviewed separately, one at a time, while constables kept an eye on the rest of the group to make sure nothing of any consequence was discussed. We went into our activities, and our reports of everyone else's activities, for the past five days. Much of it seemed, to me at least, to have happened in another life. I'm sure I contradicted myself over and over; my memory was never terrific, and it hasn't become any sharper with advancing years. And how, for heaven's sake, was one supposed to remember, or even know, what had gone on in a rambling old house with probably thirty bedrooms and innumerable nooks and crannies? The entire cast of an axe-murder film could have been hiding in Branston Abbey going about their ghoulish work all weekend, and no one would have known. 'We wouldn't even have heard the screams,' I said to myself, and didn't realize I'd spoken aloud until the rather bored detective who was questioning me jumped to the alert, and I had to explain I was just wool-gathering. I'm not altogether sure he believed me. He looked very relieved when he sent me back with the rest.

'Headache, darling?' Alan asked me presently. We had been talking about Shaw's *Pygmalion* versus *My Fair Lady*, Pat joining in with spirited opinions, and I was a little startled, but Alan's pressure on my hand warned me.

'Oh, love, I didn't want to bother you, but yes, it's been getting worse and worse.' I put a histrionic hand to my temple and hoped that was what he wanted. He sighed, stood up, and went to speak in a low murmur to the PC in the corner.

If he'd been anyone other than a distinguished retired chief constable, I doubt he'd have got by with it, but the constable, a young woman who looked to be barely out of training, was awed by the whole situation – multiple deaths in a listed building, an epic storm, and then an eminent policeman among the personnel. She licked her lips and looked around for someone to ask, but all her bosses were in other rooms.

'You're quite welcome to come along,' Alan said a little louder, 'if you feel it's necessary, but I really do need to get her to bed. She's apt to experience some nausea with these wretched things, you see, and no one would want . . .' He artistically left the sentence unfinished, and the constable gave in.

'I mustn't leave here, sir,' she said nervously, 'but I'll ask DI Collins to send someone. I hope she feels better soon, sir.'

'We both do, Constable. Thank you for being so kind.'

That almost ruined it. The PC looked as if 'kind' wasn't in her job description, and she wasn't sure she'd made the right decision. But by that time Alan had solicitously helped me out of my chair and I'd assumed, I hope, the suffering-but-brave-about-it expression of someone with an almost unbearable migraine.

We kept it up all the way to our room. One never knew when someone was watching, or listening. Once inside, Alan gestured me to the bed, wrung a washcloth out in cold water, and handed it to me. 'In case someone comes,' he said in that low tone that is so much less carrying than a whisper.

I lay down, cloth at the ready, and said, 'All right, what's this little charade all about?'

'Mostly, I wanted to get out of there. It's the first time I've ever been on the receiving end of a group interrogation, and I had no idea how wearing it is on the nerves.'

'Most unfair of you to pull rank that way. Unfair to the others, I mean.'

'Indeed. But the other thing was, I wanted you to know that they're taking Laurence away—'

'Alan!'

'Keep your voice down! You're ill, remember? Not to arrest him. I knew you'd think that, and I wanted you to know before you learned it from someone else. The police doctor is worried about that head injury and wants him in hospital, at least until they're sure there are no permanent brain injuries. He'll have a constable with him, if only because he might possibly remember something else.'

I wanted to ask if Laurence was still under any suspicion, but there was no point. We would just repeat everything we'd said before. So I just smiled and said, 'That's good. I've been worried all along about the poor man going without medical attention.'

Alan patted my hand. 'And the other news is, Dave Harrison died of drowning – there's water in his lungs – and was almost certainly pushed into the river, probably with a tree branch or something of the sort. There's a small but nasty bruise in the middle of his back, slightly abraded.'

'So that settles that, at least. He was murdered.'

'That seems to be the inescapable conclusion.'

'But what a clever way to do it! His murderer never got close enough to leave fibres or let Dave scratch him – no DNA to match up.'

'And every single one of us was manhandling tree branches that day, so evidence of bark or wood fibres on the hands is worth sweet Fanny Adams. As for the weapon, it's probably part of a fine dam somewhere downstream by now. Yes, it looks like the perfect crime. And that, my dear, is why I wish I could get you away from here. We know for certain, now, that there's a murderer on the loose in this house, and you could so easily annoy him into . . . something unpleasant.'

'Or her,' I said in an odd bit of feminism. Insist that the murderer could just as well be a woman? Maybe not quite in the spirit of the thing. And besides – 'So you find me annoying, do you?'

'Terribly.' He moved over to nuzzle my ear. 'And extremely distracting. It's a pity—'

The knock on the door sounded peremptory. We sprang apart as guiltily as if we were a couple of teenagers caught necking on the front porch. 'Come in,' he said, reaching for a tie to straighten – except he was wearing a turtleneck and sweater.

'PC Bryan, sir, just checking on Mrs Nesbitt.'

'Mrs Martin, Constable,' said Alan with a straight face.

'Oh, yes, sir?' The young woman's face reddened slightly as she looked around the room so obviously occupied by two.

I was pleased to see that the young could still blush, but it was a shame to tease her. 'I kept my own name when we married, Constable. It confuses many people.'

'Yes, ma'am. I hope you're feeling better, Mrs Martin.'

Now it was my turn to be embarrassed. I had completely forgotten our little ruse. I picked up the cloth, which had left a wet spot on the bedspread, and dabbed at my temples with it. 'Thank you. My medication is usually quite effective, if we catch the headache in time.' Which was the absolute truth.

'Um . . . good. I came to tell you, Mr Nesbitt, that we've had a call from Superintendent Westley.'

'Oh, the mobiles are back in service now?'

'Yes, sir. We told him that Mrs N— Mrs Martin is ill, and he said you may both leave if you wish. I'm afraid it won't be possible to drive out for some time, but the rail service from Shepherdsford has been restored, and there's a direct line to Sherebury.'

There was our dream come true, just like that. Home. Away from this dreadful funhouse with its skeletons and mummies that popped out on every occasion, with its murderer happy in the knowledge of having committed the perfect crime.

This house with its unhappy host and hostess, facing years, probably, of repairs and rebuilding that would never erase the memories of this weekend. This house with its complement of other guests, all of whom wanted to get home every bit as badly as we did.

Alan and I have been married only a few years, a second marriage for both of us, but we have achieved in that short time a certain level of wordless communication. I looked at him and he at me, and I made my decision. 'Please tell the Superintendent that it's very good of him, and we're grateful, but I really am feeling much better, and we would just as soon stay until . . . that is, until the drive and the roads are open.'

Alan squeezed my hand.

'I expect we'll be back downstairs shortly.' I smiled at the constable, and she smiled back and left to pass the word.

'I couldn't, Alan. Not when I'm really fine. It wouldn't be fair to the others. And besides—'

'And besides, you want to unravel the rest of this tangled web.'

'Do you mind too much?'

'I'd rather have you safe. I'd always rather have you safe, but I can't cage you up.'

'Anyway, love, with all the police in the house, I feel as safe as the Queen. No one but a fool would try anything with all those minions of the law around.'

'As an American police officer I once knew was fond of saying, however, "most criminals are not rocket scientists".'

'You're saying he – she – the murderer might try to strike again, even with all the cops around.'

'You have to consider his – for convenience' sake, let's stick to a single gender – his state of mind. If he doesn't know for certain that we now know Harrison was murdered, he must realize we soon will. He thinks he's committed the perfect crime, but doubts and fears will keep nagging at him. What if he left something at the riverbank, something incriminating? What if someone saw him? Worst of all, he knows *why* he committed the crime – and *he doesn't know if we've figured it out*.'

'We haven't. Or at least I haven't, and I've been thinking of nothing else all the time we've been here.'

'But he doesn't know that. He may think we're about to close in. Whoever he is, he's in a state of extreme nervous tension, the worse since he must conceal it. He's like one of those rockets we didn't get to set off Sunday night – just ready to explode. That's what I meant, Dorothy, when I said you might annoy him. You ask questions, you know. Lots of questions. You might just ask them of the wrong person, and set fire to that fuse, and then . . .'

'Maybe I'd better let you ask the questions.'

'That would certainly be more sensible, but I have no confidence at all that you'll remain meekly one step behind me. You have too much in common with the cats, and with the Elephant's Child. Just be very, very careful.

'And now I think your headache must be just about gone, so let's rejoin the rest, shall we?'

TWENTY-NINE

It all looked so peaceful when we got back to the library, so normal. Pat sat reading one of the classics, Ed an art book. Mr Leatherbury, looking rested, had found that book of sermons I had brought back downstairs and was reading it with every appearance of enjoyment. To each his own.

Tom and Jim sat at a chess game, playing at that glacial speed that characterizes real experts. They were, now that I came to think of it, both extremely successful businessmen, which I suppose requires something of the chess-player's mind. Joyce and Lynn, in front of the fire, were studying an old piece of needlepoint, apparently with an eye to repairing the frayed bits.

Just a normal group of people, intelligent, well-to-do, with nice manners and varied interests.

And one of them – one of us – was a murderer.

Who, who? Well, it wasn't Alan, and it wasn't I. And Tom and Lynn are some of my oldest friends. Scratch them.

That left our host and hostess, the Bateses, Ed, Pat and the vicar.

Take the easiest one first. I suppose the saintly old vicar was the least likely suspect, so there ought to be a reason why he was the villain of the piece. But for the life of me I couldn't find one. He really was the vicar, known to Pat and the Moynihans, and had held the living for years.

Suppose, though . . . I glanced at Alan, deep in last week's *Times*. I wished I could have this conversation with him, instead of just with myself, but the presence of the policeman in the corner of the room, unobtrusive though he was, effectively stopped any open speculation about the crimes.

Suppose, then, that Mr Leatherbury had known all along about the skeleton – that his predecessor had told him about it. Never mind, for now, how the previous vicar had found out. Suppose the present vicar had known all about it, including who put it there.

But, the more logical part of my brain insisted, one or the other of them would have gone to the police with the knowledge.

But maybe not, if . . . if the murderer – the original murderer – had something to do with the church. A curate? A chorister? The churchwarden? A major benefactor?

That last was the most likely. Let's see. Mr Upshawe – Laurence's father – kills his nephew so that he will inherit Branston Abbey one day. The vicar finds out. Mr Upshawe tells him that it was more-or-less an accident, really, and he – Upshawe – will leave the parish a large sum of money to replace the church roof if the vicar tells no one.

Oh, good grief. That one was as full of holes as the roof of the cloisters. For one thing, that particular Upshawe had little money. Sure, he was going to inherit the Abbey, and the estate, but it would probably take every cent he could put together just to keep the Abbey's fabric in good repair, never mind the parish church. And he didn't leave anything much in the way of money to his son, remember. Laurence had to pension off the servants because he couldn't afford to keep them on.

If Laurence was telling the truth. Always if Laurence was telling the truth. And Laurence had displayed an ability to lie.

Well, but there could have been little money left because Laurence père gave a lot of it to the church. And that was easy enough to check. Find out if the church, fifty years or so ago, had a new roof put on – or any other major repairs, I reminded myself; the roof was a figment of my imagination.

As was the whole of this scenario. Not only that, but even supposing the idea had some basis in fact, why would that give Mr Leatherbury a reason to kill Dave Harrison? I sighed and started off on another tack. Pat Heseltine.

Pat really was, on the face of it, a possible candidate for the role of Second Murderer. (I had to concede that she was too young to have done in the skeleton and/or the mummy, unless everyone was wrong about when those two unfortunates met their demise.) Pat was intelligent. She was an attorney, with the means and, I thought, the will to find out everything about everybody in Branston. Such people are dangerous, even when they don't have a face and body Helen of Troy might have envied.

She could have known about the skeleton. In fact, with the exception of Laurence, she was by far the most likely person to have known about the skeleton. The only thing was, suppose she did. Suppose she knew when and how and at whose hand the owner of the skeleton had perished. Why then would she need to kill Dave?

As for Ed Walinski – I looked at him and shook my head. Ed was a foreigner who had probably never heard of Branston Abbey until he met Jim and Joyce. How had they met, by the way? I'd never asked, but it was irrelevant. Ed was a photographer, devoted to his art. I could, just, imagine him taking pictures of the scene by the river as it played out, but I couldn't imagine him taking part. No, I should have made him the least likely suspect. Even my devious mind could not come up with a reason for Ed to kill Dave Harrison.

The trouble was, why would anybody kill Dave Harrison, except on the grounds that he was insufferable?

Well, now, there was actually an idea. I nudged Alan, who gave a start and opened his eyes.

'Aha! I thought you were much too interested in week-old news.'

He yawned. 'It's a fair cop. What's on your mind, love?' He gestured with his eyebrows in the direction of the constable.

I nodded to show I understood his warning. 'It's just that I was thinking about Julie. Are any of these stalwarts out looking for her?'

'I should think so. You remember that I have no role in this investigation.'

And it's killing you, I thought but didn't say. I contented myself with a sympathetic smile. 'But you told them she was missing, right?'

'Yes, dear,' he said, in the tone husbands have been using since Eve first asked Adam a silly question.

I kept my voice very low. 'It's just that I wondered – I mean, a spouse is usually—'

The warning look was more pronounced. 'I'm sure the detectives are taking all possibilities into account,' he said rather more loudly than necessary. 'And isn't it just about time for tea?'

It was well past teatime, actually, the police activities having disrupted our normal schedule, and I was hungry, but I couldn't get Julie out of my mind. It was terribly frustrating not to be able to talk about her to Alan, or anybody else, for that matter. But nobody could stop me thinking about her.

Where could she be – if she was still alive? Alan's idea about the tunnel was a good one, but it hadn't worked out. All the outbuildings had been checked, including the shed where she had hidden the first time. The house had been searched.

The house. This great, rambling house with thirty or so bedrooms, closets, attics – how thoroughly had they searched? And wasn't it possible, as Pat had suggested, that Julie could have been playing with us, going from one room to the next to stay hidden? I had pooh-poohed the idea at the time, but I was beginning to like it.

How could I suggest to the police that they look for her in the house? Request a word with one of them in private? I didn't want to do that without consulting Alan. Well, why not? If we were free to leave, surely we were free to have a confidential conversation. Except that it would look odd to the others if we just walked out.

I was glad the police were there, I reminded myself. Very glad indeed. But they were cramping my style something fierce.

And now more of them were arriving! I heard the whap-whap of helicopter blades drawing near, nearer, deafeningly just outside.

'What the—' Alan exclaimed, and went to the window along with the rest of us.

'Oh, no!' said Joyce, and Jim swore.

'It was inevitable,' said Tom. 'Are we allowed to talk to them?' he asked the constable who was minding us at the moment.

For the media, in force, had arrived. This was pure jam for them. The most exciting seams of the storm story had been mined and played out. They needed something to keep the readers and the viewers titillated and buying their advertisers' products, and here was a beauty of a new story. It had everything except sex and royalty, and I had no doubt the more creative members of the Fourth Estate would find a way to bring them in somehow.

The knock sounded at the door.

'I'll go,' said Joyce to the constable. 'This is still my house, regardless of what has happened here. I'll ask them to wait in the library, shall I, until your . . . er . . . your superior can decide what to do with them.'

There ensued a lovely hullabaloo. DI Bradley, the chief of the officers who had descended upon us, herded the media crowd into the library and began issuing stern instructions about all the places that were off limits to them. The men and women of the press were, by turns, intrusive, rude, noisy and insensitive, but they certainly supplied a grand distraction just when I most welcomed it.

'Alan,' I said in his ear, 'I think I know where Julie is.'

He looked at me sharply.

'I think she's in the house somewhere, probably on the third floor. I think she's been there all the time, just skipping from one room to another while we were looking for her.'

'It's possible, I suppose,' he agreed. 'But, as I recall you saying when she went missing, why would she do such a thing?'

'She's not particularly logical, you know. She's frightened of someone or something, and her idea may be to keep everyone guessing so whatever, or whoever, she's afraid of can't catch up with her.'

'Childish,' said Alan.

'Yes, but she is childish in many ways. Oh! That reminds me. Joyce said something, a while back, about her relationship with Julie. The two never got along, and something happened to annoy

Julie even more – only Joyce never said what it was. Do you think the Bill would let you ask her what it was?'

'You, my dear, are beginning to display an alarming gift for English slang. Yes, given my position as a retired officer, I imagine Her Majesty's Constabulary would allow me to interview one of the suspects.'

I was about to object to the word when I saw the twinkle in his eye. 'And can I be there?' I asked, pushing my luck.

He sighed. 'I suppose, since you are now free to do as you please and go where you please, you could sit in a corner. I don't see what Joyce and Julie's childhood have to do with anything, though.'

'I don't know that it does,' I admitted. 'It's just a loose end, and I don't like loose ends.'

So, when Joyce had freed herself temporarily from the minions of Fleet Street and the Beeb, Alan diverted her to the dining room, and I followed. He closed the door, and we all sat around the table.

'Joyce, I feel a trifle awkward, since I'm here as your guest,' Alan began, 'but my wife thinks there may be some use in asking you to finish an anecdote you began earlier.' He sketched out what I had repeated to him, and then asked, 'Would you tell us what it was that further estranged your sister?'

'Oh. I can't imagine that it's useful in any way, but I'll tell you. It's just a little embarrassing, that's all.' She took a deep breath. 'I told you,' she said, looking at me, 'that the two of us never got along. Julie was always jealous of me, of the attention I got from our parents, of my appearance – I was always prettier, though what it matters now, at our ages – well. The worst thing happened when I was nineteen. There was a great-aunt, my mother's aunt, who had quite a lot of money. She never married, and I was her first niece – named after her, as a matter of fact. She was fond of me, and I of her. We did things together, went places. I think I was almost a daughter to her, and when she died, I was really . . . well, it hit me hard. And then I found out she had left me all her money.'

She fidgeted. 'Julie was just sixteen then, a bad age for that kind of thing. She'd always felt left out, because Aunt Joyce never paid much attention to her, and she thought it was grossly unfair that I should inherit a fortune and she got nothing.'

'Oh, dear,' I said from my corner.

'Yes,' said Joyce, sighing. 'She got really mad, and even ran away from home for a little while. I didn't know what to do. I didn't really think it was unfair. I had loved Aunt Joyce, and she me, and my mother – her only other relative – didn't need or want the money. Julie had never paid Aunt Joyce the slightest attention except to whine when an expedition was planned and Julie wanted to go.'

'That might have been somewhat unfair,' I ventured.

'You'd think so, but it wasn't, really. Julie had a knack for spoiling things. If we went to the county fair, Julie would eat far too much, cotton candy and corn dogs and funnel cakes and all, and get sick and have to go home. Or we'd go to an art gallery and Julie would whine about not having fun and her feet hurt and she was sleepy and . . . well, you get the idea. She didn't really want to *do* any of the things Aunt Joyce and I did, she just wanted to tag along. So it wasn't long before Aunt Joyce and I decided it was easier for everyone to go by ourselves.'

'Yes, I see. A difficult child. But you were saying, about your inheritance . . .'

'In the end I talked to my mother about it, and made arrangements to give part of the money to Julie. You might have thought that would make her happy, but no – she wanted half. And you can call me selfish if you want to,' she added with some defiance, 'but I wasn't prepared to give in to her.'

'I don't see any reason why you should have,' I said warmly. 'You'd already done far more than you had to, legally.'

'Julie never cared a whole lot about what was legal,' said Joyce, and then covered her face with her hands. 'And how can I sit here talking about her this way, when she may be lying dead out there somewhere this very minute!'

'That's another thing—' I began, when Alan interrupted.

'I think we've taken up enough of Joyce's time,' he said. 'The media are probably slavering to talk to her again. Thank you, Joyce, for your candour. It can't have been easy for you.'

She simply shook her head, and we left her to whatever trial came next.

'And did that little exercise do any good?'

'I don't know. It cast more light on Joyce's character, anyway. But bells keep ringing at the back of my mind, begging to be answered, and when I try, they go away. Pat says those kinds of stray thoughts are like cats, who need to be ignored to appear again.'

'And how right she is. Look, love, we never had any tea, and I for one am pining away. Shall we?'

THIRTY

But we were destined that day to have a somewhat longer wait before the tea we both craved. When we entered the drawing room, we were met by DI Bradley. 'A word, sir?' He said it politely enough, but his look plainly excluded me from the conversation.

'I'll just excuse myself, then,' I said, glancing in the direction of the downstairs powder room.

I really did need to use the facilities, and when I came back into the hall, I was very glad I had, or the sight that met me might have led to a regrettable accident.

For assembled there was the whole boiling of us – guests, hosts, staff, police and the media. And in the centre of the buzzing swarm was none other than Julie Harrison.

In handcuffs.

The moment I appeared, the ladies and gentlemen of the press swarmed my way. Here was a new quarry/fount of information/victim – as you choose.

'What is your relationship to the accused?'

'Are the murders here the work of a serial killer?'

'Are you a guest here, or a resident?'

'How do you feel about ghosts?'

The last came from a young man who had, I think, detected an American accent in my brief 'No comment' replies to all queries.

For I smilingly refused to answer anything. This was a new experience for me, and not very pleasant. I knew, too, that anything I said might be twisted to suit the purposes of the reporters.

America has its own gutter press, the sort of publications you see in checkout lanes, with headlines about aliens impregnating movie stars (or political figures, depending on who's the hot news at the moment) and the latest sex scandals in Hollywood, and sometimes even rumours-reported-as-fact about British royalty. But the slimiest American 'news' papers pale by comparison with the English. Certainly there are a good many well-respected papers, *The Times*, the *Telegraph*, the *Guardian* among them. But the worst of the rags in my adopted country print not only the salacious stories you can find in America, but pictures, as well, that would be treated as pornography in many places.

Well, all of us had our clothes on, and no one, so far as I could see, had an arm around anyone inappropriate, but I still wasn't going to say anything at all. Silence can be misconstrued, but not as badly as an inadvertent remark.

I finally managed to reach Alan, who was surrounded by his own phalanx of tormentors, and was also keeping a prudent silence. I couldn't ask him what was going on, with all those eager ears listening, so I simply clung to his arm, letting them take what picture they would – who had a better right to cling, after all? – and waited.

It was only a moment until DI Bradley cleared his throat and spoke in a voice that rivalled my best quiet-the-sixth-grade efforts in my schoolteacher days long ago. 'Ladies and gentlemen! Your attention for a moment, if I may.'

His voice had a nice tone of command. He was, I thought, going to rise even further in his career. The crowd quieted and he smiled kindly.

'Now I do realize that you all want to know what has happened. Well, there's quite a story here, and it will take some time to tell. Nor have I the eloquence to do it justice. And speaking of justice, you all know that there are laws about what can and cannot be published under certain conditions.'

Murmurs ensued, and they were not happy murmurs. He couldn't be talking about the *sub judice* law, could he? Because that provision barred publication of details about a case once it had gone to trial, but we were a long way from that, surely. I looked questioningly at Alan, but he simply patted my hand.

'So, given the fact that we are dealing here with a citizen of the United States, who is under the protection of her embassy, I can say little except that we will be taking Mrs David Harrison with us to help us with our enquiries. Thank you.'

'What about Michael Leonev?' One reporter's voice rose above the others. 'I understand he's disappeared, possibly drowned.'

'Yes, that's our understanding. We will, of course, be on the lookout for him. But if he has indeed drowned, it may be some time before his body can be found. Next question?'

'They're arresting Julie?' I asked Alan, under cover of the volley of questions.

'That isn't quite what he said,' Alan answered, infuriatingly. And when I looked daggers at him, he went on, 'Let's get out of here. They're not paying attention to us at the moment; I think we can escape.'

We edged our way to the library, went in, and closed the door, and I exploded. 'Alan, what is going on? Where did they find Julie? What did he mean, help us with our enquiries?'

'Slow down, love. One thing at a time. They didn't find Julie, she found them. She simply walked down the stairs, went up to the nearest uniform, and confessed to the murder of her husband.'

I sat down.

'Alan,' I said when my head stopped whirling, 'I really, really need that cup of tea.'

'There's nothing whatever to prevent us going upstairs to make some. That would certainly be easier than getting the attention of either of the Bateses at this point, don't you agree? Let's go through the garden.'

The library was at the end of the south wing, the Palladian section of the house, and had a terrace outside the doors. I'd never used that way out, but once outside I turned to look at the amazing architecture, completely unlike the front of the house. White pillars, a small dome over the second story (this part of the house had only the two), restrained Greek-influenced decoration everywhere – 'It looks like a miniature version of the Capitol!' I said in awe, and Alan nodded agreement.

We moved down a couple of terraces, the better not to be seen from the house, rounded the west end, and entered by way of the servants hall where we had come in when we first arrived a hundred years or so ago. The elevator took us quietly to the second floor and we got to our room unobserved.

'Now tell me everything,' I demanded, and Alan did his best to comply, meanwhile turning on the kettle and setting out the teapot and appurtenances and the large box of biscuits he had raided from the kitchen – was it only last night?

'There isn't a lot more to tell, unfortunately. Almost as soon as Julie appeared and made her amazing statement, the vultures were on her, and nobody else could get a word in edgeways. The moment he could, Bradley exercised his authority, spoke a word or two in her ear, handcuffed her – and then you came on the scene and know as much as I do.'

That was profoundly unsatisfactory. 'Well, but . . . where had she been hiding all that time?'

'No idea.' He put two of those big, squishy tea bags in the pot and poured in the boiling water.

'Did she say how or why she had killed Dave?'

'Not a word.' He picked up the pot and swirled the water around.

'I admit I thought she might have done it. I tried to tell you—'

'I understood, but I had to stop you because we weren't supposed to talk about the deaths with anyone else around.'

'Well, but . . . oh, hand me a biscuit, will you? Maybe it's sugar my brain cells need. They don't seem to be functioning at all.'

Alan finished making tea in silence, poured it out, and handed me a cup prepared almost to my satisfaction, save for the unavailable milk. I drank it eagerly, drained the cup, poured myself another, and said irrelevantly, 'We should have asked them to bring us some groceries.'

'Which "them"? The police or the press?'

'Either. Both. I don't suppose they run errands for people, though.'

'Probably not. I wouldn't be surprised if Bates finds someone to send a message to some good friend in the village. If one of those mosquitoes downstairs belongs to a local rag, he'll want to keep in with the gentry, even if they are Americans. You may have your milk sooner than you think, my dear.'

'How long do you think it might be before the roads are clear and we can all leave?'

'Another day or two, I should imagine. The police can't use those helicopters forever; there are never enough to go 'round. They'll want the drive cleared and some sort of bridge rigged, and Bradley will get what he wants, sooner rather than later. He's a mover, that lad.' I nodded, and Alan finished his last cup of tea. 'I sincerely hope that by the time the road is clear, our problems will be, as well, and we can all go home.'

'But,' I said, my head swimming again, 'but I thought they *were* cleared. Julie has confessed—'

'My dear woman!' Alan turned on me a look of sheer astonishment. 'You don't mean to say you believe her?'

I opened my mouth, closed it, and glanced at the little clock on the mantel. An anachronism in the room, being of French and almost certainly eighteenth-century provenance, it was nevertheless beautiful. It showed the time to be five thirty, or nearly. 'Alan,' I said calmly, 'I think I am in need of something a little more sustaining than tea. Did you happen to bring any bourbon up with you last night?'

I sipped at it, slowly. I had no intention of repeating my folly of Sunday night. I'd barely recovered, nearly two days later. But I was feeling as though I'd been spun around rapidly, then blanket-tossed and walked through a darkened maze and left abandoned there. 'A riddle wrapped in a mystery inside an enigma,' I remarked. 'Didn't somebody say that about something?'

'Winston Churchill, referring, I believe, to Russia. Come now, Dorothy! This isn't that bad.'

'All right, tell me again, slowly. Julie Harrison has confessed to the murder of her husband. The police have taken her off, in handcuffs. But you – and presumably they – don't believe her. Explain, please.'

'I don't speak for the official police, my love, but I would be very surprised if DI Bradley believes a word of what she said. There are no flies at all on that young man.'

'I had that impression, too. He'll go far. But if he doesn't believe her, why did he arrest her?'

'Oh, you should be able to work that out, at least until you've had another few wee drams of that stuff. Think I'll have some myself.'

'Well, let's see.' I scrounged around and found some nuts to go with my bourbon. Maybe hunger was part of what was wrong with me. 'Julie hides all night, the night after Dave is killed. You find her and bring her back to the house, where she's scared to death of everybody except Mr Leatherbury. Eventually she opens up some to Pat and me. Then when we go to ask her more, she has disappeared. We look everywhere, can't find her. Then lo and behold, she comes prancing right out from wherever she's been and turns herself into the police.'

'You're doing fine so far,' said my maddening husband. 'Go on.'

'She turns herself in,' I said more slowly, 'and the police take her away . . . oh!'

'Exactly. They take her away.'

'Away from whatever has scared her so. Away from . . . from the person who really killed Dave?'

'I think the conclusion is warranted, don't you? And that's why DI Bradley let her, apparently, pull the wool over his eyes. She confesses, he takes her away, she's safe, the murderer thinks he's safe. Very neat.'

'I wouldn't have thought she was that smart,' I reflected.

'She may not be well-educated, but I think where self-preservation is concerned, our Julie is very smart indeed.'

'Except when it came to choosing a spouse. Her instincts let her down badly there,' I argued. 'And that's why I think she may be pulling a double bluff. She could have decided that Dave was such a bad bargain, she'd be better off without him. And then when his death wasn't accepted as accident, she hid out until she could work out what to do. Alan, that could explain why she was so scared of you, in particular. You represented the Law!'

'Yes, we talked about that once before, as I recall. It doesn't explain why she would be so eager to walk into the arms of the real authorities the minute they arrived on the scene.'

'Well . . . she'd had time to work out what to do. She might know that, as an American, she stood very little chance of getting into real trouble. I'll bet she's on the phone to the Embassy right this minute, especially after that very clear directive the good inspector was so careful to give her.'

'It could be you're right. It's all speculation at this point, in any case. It's been a trying day, love, and it's not over yet. What would you say to a nap till we can decently go down for dinner?'

THIRTY-ONE

As it worked out, Alan was in a moustache-twirling mood and we slept only a little, but were greatly refreshed, and much more cheerful, when we went down to dinner. Alan had told me what to expect, but it was still pleasant to find that our police presence had disappeared. 'There'll still be some officers in the house, Dorothy, but they don't intend to make themselves conspicuous. The idea is to let the real murderer think he's got away with it. He may get careless.'

The media had also departed, thanks be to God. I knew we

would find ourselves all over the evening news, if we turned on a television. No one did.

Dinner was therefore an enjoyable meal, even though we still had no fresh food. I hoped, for Rose's sake, that supplies would be forthcoming soon. An artist grows despondent when deprived of her best colours. Mr Bates was at any rate in good spirits again, serving with his usual deftness and style. Everyone was full of excited talk about going home, speculation about how soon that might be, plans for when they arrived.

Even knowing what I knew, my thoughts also turned to Sherebury. Alan had been trying at intervals to get through to our neighbour and cat-sitter, and finally achieved a static-filled connection. He handed me the phone.

'Jane? I can barely hear you. This is Dorothy. What? How are the cats?'

'Cats are fine. House is . . . but they think . . . sounds like . . . disaster . . .'

And silence. 'Hello? Hello? Are you still there?' Nothing.

'Well,' I said, handing the phone back to Alan, 'that was some use, I guess, but not much. The cats are OK, but I got the impression something disastrous had happened to the house. I wish we could get back.'

'Jane will cope,' said Alan calmly.

'She will,' I agreed. 'Jane's specialty is coping. I still want to see the worst and figure out what we're going to do.'

'Meanwhile, you can exercise your talent for – I won't say snooping—'

'You'd better not!' And I went off to snoop.

Pat was back in the library, back to Dorothy Sayers. 'I abandoned crime while we were immersed in it,' she said. 'Too topical. Now that we've light and heat and the other essentials of civilization, I can enjoy murder and mayhem again.'

'There's no murder in *Gaudy Night*,' I pointed out.

'Oh, don't you think so?' She smiled enigmatically.

'Anyway, I came to ask you something, but I'm interrupting your reading.'

'Never mind. I know the book by heart. What can I tell you?'

'Well.' I settled down in a squashy leather chair. I'd need help getting free of its embraces later, but meanwhile it was supremely comfortable. 'It's about the house – the estate, I suppose I mean. Someone, I think it was the vicar, said Laurence went to New Zealand in 1982. The Moynihans didn't buy the place until a couple of years ago. What was happening to Branston Abbey in the meantime? Surely it wasn't just sitting empty? And if Laurence was paying wages and taxes and maintenance all that time . . .'

'I wondered,' said Pat, 'when that was going to occur to you.'

I refrained from throwing a cushion at her, though I thought about it.

'My firm, in fact, handled the sale of the estate. Both times.'

'Both?' I tried to lean forward, but the chair defeated me. 'The house was sold twice?'

Pat touched the bell push. 'This story is going to require some lubrication. Yes, the house – the estate – was sold twice. Laurence never did care much for living here. Oh, thank you, Mr Bates, I'd like some brandy, please. Dorothy?'

I shook my head. I'd learned my lesson the other night. 'Just some orange juice, please. Go on, Pat.'

'Laurence,' she continued, 'had qualified as a doctor by that time, but the practice here was occupied by the same man who'd delivered most of the babies for miles around. He didn't need an assistant. Laurence was champing at the bit. As there were no opportunities for him around here, he began to look around for other practices, and someone told him they were in great need of doctors in the Antipodes. So he went out there to see for himself, and never came back. He found a city, Christchurch, that suited him beautifully, with a good hospital – he's a surgeon, you know – and took up his new life then and there.'

'He never married, then?'

'No. There was a girl here he would have quite liked to marry, while he was still in medical school, but she was a flighty little thing then, not willing to wait for years until he started earning decent money, not willing to leave Branston, sure she'd have plenty of better chances. She turned him down.'

Pat sipped thoughtfully at her brandy, and I started putting two and two together. Pat was about ten years younger than Laurence, and very beautiful, still, in middle age. When she was young . . . ah, well, she didn't seem inclined to tell me any more, and it was none of my business.

'When Laurence was settled in Christchurch he wrote to my firm, asking us to sell the estate as soon as possible. I hadn't passed the Bar yet, so I wasn't formally associated with the firm, but I knew what was happening. Laurence wanted to sell. He was less concerned with the money than with ridding himself of the responsibility. Almost all the servants had been pensioned off by then, or found better jobs, and there were no tenants on the farms or in the cottages any more, so there were few complications.

'But.' She took another sip. 'There were also few buyers for a large estate with a very old house that would require thousands of pounds spent, regularly, for maintenance. The months went by, the years. The only people living on the estate then were John Bates's father, who was the caretaker, and John. He was a small boy then, but he helped his father as much as he could. We hired cleaners and gardeners and so on, to keep the place from deteriorating, but it was all extremely frustrating.'

'So John has actually lived here all his life?'

Pat nodded.

'But aside from his family, the house was essentially empty until the Moynihans . . . but no, you said the house was sold twice.'

'Yes. A few years after Laurence left, we were beginning to consider the National Trust. They don't pay much, but they do assure that the property will remain intact and well-preserved, and the Home Secretary's office was getting a bit impatient. You know they oversee the preservation of listed buildings?'

'I do know, as it happens. My house is listed, and I had a go-round with them some years ago when it needed a new roof.'

'Then you'll understand why they were rather breathing down our necks. At that point, however, a holding company stepped up with an offer. Not a fantastic offer, but a way of getting it off our hands, and enough money to pay for some needed repairs and leave a bit for poor Laurence, who by that time had, I think, despaired of ever realizing anything from it.'

'A holding company? What did they plan to do with it?'

'They had in mind an institution of some kind, a school or retirement home or something. But apparently the plans fell through, because nothing was ever done.

'A few years later – around 2000, that would have been – the elder Mr Bates died and John took over as caretaker. He and Rose had just married, poor things, and the full responsibility of looking after the estate fell upon their shoulders.'

I shuddered. 'Not a burden I'd care to have thrust upon me.'

'Nor I. But they have done a yeoman job, prevailed where many another couple would have foundered. I doubt that even these past few days have offered the greatest challenges those two have had to face. Only a genuine love of the house could have kept them here. Now, where was I? Oh, yes, in due time the holding company decided to sell. The matter came into our hands again, and this time the Moynihans bought it.'

'I imagine everyone concerned was glad to get an offer this time.'

'Yes.'

Pat was looking at me with a rather peculiar expression. I had the feeling she was waiting for something from me.

'I suppose theirs was the only offer?'

She relaxed. Apparently that was the right question. 'No, in fact it wasn't. There was one other, but it was far below the asking price, and Jim and Joyce offered full price, with no haggling, so there was no contest, really. A pity, in a way. Most of the old estates have already passed out of the hands of the original owners, which couldn't be helped when the families died out, but I do hate to see them go to foreigners. Not that Jim and Joyce aren't perfectly nice people, but . . .' She shrugged.

'That's more the kind of sentiment I'd expect from the vicar, enamoured as he is of old houses.'

'You don't think I'm a sentimentalist? Well, perhaps the role does fit me rather oddly. Are you sure you won't have a little brandy?'

It was a clear dismissal. I said something about bed and left Pat to her Dorothy Sayers, but I wasn't sleepy.

The conversation had been interesting chiefly for what Pat hadn't said. Was she, in fact, the 'flighty young thing' who refused Laurence Upshawe's hand all those years ago? I could always ask the vicar, but he was a good friend of Pat's and might not tell me, even if he knew – the thing had happened before he came to the parish.

And even more interesting, who had underbid the Moynihans for Branston Abbey? It was easy to deduce from what Pat had said that he, she, or they were English. Could it possibly have been the vicar? Or Pat?

Hardly the vicar. The clergy in the Church of England don't usually have much more money than clergy anywhere else. There are exceptions, but very, very few could come up with the kind of money this pile must have cost – not to mention what it would continue to cost in upkeep.

Pat, then? Pat, who appeared to be cool and professional and yet hated to see the old estates fall into the hands of foreigners. Lawyers made good money, some of them, but a village solicitor?

And what on earth would a single woman do with a place this size, anyway? True, Jim and Joyce were only two people, but it was likely they planned to use the house to entertain largely, in the interests of Jim's business, whatever that was – I kept forgetting to ask Tom.

And if either Pat or Paul Leatherbury had tried and failed to buy the house, in what possible way could that fact connect with the death of Dave Harrison, let alone with a skeleton and a mummy?

I gave it up, found Alan, and had that brandy after all.

THIRTY-TWO

I must have dreamed that night, though I have no memory of what my subconscious cooked up. I only know that in the morning I knew the answer. All the answers. Who killed Dave and why, who buried the skeleton, who hid the mummy away and why – and a lot more. It remained only to prove all of it, and that might well be a big problem.

I tackled Alan over our morning tea. 'How old would you say John Bates was?' I asked, without preamble.

'Early thirties, at a guess. Why?'

'And Rose is maybe a little younger?'

'I suppose so. What does it matter?'

'Just confirming my own ideas, that's all. Are you about ready for breakfast?'

It was a beautiful day, and we had a beautiful breakfast. Alan had been a true prophet. Somehow or other John Bates had obtained fresh supplies. A bowl of fruit adorned the breakfast table, oranges and bananas and kiwis and even a couple of pineapples, quartered and then sectioned. There were fresh eggs, plainly new-laid, the yolks mounding handsomely above the whites in Rose's perfect fry-up. Milk for my tea and for the vicar's cereal.

'How is this possible?' I asked Rose in awe.

She smiled. 'John has friends. He sent a message back with the *West Kent Chronicle*, and a man brought a boat around to the water meadows this morning. I told him I'd cook him a very special lunch by way of thanks. The river's gone down a lot in

the past day or two. By tomorrow that part of the meadow will
be all mud, and by the next, anyone who wants could walk out.'

I smiled and shook my head in silent admiration, but I felt a
little panicky. I didn't have a lot of time. And I had to be very,
very careful.

As soon as breakfast was over, I sought out the vicar. I found
him, as I thought I might, sitting on the bench in the ruins of
the garden, reading the morning office.

'Please don't let me interrupt you, Mr Leatherbury,' I said.
'In fact, may I join you? I know some of the responses, at least.'

He beamed, and patted the bench beside him. 'We can share
the book. I should be delighted.'

So we read the Psalms together, and the canticles, and prayed
for peace, and grace, and I felt quite a lot better when we had
finished.

'You are an Anglican, my dear.' It was not a question.

'By adoption, as it were. I was an Episcopalian back in the
States, but we're all in the Anglican Communion. At home I
attend Sherebury Cathedral; it's right in my backyard.'

So we had a pleasant little chat about the Cathedral, and its
Dean, whom Mr Leatherbury knew, and various church practices.
Then he gave me a clear-eyed look. 'But you did not come out
here for the office. Are you cold? Shall we go inside for our talk?'

'You're right. I came to talk to you. And unless you're cold,
I'd rather talk here, where it's private.'

He inclined his head courteously and waited for me to continue.

For a moment I found that hard to do. I began tentatively. 'I
hope you'll believe that I don't ask these questions out of
curiosity. I am . . . I think I am on the verge of knowing what
has happened here, not just these past few days but over the past
many years, but I need confirmation.'

Again he nodded.

'Very well, then. Pat told me about a woman Laurence wanted
to marry, years ago. She turned him down. Was it Pat, herself?'

Somewhere a bird sang a wintry little snatch of song. Another
answered. I waited.

'Yes, it was,' said the vicar with some reluctance. 'It all
happened before I came to St Michael's, but Pat told me about
it a long time ago. We're good friends.'

I tucked away that bit of information. 'Yes, I had realized
that. She is a remarkable woman, I think. I won't tell anyone, I
promise.'

'Thank you.'

'Pat also told me that the Moynihans were not the only ones interested in buying the house at the time they did buy it. She did not tell me who the other party was, but I think I know.'

Now his face was shut.

'I thought for a bit it might have been you, with your love of old houses, but I didn't think – forgive me – I didn't think you could afford it.'

'Nor would I have bought it if I had been able to raise the money. I am a priest of the church. I dearly love beautiful old houses, but it would be most unseemly for me to live in one. Remember what Christ told the rich young ruler.'

I nodded assent. 'Then I thought of Pat, but I doubted even she, who must have a good income, had that kind of money. And a single woman – what would she do with a house this size?'

Now his eyes were wary.

'I went to bed thinking about it, and this morning I knew. Or at least I think so. It was John Bates, wasn't it?'

He said, heavily, 'I am not privy to the confidential dealings of Pat's law firm.'

'No. But you know, all the same, don't you?'

He sighed and nodded. 'It was very difficult for Pat. She knew and respected John and Rose, and knew how much love and labour they had put into this estate. She felt they, of all people, deserved to live here as owners, not mere servants. But they simply hadn't the money, nothing like enough. I believe John had been saving every penny he could, ever since he was a boy, actually, in the hope that one day it could be his. But alas, one must be a millionaire many times over to own an estate like this and keep it in proper repair. It was always a pipe dream.'

I could not speak for a while. Finally, I said, 'I hope you will pray for all of us, sir. We need it.'

'I do, and I shall.'

I had expected to feel some satisfaction. I now had all the pieces I needed to complete one part of the puzzle, but all I could feel was sadness. And as for the other part – I went to find Alan.

He was in the library, surrounded by a nest of newsprint. 'Look, love! Mr Bates managed to get some papers in this morning, along with the groceries. He is truly a man of parts.'

'Yes. Alan, what did you do with that locket? The one you found on the mummy? Annie's locket?'

If he was surprised by my lack of enthusiasm about the news-papers, he didn't remark on it. 'I gave it to the police. To DC Price, since she was the one who had to sit with the poor thing. Their experts need to take a look at it, see what they can learn from it.'

'Is she still here? DC Price, I mean?'

'No, I believe she went back with the helicopter late last night. Why?'

'Would she still have the locket, or would she have handed it over to one of her superiors, do you think?'

Alan put down his paper and gave me his full attention. 'Dorothy, what is this all about?'

'I want to know more about Annie, and that locket might tell me.' I hated being devious with Alan, but I wanted to do this my own way, and if I told him everything I knew – all right, everything I suspected – he would certainly interfere.

'Are you plotting something?'

'I suppose you could say that,' I answered reluctantly. 'Is it all right with you if I ask DI What's-his-name about the locket?'

'You're not going to get into some kind of trouble, are you?'

'What kind of trouble could I get into with police swarming all over the place?'

It wasn't an answer, and Alan knew it. He also knew that I needed my independence and that I had, so far, managed to wiggle out of whatever trouble I got myself into. I waited.

'You'll find DI Bradley in one of the third-floor bedrooms. I don't know which one. And Dorothy.'

'Yes, love?'

'Don't go and do anything stupid.'

I was sure he would consider what I was planning to be stupid, but I didn't.

Well – not very stupid, anyway.

I took the lift to the third floor. My knees were beginning to shake a little, and I didn't want them to give out on me.

There were twelve bedrooms on this floor. Heavens, I thought, what must it have been like, back in the days when all of them might be occupied at once! And no running water in those days. Hip baths, with the water having to be heated on the stove and brought up the stairs – no lift – by hapless chambermaids. And then there were the chamber pots to be emptied every morning—

I refused to follow that train of thought any further.

Which room would I choose, if I were a policeman in hiding?

Not the mummy room, because that was the obvious one. I'd choose the room next door, or the one across the hall. Close, in case someone wanted to pull something funny.

The mummy room overlooked the back of the house. That's where the helicopter would land when it came back. That's where he would be, next door, with almost the same view. And he would have stationed one of his minions across the hall, to keep an eye on the front of the house and any comings and goings there.

There would undoubtedly be someone at the ends of each wing, as well. It wasn't going to be at all easy to do what I meant to do.

If I was right.

I found DI Bradley where I expected to. He was not, at first, best pleased to see me. 'I hope, Mrs Martin, that you haven't told anyone else that I am still here. Our presence is meant to be inconspicuous.'

'And it is,' I assured him. 'Alan did tell me you hadn't left, but I simply worked out where I would be if I were you, and there you were.'

'Ah. On the principle of the missing horse.'

'Exactly.'

'Will I seem rude if I ask you, now that you have found me, to go away again? If our voices are heard—'

'Certainly.' I lowered mine another notch. 'I came for a purpose, though. There was a locket – Alan found it on the mummy's body and gave it to DC Price. Did she turn it over to you?'

'She did.'

'If you still have it, Mr Bradley, I'd very much like to see it.'

I held my breath. There was no reason in the world why he should show it to me.

The thing hung in the balance for a long moment. Then he reached into his pocket and pulled out a small plastic bag. 'The chief asked me to give every consideration to Mr Nesbitt – and to you. He apparently has a good deal of respect for your abilities, and your discretion.' He sounded extremely dubious, but handed me the bag. 'You may not take it out, you understand.'

'May I open it? Still in the bag?'

'If you can.' He sounded even more dubious. 'It's very dirty; the catch may be corroded.'

With very great care, I manipulated the locket, through the

thin plastic of its container. Getting a fingernail in the crack between the two halves, I pressed the catch.

It opened, showing itself quite clean on the inside. The tiny gold ovals on either side framed two pictures. One showed a young girl with flowing blond hair pulled back with a blue ribbon. She was beautiful, with a classic profile, lovely bones, a gracefully shaped head held high, proudly. She wore small gold hoop earrings and a locket around her neck. The other was of a man a good deal older than she, handsome in a weather-beaten sort of way. He had a stern, unsmiling face.

'Thank you,' I said, and handed the bag back. I didn't close the locket. Let that be remembered in my favour when St Peter reckons up the score.

THIRTY-THREE

Now I knew what I had to do. I didn't like it at all, and I had no idea how to go about it, except that I must do it alone.

I would have liked a little quiet time in the cloister, but the men were out there working. I peeked out from Julie's old room that had such a splendid view. I could hear the braying of saws, could see, through the holes in the roof, Ed and Mr Bates manhandling a branch of oak here, Jim hauling away a pile of debris there, Tom and Alan setting up a sawhorse, even Laurence and the vicar gathering up broken glass with gloved hands.

No possibilities there.

I went to my room, put my coat on, and went outside by the kitchen hallway. Savoury smells were coming from the kitchen, and I heard Rose humming as she worked. I felt slightly sick.

The sun was bright, but not warm. Winter was coming. The grass, even after all the rain, was becoming dry and brittle. Leaves on the few trees still standing were fading from their autumn grandeur to winter brown or gray, or falling from their living branches to lie in melancholy silence on the dying earth.

I walked south to the water meadows. Here the mud lay thick, a fetid brown slime covering all the vegetation. A dead fish, stranded by the receding waters, stared at me with its dull eye. A boat was pulled far up on the shore, its sides mud-splattered, heavy footprints all around testifying to the unloading of provisions.

Walking was treacherous. I had foolishly not worn wellies, nor had I brought my cane. I turned back. There was no respite here, either.

My head was throbbing. The pain hadn't yet begun, but the pounding was growing stronger.

So unfocused was my mind that the helicopter was in sight before I recognized the sound for what it was, and then it was too late to hide. Whether the arrivals were more police, or the media again, I didn't want to talk to them. I didn't want to talk to anybody except Alan. Alan the forbidden confidant, Alan the one person I must not even be near lest I say too much.

But the person who stepped out of the helicopter, who was helped out of the helicopter by a man with a microphone, hobbling on crutches and smiling broadly, was Michael Leonev, aka Mike Leonard.

I rubbed my eyes and looked again. It was still Mike.

He struck a pose, using one crutch like a royal staff. 'Hail the conquering hero comes!' he shouted. 'Or rather, not so terribly heroic, and not the conqueror of anything in particular – but definitely, my dear, I have arrived!'

He snapped me out of my daze. I knew everyone in the house would be out here in seconds. I ran to him, faster than I knew I could move, and pulled his head down so I could make myself heard over the rotors and the clamour of the reporters.

'Mike, listen! I'm terribly glad to see you, but all that has to wait. Can you keep everyone occupied for fifteen minutes, at least? Longer if possible, but fifteen minimum? And *in the house!* As far away from the kitchen, and from the back windows, as you can manage.'

'Dear lady! Mine not to question why, mine but to . . . yes, my dears! This thy son was dead and is alive! Kill the fatted calf! But do let's save felicitations until we're inside and I can sit down, or better yet lie down. I confess to a trifling fatigue.'

The women, being nearest, had arrived first and clustered around Mike, chattering and laughing and questioning – and being questioned by the eager media. I slipped away unnoticed and lay in wait for my quarry.

As I had half-expected, he was the last out of the cloister, walking slowly, as if reluctant to leave the work even to welcome back one we had believed dead. I cut him off from the rest.

'Mr Bates, there's something urgent in the kitchen. Can you spare a moment?'

He smiled at me, that movie-star smile, that heartbreaking smile so like the smile in the locket, and gestured for me to precede him.

When we were safely inside, I saw the last of the house party vanish up the stairs in Mike's wake. Two of the men were carrying him, to the accompaniment of great hilarity. Only then did I began to speak, very quietly, in case any policemen were within earshot.

'John, I know all about it. I know the whole story, what you did and why, but I'm not going to tell anyone just yet. You must leave, you and Rose, you must leave *now*! Take your friend's boat and go.'

'Madam, what are you talking about?' He clung to the Jeeves persona. I admired his nerve, but I could have shaken him.

'Don't waste time!' I hissed. 'There are still police in the house. They'll figure it out soon, and then it will be too late for you. You have two options: stay and be arrested for the murder of Dave Harrison, or leave this place and save yourselves.'

He had a third option, but I hoped he wouldn't think of it. We were alone in that part of the house, and he still carried the hammer he had been using in the cloister. If he kept his nerve—

But he didn't. He saw the certainty in my face and broke.

'I— it wasn't murder! I swear it. I never meant— Rose, tell her!'

We had arrived in the kitchen, where Rose was stirring a heavenly-smelling pot. She looked from one of us to the other, turned pale, and dropped the spoon. It clattered to the floor.

She started to speak, but I held up a hand. 'Rose, listen. I know everything. John's family story, his love for this house, everything. And because I have a good deal of sympathy for both of you, I'm giving you this chance to get away. If you don't take it, it means a long prison term for John, and maybe for you, too, if you're convicted as an accessory. *Please* listen!' I was near tears of desperation. 'You only have a few minutes before everyone will come back downstairs, and they may come to the kitchen. You don't have time to decide, or explain, or pack up. Just *go!*'

John put his arm around Rose. She leaned close to him as he cleared his throat. 'It's very good of you, madam, but life away from this house would have little meaning for me. I will not leave.'

Jeeves was back in perfect command of himself. 'But I cannot allow you to believe that I am a murderer. I must explain what happened. There is no great hurry. If you would come with me?'

I followed him to the part of the kitchen wing I had never seen, the Bateses' private quarters. The cozy sitting room had no fire in the fireplace – no dry wood, I remembered – but it was beautifully warm. On the mantel above the cold hearth were pictures, among them a large copy of the tiny photo I had seen in the locket.

'She was my grandmother,' said John, following my gaze. 'You probably knew that. But do please sit down, Mrs Martin.'

'I thought she must be. Did she die in childbirth?'

'She died,' said John with precision, '*of* childbirth, but not in the process. She killed herself when she realized the father of the child was not going to marry her, as he had promised.'

'The father being Harry Upshawe.'

John nodded.

'But John, who raised the child, then? The child who became your mother?'

'The child was a boy, who became my father. He was raised by the man who gave him his name, the man who should have been my grandfather, Samuel Bates.'

And the last little piece clicked neatly into place. 'They were engaged, then?'

'They were before that devil from hell came along. Annie Watkins was parlourmaid here then. There was still lots of money, and they had a large staff. Not what it had been before the wars, but big enough. It provided a lot of employment hereabouts, did Branston Abbey. Annie lived here, and that was the death of her. She fell in love with "the young master".'

His tone of voice splashed the phrase with vitriol.

'She was sure he would marry her. He was full of charm, so they say, and full of promises. But he wanted to make sure, he said, that the baby was a boy. He wanted an heir, and though the village was littered with his bastards, they all happened to be girls.

'So Annie turned down Samuel Bates and waited for Prince Charming to walk her down the aisle.'

'And instead he told her he was going to America,' I said sadly.

'He didn't even have the courtesy to tell her. She found out from one of the other servants. And then, as my grandfather –

as Samuel Bates told the story, she dressed herself in her best black, kissed her baby, and took a bottle of sleeping pills.'

'And Samuel Bates went to have it out with Harry Upshawe. Samuel worked on the estate, too, I presume?'

'Head gardener. He meant to beat Harry within an inch of his life, but . . .'

'But he went that extra inch too far, and so Harry had to be buried under the oak tree. It would be easy for a gardener to disguise the digging. And your grandmother, a suicide, couldn't be buried in consecrated ground, so Samuel walled her up in that bedroom – for spite, I suppose. But wasn't there talk, in the village and on the estate? Questions about what had become of her body?'

'There was. Samuel was a large, powerful man, and he had a temper when he'd taken a pint too much. Nobody much crossed him. And Samuel never told anyone what he had done, not even my father or me. He simply said he'd taken good care of Annie, and he hoped she'd haunt the Upshawes to the end of their days. That was why—'

I heard voices and laughter. The hungry crowds were assembling for lunch. We had very little time.

'And . . . Dave Harrison?'

'Mr Harrison,' said John, again in that cold, precise tone, 'was an arrogant fool. He thought he could push ahead his scheme about some sort of holiday camp. It would never have happened – this is a Grade One listed building – but he was about to kill Laurence Upshawe to keep him from talking about Harry. I have no great love for Upshawes, but he was of the estate. My claim as heir is better than his. I am the son of Harry Upshawe's only son. But the present Mr Upshawe did inherit, according to the law. I stopped Mr Upshawe being killed, but Harrison had already struck him with that stone. We struggled. Harrison slipped and fell in the river. He couldn't swim. I reached out a branch to him, but it was too short.'

'And you led the searchers to Laurence, so he could be found and cared for.'

'I should have taken them there sooner, but I was afraid everyone would think what you did think. I bear the guilt for that, if Mr Upshawe suffers any permanent damage. But Rose bears no blame. She knew nothing about it until yesterday. I thought it as well to tell her, with police in the house. She will carry on here until I can return.' He kissed her, then straightened his back. 'May I ask you to excuse me, madam? I must go to find a police officer.'

THIRTY-FOUR

'There was talk in the village, of course, even years later when I was old enough to understand.' Pat held the floor as we sat in the drawing room over postprandial drinks. It was our last such gathering. With a mummy, a skeleton, a recent body, and a limping dancer to transport, not to mention various pieces of evidence and, of lesser importance, a good many house guests, the police had commandeered workers from every available source to clear the drive and put a temporary bridge in place. Tomorrow we could all go home.

The media had come again, and gone again. The police had gone, taking John Bates with them. They promised to release Julie in the morning and bring her back here. I didn't envy Jim and Joyce having to deal with her.

'No one knew for certain what had become of Annie Watkins,' Pat went on. 'Some said old Samuel had disposed of her body in the convenient river. Some doubted she was dead at all, said she'd fled to cousins in Canada.'

'Not to her parents?' asked Lynn.

'She was an orphan. That's one reason she lived at the Abbey.'

'And Samuel never told anyone?' Alan asked.

'Old Samuel could be an offensive fellow in his cups. John Bates holds him in high esteem, as well he might, but the villagers didn't like him much. There were even those who said he'd walled Annie up in the Abbey alive.'

'Not so very far from the truth,' I said with a shudder.

Pat nodded. 'At any rate, I gather there began to be an odd feeling about the Abbey in the sixties, talk of ghosts and so on.'

'Was that why it was so hard to sell? I'm a bit surprised Laurence stuck it out as long as he did.'

'Perhaps there were other attractions in the neighbourhood,' I said, for her ears only.

She took a long pull at her drink and said nothing.

'What I don't see, Dorothy, is how you figured it all out.' That was Lynn again.

'It was the mummy, really, the mummy and Mr Bates's reaction to it. He's not a fainting man. Annie wasn't a pleasant sight, but neither was the skeleton, and Mr Bates dealt with it with his usual aplomb. So when he fainted at the sight of Annie, I thought it must be because he knew who she was, and had some association with her. He was far too young to have put her there, and anyway he would scarcely have showed her to us if he knew she was there. So I went about working out what the relationship might be, and . . . Bob's your uncle.'

'What will happen to him, Alan?' asked Joyce.

'It depends on whether the jury believes his story. The injury to Dave's back doesn't jibe with what Bates told Dorothy, but that could have been caused accidentally. It's a pity there were no witnesses to the thing. If I were guessing, I'd say there will be a conviction for manslaughter, voluntary or involuntary, depending on the jury's reaction. If he gets a lenient judge, he may be let off with a relatively short sentence.'

'I sure hope so!' Jim set down his glass with a thump. 'Just thinking about running this place without him gives me a backache.'

'I hope . . . that is, are you going to have unpleasant associations with the house, now?' I couldn't help feeling that if I'd left well enough alone, some of that unpleasantness might never have come to light.

'I thought about trying to sell,' Jim said frankly, 'but Joyce talked me out of it.'

'It was Rose, really,' said Joyce. 'She came to me in tears, begging us to stay on. She plans to organize a team of John's friends to do his work while he is . . . away . . . and said we would be put to no trouble.'

'She could get a far better job elsewhere,' said Tom. 'Even tonight, upset as she was, she prepared food fit for the angels.'

'I told her that,' said Joyce, fighting tears, 'and she said, "John would die in prison if he didn't know he had this house to come back to."'

It was time to change the subject. I looked across the room at our dancer, who was sitting in a chair by the fire, his foot propped up on a cushion. 'Mike, we managed to spoil your homecoming, didn't we? Or rather I did. The others have heard your story, I suppose, but I haven't.'

'Oh, I don't mind telling it again. The stripped-down story, this time. I did *rather* embroider it earlier, I'm afraid.'

'All right, you don't need to spare my feelings. I did ask you to spin it out as long as possible, and you performed nobly. It's not your fault if it did turn out not to be necessary. Go ahead and give us the penny-plain version.'

'Well, I jumped across the river, as you knew I was going to. And all would have been well if the opposite bank hadn't been so littered with leaves. I slipped on landing, and near as nothing ended up in the river. However, I managed to hang on to various bits of vegetation – what sort, I have *no* idea, not being a countryman. When I got to my feet I realized I'd damaged myself, twisted an ankle or something of the sort.'

'Mike! Were you badly hurt? Will you be able to dance again?'

'All in good time, dear lady. I was in some pain, but a dancer learns to work through that, so I started walking. I had no choice, really. I could sit there on the ground and howl till the cows came home, and no one would come to pick baby up and carry him home to mummy. Oops, sorry, poor choice of words.'

Someone snickered.

'Fortunately the road was more-or-less clear of traffic. Because I had just reached it when I stepped on something that gave way under me, and that's all I remember until I woke up in hospital in – is it Shepherdsford? That just-bigger-than-a-village place not far from here?'

The vicar nodded. He looked very tired, I thought.

'And there was a *beautiful* doctor's face looking into mine. Unfortunately he was only checking my eyes for the proper response, to make sure I wasn't dead or something. I'd been unconscious for quite some time, I gathered. Some kind person had found me by the side of the road and brought me in, and I gather all the doctors were horrified, I do mean *horrified*, my dears, when I told them how far I'd walked on what turned out to be a broken ankle.'

'Mike, enough,' I said, interrupting. 'Tell me this minute, will you dance again?'

'They say there's no reason why not, if I'm a good little boy and do as I'm told. It seems a good clean break heals much better than torn muscle tissue. In fact that ankle may end up being stronger than the other.'

He had dropped his affectations for a moment. This was a serious matter. 'I'm delighted to hear it,' I said in great relief. 'I'm waiting to see you dance Siegfried. But go on.'

'Well, that was Saturday. I was more or less *non compos mentis* for a day or so, raving like a loony, they told me, and then they eased off those *lovely* pain meds, and I remembered why I came, but there was no way they could notify anyone here, because the phones were still out. I wanted them to go and rescue poor Laurence, but they couldn't do that, either, not without a helicopter, and there was actually *none* available. You have *no* idea, my dears, what the world looks like out there. One would swear a *bomb* had been dropped, and along with all the visible damage, the villages are positively *littered* with the halt and the lame. They pushed me out of hospital the first minute they could, because they needed the bed, what with the injured pouring in from every part of the county.

'Well, I was feeling very much the fool. All those would-be-heroics, and no one could help Laurence after all. And then he turned up, not doing so badly, and told me all that had happened in my absence, and I saw what a *splendid* opportunity I had been given for publicity, so of course I notified the media – and here I am, like the proverbial bad penny.'

'And speaking on behalf of all lovers of the dance, I say, here's to your prompt recovery.' Pat raised her glass and we all followed suit.

Later Alan and I were getting ready for bed and doing all but the last-minute packing. We had managed a better connection with Jane and learned that the 'disaster' she had mentioned was our predicament at Branston Abbey, not some awful damage to our house. So I was trying to tie up the last loose ends of the Abbey problem.

I said, 'The one thing I didn't work out is what Julie was so afraid of.'

'Bates, obviously. She followed Dave and saw what happened, but not very clearly. She thought Bates pushed Dave into the river.'

'She said she didn't follow them.'

'She lied, love. She didn't want anyone to know what she knew. But while she was still suffering from hypothermia and somewhat confused, she said enough to the vicar to make him very uneasy. He came to me after Julie was "arrested" to tell me he didn't think she could have done it.'

'So you knew all along what happened!'

'Not "all along", only since her arrest. And I didn't "know" anything, only what a confused woman thought she had seen when under the influence of considerable alcohol.'

'But if you'd told me, I wouldn't have been so worried about helping John and Rose!'

'And if you'd told me what you were going to do, I'd have been able to fend you off.' He yawned and turned out the light. 'I think we're square. Anyway, if I'd told you, you wouldn't have been able to go home and tell everyone how you figured out that the butler did it.'

I threw my pillow at him.

Financial Innovation

Financial Innovation

Edited by
William L. Silber
New York University

Lexington Books
D.C. Heath and Company
Lexington, Massachusetts
Toronto   London

Library of Congress Cataloging in Publication Data

Conference on Financial Innovation, New York University, 1975.
    Financial innovation.

    Sponsored by Salomon Brothers Center for the Study of Financial
Institutions.
    Includes index.
    1. Finance—United   States—Congresses.   2. Financial
institutions—United States—Congresses. I. Silber, William L.
II. Salomon Brothers Center for the Study of Financial Institutions.
III. Title.
HG181.C653   1975   332'.0973   75-19204
ISBN 0-669-00137-6

Copyright © 1975 by D.C. Heath and Company

Published simultaneously in Canada

Printed in the United States of America

International Standard Book Number: 0-669-00137-6

Library of Congress Catalog Card Number: 75-19204

In Memory of

LR
JMR
RS
BZS

Contents

viii

Preface

The chapters included in this book were prepared for the Conference on Financial Innovation, held on April 22, 1975 under the auspices of the Salomon Brothers Center for the Study of Financial Institutions at New York University. As part of the Graduate School of Business Administration at New York University, the Salomon Brothers Center is devoted to promoting academic research on financial market phenomena. The objective is to improve our understanding of financial institutions and markets as well as to provide a common ground for discussions between the academic, government, and business communities. I would like to thank the center and the grant of the American Life Insurance Association for the financial support required to run the conference. The research environment maintained by the center is also an essential ingredient for the success of such undertakings.

Particular individuals involved in the planning and execution of the conference deserve special thanks. Nat Leff made the original suggestion to run such a symposium. Robert Kavesh served admirably as chairman, alternating between entertaining the audience and constraining the speakers. Finally, the conference could not have run as smoothly as it did without efficient orchestration by Kathy Alamo. All of these deserve part of the credit or the blame for having helped this conference take place.

W.L.S.
June 1975

What has been
Is what will be;
What has been done
Is what will be done;
Nothing is new under the sun.

Ecclesiastes I:9

Innovation in the Financial Sector: An Introduction

William L. Silber

The financial sector of the economy provides important services to producers, consumers, and investors. These include: an efficient method of conducting exchange (the payments mechanism); a set of institutions that channel saving into investment (financial intermediaries and markets); and an efficient mechanism for allocating and distributing risk (institutions that facilitate the construction of well-diversified portfolios). This book is devoted to studies of innovation in the financial sector. It focuses on the innovation of new financial instruments, institutions, markets, and practices.

Innovation means change. It usually implies progress as well, although this need not always be the case. While most economists have reserved the term for a discussion of technological improvements, it has been broadened by economic historians to include institutional change. The studies included in this book fall within this expanded framework. To the extent that real technological change induces new financial instruments and markets it is discussed below, but the analysis is by no means limited to such developments.

The chapters included here were prepared specifically for this book. The discussants' comments were presented at the Conference on Financial Innovation in April 1975. The subject matter is divided into three parts: (1) Financial Innovation: History and Theory; (2) Specific Studies of Financial Innovation; (3) Innovation and Monetary Policy: the Past and the Future. These introductory remarks are intended to set the overall framework for discussions of financial innovation, and to indicate where each of the three sections fits.

Economists who have devoted their careers to studying technological change have oftentimes looked down on their colleagues who have mastered the intricacies of macroeconomics and microeconomics. The key element in the superiority complex is that the macro-micro literature is concerned primarily with producing and then dividing the total pie of goods and services. Innovation and technological progress are concerned with expanding the total pie. And it is the latter that holds the key to massive increases in total welfare over time.

The most frequently used measure of welfare is consumption per capita. In the same vein the productivity measure generally used to indicate technological progress is output per man. Innovation in the financial sector

1

can also be reflected in that dimension. The introduction of a medium of exchange and improvements in the technology and organizational structure of the payments mechanism release resources from the exchange process, permitting an increase in production. Intermediaries and organized financial markets tend to lower the cost of capital ccnfronting entrepreneurs, thereby increasing investment and, hence, output per capita. Risk reduction via portfolio diversification would tend to reduce cost of capital as well, once again increasing output per man.

The examples just given suggest that in addition to output per capita, there should be another dimension to the effect of financial innovation on economic welfare, namely, the risk associated with the stochastic returns on real investments. When the innovation of financial instruments or practices decreases risk, only part of the story is told by the induced reduction in cost of capital and higher output per capita. Society may very well end up with a net reduction in risk bearing in addition to the fall in cost of capital. This is similar to the quality-improvement aspect of a technological change. But when dealing with the financial sector, it is crucial not to ignore this explicit and measurable (at least conceptually) dimension. The innovation of insurance contracts and the technology for constructing well-diversified portfolios would be beneficial to society from the point of view of risk bearing. Differentiated financial instruments might also produce the same type of welfare gain.

It is also worth mentioning that innovations may initially increase welfare but eventually turn out to be detrimental. A new financial instrument or market may be introduced because it yields private benefits, in spite of the existence of social costs. Such costs might take the form of increased instability in aggregate output or increased sensitivity of the financial system to exogenous shocks. Government regulation is often elicited to rectify such externalities and this, in turn, may call forth a new set of financial innovations.

The issues of how to measure the welfare gain of any innovation in the financial sector, or how to determine whether a new financial instrument, market, institution, or practice deserves the appelation "innovation" with the implication of increased welfare are crucial. Unfortunately, they are addressed only tangentially in the chapters included here. The closest one gets to an explicit treatment of welfare gains is in Part III, which addresses the question of whether new financial instruments and practices have made the conduct of monetary policy more difficult. This is an example of the kind of externalities an innovation may produce that would detract from its positive impact on economic welfare. While this book does not address the welfare implications of financial innovation, it hopefully will stimulate much needed work in the area.

The main thrust of the chapters center on: (1) the historical processes that stimulate financial innovation and the role that such innovations play in the evolution of both the real and financial sectors; and (2) the micro-economic stimuli that help explain the process of financial innovation. Of the two, the historical context has received the most attention in the literature. The work by Gurley and Shaw on financial intermediaries, for example, has its greatest value within the context of economic development. The extended time horizon implicit in historical analysis permits the researcher an opportunity to evaluate the trends that lead to and flow from a particular financial sector development.

There has been much less analysis of the process of financial innovation as viewed from the vantage point of the firm. This is in marked contrast with the extensive work on real technological change aimed at uncovering the relationship between innovation and expenditures on research and development by firms. The microeconomics of financial innovation has centered almost exclusively on the relationship between regulation and the incentive to innovate financial instruments to comply with or circumvent the regulations. Finance is, perhaps, the most heavily regulated sector in the American economy. Government legislation does, in fact, play a role in shaping the evolution of financial instruments and markets. The theoretical discussions as well as the specific studies presented here incorporate such forces but go beyond to provide a more general analysis of the stimuli to innovation.

This collection and the associated comments should be viewed as initial inquiries into the process of financial innovation. They will hopefully stimulate additional work in this surprisingly neglected area. In view of the rapidity with which financial markets have altered their characteristics during the past 15 years, it may remain a fruitful area of research for some time to come.

**Part I
Financial Innovation:
History and Theory**

Introduction to Part I

The two chapters in part I provide a historical and analytical framework for discussions of financial innovation. Chapter 1 by Lance E. Davis takes a broad look at the development of American capital markets between 1860 and 1940. A blend of long-run trends and the details of institutional evolution illustrate the forces that have shaped the American capital markets. Chapter 2 by William L. Silber sets out to provide a theoretical framework for analyzing financial innovation. After a brief description of the macroeconomic forces, a theory of financial instrument innovation at the microeconomic level is presented. The chapter concludes with some suggestive empirical evidence. The historical and microeconomic analyses of financial innovation are complementary approaches to studying the evolution of the financial sector.

1

The Evolution of the American Capital Market, 1860-1940: A Case Study in Institutional Change

Lance E. Davis

Introduction

Microeconomic theory provides the economist with most of the items in his box of tools; and while perhaps inadequate to construct castles, they have been strong and sharp enough for him to build a number of outhouses and even an award-winning home or two. On occasions, however, when the economist uses these tools, his structures, like the cathedrals of the Middle Ages, have a tendency to collapse. The present state of the economy suggests that the policy recommendations of the macroeconomist have been something less than a complete success; but as underwhelming as it is, that record is better than the batting average compiled from the policy recommendations of the growth theorists. Models built on the assumption that the institutional technology (the legal, psychological, and political strictures that govern the ways that economic units can compete and/or cooperate) is fixed appear to yield adequate predictions when the time frame of the problem is a week, a month, a year, or perhaps even a decade or two. That assumption is a less useful simplification when the period under consideration is, for example, the "postwar world," and it leads at best nowhere when the questions deal with longer time periods (for example, "the development of the American economy"). Although there are almost certainly a multitude of reasons for the present low state of growth theory, at least a part of the explanation must lie with the economist's failure to develop a theory of institutional change.

Almost every student of American economic history has noted the number and variety of financial intermediaries that have occupied the economic scene. To note is not to understand and without a theory of institutional change, it is almost impossible to explain or analyze either the timing or the pattern of those innovations. The work of J. Buchanan and G. Tullock and later extensions by L. Davis and D. North suggest a framework that may be appropriate for the problem.[1]

In brief, these authors argue that exogenous changes in the economy (technology or spatial expansion, for example) may produce potential increases in income that cannot be captured within the existing institutional

[1]Buchanan and Tullock [2]; Davis and North [6].

structure, but that can be captured by restructuring some economic institution.[2] If a person or group sees the chance to effect such a capture, they may innovate a new institutional technology just as a Schumpeterian entrepreneur would innovate within a more classical framework. Similarly, institutional innovation might come about because some person or group sees a chance to increase their income at the expense of others. Thus, institutional change may be income increasing or merely income redistributive. New institutional technologies may be invented, borrowed (with or without modification), or merely selected from a list of known but unused alternatives. The choice among competing innovations is made on the basis of profit maximization; and, depending on the costs and revenues, it may be made at the individual, the voluntary cooperative group, or the government level. The speed of innovation depends upon the potential profit, the menu of alternative institutional arrangements, and the start-up time required to bring the chosen technology "on-line." It is this model that is used here to analyze the developments in the United States capital market.

The employment of the model in the explanation of financial innovation is not without problems. The model's explanatory (or predictive) power becomes less effective the greater the redistributive and the less the income-augmenting component of the potential increase in income. When the redistributive nature of the potential gain dictates innovation at the government level, there is no natural mechanism to insure that total income will be given a dominant weight in the objective function. Moreover, theory suggests no other equally general maximand, and, as a result, the prediction about the form of the institutional innovation becomes more idiosyncratic and less sharp.

In the case of the financial sector, the importance of possible redistributive gains was recognized early, and at least since the second decade of the nineteenth century, there has been a significant amount of governmental level redistributive innovation. Moreover, the passage of time appears to have increased the rate of such redistributive regulation, and the process of innovation becomes even more difficult to analyze. Still the exercise does appear to lead to some interesting results, particularly for those cases where there are income-augmenting gains to innovation. It is on these changes that this chapter is focused.

Capital Mobilization: A Key to Development

Capital, if it is to be used productively, must be accumulated and mobilized. The economic development literature is full of discussion of the

---

[2] Such unrealized income might exist because of economies of scale, externalities, risk or uncertainty.

accumulation process but mobilization has been largely ignored.³ Frequently economists have assumed that resources withdrawn from the consumption stream are automatically available for investment. Since investment is defined as output not consumed, this conclusion follows relentlessly; however, it is less clear that understanding has been greatly advanced. In a Robinson Crusoe economy the acts of saving and investing are carried on by the same person, and accumulation is tantamount to mobilization. As the number of persons increases, however, the probability that the demand for and the supply of investable resources will be equal for every economic unit declines. If, in addition, the process of development involves not only growth in the number of economic units but spatial or industrial dislocation as well, that probability becomes even smaller. The economist whose interest is focused on current economic behavior does little violence to the problem when he assumes that there exists a structure of markets and intermediaries that smooth the flow of investable resources from surplus to deficit savings units. One hundred fifty years ago those institutions did not exist. Their innovation was a response to the profits that could be earned by capturing the increased income inherent in a reduction of risk and uncertainty discounts and in achieving certain economies of scale. More recently a substantial part of financial innovation appears to have been a response to the profits that could be realized by some form of redistribution of the existing economic pie. The nineteenth century "disinclination of capital to migrate" reflected not any great psychological attraction to home, but the rational discount of uncertain alternatives on the one hand and the absence of formal institutional channels to reduce those uncertainties on the other.

When Lincoln was elected to the presidency, the area between the Appalachians and the 100th Meridian had been settled and much of it admitted to the Union on a basis of political equality with the 13 original states. Moreover, because of developments in transportation, the area east of the Mississippi had been largely integrated into a national commodities market. The Midwest was linked with the East by both railroads and canals, the South and East used the coastal waterways to effect their close commercial ties, and both rail and riverboat provided a tenuous connection between the Midwest and the South. Not only commodities but some capital as well moved between the regions. Eastern capital had helped develop the midwestern livestock industry and factors acted to mediate the transfer of finance from the East to the southern cotton planters. In spite of these nascent developments there was no national capital market in any modern sense of the word. Nor, for that matter, was there a set of developed local capital markets, although the cities of the East and their surrounding environs were fairly well served.

³Important exceptions can be found in the work of the economic historian M.M. Poston and more recently Richard N. Cooper [5].

Such problems are not unique; they affect most all developing countries, but the United States' problems were more severe than those faced by most of its nineteenth century counterparts. Savings are generated in regions and by industries that have produced income, but a part of the demand for investment may be in regions and industries that have no earning history. The strains placed on a financial network are greater the greater the distance (industrial or spatial) is between the past and the present locus of economic activity. In the United States growth was accompanied by major shifts in both the spatial and the industrial locus. The century after 1850 saw agriculture decline from an industry that had occupied about one-half of the labor force to one that used only about 10 percent, while mining and manufacturing increased their share of workers from 15 to 25 percent and the "other" industries (largely services) grew to employ about 65 percent. At the same time the center of the nation's population moved from West Virginia to Illinois and that population became not only more western but increasingly urbanized. (The proportion living in cities of over 2,500 grew by more than four times.)

Within sectors, too, the composition of activity was changing and the shift also placed added "distance" between saver and investor. It was a period of rapid technological advance, and many of the new technologies, unlike those they replaced, were subject to increasing returns to scale. In manufacturing before 1860, with the possible exception of cotton textiles, there is little evidence that average costs were inversely related to output. In the years after, however, new technologies in milling, iron and steel production, oil refining and meat packing, to cite only a few, were marked by decreasing costs over a wide range of outputs. In the earlier period it had been possible for a firm to begin small and finance its growth out of retained earnings. With the advent of the new technology some minimum size had to be reached before a firm could become competitive, and achievement of that size often required external finance.

Although agriculture was becoming less capital intensive, it was becoming more finance intensive. In the early nineteenth century land clearing absorbed the bulk of the industry's capital. While total capital requirements were large in relation to output, there were few scale economies and the requirement could often be met internally.[4] As the agricultural frontier passed from the forests of the old northwest territory to the plains of the central states, the size and form of the requirements changed. The capital needed for land clearing declined, but the cost savings inherent in the new mechanical planting and harvesting equipment forced a farmer to adopt these devices if he was to be competitive—and in the absence of prior accumulation, adoption required finance.

[4]The farmer could reduce his consumption of leisure and use the released time to "clear the south forty."

The financial demands of the postbellum decades did strain the financial network, but to conclude there was strain is not to argue that there was no financial infrastructure. In 1860 there were over 1,500 commercial banks, almost 300 mutual savings banks, about 50 life insurance companies, and a number of savings and loan associations. In addition, the New York Stock Exchange had been in existence for almost 70 years and by 1860 handled several million shares annually in over 100 corporations. It is, however, to argue that the structure was inadequate to deal with the economy of the 1850s, let alone to respond adequately to the demands placed on it by the economic developments of the next half century. The inadequacy is reflected by high interregional and interindustry differentials in the cost of finance and by the importance of informal arrangements (and the magnitude of the profits attached to those arrangements) in the provision of finance for new areas and activities.

The existence of 1,500 commercial banks suggests that there was an institutional structure that in principle could have been capable of meeting the mobilization demands of the American economy. For a number of reasons it proved inadequate. The nation's political structure had been established before there was any real national economy, and the bank charter laws reflected the focus on local economic activity. With two noteworthy exceptions, commercial banks were chartered by state governments, concentrated most of their loan activities in local markets, and resisted most suggestions that they cooperate with other banks—even those in the area state, let alone those in other states. Moreover, while early commercial banks, in response to increasing demands, had begun to move into the long-term credit market, the financial debacle of 1837 and the depression of 1839-42 wrought such havoc with the system that the movement was largely halted. State governments began to impose legal constraints on long-term investments, and even in states not so restricted, the bankers themselves began to display an increasing preference for short-term loans. For example, the Forestal system prohibited long-term loans by Louisiana banks, and banks chartered under the National Banking Act were not permitted to make mortgage loans. Thus, at the beginning of our period, legal and psychological constraints had combined to limit the mobilization activities of commercial banks to the local area in which the bank was located and within that area to the mobilization of short-term finance.

The withdrawal of the commercial banks left the long-term loan market to savings banks and life insurance companies. The savings banks had been important and had played a role in mobilizing long-term credit in the Northeast. In Boston they had aided the movement of funds to the textile industry; in New York they had made funds available to the Erie Canal when most savers thought the enterprise too risky; and further south they had helped make Baltimore a major commercial entrepôt. It is possible that the savings banks could have provided the institutional technology for effecting the mobilization of long-term capital, but they did not. Rooted in philanthropy, they were organized by eastern businessmen who wanted to inculcate the virtues of thrift into the working classes. The banks had grown rapidly in the northeastern part of the United States, but they never were important elsewhere. It would be interesting to explore the reasons for the failure to spread geographically, but it may merely reflect the dominance of agriculture (and thus the dearth of either businessmen or workers) in the other regions at the time the philanthropic fervor was at its peak. The fact remains, however, that as late as 1930 of the 606 mutual savings banks in the United States, only 24 were located south of Washington, D.C. or west of Pittsburgh. Moreover, the same philanthropic philosophy that underlay their establishment acted to limit their ability to mobilize capital effectively. Since they were semiphilanthropic, they were frequently the object of government regulation and such regulations often included some limitation on the geographical scope of their investment activities. Even when there were no legal restrictions, the banks' managers were most interested in the safety of their deposits (since the purpose of the whole exercise was to prove to the poor that savings could be both safe and profitable), and they tended to avoid investments in uncertain activities, whether the reason for the uncertainty was geographical distance or lack of a financial history. The effects of this bias were compounded by the usury laws that normally left the equilibrium rate (particularly for risky endeavors) above the legal limit.

Nor were the life insurance companies able to provide the institutional structure necessary to arbitrage the long-term capital markets. The first mutual did not begin to write insurance until the early 1840s, and by 1860 the 43 mutual and stock companies had combined assets of only $36 million. The innovations of tontine and industrial insurance that were to underwrite almost exponential growth in the ensuing decades were still in the future. Like the savings banks they frequently faced legal regulation designed to keep their investments close to home. Even when there were no legal constraints, they shared with other surplus savings units the uncertainty about "foreign" investments and the substantial costs of gathering the information required to reduce that uncertainty.

Emergence of National Markets

Although the evidence is meager, it does suggest that both the long- and the short-term capital markets were largely local and the finance industry lacked the institutional infrastructure necessary to provide a working national market. If a national market had existed, the price of finance net of risk differentials should not have differed between regions or industries by more than the cost of transport, and the profits accruing to firms engaged in interindustry or interregional financial arbitrage should be no higher than those earned in any competitive industry. Differentials were higher and so were profits.

Granted that appropriate risk differentials are hard to estimate, in 1870 farm mortgage rates were averaging about 7 percent in New York, 10 percent in the states of the Old Northwest Territory, and 12 percent in Kansas and Nebraska.[5] The net (after losses and costs) rates of return on national bank portfolios (a figure that might be viewed as a proxy for short-term interest rates) averaged for the two years 1869-70 over 3 percent in New York City and about 13 percent on the West Coast.

Moreover, the qualitative evidence suggests that there were very large profits to be earned by any individual who could successfully overcome the "disinclination of capital to migrate." Andrew Carnegie's fortune was not based on his ability to make better steel than his competitors, but on his ability to transfer capital to steel production.[6] The same is true of John D. Rockefeller, whose fortune was much more closely associated to his connections with the Cleveland (and later New York) banking communities than it was with any particular oil refining skill.[7] Similarly, J.P. Morgan's fortune was the product of his ability to mobilize capital across a number of industries and regions in response to potential profit opportunities, and in those instances where he moved into sectors already well served by the existing capital markets (ocean shipping, for example), his "magic touch" produced no abnormal profits.[8] Admittedly, these three are hardly typical, but a careful reading of the economic history of the latter nineteenth century suggests that informal arrangements were very important in the transfer of capital into new economic activites. Moreover, the rewards earned by the few individuals who were capable of effecting such arrangements attest to the monopoly profits available in an industry where the absence of an institutional structure makes entry difficult.

If the evidence suggests that such an institutional structure did not exist in 1860, the same data suggests that by the middle of the twentieth century the structure was mature and stable. By that time the American domestic financial network was probably the most sophisticated in the world. Interregional interest differentials had largely disappeared, and when in the

---

[5] See, for example: Bogue [1], Hoecker [14], and Ladin [18].

[6] Carnegie [3].

[7] Nevins [23].

[8] Hovey [15].

mid-thirties, federal law forced investment banks to divest themselves of their commercial banking subsidiaries, most of the Morgan partners preferred the latter activity in spite of its relatively competitve character to the one in which the House's fortunes had been rooted. These changes are the result of a number of financial innovations—innovations that were themselves responses to the profit opportunities presented by the developing economy.

The withdrawal of the commercial banks from the long-term capital market makes it necessary to break the history of the institutional innovation in the financial sector into two parts: that concerned with the long- and that relevant to the short-term market. In both cases the years after Appomattox saw a movement toward a single, closely-integrated, national capital market, but the development of the short-term market was more rapid. Thus, while outside the South the economy had a single, national short-term market by the outbreak of World War I, the long-term market, though operating much more easily than it had 50 years before, was still not integrated into a single unit. That objective was not achieved for another two decades.

Development of the Short-term Market

Institutional development in the short-term market was based on the already existing commercial banking system. The organizational costs of innovation are reduced if the new institution can make use of some already existing structure. Although use of existing structures was less in the United States than in other places (the United Kingdom, for example), the banks did remain the point of contact for both surplus and deficit units, a fact that was reflected in their continued rapid expansion.[9] In Canada and the United Kingdom the development of nationwide branch banking was the institution that ultimately provided interregional mobility of short-term capital. In those environments that technology proved superior; not only were organizational costs lower, but there was no need to place an additional administrative layer between the capital surplus and the capital deficit unit. In the United States that innovation was not on the legal menu of alternatives. State laws, when they permitted branching at all, prohibited it across state lines, and the national banks were granted no greater leeway.

In spite of these legal constraints, innovation did take place. Evidences of this movement are visible in the gradual reduction in interregional, short-term interest differentials.

Although not without problems, the net rate of returns on national bank

---

[9]Their numbers and size increased about ten times as rapidly as did population in the years between 1865 and 1914.

portfolios can be taken as a proxy for short-term interest rates.[10] An index of the variance in the regional relatives of rates for the six regions reported by the Comptroller of the Currency are displayed in Table 1-1.[11] Although the movement is not unidirectional, that index had fallen to about one-fifth its initial level by the outbreak of World War I; and, perhaps equally important, it shows little further downward drift over the last few years of the period. Periods of financial crisis or economic distress (particularly periods of agricultural distress) tended to increase the variance, but the trend across cycles is downward, but downward at a decreasing rate. Since there are far fewer observations, the data for reserve city banks are more difficult to interpret. For those banks, however, it appears that the process of intermarket integration was even faster than for those in smaller cities.[12]

The improvement was not uniform across regions. For the nonreserve city banks, rates in the New England and Middle Atlantic states came together by the end of the 1870s, but it was the 1890s before there was near equality between rates in those regions and those in the middle western states. Even at the end of the period, rates in the other three regions

---

[10]In a recent article it has been observed that gross returns are a much better proxy. Gross returns are' however, available only for the period after 1889, and focusing only in movements of the gross measure leads to possibly erroneous conclusions about the dating of the emergence of a national market. Both gross and net measures include, unfortunately, some risk differential, and when distress is localized, risk differentials will move apart. The 1890s was a period of severe distress on the plains, and regional rates (both gross and net) tended to move apart. The net series then shows closing until the 90s, then movement apart (as regional risk differentials increased) and finally closing again in the decade 1900-1910 as the western drought subsided. The gross series, starting as it does in 1889, shows large differences, differences that disappear in the first decade of the twentieth century. Interpretation of the net series suggests a gradual movement toward a national market over the entire 40-year period; the gross series suggests that the movement was the product of the last ten years.

[11]The regions are those of the Comptroller of the Currency (see Appendix 1A).

[12]In her comments (see pp. 45-51) Mrs. Schwartz has suggested that the reader would benefit from some measure of the interregional variance in the capital markets at the present time. That request is not easy to meet; but for the period beginning in mid-1967, the *Federal Reserve Bulletin* does report average bank rates on short-term business loans for 35 "financial centers" on a regional basis. These regions are not identical with those used by the Comptroller of the Currency but they are somewhat analogous. If New York City is excluded, the series provides a four-times-a-year weighted average of loans made in seven cities in the Northeast, eight in the North Central, seven in the Southeast, eight in the Southwest, and four on the West Coast.

The interest relatives were employed to provide some adjustment for trend, and since the barriers to capital movement should have been absolute not relative they provide a downward bias in the degree of capital market improvement as long as the trend in the rates is downward. Since rates rose substantially between 1914 and the mid-1960s, movements in the variance of the relatives become difficult to interpret. Thus, these comparisons will be based on an index of the variance in the rates rather than the relative variance.

For the six years 1968 through 1973 the variance of the Federal Reserve series was 0.025. Again it is not quite clear what the base of comparison should be, but if reserve cities are somewhat analogous to "financial centers" and if the South is excluded the variance for the period 1912-14 average- 0.041.

Table 1-1
Index of the Variance of Regional Interest Relatives, Net Returns Nonreserve City Banks, Comptroller Regions

1869	0.163	1881	0.107	1893	0.094	1905	0.119
1870	.065	1882	.084	1894	.016	1906	.045
1871	.378	1883	.034	1895	.048	1907	.045
1872	.331	1884	.083	1896	.050	1908	.047
1873	.027	1885	.086	1897	.073	1909	.052
1874	.058	1886	.039	1898	.035	1910	.052
1875	.131	1887	.017	1899	.012	1911	.036
1876	.096	1888	.111	1900	.018	1912	.027
1877	.173	1889	.062	1901	.037	1913	.034
1878	.129	1890	.031	1902	.085	1914	0.059
1897	.198	1891	.048	1903	.042		
1880	0.106	1892	0.033	1904	0.038		

Source: Davis [8], Table 5, unweighted rate. Reprinted with permission.

remained above the low three, but the gap between them was much smaller than it had been earlier. For the South alone there is little evidence of market integration. That region had been characterized by relatively low rates at the beginning of the period, but at the end they were among the highest in the nation. For the reserve cities the pattern is similar, but if cyclical fluctuations are ignored, integration appears to come five to ten years earlier.

The regional differences in interest rates meant profits to those who could arbitrage the markets. Legal constraints made it difficult to innovate within the banking sector, but those constraints were ineffective outside the sector. While at times invention must precede innovation, at other times it is only necessary to borrow a technology that has proved itself elsewhere. In Great Britain before the emergence of the system of national branching, spatial relocation of capital had been effected by the activities of the discount house. The discount house bought commercial paper from the banks in high interest areas and sold it to banks in areas of excess capital supply, and it was the institution that had produced capital market integration in the United Kingdom. In the period 1830-70 those houses had purchased paper in the midlands and the North and sold it in London and the South. The institution ultimately proved unable to compete with the system of nationwide branching, and by 1880 had been largely replaced by that "more efficient" institution.[13] In the United States, however, while national branching would probably have proved the institution of choice,

[13]For a discussion of the discount house, see King [16]. For a discussion of the emergence of a short-term paper market in the United Kingdom and its effects on interest differentials, see Davis [7].

legal constraints moved it outside the choice set. The system that did emerge was the commercial paper house—an institution similar to the British discount house.

The first American commercial paper house—an institution designed to purchase commercial paper in banks in high interest areas and resell that paper to banks in low interest areas—was founded in the Northeast in the 1840s.[14] Because of the high cost of gathering the information needed to determine the quality of the offered papers, spatial expansion was slow. In Great Britain distances were smaller and the business community more closely knit; these facts certainly made that information less costly. With the increasing trade between regions and the emergence of institutions designed to exploit the inherent economies of scale in information gathering (Dun and Bradstreet, for example), costs fell and potential profits rose. The commercial paper industry began to expand out of the East. Expansion took it to Indianapolis in 1871, and by 1880 there were firms in Chicago, Minneapolis, and Milwaukee as well. By the end of that decade Kansas City had been added to the list, and by the turn of the century the West Coast cities of Los Angeles, San Francisco, and Seattle. The next decade saw the inclusion of Wichita and Dallas. "By 1913 it could be said that the commercial paper houses had branches or representatives in 'all the large cities' of the United States."[15]

Unlike the informal transfer arrangements where the system depends upon a structure of highly personal relations that are almost impossible to duplicate, formal institutional arrangements can be copied. Since there are no patents to protect new institutions, the profits that accrued to the first financial innovators induced further entry. By 1900 there were, for example, nine or ten firms in both Chicago and Minneapolis, and the competition squeezed profit margins. Commission charges that had averaged one-half percent in 1870 had fallen to near zero by 1910. The search for profits induced the firms to extend their operations into more and more distant areas. The search was facilitated by falling information costs since operations in one area made it easier to obtain information about neighboring areas. The result was, on the one hand, westward expansion and, on the other, movement within a region from the large cities to smaller cities and towns. A region by region examination of the decline in interest differentials indicates that those declines are closely associated with the entry of a commerical paper house into an area (see Table 1-2). The rates close first between those in the region's cities, and those prevailing in "national" markets and then, after a lag of five to seven years, the differences between "country" and "national" rates tend to disappear as well. Outside the South the commercial paper houses appear to have provided the mecha-

---

[14]For the best history of the commercial paper house, see Greef [13].

[15]Greef [13], pp. 39-40.

Table 1-2

Interregional Interest Differential and the Penetration of the Market for Commercial Paper

(1)	(2)	(3)	(4)
1	1860-2	1870-1	1870-2
3	1910-1	NC	NC
4	1880-1	1880-1	1880-2
5	1890-2	1890-2	NC
6	1900-2	1910-1	1910-1

Note:

(1) Region.

(2) Date of market penetration into cities in region.[a] Periods are half decades (e.g., 1860-2 = 1865-9).

(3) Date of reduced differential between city rate and city rate in Region 2.

(4) Date of reduced differential between country rate and country rate in Region 2.

[a]Market penetration dates are from Greefe [13].

nism for transferring short-term capital across substantial distances. The "festive note broker" may have been the bane of the midwestern banker's life (and certainly of his monopoly position), but he played a major role in the development of a national short-term capital market.

One final word: Although a national short-term market had largely emerged by 1914, institutional innovation did not stop. While the commercial paper houses continued to operate, their importance diminished (how many remember that Goldman-Sachs was originally a commercial paper house?) as new and more efficient institutions replaced the old. Just as the discount houses in the United Kingdom could not compete with national branch banking, the commercial paper houses found it more and more difficult to compete with the capital mobilizing activities of the national borrowing firm. In Great Britain the branch bank in the high interest area could draw funds from branches in low interest regions. In the United States the national firm could borrow in the low interest eastern cities and make those funds available to its offices in the high interest West.

Development of the Long-term Market

In the long-term market there existed no institutional counterpart of the commercial bank. Innovation there had to include not only mobilization but the accumulation and distribution of the mobilized funds as well. At the same time there were probably more uncertainties attached to long-term lending, since repayment was tied to the success of a much wider variety of activities. Perhaps because the innovation was necessarily more complex, perhaps because the uncertainties to be overcome were larger, the regional differences were greater at the beginning of the period and the evolution of the national market, both spatial and industrial, was slower.

The quantitative evidence is even more fragmentary for the long-term market than it was for the short-term. There was no counterpart of the Comptroller of the Currency to require that a major subset of the dominant institutions (savings banks, land mortgage companies, life insurance, etc.) file periodic reports. What evidence there is, however, appears to substantiate the existence of significant interregional interest differentials and suggests that there was a movement toward a national market over the last third of the nineteenth and the first third of the twentieth century.

There are data on the balance sheets (if not the income statements) of reporting private and savings banks; and evidence drawn from them appears to support the hypothesis. The institution's portfolio contained both loans and formal securities (most frequently government and railroad bonds). If both securities and loans were traded in the same spatial market, there should be little regional variation in the proportion of each type of asset held. If they were traded in different markets and if, as appears reasonable, securities were traded in a broader spatial market than loans, one would expect regional differences in the ratio of loans to securities plus loans, as institutions in high interest regions biased their portfolios toward those higher yielding assets. An analysis of the portfolios of reporting banks indicates that there were significant regional variations in portfolio composition, and the variations were in the expected direction. Savings and private banks in the East had a lower proportion of their assets invested in loans than did their counterparts in the West. Moreover, although the difference persists throughout the period, it becomes less.

The sparse interest rate data tell the same story. A comparison of mortgage rates in selected counties indicates that in any year rates were higher the further west was the county, but that the intercounty differentials got smaller as time passed. The continuous data reflects conditions in only a few counties, but for the decade of the 1880s, an annual survey of mortgages consummated was included as part of the Eleventh Census. Those figures indicate that there were substantial regional differentials and that rates were lowest in the New England and the Middle Atlantic states and highest in the Mountain and Pacific (see Table 1-3) states. The interregional variance was greater for urban than for rural mortgages, but both declined by about half over the decade. The high variances for urban mortgages is somewhat surprising, but it almost certainly reflects institutional change already underway in the agricultural sector.[16]

Since 1910 the Department of Agriculture has collected an annual series

[16]As we shall see, both land mortgage banks and insurance companies had begun to move capital into farm mortgages by the 1880s.

Table 1-3
Regional Interest Relatives

Region	Year:	1880	1881	1882	1883	1884	1885	1886	1887	1888	1889
					Acres Mortgaged						
NE		71	72	74	75	76	74	73	75	77	78
MA		71	71	73	73	73	73	72	74	73	75
ENC		87	84	86	87	89	89	87	88	88	88
WNC		107	107	109	110	110	109	109	112	110	112
SA		86	87	89	90	92	93	92	94	94	93
ESC		94	94	96	99	97	99	99	96	97	99
WSC		106	108	109	111	115	113	115	117	114	114
Mt.		142	142	130	126	123	130	127	123	127	125
Pac.		139	129	130	124	129	128	124	117	121	118
σ^2		604	534	411	344	355	390	373	305	313	288
					Lots Mortgaged						
NE		69	69	71	72	71	71	72	73	74	76
MA		67	68	70	70	69	70	69	71	71	72
ENC		82	81	82	83	83	84	84	85	86	88
WNC		108	107	107	109	107	109	107	108	108	105
SA		81	84	86	85	88	88	88	89	90	92
ESC		85	88	92	91	89	90	90	92	95	96
WSC		101	104	107	109	110	111	111	113	113	113
Mt.		176	173	169	161	159	153	153	148	147	141
Pac.		130	127	118	118	122	121	121	119	121	120
σ^2		1078	985	834	721	719	686	629	542	525	429

Source: Eleventh Census of the United States; regions are present census classifications.

of farm mortgage rates by state (see Table 1-4). The series is for mortgages in place not mortgages made, and is, therefore, not strictly comparable to the Eleventh Census series on acres mortgaged. The latter series is more responsive to capital market changes since fluctuations in the former are dampened by the stock of existing mortgages. Both do, however, reflect the same underlying trends and the USDA figures show a continuation of the general patterns established earlier, although there were some important changes in the capital markets between 1890 and 1910. In the earlier period the rates in the East, West, and North Central regions were above those in the Northeast, but by 1910 they were almost equal.[17]

The USDA data show a falling trend in the interregional variance over the first 25 years of the study, and by the mid-1930s that figure was only one-ninth its 1910 value. Although the decline was not continuous (the agricultural depression of 1920-22, for example, produced a short reversal),

[17]In the 1880s the two eastern regions averaged 74 percent of the national average while the two western regions averaged 98 percent. For the period 1910-15 the figures were 86 percent and 88 percent.

Table 1-4
Regional Interest Relatives, Farm Mortgages in Place, 1910-48

Year	NE	MA	ENC	WNC	SA	ESC	WSC	Mt.	Pac.	Avg.	σ²
					Region						
1910	88	83	86	88	102	109	117	122	108	6.5	0.188
1911	88	83	85	88	102	108	115	120	108	6.5	.173
1912	86	85	85	89	102	109	114	118	108	6.5	.160
1913	89	86	86	91	103	109	116	120	106	6.4	.153
1914	88	86	88	91	103	106	116	122	108	6.4	.157
1915	88	86	88	91	103	103	117	122	108	6.4	.158
1916	88	86	89	92	103	103	117	120	108	6.4	.144
1917	88	86	89	91	103	102	117	119	108	6.4	.141
1918	89	87	90	92	103	102	116	117	108	6.3	.120
1919	89	89	90	92	103	100	114	116	106	6.3	.100
1920	89	89	90	92	103	100	114	114	105	6.3	.092
1921	90	89	92	94	103	100	114	114	106	6.3	.084
1922	92	89	94	95	105	102	117	116	108	6.4	.098
1923	89	88	92	94	102	98	114	112	105	6.5	.082
1924	92	91	94	95	102	98	113	114	106	6.4	.059
1925	92	91	94	95	100	97	111	113	105	6.3	.049
1926	92	92	95	95	103	98	110	111	105	6.3	.045
1927	92	92	94	94	103	97	108	110	105	6.3	.037
1928	94	94	95	94	103	98	108	110	105	6.2	.037
1929	94	94	94	92	103	98	106	108	105	6.2	.034
1930	96	96	96	92	103	100	108	110	107	6.1	.037
1931	96	97	96	92	103	100	108	110	107	6.1	.036
1932	96	97	96	92	103	100	108	110	107	6.1	.036
1933	96	97	96	92	103	98	108	110	107	6.1	.037
1934	97	97	95	93	100	97	105	107	107	5.9	.025
1935	98	100	96	95	98	96	104	105	105	5.6	.015
1936	102	102	94	94	100	96	104	106	106	5.2	.020
1937	102	102	94	94	100	96	104	106	106	5.2	.020
1938	102	102	94	92	98	96	104	106	108	5.1	.027
1939	102	102	94	92	100	98	104	106		5.1	.032
1940A	100	100	92	92	98	96	104	104	106	5.2	.024
1941A	102	102	94	92	100	98	104	104	108	5.1	.023
1940B	104	104	96	91	104	102	96	102	104	4.7	.024
1941B	104	104	96	91	102	102	96	102	104	4.6	.024
1942	104	104	93	91	102	102	96	100	104	4.6	.022
1943	104	104	96	93	102	104	98	102	104	4.5	.016
1944	104	104	96	91	102	102	96	100	104	4.5	.019
1945	104	102	96	93	102	104	98	102	104	4.6	.019
1946	102	100	92	90	104	104	97	102	102	4.8	.024
1947	104	100	94	91	106	106	98	102	102	4.7	.024
1948	104	100	96	91	109	106	98	102	100	4.7	0.029

Source: Lingould and Brown [19] and Yarnall [28].

Note: A = Lingould and Brown figures for 1940-41.
     B = Yarnall figures for 1940-41.

it was downward in 19 of the 25 years between 1910 and 1935; moreover, there appears to have been some acceleration after 1916.

On a region-by-region basis, the data show a continuation of the trends established in the nineteenth century. Rates in the South continued to hang above the national average. The 1910 rates are highest in the Mountain and Pacific states, but market integration continued, and by 1940 rates in those regions were only slightly above the national average. It appears that for farm mortgages at least, a national long-term market had emerged by the mid-thirties.

If geographic expansion had strained the financial network, the end of that expansion would by itself reduce the strain and reduce regional differences somewhat even in the absence of institutional innovation. The evidence indicates that there was substantial innovation, and that developments were both swifter and more complete than one would expect from attrition alone.

The postbellum period was marked not only by regional but by intersectional shifts as well. For the period after 1880 we have the benefits of S. Kuznets' aggregate data on the demand for capital, and they indicate that agriculture's share of the allocatable stock of business capital stock declined from one-third to one-fifth, and the share of regulated industries fell from 50 to 44 percent, and the share of mining and manufacturing rose from 10 to 40 percent.[18] Nor were these new demands met by any great increase in internal financing. The trend in the ratio of internal to total finance for the business sector was slightly upward, but almost all of that increase can be traced to the recent increase in internal finance in the agricultural sector. It was innovations in the capital markets that made it possible to meet the majority of the shifting and increasing capital demands of the business sector. Between 1870 and 1930 innovation took place both in intermediation and in the formal securities markets. More recently, it appears that increases in total income that could be captured from further innovation have begun to decline. Although innovation has continued, after 1920 new institutional technologies in the domestic market were ever more frequently designed to redistribute rather than increase income or to move funds from saver to consumer rather than from saver to business.

Interregionally, the most important events of the post-1870 decades were the agricultural (and later industrial) development of the Midwest and Far West and the related increasing demand for capital in those regions. The increasing flow of capital from the east to the west was channeled through the institutional conduits established by land mortgage companies, life insurance companies, and, later, a series of government institutions designed to aid agriculture. The major barrier to interregional capital flows was the uncertainty discounts attached to investments far removed from the knowledge of the saver and the high costs associated with obtaining information that would permit those discounts to be reduced. The information industry is marked by increasing returns to scale. If innovation could

[18]Kuznets [17].

permit those economies to be captured, capital would flow much more easily; and a part of the resulting increase in income could accrue as profits to the successful innovator. A search of the menu of private institutional alternatives that were available in the last quarter of the nineteenth century suggests that either life insurance or land mortgage companies could have provided the requisite institutional structure. A detailed examination of the relative cost structure of the two indicates that in the long run it would probably be the insurance companies that would prove competitively stronger.

Land Mortgage Companies: A Temporary Phenomenon

In the long- as well as in the short-term market, the Northeast remained the surplus savings area, and the usual instrument of capital transfer—for agriculture at least—remained the mortgage loan. Since commercial bankers were often precluded by legal or psychological strictures from making mortgage loans, individual lenders dominated the market.[19] The formal security markets were not sufficiently developed to provide an alternative institutional instrument, and even today the average size of an agricutural enterprise precludes any important reliance on those formal markets.

Mortgages were a fairly uncertain form of investment. Their quality varied not only with the general state of agriculture, but also with the quality of the individual farm—to say nothing, since foreclosure and resale is a resource-consuming activity, of the quality of the individual farmer. Knowledge of individual enterprises is expensive to acquire, but for any given locality it is often a matter of general knowledge in the business community. The local banker, because of his personal knowledge, should have been particularly well-placed to act as a mortgage broker. At times he did, but as we have seen, he could not use the existing institutional structure.

Potential eastern investors observed the interest differentials, and some of them employed agents to seek out desirable mortgages. However, that channel was only open to those with large personal accumulation, since the marginal return had to be large enough to cover the entire search cost. Once an agent had gathered enough information on local conditions to satisfy his employer, the costs of distributing that information to others was not high. Recognizing this source of increased income, many agents went from working for one investor to serving the needs of a group, and they served the expanded group at a much lower average cost than they could have served "a single master." Search costs would be further reduced if the

---

[19]In Tippecanoe County, Indiana, for example, in the period 1865-80, individuals made 83 percent of mortgage loans. Similar figures hold for the other western counties where mortgages have been studied in detail!

accumulation of investable funds was centralized. A visit to a single eastern office could provide the potential investor with information from a number of agents in different western areas and provide him with an inexpensive way to place his order for a mortgage. Eastern offices of western agents were the second step in the innovation process.

While the office and its linked agents reduced the uncertainty attached to investment in a particular western farm mortgage, unless the investor bought a portfolio of mortgages, he was not insured against the risk of individual failure. But different institutional arrangements can produce different levels of risk, and it was only a short step from the agent with office to an institution that, instead of selling mortgages, issued formal securities against a portfolio of those assets. There was, of course, no insurance against a general agricultural depression or a natural disaster involving a major section of the country. The new institution did reduce risk and as a result made mortgage credit available more cheaply. The land mortgage company was born. The institutional form was not invented in the United States but borrowed from Europe.

The first steps in the innovation process date from the 1870s when agents began to channel finance into the farms in Iowa, Minnesota, and eastern Kansas and Nebraska. While the J.B. Watkins Land Company— probably the earliest of the prototype institutions—began in 1870, it was 1881 before the Iowa Land and Trust Company of Des Moines issued the first debentures against a portfolio of mortgages; and it was not until the middle of the decade that the practice became common.[20] Thereafter growth was rapid, and the names of 167 companies were listed with the appropriate New York department in 1891.

A thorough study of the land mortgage industry is still to be written, but it appears that the firms in the industry were quite successful. The companies reporting in Massachusetts in 1891 showed average dividends of about 9 percent, and as they tended to retain a part of their earnings, total profits were almost certainly larger. An analysis of companies reporting in New York indicates that total profits were in the neighborhood of 20 percent per year.[21]

In spite of their profitability, the long-term impact of the land mortgage companies was relatively small. In 1893 the 65 companies licensed to do business in Massachusetts, Rhode Island, and Connecticut had total assets of $109 million, equity of $25 million, and loans of $72 million.[22] If we assume that there were 200 firms (20 percent more than listed in the New York enumeration) and that the 65 were of average size (they probably were among the largest), the figure suggests a total loan commitment of

[20]For a history of the J.B. Watkins Company, see Bogue [1].

[21]See Frederiksen [10].

[22]Ibid.

about $222 million. That figure compares with the mortgage loans of life insurance companies of $386 million, of which $217 million were in the major market areas served by the land mortgage companies. At the peak of their activity, the new institution shared the western mortgage business (perhaps as an equal but more likely as a junior partner) with the life insurance companies. The early 1890s were the high water mark of the institution's growth, within three or four years the entire industry had disappeared with hardly a trace.

The failure of the institution to become as important in this country as it had in Europe can probably be traced to two causes. In the short run the formal capital markets were less developed here, and those that existed were biased towards governments, railroad shares, and utilities. Listing was difficult (none of the land banks was listed on the New York Exchange) and penetrating the portfolios of the typical eastern investors even more difficult. In the long run they were unable to compete with the life insurance companies.

Life Insurance Companies and Capital Mobilization

The land mortgage company evolved as a specialized institution designed to transfer eastern savings into western agriculture. The life insurance company had been designed to sell life insurance, but given the competition for business and the time distribution of its premium and insurance payments, a company needed investment almost as much as the western farmers needed mortgage credit. The decades after 1870 saw the successful innovation of tontine and industrial insurance, and while the increased sales meant rapid growth and large administrative salaries, it also meant the rapid accumulation on investable funds. By the end of the century the industry's assets had risen from slightly over $100 million in 1866 to more than $1.7 billion.

In the late nineteenth century there was a general relaxation of the legal constraints on the investment policies of life insurance companies, and the managers were quick to take advantage of the profits available in spatial capital mobilization. Because of the regulation and the uncertainties attached to distant investment, most firms had originally centered their portfolios close to their home offices. With the removal of those constraints and as reports from sales offices in other areas increased their knowledge of those places, management began to shift its portfolios toward regions of higher return. The Northern Mutual Life Insurance Company of Milwaukee, Wisconsin provides an excellent illustration of this behavior. The firm was founded in 1857 and received legal permission to invest in mortgages outside of Wisconsin in 1863. In spite of the change, few loans were made outside the Milwaukee area, let alone outside the state. In 1864 even Saulk County seemed too far removed to consider without careful study. The first out-of-state loans were not made until 1867, but once the decision was made, regional diversification went swiftly. In 1873 more than one-quarter of their loans were made on land outside the East North Central region, and by 1907 that proportion had risen to 56 percent.[23] The Northwestern's experience appears to be confirmed by the aggregate data. M. Pritchett has allocated the industry's investments by region, and the results are displayed in Table 1-5.[24] His study encompassed the portfolios of 322 companies, and while it is not possible to provide a year-by-year, region-by-region breakdown of the total assets of the companies included, there was clearly a predominantly eastern bias in the location of those companies. Over the 26 years for which regional data have been collected, the proportions of investments in the northeast (regions 1 and 2) declined from about three-quarters to about 40 percent of the total, those in the upper Midwest (regions 3 and 7) increased by about half, and while the absolute levels outside the Southwest (region 6) were not large, there were marked percentage increases in all of the other regions. A very similar story is reflected in the trends in each of the asset categories (mortgages, bonds and stocks).

It is interesting to note that Pritchett's data shows not only a westward shift in the locus of investment, but also a substantial change in the institutional instrument used to effect that transfer. In 1874 mortgages represented three-quarters of the regionalized investments while bonds made up only 15 percent (and three-fourths of those were governments) and equities 3 percent. By 1900, although the industry's holdings of mortgages had doubled, the share of those loans in the total had fallen to less than one-third. Meanwhile bonds had risen to one-half and stocks to 6 percent. Moreover, of the bond investment, only 12 percent were government and rails accounted for 70 percent. Clearly, the ability of the insurance companies to mobilize credit effectively was aided by collateral developments in the formal securities markets.

Pritchett does not report earnings by regions or by companies but in a much earlier work, I. Zartman provided that data for a sample of 29 firms for the period 1887-1904.[25] The data (see Table 1-6) indicate that the interregional variance in returns declined over the period of Zartman's study, but we have already seen a similar decline in the more general mortgage series. If firms initially tended to invest close to home, the variation between rates by location of lender should be similar to the

---

[23] See Williamson and Smalley [27].

[24] M. Pritchett [24].

[25] See Zartman [29]. While the data are not the best, there is at least one company in four of the nine census regions.

Table 1-5

Regional Investments of Life Insurance Companies, Percent of All Allocable Assets

Region	1	2	3	4	5	6	7	8	% Allocated
Year					*All Asset*				
1874	13.9	60.0	14.9	0.4	0.4	1.5	8.5	0.3	69.5
1880	12.1	50.4	25.3	0.4	0.5	4.1	6.6	0.3	70.9
1890	5.9	38.5	24.1	1.9	2.1	10.0	13.3	1.1	86.5
1900	6.7	33.3	19.7	2.8	2.9	11.9	13.3	3.3	87.6
					Mortgages				
1874	12.6	59.4	15.6	0.03	0.04	1.4	10.8	0.03	
1880	8.5	46.8	31.2	0.00	0.08	2.0	11.4	0.03	
1890	3.8	42.7	31.0	0.16	0.58	9.5	12.0	0.26	
1900	4.6	34.3	29.1	0.87	1.90	11.8	16.3	1.00	
					Bonds				
1874	18.6	54.2	17.0	2.3	2.5	1.8	1.6	2.0	
1880	15.5	59.6	14.6	0.7	1.4	6.1	0.9	1.1	
1890	6.0	28.6	21.8	5.1	5.1	11.9	18.6	2.1	
1900	7.6	28.3	19.2	5.2	4.7	15.0	15.5	5.8	
					Stocks				
1874	48.6	23.6	22.2	0.3	0.0	0.3	4.1	0.0	
1880	51.5	42.6	4.4	0.4	0.0	0.1	0.0	0.0	
1890	21.6	40.5	15.4	0.6	1.1	4.9	14.7	1.3	
1900	18.2	55.2	13.9	1.0	1.1	2.6	6.5	1.5	
					Percent of Companies				
1843–1900	11.4	41.6	15.8	5.2	8.7	8.4	6.8	1.9	

Source: Pritchett [24]. Reprinted with permission.

variance in the regional rates. If those firms continued to pursue the same pattern over the period, the variance in the insurance series should decline with the variance in the general series. The data, however, seems to indicate that the insurance series declined more rapidly. One could hypothesize that the life insurance companies recognized the profits in interregional mobilization, responded to those perceived profits by shifting their portfolios towards higher yielding regions, but were, in the late nineteenth century, still too small to completely arbitrage out these differences.[26]

[26]For the first three years of the 1880s the ratio of general (census) to company (Zartman) variance averaged 3.1; for the last three years, 2.0.

Table 1-6

Regional Variation in Relatives of Mortgage Rates of Interest by Region of Lending Company, 1877-1904

Year	$\sigma^2 LI$	σ^2 Census	Year	$\sigma^2 LI$
1877	0.866		1891	0.202
1878	.272		1892	.504
1879	.680		1893	.182
1880	.449	0.899	1894	.245
1881	.194	.703	1895	.081
1882	.178	.651	1896	.079
1883	.158	.316	1897	.146
1884	.209	.595	1898	.037
1885	.451	.603	1899	.038
1886	.267	.544	1900	.030
1887	.156	.385	1901	.025
1888	.330	.446	1902	.046
1889	.182	0.371	1903	.022
1890	0.086		1904	0.017

Source: Life Insurance figure from Zartman [29]. Census from Eleventh Census. Regions are New England, Middle Atlantic, East North Central, and Pacific.

While most companies had offices in the East, they did not limit their business to that area. Although there had been some concern about high southern mortality rates, there was hardly any hesitation to sell insurance in most any other part of the country. This willingness is attested both by our knowledge of individual firms and by Pritchett's aggregate data (see Table 1-7). Once the decision to expand the sales area had been made, the costs of geographic dispersion in the investment portfolio were reduced. Sales meant offices and agents and with those innovations came reductions in the cost of acquiring information and in supervising local investments. States often required a "foreign" firm that wanted to sell insurance to make some minimum investment in the state. Not only did such a requirement force spatial relocation, but it provided compulsory education for the firms' investment committees as well. Given the joint cost nature of the diversification expense, the costs of mobilization for the life insurance companies were probably less than for alternative institutional structures (the mortgage banks, for example).

Once the decision had been made to shift funds into western agriculture the transfers were substantial. Poor's regions 3, 6, 7, and 8 represent the areas of increasing agriculture demand and the major areas served by the mortgage banks. The magnitude of the mortgage investments of the insurance companies is shown in Table 1-8. From the mid-1870s to the mid-1880s, the proportion of total life insurance assets invested in all (farm and nonfarm) western mortgages rose from 15 to 20 percent; and, in spite of the

Table 1-7

Percentage Distribution of Premium Income by Region, Life Insurance Companies, 1874-1900

Region:	1	2	3	4	5	6	7	8	Foreign
Year									
1874	21.4	47.8	21.6	0.7	1.8	1.0	1.9	1.4	2.5
1880	16.8	45.6	20.6	1.8	3.1	2.6	2.9	3.9	2.7
1890	12.6	36.2	16.9	2.2	4.4	7.5	4.2	3.2	12.8
1900	11.3	37.1	17.5	4.3	5.1	6.3	4.1	3.1	11.1

Source: Pritchett [24]. Regions are from Poor and Poor [25].

Table 1-8

Life Insurance Companies, Western Mortgages, 1874-1900

	(1) Western Mortgages	(2) Total Assets	(3) (1)/(2)		(1) Western Mortgages	(2) Total Assets	(3) (1)/(2)
1874	62.0	425.9	14.6	1888	137.6	629.0	19.9
75	68.1	434.8	15.7	89	148.0	737.9	20.1
76	68.5	438.0	15.6	1890	173.3	796.3	21.8
77	76.5	438.9	17.4	91	185.3	865.7	21.4
78	77.5	443.5	17.6	92	191.6	950.2	20.2
79	83.7	447.1	17.5	93	216.6	1018.7	21.3
1880	79.7	462.3	17.2	94	229.3	1112.0	20.6
81	77.1	476.1	14.1	1895	234.7	1196.1	19.6
82	80.0	479.7	16.7	96	253.3	1280.0	19.8
83	96.9	508.9	19.0	97	255.4	386.0	18.4
84	107.4	529.6	20.2	98	257.8	1509.5	17.1
1885	115.3	562.4	20.3	99	259.0	1641.8	15.8
86	134.8	595.6	22.3	1900	294.5	1826.5	16.1
87	135.5	631.9	21.4				

Source: Pritchett [24]. Regions are from Poor and Poor [25].

very rapid growth of the industry, that proportion remained constant until the middle of the next decade. (During that period the volume of western mortgage credit rose from $62 million to $250 million.) For the remainder of the century, although the percentage of total assets invested in western mortgages fell, the volume continued to rise, and it reached $294 million in 1900.

The two institutional developments had done much to reduce interregional variance in interest rates, and it is possible that had nothing occurred to interfere, a national long-term market might have emerged by the beginning of World War I. Between 1875 and 1890, however, the demand for capital had shifted from the grasslands of Iowa and Kansas to semiarid plains beyond the 100th meridian, and an increasing proportion of mortgage credit was directed into that latter section. With rain profits were high and mortgages secure, and beginning in the mid-eighties a prolonged drought gripped the area. The drought brought declining incomes, multiple defaults and frequent foreclosures. Foreclosures are never costless, but in this instance the reason for default was the inability of the foreclosed unit to make a profit regardless of its management. The lending institutions themselves were threatened.

As an institution, the life insurance companies were better able to stand the economic pressure than were the mortgage banks. The latter institutions had provided investors with less risk by substituting a portfolio of mortgages for a single mortgage, but that portfolio was never better than the average mortgage it contained. For the insurance company, the risk was spread not only over a portfolio of western mortgages, but over mortgages in the East and South and over the symbolic capital issues of a number of other industries as well. While they were not as profitable in periods of western prosperity, neither were they as unprofitable in the long period of drought. The populist movement was one political manifestation of farm depression and the demise of the mortgage banking industry was one economic consequence. By 1896 all of the 167 firms listed in the New York report of 1891 had either gone into bankruptcy or withdrawn from the industry. For the insurance companies the decade saw falling investment income and a portfolio of lapsed mortgages, but relatively few bankruptcies.[27]

Intermediation: Pension Plans and the Government

Innovation did not cease in 1900, and for the more recent past it is possible to draw on the work of S. Kuznets and of R. Goldsmith for the aggregate statistics of institutional evolution.[28] Their conclusions are fairly consistent with the predictions of the model of institutional change, although the movement toward redistributive institutions makes those predictions less sharp. Over the first four decades of the twentieth century, in addition to the continued growth in both absolute and relative terms of the life insurance industry, the institutional environment was marked by the innovation of a number of pension plans, both public and private; by a series of

[27]For the industry investment income averaged 5.9 percent over the three years 1883-85 and fell to 4.5 percent in the three years 1893-95.

[28]R. Goldsmith [12], and S. Kuznets [17].

government institutions often designed to effect some income redistribution but in the process also serving some intermediation function; and by a number of institutions capable of transferring resources from saver to consumer. Both the interest series and the pattern of recent innovation suggest that by the mid-1930s the United States had an integrated national long-term capital market and that the profit potential in the traditional areas of mobilization had been exhausted. Thus, while domestic innovation in response to perceived profits continued, its nature differed, at least by degree, from the earlier developments focused as they were on transferring capital to a developing business sector.

By mid-century pension funds had grown to command over 10 percent of all assets held by financial intermediaries (compared with the 13 percent held by life insurance companies). Like the life insurance company, the pension fund was not an institution whose primary function was improvement of the capital market, but like the life insurance company, it was an institution with the ability to affect that market. In 1952 about five-sixths of the assets were held by government funds and the rest by private. At least a part of the explanation of the innovation of the government institutions almost certainly lies in a desire to redistribute income, and for an explanation of the timing of that innovation it is necessary to look at changes in the political as well as the economic environment.

The fact that a pension scheme was the redistributive instrument chosen when coupled with the evidence of innovation of similar institutions in the private sector suggests that consumers may have altered their preference for present as opposed to future income and/or that the costs of acquiring future relative to present income may have changed. Although a detailed account of the emergence of these new institutions is beyond the scope of this chapter, casual empiricism suggests that there may have been both preference and cost changes. As Goldsmith has pointed out, there were long-term shifts in the economy that would likely produce such taste changes.[29] The shift from employer to employee status made it more difficult for an individual to choose the date of his own retirement; and increasing length of life meant a greater concern about postretirement income. At the same time increases in the level of real income must have reduced the opportunity cost of deferred income. In the short run the spectre of 14 million unemployed must have made nearly everyone more aware of the problems of unemployment in a specialized economy, whether the income loss was associated with depression or forced retirement. These concerns were probably greater among lower income groups, and during the 1930s changes in the political environment reduced the costs of effecting those taste changes. The victory of the Democratic farmer-labor-black coalition greatly increased the political power of those most concerned

[29]R. Goldsmith [12].

and their ability to effect governmental institutional innovation. At the same time the emergence of a more powerful trade union movement (also a result of the new political coalition) provided the institutional structure to effect changes in the private sector. At a different level the increasingly progressive income tax must have provided an economic incentive for substituting future for present income independent of any taste or cost change.

These innovations have, however, done little to increase mobility and may have actually reduced it. Government pension funds were invested almost entirely in government bonds, and the contribution of those institutions to mobilization was minimal. The record of private funds is better, but they are sometimes regulated and, when not, frequently subject to peculiar noneconomic biases in their investment decisions. Of more importance from the point of view of mobilization were the government owned or supported lending institutions.

In terms of spatial mobility the first and probably the most important of the government institutions were the products of the Federal Farm Loan Act of 1916. The act established two parallel institutions supervised by the Federal Farm Loan Board (a Treasury bureau): federal land banks to provide money at cost to national cooperative farm loan associations and privately owned joint stock banks to lend money directly to the farm sector. To assure "equality" the nation was divided into 12 districts and the system was designed to provide a supply of capital on more or less equal terms to each.[30] While growth was relatively slow and critics charged corruption and incompetence, the impact on interregional mortgage differentials was immediate. The trend toward regional equality was rooted in the nineteenth century, but with the innovation of the new institution, the rate of closure increased dramatically. By the mid-thirties the index of interregional variance had declined to about one-ninth its 1910 level and about one-seventh the level of 1916. The proportion of all farm mortgages held by federal land banks rose to about 12 percent in the late 1920s, remained at that level until 1933, then tripled. The banks continued to hold that fraction until the outbreak of World War II. The proportion held by the joint stock banks rose to about 6 percent in 1928, remained at that level until 1933, then gradually fell to zero at the end of the decade.[31] In comparison, life insurance companies (the largest class of institutional investors in 1916) held between 10 and 15 percent from 1910 to 1925; that figure rose to about 20 percent over the next ten years, then dropped back to its original level by 1940. The federal agencies by the twenties had equalled the insurance companies, and during the thirties they were twice as important. Since the

[30]G. Soule [26].

[31]Lingould and Brown [19].

government institution pursued a low and relatively equal rate policy in all regions, it is not surprising that interregional rates continued to narrow in spite of the agricultural depression of 1921-23 and the general depression of the thirties. Since widespread foreclosures in the latter period had left the insurance companies with portfolios full of farms rather than mortgages and since the loans that produced those foreclosures were among the best, it appears that the political decision to redistribute income may have had the effect of reducing interest differentials below the levels that would reflect risk alone.

The other federal credit agencies (including the intermediate-term credit bank for agriculture established in the 1920s, the Reconstruction Finance Corporation, a product of the Hoover years, and the myriad of credit institutions that began during the Roosevelt presidency) almost certainly had similar effects. By absorbing the riskiest loans and by charging nearly the same rate in every part of the country, the governmental institutions have, perhaps artificially, guaranteed the emergence of a single long-term capital market. In the case of agriculture, for example, the government concentrated its loans among the highest risk borrowers and in the regions that otherwise would have had the largest excess demand for finance. As a result, the gradual withdrawal of the government from the farm mortgage market in the 1940s was at the expense of the low-risk borrowers and of borrowers in areas of less excess demand. As a result withdrawal did not produce an increase in interregional interest differentials.

It has been argued that legal changes coupled with governmental innovation has affected the mortgage market. In 1914 the Comptroller of the Currency permitted national banks to make mortgage loans, and that decision should have caused the commercial banks to increase their holdings of mortgages. The effects are not, however, obvious in either the farm or the nonfarm mortgage data. Commercial bank holdings of farm mortgages rose in absolute terms, but not as a percentage of total farm mortages (they remain constant at about 15 percent from 1912 to 1925). In the case of nonfarm mortgages, bank holdings double (from 5 to 10 percent) in the first decade of the century, but do not change again until 1930. There was some small increase during the depression, but the major movement of commercial banks into the mortgage market does not occur until after 1940. The innovation of government loan guarantee programs was important but changes in legal constraint were not. The absence of any obvious effect of that change is surprising and in need of further explanation.

The shift from mobilization for business to mobilization for consumer use can be seen in the behavior of the household sector. Kuznets' data show that in the decade 1900-1909, 65 percent of the sector's capital formation was financed internally; by the twenties that figure had fallen to less than 40 percent, and in the immediate post-World War II decade it was something just above 25 percent. In addition, there was of course almost no finance available to support consumption at the turn of the century. Consumer finance dates from the end of World War I, but by 1929 it accounted for 30 percent of short-term household credit. That figure reached 40 percent in 1939 and 60 percent ten years later. While commercial banks were responsible for a majority of the loans, new institutions—sales and personal finance companies—held about 15 percent of all household short-term debt by 1949.

Securities Markets and Investment Banking

Innovation in the financial sector was not confined to intermediation, there were developments in the formal markets as well. Although there were subsidiary markets in a number of cities, 1850 had already seen the centralization of the nation's security markets in New York City. The market at midcentury was, however, very different from the market that had emerged by the end of World War I. In 1856, for example, the securities of 106 firms were traded on the New York market. Forty-two of those firms were railroads and 35 were banks while only 20 were "industrials." In addition, in spite of its national character there was a decided local bias in the geographic distribution of the securities traded. The banks were almost all from New York City and the industrials were almost entirely from the Middle Atlantic states. Only the rails displayed any regional diversity. In that sector firms in the East North Central region actually outnumbered those from the two eastern regions (21 to 19 with one southern and one foreign).[32]

An efficiently operating market can increase direct saver-user transfers by (1) reducing the search costs in the marketing of new issues; and (2) by increasing liquidity and, therefore, in a risk-averse society, increasing the perceived net rate of return. The market also plays the same dual role for the intermediaries, especially in a period when those intermediaries are both small and institutionally immature.

Both the number and diversity of the issues traded on the exchange increased. The number of firms whose securities were traded reached 270 in 1900, 380 in 1920, and almost 1,200 in 1930. Total volume reached 54 million shares in 1875, 115 million in 1882, 265 million in 1902, and after continuing at about that level until the end of World War I, 1,125 million in 1929. Nor was the increase concentrated in the same industrial sectors. Utilities became important in the seventies and eighties, and in the last decade of the nineteenth century, industrials also began to play a significant role in the market's activities. While few industrials were listed before the

[32]Myers [21].

late 1880s, the innovation of preference shares to that class of issue greatly increased their importance. In the period 1890-93 the new industrial issues listed about equaled the new rail issue listed. Industrials continued to grow in importance with the large issues that were triggered by the merger movement of 1897-1902 and slightly later by the innovation of formal underwriting to industrial securities. J.P. Morgan and Company underwrote the first issue of preferred shares in 1898, and after 1902 the practice became common.[33] In 1893 the directors of the Sun, Fire and Life Insurance of London ordered their American subsidiary to sell their holdings of Proctor and Gamble bonds because "the Committee prefer in general to hold securities which are regularly quoted and dealt in, which very few of the best industrial bonds appear to be."[34] In 1898 Morgan underwrote the first industrial issue, and in 1902 his firm successfully marketed the United States Steel issue. Still, it was 1919 before the New York banks began to treat industrials equally with other securities when offered as collateral for call loans.[35]

Two very different kinds of development underwrote this growth in the formal security market. External to the financial structure, the nature of the economy was changing. Industry was growing in importance, and there were more and better information systems that reduced the uncertainties attached to investments in that sector. There were also institutional changes within the financial sector. For example, it appears that the introduction of preferred shares greatly speeded investor acceptance of new types of issues. In a world still marked by considerable uncertainty, investors seemed more willing to absorb issues whose yields were shielded from the whims of a largely unknown management.

On a more general level, the market's development was supported by parallel innovation in investment banking. Before the 1860s investment banking was carried on as one of a number of activities of unspecialized general banks, but with the innovation of specialization, the industry grew quickly. Because of his success in marketing government bonds, Jay Cooke became the prototype of the new investment banker, and at the war's end he turned from governments to railroad bonds. Cooke proved that there were profits in long-term capital mobilization if the proper institution could be found, and his experience suggested he had found it. His success induced a number of firms to copy his specialized institutional design. Typically the specialized bankers were not new firms but tended to come either from old New England commercial-financial firms (Lee, Higginson and Kidder Peabody, to name two) or from the generalized banking activities owned by immigrant German Jews (Kuhn Loeb and J. & W.

[33]Navin and Sears [22].

[34]See [20].

[35]Carosso [4].

Seligman, for example). Both Cooke and his followers profited from the war and the postwar railroad boom. The crash of 1873 pushed Cooke into bankruptcy and temporarily halted growth, but under the leadership of J.P. Morgan and the revitalized Kuhn Loeb and Company, many of the old and a number of new firms began to grow and expand.[36]

The early investment banker developed a close personal relationship with his customers, and on the basis of these informal ties, he marketed the symbolic capital of an ever-increasing number of new companies. Purchases helped educate the saver to the profitability of paper investments and made him better aware of the existence of the paper bought and sold on the formal markets. At the same time those formal markets provided that investor with greater liquidity not only for shares bought on the market but for many of those acquired through the informal markets. As late as 1880 there were relatively few persons residing outside the Northeast who were willing to hold paper securities, and even in the Northeast there were those who would buy only if they were able to deal personally with a representative of a trusted investment bank. As the 1900s became the 1910s and the 1910s the 1920s, the situation changed. People in continually broadening geographic areas and occupational classification began to purchase securities, and when those investments proved profitable, they came to depend more on the formal and less on the informal marketing arrangements.[37] In its formative (and most profitable) years the investment bank had served a double function. It acted to underwrite and, therefore, reduce the risk associated with attempts to raise capital through the sale of formal securities and by placing itself between saver and user, it reduced the uncertainties attached to "foreign" investments. The former activity continued but success in the latter sphere made the second function itself largely unnecessary. Profits in investment banking undoubtedly declined, but the education that the institution had provided made the formal markets a more effective agent in the capital mobilization process. During World War I marketing efforts in support of the government bonds increased still further membership in the group willing to hold symbolic capital, and these new recruits, when added to the original total, provided the basis for the great bull market of the twenties.

The aggregate also confirm the development and penetration of the formal capital markets. The almost tenfold increase in the number of shares traded between 1900 and 1929 was in part reflected in the share of equity in total external finance for the nonfinancial corporate sector, a figure that rose from 31 percent in the decade 1900-1909 to 43 percent in the decade

---

[36]Ibid.

[37]As early as 1905 the spatial growth was the subject of comment by a New York banker who said, "The whole Mississippi Valley gives promise that in some day, distant perhaps, it will be another New England for investments. There is a developing bond market there which is of constant astonishment to eastern dealers." Frank Vanderlip, quoted in Edwards [9].

1920-29.[38] The Crash and Depression resulted in a decline in new equity issues and the number of transactions; and as late as 1950 neither figure had returned to its 1929 peak. In spite of the collapse, even in the 1930s, there was still a functioning national securities market. For the period 1931-40, for example, sales on the New York Exchange averaged 404 million shares, a level higher than was traded in 1921-25.

In any assessment of the importance of the developments of the formal capital markets, the relationship between those markets and developments in intermediation should be kept in mind. Goldsmith's figures indicate that in 1900 one-third of all domestic corporate bonds and 8 percent of the outstanding equity of those corporations were held by financial intermediaries. By 1929 these figures had increased to one-half and 13 percent, and by 1952 to over 90 percent and to one-fifth.[39] It does not seem unreasonable to infer that the direct contributions of the formal security markets to the mobilization of domestic capital had been fairly well worked out by 1929—the framework of an effective institutional structure was in place.

Taking all of the evidence together it appears that the strains placed on the capital markets by the geographic and industrial dislocations of the nineteenth century had been largely worked out by the third decade of the twentieth. The process of geographic and industrial growth in the nineteenth and early twentieth century generated potential profits that could be captured by successful institutional innovation, and attempts to garner those profits spawned a large number of new institutional technologies. Some like the life insurance companies took root and continued to grow; others—the land mortgage companies, for example— flourished briefly and dropped by the wayside, replaced by more efficient substitutes; still others failed to achieve any noteworthy history at all. The successful innovators accrued short-run profits, but imitation and further innovation cut into those rents. The product of that competition was a national capital market. The local bankers in the West bewailed the arrival of the commercial paper house but interregional interest differentials disappeared, there were few twentieth-century counterparts of Andrew Carnegie whose fortune lay rooted in his ability to personally mobilize capital, and no single firm today dominates the investment banking system like the House of Morgan did in the last quarter of the nineteenth century.

The aggregate data too support these qualitative judgments about the maturity of the domestic financial network. The rate of growth of the financial intermediaries has slowed down since 1929. Within the sector the value of assets rose more rapidly than the number of intermediaries—an indication that growth was concentrated on existing rather than focused on the innovation of new institutional forms. Finally, there is a trend towards more equal spatial density in the location of those intermediaries—once

[38]Kuznets [17].

[39]Goldsmith [11].

again evidence that the spatial disequilibrium was being ironed out. The innovation that has occurred suggests that the largest profits are no longer concentrated in the spatial and industrial mobilization of business capital. The rise of income redistributing institutions reflects political rather than economic forces. The pension funds were not an institutional response to potential profits in the financial sector, and, unlike the insurance companies, their growth has not been associated with profits from mobilization. Finally, the development of institutions designed to transfer resources from savers to consumers moves few funds towards the business sector, regardless of industry or location. While some of these developments are the products of political decisions, the type of innovation in the private sector suggests that, after 150 years of evolution, there are no longer large profits to be captured in the traditional areas of domestic mobilization.

Appendix 1A

Three different regional classifications have been used by the authors cited in this paper. These classifications are summarized below.

I. Census
  1. *New England*
     Maine, New Hampshire, Vermont, Massachusetts, Rhode Island, Connecticut
  2. *Middle Atlantic*
     New York, New Jersey, Pennsylvania
  3. *East North Central*
     Ohio, Indiana, Illinois, Michigan, Wisconsin
  4. *West North Central*
     Minnesota, Iowa, Missouri, North Dakota, South Dakota, Nebraska, Kansas
  5. *South Atlantic*
     Delaware, Maryland, District of Columbia, Virginia, West Virginia, North Carolina, South Carolina, Georgia, Florida
  6. *East South Central*
     Kentucky, Tennessee, Alabama, Mississippi
  7. *West South Central*
     Arkansas, Louisiana, Oklahoma, Texas
  8. *Mountain*
     Montana, Idaho, Wyoming, Colorado, New Mexico, Arizona, Utah, Nevada
  9. *Pacific*
     Washington, Oregon, California
II. Comptroller of the Currency
  1. *New England*
     Maine, Vermont, New Hampshire, Massachusetts, Connecticut, Rhode Island
  2. *Eastern*
     New York, New Jersey, Pennsylvania, Delaware, Maryland, District of Columbia
  3. *Southern*
     Virginia, West Virginia, North Carolina, South Carolina, Georgia, Florida, Alabama, Mississippi, Louisiana, Texas, Arkansas, Kentucky, Tennessee

41

4. *Middle Western*
   Ohio, Indiana, Illinois, Michigan, Wisconsin, Minnesota, Iowa, Missouri
5. *Western*
   North Dakota, South Dakota, Nebraska, Kansas, Montana, Wyoming, Colorado, New Mexico, Oklahoma
6. *Pacific*
   Washington, Oregon, California, Idaho, Utah, Nevada, Arizona

III. Poor's
   1. *New England*
      Maine, New Hampshire, Vermont, Massachusetts, Rhode Island, Connecticut
   2. *Middle Atlantic*
      New York, New Jersey, Pennsylvania, Delaware, Maryland, District of Columbia
   3. *Central Northern*
      Ohio, Michigan, Indiana, Illinois, Wisconsin
   4. *South Atlantic*
      Virginia, West Virginia, North Carolina, South Carolina, Georgia, Florida
   5. *Gulf and Mississippi Valley*
      Alabama, Mississippi, Tennessee, Kentucky, Louisiana
   6. *Southwestern*
      Missouri, Arkansas, Texas, Kansas, Colorado, New Mexico, Oklahoma
   7. *Northwestern*
      Iowa, Minnesota, Nebraska, North Dakota, South Dakota, Wyoming, Montana
   8. *Pacific*
      Washington, Oregon, California, Nevada, Idaho, Arizona, Utah

References

[1] Bogue, A., *Money at Interest*, Lincoln, University of Nebraska Press, 1969.
[2] Buchanan, J., and Tullock, G., *The Calculus of Consent: Logical Foundations of Constitutional Democracy*, Ann Arbor, University of Michigan Press, 1962.

[3] Carnegie, A., *Autobiography of Andrew Carnegie*, Boston, Houghton Mifflin, 1920.

[4] Carosso, V.P., *Investment Banking in America: A History*, Cambridge, Harvard University Press, 1970.

[5] Cooper, Richard N., *Economic Mobility and National Economic Policy: The Wicksell Lectures*, 1973.

[6] Davis, L., and North, D., *Institutional Change and American Economic Growth*, New York, Cambridge University Press, 1971.

[7] Davis, L., "Capital Immobility, Institutional Adaptation, and Financial Development," *Zeitschrigt Fur Die Gesamte Stattswissenschaft*, February 1968.

[8] Davis, L., "The Investment Market, 1870-1914: The Evolution of a National Market," *Journal of Economic History*, 1965.

[9] Edwards, G.W., *The Evolution of Finance Capitalism*, Clifton, N.J., Augustus M. Kelley, 1967.

[10] Frederickson, D.M., "Mortgage Banking in the United States," *Journal of Political Economy*, 1894.

[11] Goldsmith, R., *Financial Intermediaries in the American Economy since 1900*, Princeton, Princeton University Press, 1958.

[12] Goldsmith, R., *A Study of Savings in the United States*, National Bureau of Economic Research, 1956.

[13] Greef, A.O., *The Commercial Paper House in the United States*, Cambridge, Harvard University Press, 1938.

[14] Hoecker, R., "A Study of the Farm Mortgage History in Lansing Township, Tompkins County, New York," Cornell University M.A. Thesis, 1939.

[15] Hovey, C., *The Life of J. Pierpont Morgan*, Sturgis and Walton Co., 1912.

[16] King, W.T.C., *History of the London Discount Market*, Routledge and Sons, 1936.

[17] Kuznets, S., *Capital in the American Economy; Its Function and Financing*, National Bureau of Economic Research, Princeton, Princeton University Press, 1961.

[18] Ladin, J., "The Source of Mortgage Credit for Tippecanoe County 1865-1866," *Agricultural History*, 1962.

[19] Lingould, H.T., and Brown, W.O., "Interest Charges Payable on Farm Indebtedness in the Unites States, 1910-1940, U.S. Department of Agriculture, 1942.

[20] *Minutes of the Joint Finance Committee, Sun Fire and Life Companies*, March 6, 1893.

[21] Myers, M., *The New York Money Market: Vol. 1, Origins and Development*, New York, Columbia University Press, 1959.

[22] Navin, R., and Sears, M., "The Rise of the Market for Industrial Securities, Minutes, 1887-1902," *Business History Review*, 1955.

[23] Nevins, A., *John D. Rockefeller*, New York, Charles Scribner's Sons, 1959.

[24] Pritchett, M., "A Study of Capital Mobilization: The Life Insurance Industry in the Nineteenth Century," Ph.D. Dissertation, Purdue University, 1970.

[25] Poor, H.W., and Poor, H.V., *Poor's Manual of Railroads in the United States*, Poor's Manual, Company, 1917.

[26] Soule, G., *Prosperity Decade: From War to Depression; 1917-1929*, Rinehart, 1947.

[27] Williamson, H.F., and Smalley, O., *Northwestern Mutual Life: A Century of Trusteeship*, Evanston, Ill., Northwestern University Press, 1957.

[28] Yarnall, S.I., "Farm Mortgage Charges and Interest Rates 1940-48, U.S. Department of Agriculture Bulletin no. 8210.

[29] Zartman, I., *Investments of Life Insurance Companies*, Henry Holt, 1906.

Comment: The Evolution of the American Capital Market, 1860-1940: A Case Study in Institutional Change

Anna J. Schwartz

Lance Davis recapitulates in this chapter his 1965 *Journal of Economic History* essay, "The Investment Market, 1870-1914: The Evolution of a National Market," and extends it a decade back to the eve of the Civil War and two and a half decades forward to the eve of World War II. Below I review the main propositions and offer general criticisms of their design and of the evidence on which they are based.

The Main Proposition

This long and diffuse chapter can be summarized under six heads: (1) the focus of the chapter; (2) the capital market at the outset of the period covered; (3) the capital market at the close of the period; (4) the development of the short-term national capital market; (5) the development of the long-term national capital market; (6) capital market developments other than the promotion of capital mobility.

 1. *The focus of the chapter* is on financial innovation that promoted capital mobility, smoothing its transfer from surplus to deficit savings units in different geographical and industrial locations. The chapter argues that before 1920 (at another point, 1900 is mentioned as the dividing line), financial innovation in the United States was a response to income increasing opportunities that exogenous changes in technology or spatial expansion generated; thereafter, those opportunities to increase total income declined, and "a substantial part of financial innovation" was a response to income redistributive opportunities available "at the expense of others" (p. 10), or involved the movement of "funds from saver to consumer rather than from saver to business". Financial innovation need not be original in conception: it may be borrowed from other countries and adapted to local conditions. It may also be a well-known technique not therefore put to use.

 2. *At the outset of the period, in 1860,* the United States is described as having "no national capital market in any modern sense of the word" nor has it developed local capital markets. Commercial banks in 1860 mobilized capital locally and for short-term use only. Mutual savings banks and life insurance companies confined their long-term investments, for legal or

philosophical reasons, to uses of funds with relatively certain outcomes. Usury laws also discouraged risky investments since the equilibrium rate on such uses exceeded the legal limit. The evidence that a national market did not exist is said to be "high interregional and interindustry differentials in the cost of finance and . . . the importance of informal arrangements (and the magnitude of the profits attached to those arrangements) in the provision of finance for new areas and activities". "If a national market had existed, the price of finance net of risk differentials should not have differed between regions or industries by more than the cost of transport, and the profits accruing to firms engaged in interindustry or interregion financial arbitrage should be no higher than those earned in any competitive industry. Differentials were higher and so were profits". The firms that did engage in the transfer of capital are said to have earned "monopoly profits available in an industry where the absence of an institutional structure makes entry difficult".

3. *The history of financial innovation in the post-Civil War period,* according to Davis, accounts for the development of a "single, national short-term market by the outbreak of World War I" and of a "single, closely-integrated, national [long-term] capital market" two decades later. The evidence that a national market did exist is that "interregional interest differentials had largely disappeared" by the aforementioned dates. It is argued that "profits in investment banking undoubtedly declined", and as proof the fact is adduced that when J.P. Morgan & Company was forced to divest itself of its commercial bank activities, most of the partners opted for commercial banking, in spite of the competition (p. 16). There is a strong suggestion that an era of financial innovation in the service of spatial and industrial mobilization of business capital has come to a close: since 1929 innovation of new institutional forms is said to have declined; the rate of growth of the number of financial intermediaries, though not of the value of their assets, has declined; and the spatial density of the location of the intermediaries has become more equal.

4. *What were the innovations in the short-term capital market that led to a national market by World War I?* In the United States, unlike the case of the United Kingdom, branch banking was not "on the legal menu of alternatives"; the regulatory agencies, moreover, are said to have discouraged interregional mobilization of capital; the sole innovation that encouraged capital transfers from high interest to low interest areas that is cited was the commercial paper house. The evidence offered for the development of a national market by 1914 is two-fold: (1) a downward trend in the variance of regional rates of return on capital in nonreserve city national banks, 1869-1914, that is described as lowering the variance "to about one-fifth of its initial level" by 1914; (2) a table citing the dates of the entry of a commercial paper house into an area and the subsequent dates when

the interest differentials between a region's cities decline, and still later dates when the interest differentials between a region's country districts decline. The discussion of the short-term capital market concludes with a reference to the elimination of the commercial paper house as an effective force by the rise of the national borrowing firm that borrowed in low interest eastern cities and transferred the funds to its offices in the "high interest West". The chapter cites no date for the rise of the national borrowing firm.

5. *More attention is devoted to the emergence of a national long-term capital market*. The problems for innovation to overcome are described as more complex, not only providing for mobilization but also for accumulation of funds; the absence of an institutional counterpart of the commercial bank; the greater uncertainties in long-term lending. Although quantitative evidence is fragmentary, the regional differences in long-term yields "were greater at the beginning of the period" than in the short-term capital market (p. 21), and the development of the national market was slower. Two influences on the narrowing of the differentials are referred to: (1) the end of geographical expansion; (2) institutional innovation. The first is dismissed and the influence of "substantial innovation" credited with the satisfaction of the increasing capital demands of the business sector and of the shift of the demand from the East to the West. Institutional developments in intermediation of the interregional shift in capital demand are discussed at some length. Why mortgage land companies that pioneered the issue of debentures against a portfolio of mortgages did not flourish in this country, although they did in Europe, is described. They were displaced by the life insurance companies, which succeeded in transferring eastern savings into western agriculture. In addition to these private institutions, the role of the federal land banks and the Federal Farm Loan Board in pursuing "a low and equal rate policy in all regions" (p. 34) is referred to as having reduced interregional variance in mortgage loan rates. The loosening of the legal constraint on mortgage loans by national banks in 1914 was less important than the government loan guarantee programs established much later in inducing banks to acquire such assets.

Let me now refer to the evidence offered in support of the theme of the gradual evolution of a long-term national market. First, Davis notes (without citation) regional differences in the ratio of loans to securities plus loans of reporting private and savings banks. Institutions in the East had a lower proportion of assets invested in loans than did their counterparts in the West, presumably because loans were higher yielding in the West, and while the differences persisted, they narrowed. Second, he gives a table of regional relatives of mortgage rates of interest on acres and lots, drawn from the Eleventh Census, for the decade of the 1880s, showing greater interregional variance for urban than for rural mortgages, with both declining about half over the decade. Third, he gives a table of regional relatives of interest on farm mortgages in place from statewide data compiled annually by the Department of Agriculture since 1910, showing a falling trend in the interregional variance. Fourth, for four dates between 1874 and 1900, he gives the percentage of all allocable assets of a small sample of life insurance companies invested in mortgages, bonds, and stocks, by region, showing a redistribution from the Northeast to other regions, with the percentage distribution of premium income, by region, of these companies, at those dates, showing some gradual increase in geographic dispersion. In addition, for a sample of 29 life insurance companies in four regions, he gives the variance of relatives of mortgage rates of interest by region of the lending company, showing a decline for the period 1877-1904. Finally, he shows the percent of total assets of these companies invested in western mortgages, over the same period, an upward trend until 1890, subsequently reversing itself.

Following the treatment of the institutions involved in the interregional shift in capital demand, there is a briefer discussion of developments in the formal securities market that assisted the business sector in obtaining external finance. Two innovations are singled out; formal underwriting of industrial securities and the introduction of preferred shares by J.P. Morgan in 1898. Underwriting of industrials was a response to the growing importance of industry and preferred shares "speeded investor acceptances of" the new issues. As a result, "both the number and diversity of the issues traded on the exchange increased". Investment banking was the institutional vehicle that served the capital mobilization process. Financial intermediaries in general were important because they held a significant share of all domestic corporate bonds, although not of equity.

6. *Institutional evolution since 1900, Davis says, has been marked by a movement toward redistributive institutions,* in which he includes pension plans, both public and private, and other government institutions that may also serve some intermediation function, but are mainly designed to effect redistribution, and by a movement towards institutions transferring resources from saver to consumer, in contrast to earlier ones that transferred resources to a developing business sector (pp. 32-33). He speculates on the possible reasons for the emergence of pension plans, and notes that they have done little to increase mobility and may have reduced it. He does not regard the rise of these institutions as a response to potential profits in the financial sector. As for the consumer finance industry, a post-World War I development, the commercial banks, and two new institutions, sales and finance companies, nurtured it. The industry presumably was created in response to potential profits, but its existence confirms for Davis that "there are no longer large profits to be made in the traditional areas of mobilization".

General Criticisms

Let me say at the outset that I believe that a national capital market has evolved in the United States although it did not exist in 1860, but I do not believe that Davis has gone about demonstrating the case for this hypothesis in an effective manner. The earmark of a national market for Davis appears to be the absence of interregional interest differentials. Before embarking on any historical investigation, does it not seem obvious that he should first have examined the variance of interregional interest differences currently, when presumably there is no question that the capital market is national? It may come as a surprise to him that interregional interest differentials may still be observed. Each issue of the *Federal Reserve Bulletin*, for example, contains a table of rates on business loans of banks in New York City and six other regions, at quarterly intervals, showing short-term, revolving credit, and long-term loans, classified in five sizes. Differentials in 1974 between regions vary from under 1 percent to nearly 6 percent. It has long been known that the wide variation in rates on loans that may be observed even currently reflects differences in size of loan and other characteristics more than it reflects differences in city or region. Here we have current Federal Reserve data that standardize for size of loan but not for other characteristics, and so interregional differences still appear. Are they true interregional differences or the reflection of heterogeneity in the group of loans that are priced? No one can say. Had Davis taken the current variance as a benchmark, at least one would have some criterion by which to judge the variances that he reports for earlier dates. It is certain that the declining trend in the variances that he reports cannot be interpreted simply in the manner that he suggests. The trend may reflect the closing of interregional differences but may equally well reflect increasing homogeneity of loan characteristics among regions.

It appears to me also that Davis exaggerates the extent of the decline in the variances. Until the middle 1880s, the national bank variances are indeed at a higher level than subsequently. There is no real downward movement over the balance of the pre-World War I variances. Davis acknowledges that the movement is not unidirectional but interprets increases in the variance as cyclical in nature. It may be that during business contractions loan characteristics become more dissimilar, and hence widen the spread in interest rates that is observed. Accordingly, I am also dubious about the validity of the table showing dates when interregional differences are said to close.

Let me also note that I do not believe that Davis was well advised to pinpoint the date of the establishment of a national market. He says that it was 1914 for the short-term market. What are we to make of the differential in Federal Reserve discount rates between most districts that characterized the 1920s and that encouraged rate trading across district lines? It also seems to me that mention only of the commercial paper house as promoting the rise of a national market is unduly restrictive. The development of correspondent bank relationships, the development of lending on the New York call loan market by interior banks, the creation of clearing houses, the distribution of Treasury deposits geographically, bank sales of drafts on the interior, to mention only a few, are important factors that contributed to the rise of a national money market before World War I; thereafter, I would also mention the beginnings of the federal funds market in the 1920s.

The notion that it was the legal prohibition of branch banking in the United States that prevented development along lines observed in other countries seems to be doubtful. The law reflected the underlying economic reality that, in most sections of the United States before 1914, branch banking would not have been a profitable way of organizing banks: funds would have moved to the branches from the parent bank with no basis for a return flow. Where branch banking took hold, the law did not prevent the development. If national branch banking would have been the institution of choice, the law would have reflected that consensus. Davis, moreover, misstates what the Comptroller of the Currency ruled in 1890 regarding the sale of certificates of deposit by banks in high interest areas to banks in low interest areas. He did not move to stop the practice, as Davis has it. The Comptroller objected only to the misclassification of such sales as deposits, when in fact they were interbank loans.

Most of the points I have made with respect to the short-term market apply also to the long-term market. I do not accept Davis' dating of the emergence of a national market in 1933. I would want to know the size of the variance interregionally in the current long-term market. I am also doubtful that the private investment banking houses before 1910 were reaping monopoly gains. The risks they took were commensurate with their returns. I do not understand why Davis believes that the absence of an institutional structure made entry difficult into the investment banking business.

The fact that interregional differences in interest rates were greater at the beginning of the period in the long-term than in the short-term market undoubtedly reflects higher risk differentials on mortgage loans than on commercial loans, not necessarily a difference in the degree of nationalization existing at the start. As the risk differentials declined between frontier regions and regions that were settled earlier, the variance also declined. As Davis himself notes, the quality of mortgages varied "not only with the general state of agriculture, but also with the quality of the individual farm, to say nothing . . . of the quality of the individual farmer". None of the mortgage interest figures he presents standardizes for these differences, so one really cannot say what is being compared in the regional averages. I am doubtful that the mid-thirties figure of interregional variance is a reliable basis for arguing that it was the impact of the Federal Farm Loan Act that produced a closing of interregional mortgage differentials. It was more likely the consequence of the generally low level of depression mortgage rates.

One point that Davis might have discussed is the reason he computed relatives of the interest rates before calculating the variance. He did not calculate the variance directly from the actual interest rate figures. Presumably the choice of procedure was dictated by the desire to avoid bias in the variance attributable to trend in interest rates. But this is a matter Davis should have dealt with explicitly instead of passing over it in silence.

The discussion of developments in the formal securities market is rather sketchy. In addition to the two innovations Davis mentions, he might also have referred to the role of the trust companies as institutional investors, their nationwide operations, the development of syndicates to purchase or underwrite an issue, the advertising of new issues, the installment plan for retail purchase of securities, and similar items.

The shift in the focus of the chapter from financial innovation to promote capital mobility to innovation to effect redistribution of income and to shift resources to consumers in my view should not have been made. The chapter would be more unified if Davis had concentrated on the capital mobilization theme and ended by a discussion of post-World War II financial innovation directed at a world capital market. The same issues can be treated from the standpoint of intercountry variance as of interregional variance.

Reference

Davis, Lance E., "The Investment Market, 1870-1914: The Evolution of a National Market," *Journal of Economic History* 25 (3), September 1965, pp. 355-99.

2 Towards a Theory of Financial Innovation

William L. Silber

Introduction

The structure of the financial sector of an economy is described by its institutions, instruments, and markets. Changes in the financial structure occur when new financial institutions emerge, or when new financial instruments or new markets are innovated. J.G. Gurley and E. Shaw [23] discussed the impact of a particular group of financial institutions, financial intermediaries, on economic development. Recently, L.E. Davis and D.C. North [14] developed a more general theory of institutional change, and applied it in a number of areas including the financial sector. Part I of this chapter continues in this direction and focuses on the interrelationship between financial sector innovations and real economic performance from a macroeconomic standpoint. Within the financial sector the relationship between institutions, instruments, and markets is examined in detail.

The main concern of this study, however, is with the microeconomics of innovation in financial structure. Part II discusses the factors leading to innovation of new instruments and/or practices by financial firms. After a theory of instrument innovation is suggested, we attempt an analysis of its empirical validity within an historical context. Our understanding of the financial sector will be greatly enhanced if our theory identifies the common elements in such diverse financial innovation is, for example, the introduction of industrial insurance in 1875 and negotiable certificates of deposit in 1961.

The study of innovation of financial instruments and practices is not nearly as well-developed as its counterpart in the real sector. The theoretical and empirical work by J.A. Schumpeter [51], E. Mansfield [35], J. Schmookler [50], and F.M. Scherer [49], to name a few, on innovation in the real sector is well known. The similarities and differences in financial sector innovation compared with real sector innovation is discussed in Part II.

This study was conducted under the American Life Insurance Association Grant to the Salomon Brothers Center for the Study of Financial Institutions, New York University. Helpful comments were received from Kenneth Garbade, Stephen Goldfeld, Michael Hamburger, Dwight Jaffee, Herman Krooss, Nat Leff, and Lawrence Ritter.

Part I

Characteristics of the Financial Sector

This section describes some of the key characteristics and institutions of the financial sector of the economy. The basic functions of money, financial assets, secondary markets, and financial intermediaries, and their relationship to real economic activity are reviewed. This sets the framework for describing the macrostimuli to financial sector evolution in the next two sections.

The utility of money, where money is often considered the most fundamental financial instrument, is rooted in the exchange process of the real sector. K. Brunner and A.H. Meltzer [8] have shown that as long as economic units exchange real goods among themselves, and as long as uncertainty exists, the cost of exchange can be reduced if one good serves as a medium of exchange. Whether full-bodied commodity money is called a "financial asset" or whether that term is reserved for fiat money is not discussed here. We note only that the innovation of money responds to a stimulus in the real sector and in turn influences the potential path of real economic activity. The latter occurs because, as the cost of exchange is reduced, production and/or leisure can increase.

The emergence of securities (equities and debt instruments) is an unambiguous financial innovation. As long as there exist "deficit" units that want to spend more than their current income and accumulated wealth permits and "surplus" units that want to spend less than their current income, financial assets and liabilities will be created. Deficit units issue "primary" securities that are purchased by surplus units. Purchasing power over real resources is redistributed. This reallocation of real resources from less useful or less productive activities to more useful or more productive activities is a major contribution of the financial sector to real economic activity.

In order to facilitate the transfer of funds between saver-lenders and investor-borrowers, a market in primary securities might emerge. Economic units might find it profitable to become brokers between borrowers and lenders, collecting and disseminating information between potential sources and uses of funds. Such brokerage (or dealer) services in the primary securities market do, in fact, exist in the form of investment banking firms.

The development of a market for primary securities is perfectly analogous to the emergence of a market for any good. Indeed, classical economists included the market for the loanable funds *represented* by such securities within the conceptual framework of the real sector of the economy. It is important to distinguish this "distribution" market for primary securities from secondary markets in such securities.

Secondary markets permit holders of financial assets to dispose of the security at their own discretion, rather than depending on the redemption schedule of the issuer. Secondary markets provide liquidity to holders of securities, where liquidity is defined as the ability to turn an asset into cash quickly with little loss in value. A security holder is willing to pay for such liquidity services because, as long as there is uncertainty over the time horizon he wishes to hold the security (his holding period), such liquidity services increase the flexibility of his consumption opportunities. Deficit units also have an interest in the existence of secondary markets for their securities since the interest rate demanded by lenders is less the greater the marketability of the security. The innovation of secondary markets for financial assets lowers interest rates, and, therefore, has an impact on the real sector.

The existence of a secondary market for a financial asset changes the nature of the security issued by the deficit unit. By transforming a relatively illiquid asset into one with greater liquidity, the characteristics of the security differ from the characteristics of the underlying real investment. To society as a whole, of course, the mere existence of a secondary market could not transform an illiquid real investment into a liquid security. But a secondary market takes advantage of the different needs for liquidity by individual economic units at different moments in time. This relationship becomes clear once it is recognized that liquidity vanishes with a sudden preference by *all* economic units to liquidate their financial assets at a particular point in time.

The innovation of securities and markets to facilitate the movement of savings into the most profitable investments is one function of the financial sector. The stochastic nature of returns on real investment adds another dimension to the financial sector. The celebrated article by K.J. Arrow [4] underscored the role of securities and securities markets in the allocation of risk bearing in the economy. It is well-known that *risk*, defined as variance of returns, can be reduced through diversification, that is, by holding a portfolio of different securities whose stochastic outcomes are more or less independent of each other.

Without a financial sector such diversification to reduce risk could be undertaken by a firm's choice of real investment projects. There is no doubt that some nonfinancial diversification does, in fact, occur. But "direct diversification" is a less efficient way to lower risk compared with financial diversification. If a firm combines, say, two investments with negative covariance of returns, all individuals are then forced to hold these two investments in the *same* proportion. With diversity of preferences among economic units, this shrinkage of the opportunity set is inefficient. Financial claims, on the other hand, can be held by individuals in different proportions. A second disadvantage of direct diversification stems from conflicting criteria that may emerge from factors determining the optimum size of a productive organization (see A.A. Alchian and H. Demsetz [2]) . The financial sector provides the additional *option* of separating the "size of firm" decision from risk-diversification considerations.

The continued evolution of financial institutions and instruments is best explained within the context of risk reduction. Financial intermediaries emerge because, given transactions costs, their size gives them a comparative advantage over individuals in the effort to reduce risk via diversification. To the extent that there are economies of scale in the acquisition of information or expertise they can further lower risk. The myriad of financial instruments (equities, bonds, preferred stock, deposits, etc.) issued by firms in the real sector as well as financial firms helps to distribute exposure to risk among economic units more efficiently.

Macroanalysis of Financial Sector Development

The discussion outlined above suggests a number of conditions in the real sector that may lead to opportunities for financial innovation. These include: (1) factors that alter the size and/or composition of surplus and deficit units, such as an increase in total saving or shifts in the composition of real expenditures; (2) technological progress, such as computers and financial theory that alter the costs of specific financial services; and (3) changes in risks or attitudes towards risk, such as increased uncertainty over the future course of inflation or increased (decreased) instability in real economic activity.

Financial innovation will occur to the extent that these factors lead to profitable or "utility increasing" opportunities. Whether an individual firm is induced to innovate or whether collective action or government intervention is required, is an important issue, and is discussed by L.E. Davis and D.C. North [14]. We will indicate by specific example some of the conditions leading to collective action and/or government intervention.

Financial innovation need not stem from purely real sector phenomena. Distribution of risk bearing might be improved by the creation of new financial claims that cater to changing utility functions or altered competitive relationships. Indeed, much financial innovation by individual firms is no doubt aimed at altering the competitive nature of the financial markets. By moving from a purely competitive position to one with some monopoly power a financial firm might be able to increase its profits (at least for a while). Furthermore, reducing the risk associated with a financial transaction itself is another source of innovation. A sudden preference for increased liquidity may lead to new types of financial assets or new markets. As in the case of innovations generated from the real sector, financial firms will perceive these forces in different ways, as we will see in Part II.[1]

The process of financial development is best illustrated by way of example. Specific hypotheses will emerge regarding the innovation of instruments, markets, and institutions. The interrelationship between these three aspects of the financial sector can then be discussed.

A new financial instrument can be stimulated by any of the forces just discussed. An increase in a particular category of real expenditure, such as residential construction, may lead to deficit units supplying a new type of instrument in order to attract funds at lower cost. In this case a debt instrument with first claim on the real property it is used to finance would be introduced. Lenders might be willing to lower the interest charges on such loans to the extent that the risk of such a new instrument reduces total portfolio risk. Similarly, as long as lenders perceive differences between federal, state-local, and corporate issuers, deficit spending by any of these groups will lead to a new category of securities.

A second example of innovation concerns the financial firm's response to a new risk in the economy. Increased interest rate variability or uncertainty over inflation may induce firms to innovate financial assets that protect individuals from such uncertainties. The objective, of course, is to increase the firm's profitability. For now let us assume that the creation of new financial instruments occurs either as a result of the emergence of a new deficit unit, such as state-local governments, or as an attempt by various economic units to improve their competitive position for funds via product differentiation.[2]

The creation of new financial instruments raises the question of whether secondary markets for such instruments will develop. The ease with which secondary markets are created influences the yields on new securities, since the marketability of a security is an important determinant of its yield. The ease with which new secondary markets are established, therefore, also determines the rate at which new instruments are innovated. For if secondary markets are very costly to establish, then yields on new

---

[1] We have not discussed innovation that responds to government regulation as yet. Financial innovation does, indeed, respond to regulation as we will see. The welfare implications of such financial innovation are unclear. To the extent that the regulation succeeds in promoting a socially desirable objective it would appear that circumventing such regulations via innovation reduces welfare. But optimum regulatory policies should, in fact, anticipate private sector reactions, in which case the induced innovations would promote social objectives.

[2] Differentiated financial instruments are often ascribed to imperfections in the capital markets and government regulation (see Gurley and Shaw [24]). In the absence of imperfections it still seems correct to expect an efficient financial sector to have various types of financial instruments (equities, preferred stock, convertible bonds, and so on) as long as individual economic units have different preference functions. Product differentiation by financial firms appears to permit a redistribution of risks among economic units so that the subjective risk borne by the economy is minimized.

categories of securities will be higher and borrowers may find it more attractive to finance their expenditures with existing securities. We turn now to a specific analysis of the interrelationship between instruments and markets. This will also lead to a discussion of intermediaries and markets.

Instruments, Markets, and Intermediaries: Some Interrelationships

The work by H. Demsetz [15] and S.M. Tinic [55] on the economics of liquidity services helps define the conditions that determine the likelihood of a secondary market being established. A comparison of the revenues from operating a secondary market with the costs will determine the expected profitability of such an institution. We first look at the revenues and then turn to the cost side.

The revenues accruing to the operation of a secondary market are determined by the price that people are willing to pay for such services and the volume of securities traded at such prices. The volume side of the picture explains the importance of a large quantity of a security outstanding for the operation of a secondary market. The price that economic units are willing to pay is determined by the marginal utility of liquidity services. One factor that obviously influences the marginal utility of liquidity services is the existing level of liquidity from other sources. The existence of highly liquid assets will, ceteris paribus, discourage the establishment of secondary markets for new securities. Of particular interest on this score is the liquidity provided by financial intermediaries, and therefore, the relationship between intermediaries and markets.[3]

The ability of financial intermediaries to diversify more efficiently than individuals and therefore to reduce the subjective risk borne by the economy was stressed above. Intermediaries can, therefore, issue liabilities that are less risky than the primary securities issued by deficit units. In addition, intermediaries are also able to take advantage of the offsetting needs for funds by different economic units. Financial intermediaries can, therefore, also issue liabilities with greater liquidity than the primary securities purchased, that is, they can promise to redeem their liabilities for cash on short notice even without resorting to secondary markets. In other words, intermediaries perform some of the same functions as secondary markets. In our context the marginal utility of liquidity services in the form of new secondary markets is lower in the presence of

---

[3]The size of real money balances held by society clearly affects the marginal utility of liquidity services. The relationship between money balances and secondary markets within the context of the optimum quantity of money literature is explored in W.L. Silber [52].

financial intermediaries. This may be a partial explanation for the difficulty underdeveloped countries have encountered in establishing secondary markets.[4] Most of these countries have transplanted the financial intermediaries that have evolved in developed countries. Given such intermediaries, the subsequent difficulty in promoting secondary markets is not too surprising.[5]

The cost side of secondary markets is influenced by many factors, such as those associated with inventory-carrying by market makers (Tinic [55, pp. 80-83]). The key to historical changes in costs, however, is likely to be most dependent on changes in the state of technology in communications and information. The more advanced the technology, the lower the cost, and the smaller need be the volume of the security outstanding in order to justify a secondary market. The homogeneity of the security is relevant as well since it helps define the size of the market. To the extent that increased information and communication permits market makers to group securities into homogeneous classes there may be further inducements to secondary markets as a result of technological breakthroughs in information and communication.

An example of size of market and the degree of homogeneity of a security is the mortgage market. Although the volume of mortgages currently outstanding exceeds the volume of corporate bonds in the United States, the lack of uniformity in the mortgage contract and the inability to standardize credit ratings has acted as a barrier to the operation of a secondary market. In essence, there are many small mortgage markets rather than one large one.

A collective attempt at standardizing the mortgage contract and the establishment of uniform credit evaluation for mortgages (and the ability to store and transfer such information) would increase the feasibility of a secondary market. This has, in fact, occurred quite recently with the Federal National Mortgage Association and the secondary market in FHA mortgages and the Federal Home Loan Mortgage Corporation and conventional mortgages. This leads directly to the issue of whether secondary markets are public or semipublic goods that require collective or government action.

[4]For a discussion of secondary markets in underdeveloped countries see R.C. Porter [43], [44].

[5]A complementary relationship also exists between intermediaries and markets, if only because intermediaries need markets for at least some of the primary securities they hold. Intermediaries also increase the total volume of securities outstanding by lowering the interest rate charged to deficit units. The "size effect" is beneficial to potential secondary markets. If permitted to develop on their own, perhaps the complementary relationship dominates and the dynamics are such that secondary markets grow with intermediaries. Alternatively, perhaps they both respond to other forces, such as an increase in aggregate saving or real technological progress that makes both intermediaries and markets more profitable to operate.

Whether the establishment of a secondary market, or, for that matter, any market, requires collective action or government intervention depends upon whether the use of a market is characterized by either nonexcludability or jointness of consumption.[6] Either of these characteristics produces a divergence between private and social costs and/or benefits, and therefore requires collective action. A market produces the service of bringing buyers and sellers together. It gathers and disseminates information about prices of recent trades as well as bid and ask data for potential exchanges. It also provides a forum for initiating and consummating actual trades. It is clearly possible to exclude individuals from the use of both of these market services. In other words, someone could charge for the privilege of using the information and trading facilities of a market. Hence, a market does not have the characteristic of nonexcludability. On the other hand, market services do appear to be characterized by jointness. For example, one person's access to price and bid-ask information does not infringe on another person's use of that information.[7]

It is important to emphasize the term collective action rather than government intervention since private individuals, acting as a group, could produce the socially optimal level of market-making services. For example, all issuers of, say, corporate bonds would benefit if a secondary market were established. It is conceivable, therefore, that a group of large firms would jointly assure a potential market maker of an adequate volume of debt financing to justify the operation of a secondary market. Something like this occurred when the negotiable certificate of deposit (CD) was introduced in 1961 by New York City banks. In particular, a sufficiently large volume was assured to brokerage firms so that they agreed to make a market in that security.[8]

---

[6]These are the two characteristics of public goods as discussed in R.A. Musgrave and P.B. Musgrave [40]. Nonexcludability refers to the impossibility of limiting the consumption of a particular good to an individual. The classic example is national defense. In particular, if one person protects himself against nuclear attack, all of those surrounding him are similarly protected. They cannot be excluded from consuming the good as is possible in "normal" goods. Jointness refers to the ability of two or more people to consume jointly the good or service without reducing each other's utility. These two characteristics often go together (as with national defense) but sometimes they do not (as with a bridge or highway that has jointness but does not suffer from nonexcludability).

[7]It is less clear that the trading initiation and execution function of a market is characterized by jointness. In particular, if one executes a trade with another based on the information provided, there are fewer people (or fewer dealer funds) left over for a second person to trade with. On the other hand, this "erosion of jointness" is similar to the case of a bridge (the classic public good as a result of jointness). Since there are indivisibilities in providing the services of a bridge (it is very expensive to justify for one economic unit) there is likely to be jointness in consumption until the bridge becomes crowded, at which point jointness in consumption disappears. The ability to initiate and execute a trade in an established market has similar characteristics. It seems reasonable to conclude, therefore, that both services provided by a market exhibit jointness and therefore require collective action.

[8]See R. Fieldhouse [17].

A second example is the introduction of the automated quotation system for over-the-counter securities (called NASDAQ) by the National Association of Securities Dealers in 1971. Such trade associations are ideal vehicles for collective action of the type described. In instances where the individual issuers of a category of securities are too small or are fragmented, the government might have to intervene in order to promote market-making activities. The mortgage market cited above is a good example.

The Need for a Micro Approach

There are a number of hypotheses that could be tested empirically in light of the discussion thus far. This is especially true with respect to secondary markets. A historical comparison of secondary market development today versus that of a century ago, with the implied differences in the technology of communication and information, is straightforward. Similarly, a comparison of secondary markets in underdeveloped economies with and without financial intermediaries as well as the importance of government intervention in the process is another area of potential empirical work. Aside from the studies by R.L. Sandor [48], R.C. Porter [43] and G.A. Akerlof [1], little analysis of secondary market development has been undertaken.

While this approach is capable of confirming or denying the interrelationships discussed above, it is more fruitful at this point to develop a microanalysis of the innovative process in the financial sector and to test its validity. As we mentioned above, the macrostimuli to financial innovation are perceived in different ways by financial firms. There may also be a difference between the dynamic reaction of a firm to a particular stimulus and a comparative statics analysis of the innovative process on a macro level. We leave, for now, the overview of financial sector evolution and turn to the innovative process from the standpoint of the financial firm.

Part II

Innovation: The Approach and Relevant Literature

The objective in the remainder of this chapter is to analyze financial innovation from a microeconomic standpoint. There are a number of components to the analysis. In this section the theory of innovation in the real sector is examined for its potential financial sector implications. We then

62

turn to the theory of behavior of the financial firm to provide a framework for decision making with regard to innovation of financial instruments and practices. The impact of regulation on innovations is dealt with in particular detail because of its apparent importance in recent historical periods. Finally, the concluding sections present a suggestive analysis of the characteristics of actual innovations and an historical evaluation of their proximate causes.

Innovation has been given very specific and somewhat more general meanings. J.A. Schumpeter [51] used the term in a very special way, relating it to the implementation of a new process or method that alters the production possibilities of a firm. The term has been used more broadly by E. Mansfield [35], J. Schmookler [50], and F.M. Scherer [49]. These writers distinguish between process innovation and product innovation, that is, the introduction of a new product. Futhermore, there are major innovations and minor or routine innovations. It would seem that a "routine product innovation," such as discussed by K.E. Knight [31], is very much like product differentiation by firms within an oligopolistic or monopolistically competitive industry. To the extent that this is correct, the theory of monopolistic competition is a relevant analytical framework for explaining part of the innovative process.[9]

The hypotheses aimed at explaining innovation are as diverse as the types of innovations under scrutiny. Schumpeter argued that large firms (especially those with monopoly power) were most likely to innovate, because the cost of failure could more easily be absorbed. Others have suggested that the small competitive firm is the most likely innovator as it attempts to break into established markets. J. Schmookler [50] is noted for his hypothesis that innovations tend to rise and fall with the sales of the product that they produce.[10] These alternative hypotheses can only be resolved by empirical tests, such as those conducted by Mansfield [35].

There has also been interdisciplinary work by behavioral scientists and economists on the characteristics of the innovative firm. R.M. Cyert and J.G. March [13], S.W. Becker and F. Stafford [5], and K.E. Knight [31] mention two types of innovative pressures: (1) success-slack innovation and (2) failure-distress innovation. Under the first category the successful organization can afford to devote resources aimed at radical innovation. Under the second category an organization faced with adversity or failure will be induced to innovate. The objective of the organization or firm under both types of innovation is utility maximization, although it is usually stressed that there are other factors besides profits and variance of profits that influence behavior, such as firm growth and market share (these either enter as part of the firm's objective function or are constraints on its behavior).

[9]Many innovations in the financial sector fall into this category.

[10]An excellent survey of alternative theories of innovation is chapter 15 in F.M. Scherer [49].

A study by R.R. Nelson and S.G. Winter [41] attempts a more formal integration between organizational theory and technological change. Their "evolutionary" theory of innovation stresses an incremental search process that is triggered by a firm's rate of return falling below target levels.

In contrast with the extensive treatment of the microeconomics of innovation in the real sector, the literature on financial innovation is quite sparse. Of the studies mentioned above, only Becker and Stafford [5] examined innovation by financial firms. Their study was based on a questionnaire survey of the practices of savings and loan associations in Cook County, Illinois during the 1961-63 period. It is surprising that no subsequent empirical work has been done. On the theoretical front there have been some very specific inquiries into the effects of financial innovations. We will discuss these as a point of departure for our framework of financial innovation.

Financial Innovation: What It Means

When dealing with innovation in the real sector it is possible to limit the scope of analysis by an objective criterion: an innovation is a new product or process that qualifies for patent protection. There is simply no such counterpart in the financial sector. But economists concerned with the study of innovations in the real sector have pointed out the dangers of relying solely on patent data, for example, Mansfield [35] and Scherer [49]. Certainly those who discuss routine product innovation have no such objective criterion.

In analyzing financial innovation we have no choice but to create our own criterion. The best we can do is to generalize the accepted use of the term as it has been employed in specific financial market developments, such as: the emergence of negotiable certificates of deposit (CDs) and Eurodollars during the 1960s (A.J. Meigs [37]); the computerization of the demand depositor-banker relationship (G.W. Mitchell [38]); the introduction of term loans into bank portfolios and the growth in the practice of amortizing mortgage loans during the 1930s (H. Krooss and M. Blyn [32]); and the introduction of industrial insurance (1875) and group insurance (1911) by the life insurance industry (*Life Insurance Fact Book* [33]). The list could, of course, be extended considerably.

A number of characteristics of these innovations are worth mentioning. There is a distinction between process innovation (e.g., computers in banking) and product innovation (e.g., negotiable CDs) in the financial sector similar to the distinction in the real sector. Most innovations do not create something totally new. Rather, they combine existing financial technology in a new way (e.g., adding negotiability to a nonnegotiable instrument). The term innovation is also extended to the use of an already existing financial instrument by a firm or an industry that previously did not deal in such instruments. And here again an analogy with the real sector is appropriate, that is, an invention may exist but not be innovated until stimulated by a specific set of circumstances.

In terms of a general criterion, we might appeal to the judgment of industry experts and financial specialists as to what constitutes an innovation.[11] The principle laid down by T. Gaines [19] is as follows: "An innovation is a change in techniques, institutions or operating policies that have the effect of altering the way an industry functions." An alternative is S.W. Becker and T.L. Whisler's [6] criterion: ". . . the first or early use of an idea by one of a set of organizations with similar goals."

Given the similarities and differences between real sector innovation and financial innovation just discussed, let us try to present a somewhat more formal analytical framework.[12] We will then return to our discussion of the characteristics of such innovation.

A General Theory of Financial Innovation

Many have argued that financial innovation is largely a response to regulation. The emergence of negotiable CDs, the development of the Eurodollar market, and the introduction of bank-related commercial paper are all credited to interest rate ceilings under Regulation Q. The regulation theory of innovation has been articulated most clearly (and rather elegantly) by S.I. Greenbaum and C.F. Haywood [21]. While this hypothesis has merit, it is too narrow to explain properly the evolution of financial instruments. Regulation turns out to be just one element of a more general category of innovation-generating phenomena.

Our basic hypothesis is that innovation of financial instruments and practices occurs in an effort to remove or lessen the financial constraints imposed on firms. Government regulation does, indeed, impose con-

---

[11]It is interesting to note that the Becker and Stafford study mentioned above used a survey of experts in the field (University of Chicago business economists!) to compile their list of innovative practices. The Rand Corporation routinely uses survey techniques to identify innovations. Indeed, its Delphi technique is specifically aimed at deriving a consensus of expert opinion (see D. Gabor [18]).

[12]While we have made use of the analogy between innovation in the real sector and the financial sector there is one key difference that must be reemphasized. The ability to preserve property rights over an innovation by patent, trademark, or copyright does not extend to financial innovation. Scherer [49] cites the purpose of such protection: "to promote invention, to encourage the development and commercial utilization of inventions and to encourage investors to disclose their inventions to the public." However, even as applied to the real sector, Scherer questions the need for such patent protection. In particular, innovative profits may be a sufficient inducement simply because of "natural imitation lags, advantages of competitive product leadership and the existence of nonpatent barriers to the emergence of a competitive market structure." In the financial sector it is precisely these natural forces that act as an incentive to innovation.

straints and thereby induces innovation. But the behavior of the financial firm is constrained by other factors as well—including self-imposed constraints and market-imposed constraints. To understand the type of constraints faced by the firm as well as the nature of the changes that trigger innovation, it is necessary to briefly review the literature on behavior of the financial firm.

Models of the financial firm are aimed at explaining the portfolio composition of such institutions and, where relevant, the interest rates offered on the firm's liabilities or the rate charged on its assets. Financial institutions are assumed to maximize utility, subject at least to the balance sheet constraint that the sum of all assets minus liabilities and capital equals zero. There may be other explicit constraints built into the optimization problem such as a target rate of growth for total assets, various regulatory requirements (such as, reserves must equal at least x percent of total deposits in the case of commercial banks) or self-imposed liquidity requirements specifying the desired percentage of the total portfolio in some particular asset.

In addition to these explicit constraints on the firm's behavior, the markets surrounding the financial firm define two sets of data: (1) the policy tools that the firm can vary at its discretion in order to reach an optimum; and (2) the parameters that the firm must accept as part of the optimization problem. The latter set of data constrains the behavior of the firm. Specific examples are as follows: A financial firm facing perfectly competitive markets for both its assets and liabilities views interest rates on these instruments as parameters and uses quantities purchased and sold as its policy tools. This view of the behavior of the financial firm is presented by M. Parkin [42]. A firm facing imperfectly competitive markets for its assets and/or liabilities accepts the associated demand and supply functions as parameters and uses the interest rate offered on deposits and the rate charged on its loans as policy tools. The models of M.A. Klein [30] and J.J. Pringle [45] incorporate specific assumptions regarding imperfectly competitive markets confronting financial institutions. Finally, some firms may view the inflow of funds as a constraint and concentrate only on the optimum distribution of funds among alternative assets. This is the formal assumption of portfolio choice in H. Markowitz [36] and has been incorporated in a number of empirical studies, such as S.M. Goldfeld [20] and P.H. Hendershott [25].[13]

These models of financial firm behavior permit us to specify the conditions that are likely to induce innovation. New financial instruments or practices will be innovated when there is an exogenous change in the

---

[13]There are three possible justifications for viewing liabilities as a constraint: The public's demand for these liabilities may be insensitive to the rate offered; the rate offered may be fixed exogenously (either by regulation or oligopolistic agreement); or the cost associated with trying to control deposits may exceed the expected increase in utility. The latter could occur when deposit flows are sufficiently large to justify the firm's sole preoccupation with the distribution of inflows among alternative assets.

constrained optimization of the firm that stimulates a search for new policy tools. There are two types of changes that induce firms to undertake the search costs required to modify its traditional policy tools. In one case exogenous changes in constraints force a reduction in the utility of the firm and the firm innovates in an effort to return to its previous level of utility. This clearly falls into the category of "adversity-innovation" mentioned above. In the second case innovation responds to an increase in the cost of adhering to a constraint. In a programming context this corresponds to an increase in the shadow price of the constraint. Both of these conditions create a strong incentive to remove or modify the constraints. If set internally, the firm may simply suspend or revise the constraint. If the constraint is imposed externally, for example, by market forces or by government regulation, the firm will attempt to circumvent the constraint by altering the opportunity set it faces.

This constraint-induced innovation hypothesis requires further specification if it is to be relevant operationally and if it is to be tested empirically. After all, the financial firm is constantly responding to changing yields and risks, as well as inflows and outflows of funds, by using its conventional policy tools. How are these "normal" stimuli and responses to be distinguished from those falling into the innovation category? The search costs inherent in reexamining the firm's policy weapons and the nature of its financial assets and/or liabilities for potential innovation suggest that this route will be chosen only when the "normal" reduction in firm utility becomes "abnormal." Similarly, the innovation route will be chosen only when the shadow price of a constraint becomes "abnormally" large. The term "abnormal" is best understood in an historical context. In particular, a firm sets its goals (and "normal" policy reactions) in terms of its historical experience. It then reevaluates its position when conditions change significantly.

The constraint-induced innovation hypothesis can now be given a time dimension. As the cost of adhering to a constraint rises over time or as the financial firm experiences continued decreases in utility over time, it will undertake or intensify the search for new financial instruments and/or practices. The sharper the rise in the shadow price or the reduction in utility, the greater will be the innovative effort. We expect, therefore, a time lag between the initial stimulus to innovate and the actual innovation. The time lag should be shorter, however, the greater the change in initial conditions.

Specific Causes of Financial Innovation

The theory of financial innovation just outlined is best illustrated at this point via some examples. Indeed, it is now easy to explain the genesis of the regulation theory of financial innovation. The most abrupt change faced by firms would appear to be the imposition of regulations by government or government agencies. The legislation of the 1930s aimed at the banking system and financial intermediaries is a perfect example.

A more subtle (hence more interesting) type of regulation-induced innovation is the rising cost of adhering to an existing regulatory constraint. The best example of this is interest rate ceilings imposed on the deposits of commercial banks, which become more costly as interest rates on other financial instruments rise. The perception of the rate-ceiling constraint by the bank will differ depending upon whether (for example) the time deposit market is, (a) perfectly competitive, or (b) imperfectly competitive. In the former case the bank's desired demand for time deposits (at the constrained rate) exceeds the actual amount it receives; in the latter case one of its policy tools has been immobilized, that is, it can no longer set the time deposit rate at its optimum level.

The innovative response is likely to be different in each case as well. The bank facing a competitive market finds itself in a corner solution and is likely to try to innovate a new source of funds. The bank that had some monopoly power was just deprived of one of its discretionary tools and is likely to respond by innovating another. One possibility is to try to en-dogenize some heretofore exogenous item in its balance sheet. It would appear that the innovation of CDs, Eurodollars, and bank-related commercial paper fall into this second category, that is, endogenizing an exogenous item in bank portfolios. A more careful examination of this point should be undertaken, however.

Innovation might also be generated by declining demand for a particular category of a firm's assets. This is most likely to occur when there exists significant expertise in the firm concerning the class of borrower associated with the asset. More generally, as the interest rate on a particular asset category declines, the labor resources administering such assets (loans) will try to maintain their submarket for funds by altering the characteristics of the asset. A specific example is the introduction of term loans into the portfolios of commercial banks in the 1930s. As in this example, the incentive to innovate by modifying asset characteristics is greater, the larger is the fixed investment (including human capital) in a particular market.

Declining growth in total sources of funds is another likely cause of innovation. A firm may accept its total sources of funds as a constraint as long as the inflow is growing at a minimum (target) growth rate. When growth falls below that rate the firm will undertake policies to achieve its desired growth target. One possibility is to vary (increase) the return offered on its liabilities. But under certain conditions this will not be desirable such as when the public's demand for these liabilities is inelastic or if the firm is in an oligopolistic market so that it cannot increase its share of funds by open price competition. Under such circumstances the financial firm will be induced to innovate a new financial product in order to attract funds. Since growth targets are likely to be set with reference to historical experience, it is likely that a drop in the rate of growth in the liabilities/capital account compared with past growth rates makes the constrained optimization unacceptable and pressures to innovate emerge.[14] A detailed example of product innovation by life insurance companies presented below illustrates this type of innovative pressure.

The risk dimension of the firm's utility function and the stochastic nature of the constraints confronting the firm provide another source of innovation. A change in the riskiness of one (minor) security in the firm's portfolio can be dealt with by changing the asset proportions in the portfolio. A far more difficult situation confronting the firm is a fundamental change that affects the riskiness of all securities at the same time or a change in the riskiness of major items in the firm's balance sheet, for example, total deposits. Such risks cannot be easily diversified away (if at all) and the institution turns to innovation to restore risk to its previous level.

A good example of risk-induced innovation is when the market for a firm's liabilities changes from monopoly to perfect competition. Interest rate variability then begins to affect the variance of the firm's profits. One way to restore certainty to the firm's profitability is to tie the yield on the firm's assets to the stochastic interest rate paid on liabilities. This is precisely the description of the process involved in moving from the "administered" prime rate on bank loans of the 1960s to the "floating" prime rate of the 1970s. It is no accident that this corresponds roughly to the emergence of a highly competitive market for bank (time) deposits.

Most of the examples of innovation just given have been responses to decreases in utility. As indicated above, this corresponds to *adversity innovation* as discussed by behavioral scientists. *Success innovation* has been used in reference to the slack that a successful firm maintains with the hope that such "surplus" resources generate innovative-type planning. We can extend that term to include the innovations that respond to rising shadow prices on constraints, especially self-imposed constraints. For example, a firm that accepts total liabilities as a constraint at one set of asset yields might be unwilling to do so at a higher set of yields. Rising asset

---

[14]There are at least two reasons suggesting that financial firms will be concerned with decreases in total growth. The fixed costs (including human capital) discussed above help determine the most efficient size of firm operations. A target rate of growth over some specific time horizon is likely to be set in order to achieve the minimum cost level of operation. Second, transactions costs are lower in making marginal portfolio adjustments to normal stimuli when inflows of funds can be used. In this case only one transaction fee must be paid while in a portfolio of little or no growth, two transaction fees (a purchase and a sale) are incurred.

yields over time may, therefore, lead a firm to innovate a new source of funds, especially if the public's demand for its liabilities is inelastic (or if the market is oligopolistic).

This category of success-innovation can also include the exploitation of technological developments that might reduce costs drastically or substantially change the nature of the financial service provided. It would seem that only a highly profitable firm would have the resources needed to undertake such high-risk, long-term prospects. Technological developments include physical technology such as computers, analytical technology, such as the construction of efficient market portfolios (see F. Black and M. Scholes [7]) and "miscellaneous" technology such as the development of mortality tables by insurance companies for particular classes of the population.

Empirical Evaluation of Financial Innovation

A number of specific examples of financial innovation were presented in the previous section. These provided illustrations of the constraint-induced innovation hypothesis spelled out earlier. To set the stage for current and future empirical investigations let us summarize the conditions we expect to be associated with financial innovation as well as the type of innovation that occurs in response to these stimuli.

Financial innovation should be induced by any of the following conditions facing the firm: (a) imposition of regulatory constraints; (b) exogenous decreases in its rate of growth; (c) an exogenous increase in the variability of major items in its balance sheet; (d) a change in the competitive nature of the markets facing the firm; (e) sharply rising yields on the assets in the firm's portfolio; and (f) a technological breakthrough that has the potential of significantly altering the opportunity set or cost functions of the firm. These conditions are more likely to induce new financial instruments when the market structure is oligopolistic.

The innovative response to these stimuli should occur with some time delay. The type of response or the objective of the innovations include: (a) endogenizing an exogenous item in the firm's balance sheet (by modifying the instrument or accepted practices with respect to it); (b) introducing an existing financial instrument from another country or industry into the firm's portfolio; (c) somewhere between (a) and (b) is the attempt by the firm to generate demand for credit or demand for its liabilities by modifying an existing asset or liability in its portfolio. Innovations falling into category (c) are, unlike (a), only aimed at expanding balance sheet constraints rather than creating an additional policy tool for the firm.

We can now turn to a more comprehensive survey of actual financial innovation. The empirical evidence is presented in two parts. First, an illustrative historical categorization of selected innovations by United States financial institutions is set forth. This will be followed by a somewhat more detailed analysis of innovations in the life insurance industry. The former is aimed at evaluating the usefulness of the analytical classification scheme set forth above. The latter is an example of the type of empirical work needed to establish properly the causes of specific innovations.[15] The life insurance industry receives special attention because it has shown considerable innovative activity (beginning in the middle of the nineteenth century) and because in contrast with, say, commercial banking, much fewer regulations have impinged on firm behavior. Furthermore, there are many well-documented historical studies of the major firms in the industry.

Table 2-1 presents an *incomplete* list of innovations by *selected* financial institutions.[16] It is meant to be suggestive rather than comprehensive. The references cited are the primary sources that mention the various items as innovations. The classifications by type of innovation and the apparent causes are based on the framework presented above and the discussion set forth in the source documents. The type of innovation is more easily identified than the cause of the innovation. All that is required is information on the previous status of the new instrument (e.g., whether it was an exogenous item in the institution's portfolio) and some judgment as to whether the innovation was aimed at providing the institution with a new policy tool as opposed to, say, expanding its sources of funds. To isolate the cause of the innovation properly, however, often requires the application of formal mathematical and statistical techniques.[17] In both cases our

---

[15]There are two types of empirical studies that are appropriate for analyzing financial innovation. A time series of innovations in a particular industry can be studied, for example, innovations in commercial banking or savings banking between 1870 and 1970. The causes of the innovations in the industry and their rates of diffusion can be investigated in this context. (See W. Rudelius and G.L. Wood [47] for an attempt at measuring the rate of diffusion of selected life insurance innovations.) Cross-section analysis of firm practices at a particular moment in time lends itself to a more intensive analysis of firm characteristics associated with innovative activity. Our empirical investigation uses the time series approach.

[16]While our analysis is limited to financial firms, the same type of pressures might impinge on nonfinancial corporations, thereby leading to financial innovation within the real sector of the economy. The credit activities of large manufacturing and retail corporations (General Motors and Sears Roebuck) suggest that innovation by such institutions is worth special attention (see C.A. Christophe [10]).

[17]A specific example using mathematical programming techniques to identify the causes of financial innovation is as follows. Table 2-1 attributes the innovation of CDs as well as six other bank instruments of the 1960s to rate regulation. It also types these innovations as efforts to endogenize heretofore exogenous items in bank balance sheets. The historical explanation is that CDs emerged as a result of three factors that developed during the 1950s: a slowdown in the growth of bank deposits (both demand and time); an increase in bank loan demand; and the rundown of the government bond portfolio (see M. Kimbrell and A.A. Dill [29]). The key to the slow growth in bank deposits is rising rates on open market securities and the ceilings on the rates that could be offered on demand and time deposits. Rising asset yields and the

initial investigation turned up uncertainties, and these are indicated in the table.

It is beyond the scope of this chapter to try to justify each of the entries in Table 2-1. The classification scheme does, however, present an outline for substantial empirical research. Our example with the life insurance industry follows.

Life Insurance Innovations: Tontine, Industrial, and Group Insurance

The introduction of tontine insurance in 1868, industrial insurance in 1875, and group insurance in 1911 were major innovations in the life insurance industry. Each type of policy was a significant departure from existing policies in the United States, although the tontine and industrial forms of insurance were known in Europe. There are very specific explanations of each of these innovations as presented by life insurance historians. We will review these very briefly and then see to what extent our more general approach can account for these innovations.

The tontine policy was introduced in 1868 by the Equitable Life Assurance Society.[18] The key advantage of the tontine policy from Equitable's standpoint was its deferred dividend feature. The innovation of the tontine stemmed from competition between Equitable and the leading company of that period, Mutual Life. This rivalry was intense because of the former association of the president of Equitable (Henry B. Hyde) with Mutual Life. The immediate cause of the tontine was the substantial reduction in Equitable's surplus in 1865 in order to pay a dividend. This, in turn, was a response to Mutual Life's newly introduced annual dividend policy. This

increase in demand for commercial loans would have triggered the innovation of a new source of funds earlier than 1961 were it not for the excessively large government bond portfolio (a legacy of World War II) that banks were able to use as a discretionary source of funds. As these pressures intensified banks were induced to alter the characteristic of a relatively minor item on the liability side of the balance sheet—nonnegotiable corporate CDs (approximately $1 billion until 1961). The innovation of the secondary market for CDs and the spread of negotiability permitted banks a new discretionary source of funds (see T. Gaines [19]). These hypotheses can be formally tested by looking at bank portfolio behavior from a mathematical programming standpoint. The argument can be stated as follows: innovation of CDs and other money market instruments resulted from rising shadow prices attached to the demand and time deposit constraints as well as the rising shadow price associated with constraints on the size of the government bond portfolio. By constructing a programming model of bank portfolio behavior and evaluating it over the 1950-70 time interval using historical data, one could see whether the shadow prices of the constraints rise significantly immediately before the innovation. A New York University doctoral dissertation is currently approaching bank innovations in this way.

[18]The tontine was an arrangement whereby a group of people deposited a sum of money to be divided among the survivors at some specific date in the future (see H. Krooss and M. Blyn [32, p. 36]). Various modifications of this general scheme were introduced by United States insurance companies.

Table 2-1
Classifying Financial Innovations

Innovation (Date)	Reference	Type of Innovation (Objective)	Cause of Innovation
1. Commercial banks			
a) Enter investment banking (1908)	[32, p. 157]	(2)	Portfolio regulation
b) Trust subsidiaries (1913)	[32, p. 155]	(2)	Portfolio regulation
c) Consumer loans (1928)	[29, p. 97]	(3)	Weak loan demand
d) Term loans (1933)	[46], [27]	(3)	Weak loan demand
e) "Computer banking" (1950s)	[38]	(4)	Available technology
f) Negotiable CD (1961)	[37, p. 168]	(1)	Rate reg.; exp. loan dem.
g) Subordinated debentures (1963)	[37]	(1)	Rate regulation
h) Short-term promissary n. (1965)	[37, p. 168]	(1)	Rate regulation
i) Eurodollars (1966)	[37, p. 168]	(1)	Rate regulation
j) Evolution fed. funds mkt. (1960s)	[37, p. 168]	?	?
k) Credit cards (1960s)		(4)	Technology
l) Bank-related comm. paper (1969)	[29]	(1)	Rate regulation
m) Loan RPs (1969)	[29]	(1)	Rate regulation
n) Working capital accept. (1969)	[29]	(1)	Rate regulation
o) Floating prime (1971)	——		Change in competition
p) Floating rate notes (1974)	——	Reduce risk (3)	Rate regulation

2. Savings banks			
a) Savings bank life ins. (1907)	[34]	(2)	Regulatory change
b) Christmas Clubs (1911)	[34]	(3)	?
3. Savings and loan associations			
a) Serial plan (1850)	[54, p. 28]	(3)	Orig. charter too confining
b) Permanent plan (c. 1880)	[54, p. 29]	(3)	"
c) Brokerage of sav. accts. (c. 1950)	[16]	(3)	Rising yields
d) Mortgage participations (1957)	[16]	?	"
4. Life insurance companies			
a) Tontine (1868)	[32, p. 107]	(2)	Declining surplus
b) Industrial ins. (1875)	[11, p. 109]	(2)	Slowdown in growth
c) Group insurance (1911)	[11, p. 109]	(3)	"

Notes: Types of Innovation.

(1) Endogenizing an exogenous item in the firm's balance sheet (by modifying the instrument or accepted practices with respect to it).
(2) Introducing an existing financial instrument (from another industry or another country) in the firm's portfolio.
(3) Attempting to generate demand for credit or demand for liabilities by modifying an existing asset or liability in the portfolio.
(4) New item.

reduction in surplus brought Equitable to the brink of bankruptcy. The immediate purpose of the tontine, therefore, was to replenish Equitable's surplus account.[19] Of longer term significance, of course, was the effectiveness of the tontine policy in attracting new business.[20]

Industrial insurance was innovated by the Prudential Insurance Company in the year it was established, 1875. Prudential used this new form of insurance, which appealed to low-income working classes,[21] as a means of breaking into an insurance industry that was dominated by a few large firms. For three years Prudential was the only issuer of industrial insurance. In 1879, however, two major companies, Metropolitan and John Hancock, introduced industrial insurance. It is this development that turns out to be most instructive from our standpoint. Both of these companies had been experiencing severe declines in growth immediately prior to their entry into the industrial area. So vigorous was Metropolitan's thrust in that direction that it became the leader in industrial insurance by 1891.[22]

Group insurance was first written in 1911 by Equitable. Some have argued that the labor union movement provided a strong impetus to both management and insurance industry officials to introduce a form of insurance aimed specifically at the growing urban work force.[23] More important from our point of view was the declining growth rate experienced by Equitable between 1900 and 1910 and its relatively inferior growth record over the interval compared with other firms.

Let us now take a more detailed look at whether these innovations were responses to identifiable pressures, such as declining growth and/or rising interest rates. The fact that the industry can be described as an oligopoly suggests that open price competition was discouraged; hence, growth deficiencies and rising interest rates were likely to be met by innovation of instruments and practices.[24] The lengthy time horizon inherent in the life insurance industry, together with the considerations set forth in footnote 14 above, also suggest that decreases in total growth are likely to be associated with innovation.

---

[19]A summary of this episode is found in R.W. Cooper [12].

[20]R.C. Buley [9] reports that within 20 years of Equitable's introduction of the tontine, 75 percent of all companies issued some form of that policy. Furthermore, Equitable moved from the 20th largest insurance company in 1860 to 7th in 1875 and 2nd in 1880.

[21]Existing ordinary policies were not written in small denominations and premiums were large and infrequent. Fraternal organizations did provide a form of insurance to low income groups but their methods were haphazard.

[22]See M. James [28].

[23]See D.W. Gregg [22].

[24]We have data on total insurance in force for six firms: Metropolitan Life, John Hancock, Equitable Life, Mutual Life, New York Life, and Prudential. The six firm concentration ratios for 1880, 1900, and 1920 were 52.3 percent, 60.8 percent, and 50.7 percent, respectively (data sources are described in the notes on Tables 2-2 through 2-7).

Tables 2-2 through 2-6 present the annual rates of growth (between 1860 and 1940) in total assets of all insurance companies combined,[25] Metropolitan Life, John Hancock, Equitable, and Mutual Life. Table 2-7 gives the average yield on government and corporate bonds over the same period.[26] Tables 2-2 through 2-6 also include a bracketing of the growth rates into different periods, with the changes determined by a visual inspection of the data. The arrow at the beginning of each bracket indicates the direction of the change in the rate of growth compared with the previous period. Observations set off by parentheses are "outliers" within that period (or between periods). Dates of various modifications in the insurance contract as well as important regulatory changes (1905 Armstrong Investigation) are also noted.

The introduction of the tontine in 1868 is not accompanied by any noticeable decrease in total asset growth of any of the individual companies or of all companies combined. Interest rates also showed little trend in the preceding two or three years. Upon reflection, it is not too surprising to find the innovation of the tontine policy unaccompanied by either of these financial pressures. As mentioned above, the unique feature of the tontine from the innovator's standpoint was its deferred dividend feature, and that characteristic of the innovation was directly related to a very specific financial constraint—the decline of the surplus account.

The behavior of total asset growth surrounding the introduction of industrial insurance is strongly supportive of the constraint-induced innovation hypothesis. Table 2-2 shows a steady decline in growth of total assets for the entire industry between 1870 and 1875, and then virtual zero growth between 1876 and 1879. Prudential was established in 1875 and it chose to introduce industrial insurance, perhaps in light of the slowdown in overall industry growth. Tables 2-3 through 2-6 indicate quite clearly that the two companies (Metropolitan and John Hancock) with negative growth between 1877 and 1879 introduced industrial insurance while the others (Equitable and Mutual Life) with positive growth (even though substantially below the preceding years) did not follow. A glance at Table 2-7 indicates a modest role, if anything, from the interest rate side of the picture.

In light of these findings we might modify the constraint-induced innovation hypothesis to take account of the *relative* adversity of firms, at least within an oligopolistic industry. Those firms under most severe pressure are likely to innovate more quickly than the others.

---

[25]The data for *all* insurance companies combined is actually for *all* insurance companies authorized to do business in New York State. These firms represent 95 percent of total insurance in force.

[26]Tables 2-2 through 2-7 are based on data prepared by Maia Greco as part of her masters project at the Graduate School of Business Administration, New York University.

Table 2-2
Annual Rate of Growth in Total Assets, All Insurance Companies

	Year	% Change Gross Assets		Year	% Change Gross Assets
Agency system	1860	17.4		1900	9.4
	1861	10.6		1901	9.0
	1862	13.0		1902	9.7
	1863	25.6		1903	8.0
	1864	29.6	Armstrong	1904	10.3
	1865	31.0	investigation	1905	8.0
	1866	42.6		1906	7.6
	1867	37.1	Policy	1907	(2.3)
Tontine	1868	39.6	modifications	1908	9.8
	1869	30.0		1909	8.2
	1870	18.3		1910	6.5
	1871	12.3	Group	1911	6.7
	1872	11.1		1912	5.9
	1873	7.5		1913	5.8
	1874	7.5		1914	5.0
Industrial	1875	4.1		1915	4.6
	1876	1.1		1916	6.1
	1877	−2.8		1917	6.3
	1878	1.2		1918	8.2
	1879	0.1		1919	(3.1)
	1880	4.1		1920	7.4
	1881	2.7		1921	7.3
	1882	4.7		1922	8.1
	1883	4.9		1923	8.3
	1884	4.2		1924	9.5
	1885	6.6		1925	11.2
	1886	7.0		1926	11.2
	1887	6.3		1927	11.2
	1888	2.7		1928	10.8
	1889	13.9		1929	9.4
	1890	8.1		1930	7.9
	1891	8.8		1931	7.0
	1892	10.3		1932	3.4
Policy	1893	7.5		1933	1.7
modifications	1894	8.7		1934	4.6
	1895	8.2		1935	6.5
	1896	7.5		1936	7.1
	1897	8.6		1937	5.5
	1898	8.8		1938	5.7
	1899	8.6		1939	5.5
				1940	5.3

Source: Annual Reports Department of Insurance of the State of New York, 1860-1940.

The innovation of group insurance in 1911 is best understood in this light. For each of the four firms, the growth rate slowed at some point between 1905 and 1910. The Armstrong Investigation in 1905 and the panic of 1907 were contributing factors. The two firms most adversely affected were Equitable and Mutual Life. As can be seen in Table 2-5 Equitable

Table 2-3

Annual Rate of Growth in Total Assets, Metropolitan Life

	Year	% Change Gross Assets		Year	% Change Gross Assets
Tontine	1868	27.8		1904	21.2
	1869	48.8		1905	18.4
	1870	40.2		1906	16.3
	1871	32.3		1907	12.4
	1872	29.0		1908	19.0
	1873	11.7		1909	17.4
	1874	16.2		1910	13.3
	1875	5.7		1911	12.5
	1876	9.8		1912	12.7
	1877	−2.7		1913	12.6
Industrial	1878	−0.1	Group	1914	10.2
	1879	−3.0	(own employees)	1915	9.2
	1880	−3.8		1916	12.7
	1881	1.3	Group	1917	15.8
	1882	1.5		1918	10.1
	1883	9.2		1919	11.5
	1884	5.3		1920	13.4
	1885	20.9		1921	13.7
	1886	33.1		1922	12.9
	1887	32.4		1923	13.6
	1888	28.1		1924	13.7
	1889	36.7		1925	13.9
	1890	25.4		1926	13.7
	1891	26.4		1927	13.3
	1892	21.4		1928	12.9
	1893	16.9		1929	11.7
Established	1894	15.4		1930	10.0
intermediate	1895	14.6		1931	8.5
branch	1896	19.7		1932	5.0
	1897	18.7		1933	2.4
	1898	19.6		1934	4.4
	1899	17.4		1935	5.1
	1900	21.7		1936	6.1
	1901	20.3		1937	5.0
	1902	18.3		1938	4.7
	1903	18.5		1939	4.0
				1940	4.2

Source: Annual Reports of the Department of Insurance of the State of New York, 1867-1940.

introduced a series of policy changes beginning in 1908 (including opening an industrial insurance department) culminating with the innovation of group insurance in 1911. Mutual Life, on the other hand, did not even follow the group policy innovation. The only explanation is offered by S.B. Clough [11, p. 244], which cites the explicit antigrowth policy of Charles A. Peabody, president of Mutual Life between 1905 and 1927. Once again, interest rate movement between 1905 and 1911 seem to play a modest role in the pressure to innovate group insurance.

Table 2-4
Annual Rate of Growth in Total Assets, John Hancock

	Year	% Change Gross Assets		Year	% Change Gross Assets
	1867	68.2 ⌉		1904	16.9
	1868	37.3		1905	16.5
	1869	30.6		1906	15.1
	1870	21.0		1907	13.0
	1871	12.9		1908	18.0
	1872	13.3 ⌟		1909	14.3 ⌟
	1873	2.9 ⌉ ↓		1910	12.7 ⌉ ↓
	1874	3.9		1911	13.3
	1875	4.3		1912	13.0
	1876	2.3 ⌟		1913	12.1
	1877	0.4 ⌉ ↓		1914	10.7
	1878	−2.0		1915	9.5
Industrial	1879	−3.3		1916	11.2
	1880	−3.5		1917	10.6
	1881	−2.4		1918	(9.6)
	1882	0.1 ⌟		1919	(8.9)
	1883	2.6 ⌉ ↑		1920	13.4
	1884	1.8	Double indemnity	1921	13.3
	1885	4.7		1922	11.8
	1886	4.6		1923	11.7
	1887	6.8		1924	11.3
	1888	8.1		1925	10.7
	1889	7.0 ⌟		1926	10.6
	1890	11.8 ⌉ ↑		1927	10.6
Weekly	1891	10.4		1928	10.0
premium plan	1892	15.5		1929	9.3 ⌟
	1893	14.5		1930	7.7 ⌉ ↓
	1894	15.2		1931	6.4
	1895	14.9		1932	2.9
	1896	15.1		1933	2.5
	1897	18.9		1934	4.0
	1898	11.9		1935	7.1
	1899	16.0		1936	8.9
	1900	16.5		1937	7.6
	1901	16.6		1938	7.7
	1902	17.8		1939	6.4
	1903	17.2		1940	7.8

Source: Annual Reports of the Department of Insurance of the State of New York, 1866-1940.

The data, with some charitable interpretations, do tend to support the constraint-induced innovation hypothesis discussed above. But there is still another test to which our analysis must be put. In particular, are there any periods in which firm growth declined noticeably but did not result in innovation? If financial constraints occur with regularity but innovation is relatively infrequent, our evidence is hardly worth the name.

The growth in total assets of all firms presented in Table 2-2 shows only one period of decline aside from the cases just discussed, and that is associated with the Great Depression. All of the firms experienced a similar

Table 2-5

Annual Rate of Growth in Total Assets, Equitable Life Assurance Society

	Year	% Change Gross Assets		Year	% Change Gross Assets
	1860	42.9		1900	8.8
	1861	29.4		1901	8.7
	1862	53.6		1902	8.5
	1863	80.6		1903	5.9
	1864	75.2		1904	8.6
	1865	54.8		1905	0.3
	1866	94.0	Industrial	1906	3.6
	1867	66.5	department	1907	−0.3
Tontine	1868	50.7	and other	1908	(8.3)
	1869	36.1	changes	1909	−3.7
	1870	25.9		1910	2.6
	1871	19.3	Group	1911	2.5
	1872	21.3		1912	1.8
	1873	16.8		1913	2.4
	1874	14.4		1914	1.8
	1875	11.6		1915	2.1
	1876	8.0		1916	3.0
	1877	7.1		1917	2.6
	1878	5.9		1918	(6.1)
	1879	5.7		1919	(−2.0)
	1880	10.0	Endowment policy	1920	4.6
	1881	8.3	Retirement annuity	1921	4.5
	1882	8.3		1922	1.3
	1883	9.6		1923	3.5
	1884	9.9		1924	5.6
	1885	13.9		1925	9.2
	1886	13.4		1926	9.7
	1887	11.6	Group annuity	1927	11.2
	1888	12.5		1928	11.3
	1889	12.9		1929	9.6
	1890	10.9		1930	8.9
	1891	14.0		1931	9.0
	1892	13.0		1932	5.1
	1893	10.4		1933	3.3
	1894	10.1		1934	9.0
	1895	9.1		1935	9.6
	1896	7.9		1936	9.3
	1897	9.5		1937	6.1
	1898	9.3		1938	7.4
	1899	8.4		1939	6.2
				1940	6.8

Source: Annual Report of the Department of Insurance of the State of New York, 1859-1940.

decline in growth but in no cases were there any innovations. This is not too disturbing, of course, given the very specific circumstances surrounding the Great Depression. The decline in interest rates—beginning in 1929—is an obvious offsetting pressure.

Some firms experienced moderate declines in growth between 1892 and

Table 2-6
Annual Rate of Growth in Total Assets, Mutual Life

	Year	% Change Gross Assets		Year	% Change Gross Assets
	1860	16.1 ⌉		1900	7.9
	1861	11.4		1901	8.3
	1862	13.8		1902	8.4
	1863	15.7		1903	5.1
	1864	17.5		1904	9.8
Survivorship policy	1865	15.0 ⌋		1905	6.8
Installment policy	1866	29.0 ⌉ ↑		1906	5.3 ⌋
	1867	29.7		1907	(−0.3)
	1868	29.3		1908	(10.4)
	1869	21.2		1909	2.7 ⌉ ↓
Tontine	1870	18.3 ⌋		1910	2.4
	1871	15.6 ⌉ ↓		1911	2.4
	1872	13.6	Disability	1912	2.1
	1873	11.9	benefits	1913	1.2
	1874	10.5		1914	0.5
	1875	8.8 ⌋		1915	1.1
	1876	4.5 ⌉ ↓		1916	1.7
	1877	3.3		1917	1.5 ⌋
	1878	2.5		1918	(6.2)
	1879	1.6		1919	−1.9 ⌉ ↓
	1880	3.8		1920	1.3
	1881	3.3		1921	1.0
	1882	3.4		1922	2.0
	1883	3.2		1923	1.0
	1884	2.7		1924	2.6 ⌉ ↑
	1885	4.7		1925	4.5
	1886	4.8		1926	7.0
	1887	4.0 ⌋		1927	8.0
	1888	6.1 ⌉ ↑		1928	7.6
	1889	8.1		1929	6.9
	1890	8.0		1930	6.2
	1891	7.9		1931	5.1 ⌋
	1892	9.5		1932	1.9 ⌉ ↓
Continuous	1893	6.8		1933	−0.7 ⌋
installment	1894	9.4		1934	3.6 ⌉ ↑
	1895	8.6	Endowment	1935	6.8
	1896	6.8	annuity	1936	5.6
	1897	8.1		1937	3.1
	1898	9.4	Juvenile insurance	1938	3.7
	1899	8.8		1939	3.2
				1940	2.8

Source: Annual Report of the Department of Insurance of the State of New York, 1859-1940.

1895 (except for John Hancock). In 1919 there was another interruption in growth (except for Metropolitan Life). While there were a number of contract modifications during both of these periods it is not clear that they can be associated with these constraints. These intervals seem neither supportive nor damaging to our case.

Table 2-7

Interest Rates on Government, Corporate, and Municipal Bonds (Annual Average)

Year	U.S. Govt.	RR Bonds	Year	U.S. Govt.	Prime RR & Corp.	Year	U.S. Govt.	L-T Corp. & Munc.
1860	5.57	6.04	1890	3.26	3.68	1921	5.09	5.16
1861	6.45	6.33	1891	3.38	3.84	1922	4.30	4.49
1862	6.25	5.52	1892	3.46	3.72	1923	4.36	4.51
1863	6.00	4.77	1893	3.56	3.73	1924	4.06	4.51
1864	5.10	4.83	1894	3.51	3.62	1925	3.86	4.50
1865	5.19	6.02	1895	3.56	3.46	1926	3.68	4.36
1866	5.17	6.37	1896	3.78	3.50	1927	3.34	4.18
1867	4.97	6.32	1897	3.54	3.33	1928	3.33	4.19
1868	4.62	6.26	1898	3.58	3.26	1929	3.60	4.47
1869	4.07	6.55	1899	3.54	3.24	1930	3.29	4.31
1870	4.24	6.41	1900	3.47	3.31	1931	3.34	4.15
1871	4.18	6.35	1901	1.98	3.28	1932	3.68	4.61
1872	3.70	6.18	1902	1.93	3.34	1933	3.31	4.19
1873	3.51	6.20	1903	1.97	3.55	1934	3.12	3.83
1874	3.42	5.91	1904	2.08	3.57	1935	2.79	3.44
1875	3.30	5.45	1905	2.03	3.51	1936	2.65	3.11
1876	3.66	5.16	1906	2.03	3.65	1937	2.68	3.12
1877	3.81	5.18	1907	2.33	3.92	1938	2.56	2.90
1878	3.97	5.11	1908	2.39	3.90	1939	2.36	2.77
1879	3.96	4.77	1909	2.57	3.78	1940	2.21	2.70
1880	3.63	4.46	1910	2.76	3.87			
1881	3.13	4.13	1911	2.70	3.93			
1882	2.91	4.20	1912	2.71	3.95			
1883	2.88	4.23	1913	2.83	4.14			
1884	2.76	4.15	1914	2.79	4.11			
1885	2.68	3.98	1915	2.79	4.18			
1886	2.43	3.81	1916	2.57	4.10			
1887	2.32	3.80	1917	2.95	4.41			
1888	2.27	3.69	1918	3.05	4.82			
1889	2.13	3.51	1919	3.02	4.84			
			1920	2.90	5.27			

Source: Homer [26].

Future Research on Financial Innovation

We have presented a framework for discussing innovation in the financial sector of the economy. Our attention was devoted almost exclusively to analyzing the innovation of financial instruments and practices by financial firms. Our theoretical model appears capable of explaining the common features of apparently unrelated financial innovations. Empirical evidence on the determinants of such innovation by life insurance companies has also been set forth. As we have pointed out, this is the direction that future research on financial innovation must take. Historical studies of individual financial institutions applying mathematical-statistical techniques to the available data promises additional insights into the innovative process.

A natural extension of these investigations would be to examine the process by which real technological advances are adopted by financial firms. Are the factors that trigger such innovation similar to the ones that generate instrument and practice innovation? Parallel research on these various aspects of innovation in the financial sector should add significantly to our understanding of the evolution of the financial sector.

References

[1] Akerlof, G.A., "The Market for 'Lemons': Quality Uncertainty and the Market Mechanism," *Quarterly Journal of Economics*, August 1970.

[2] Alchian, A.A., and H. Demsetz, "Production, Information Costs and Economic Organization," *American Economic Review*, December 1972.

[3] *Annual Reports of the Department of Insurance of the State of New York*, Superintendent of the Insurance Department of the State of New York, Albany, 1859-1970.

[4] Arrow, K.J., "The Role of Securities in the Optimal Allocation of Risk Bearing," *Review of Economic Studies*, Volume XXXI (2), 1964.

[5] Becker, S.W., and F. Stafford, "Some Determinants of Organizational Success," *Journal of Business*, October 1967.

[6] Becker, S.W., and T.L. Whisler, "The Innovative Organization: A Selective View of Current Theory and Research," *Journal of Business*, October 1967.

[7] Black, F., and M. Scholes, "From Theory to a New Financial Product," *Journal of Finance*, May 1974.

[8] Brunner, K., and A.M. Meltzer, "The Uses of Money: Money in a Theory of an Exchange Economy," *American Economic Review*, December 1971.

[9] Buley, R.C., *The Equitable Life Assurance Society of the United States*, New York, Appleton-Century-Crofts, 1967.

[10] Christophe, C.A., *Competition in Financial Services*, New York, First National City Corporation, 1974.

[11] Clough, S.B., *A Century of American Life Insurance*, New York, Columbia University Press, 1946.

[12] Cooper, R.W., *An Historical Analysis of the Tontine Principle*, Philadelphia, S.S. Huebner Foundation for Insurance Education, 1972.

[13] Cyert, R.M., and J.G. March, *A Behavioral Theory of the Firm*, Englewood Cliffs, N.J., Prentice-Hall, 1963.

[14] Davis, L.E., and D.C. North, *Institutional Change and American Economic Growth*, Cambridge, Cambridge University Press, 1971.

[15] Demsetz, H., "The Cost of Transacting," *Quarterly Journal of Economics*, February 1958.

[16] Ewalt, J., *A Business Reborn: The Savings and Loan Story 1930-1960*, Chicago, American Savings and Loan Institute Press, 1962.

[17] Fieldhouse, R., *Certificates of Deposit*, Boston, The Bankers Publishing Company, 1962.

[18] Gabor, D., *Innovations: Scientific, Technological and Social*, Oxford University Press, 1970.

[19] Gaines, T., "Financial Innovation and the Efficiency of Federal Reserve Policy," in *Monetary Process and Policy* (G. Horwich, ed.), Homewood, Ill., R.D. Irwin, 1967.

[20] Goldfeld, S.M., *Commercial Bank Behavior and Economic Activity*, North-Holland Publishing Company, 1966.

[21] Greenbaum, S.I., and C.F. Haywood, "Secular Change in the Financial Services Industry," *Journal of Money, Credit, and Banking*, May 1974.

[22] Gregg, D.W., *Group Life Insurance—An Analysis of Concepts, Costs and Company Practices*, Philadelphia, S.S. Huebner Foundation for Insurance Education, 1962.

[23] Gurley, J.G., and E. Shaw, "Financial Intermediaries and the Saving-Investment Process," *Journal of Finance*, May 1956.

[24] Gurley, J.G., and E. Shaw, *Money in a Theory of Finance*, The Brookings Institution, 1960.

[25] Hendershott, P.H., "A Flow of Funds Model: Estimates for the Non-bank Finance Sector," *Journal of Money, Credit and Banking*, November 1971.

[26] Homer, S., *A History of Interest Rates*, New Brunswick, N.J., Rutgers University Press, 1963.

[27] Jacoby, N.H., and R.J. Saulnier, *Term Lending to Business*, Washington, National Burueu of Economic Research, 1942.

[28] James, M., *The Metropolitan Life—A Study in Business Growth*, New York, The Viking Press, 1947.

[29] Kimbrel, M., and A.A. Dill, "Other Sources of Funds," in *The Changing World of Banking* (Prochnow and Prochnow, eds.), New York, Harper & Row, 1974.

[30] Klein, M.A., "A Theory of the Banking Firm," *Journal of Money, Credit and Banking*, May 1971.

[31] Knight, K.E., "A Descriptive Model of the Intra-Firm Innovative Process," *Journal of Business*, October 1967.

[32] Krooss, H., and M. Blyn, *A Short History of Financial Intermediaries*, New York, Random House, 1971.

[33] *Life Insurance Fact Book*, New York, Institute of Life Insurance, 1973.

[34] Lintner, J., *Mutual Savings Banks in the Savings and Mortgage Markets*, Cambridge, Harvard University, Graduate School of Business, 1948.

[35] Mansfield, E., *The Economics of Technological Change*, New York, W.W. Norton & Co., 1968.

[36] Markowitz, H., *Portfolio Selection: Efficient Diversification of Investments*, New York, John Wiley & Sons, 1959.

[37] Meigs, A.J., "Recent Innovations in the Functions of Banks," *American Economic Review*, May 1966.

[38] Mitchell, G.W., "Effects of Automation on the Structure and Functioning of Banking," *American Economic Review*, May 1966.

[39] Modigliani, F., and R. Sutch, "Innovations in Interest Rate Policy," *American Economic Review*, May 1966.

[40] Musgrave, R.A., and P.B. Musgrave, *Public Finance in Theory and Practice*, New York, McGraw-Hill, 1973.

[41] Nelson, R.R., and S.G. Winter, "Toward an Evolutionary Theory of Economic Capabilities," *American Economic Review*, May 1973.

[42] Parkin, M., "Discount House Portfolio Selection," *Review of Economic Studies*, October 1970.

[43] Porter, R.C., "The Birth of a Bill Market," *Journal of Development Studies*, April 1973.

[44] Porter, R.C., "Narrow Security Markets and Monetary Policy: Lessons from Pakistan," *Economic Development and Cultural Change*, October 1965.

[45] Pringle, J.J., "A Theory of the Banking Firm: Comment," *Journal of Money, Credit and Banking*, November 1973.

[46] Ritter L.S., "Commercial Bank Liquidity and Medium and Longer-Term Bank Loans in the United States," *Banco de la Republica*, Bogota, Colombia, June 1957.

[47] Rudelius, W., and G.L. Wood, "Life Insurance Product Innovations," *Journal of Risk and Insurance*, June 1970.

[48] Sandor, R.L., "Innovation by an Exchange: A Case Study of the Development of the Plywood Futures Contract," *Journal of Law and Economics*, April 1973.

[49] Scherer, F.M., *Industrial Market Structure and Economic Performance*, Skokie, Ill., Rand McNally, 1973.

[50] Schmookler, J., *Invention and Economic Growth*, Cambridge, Harvard University Press, 1966.

[51] Schumpeter, J.A., *Business Cycles*, New York, McGraw-Hill, 1939.

[52] Silber, W.L., "Money, Markets, and Intermediaries: Some Interrelationships," Working Paper Number 32, Salomon Brothers Center for the Study of Financial Institutions, New York, New York University, March 1975.

[53] Stalson, J.O., *Marketing Life Insurance*, Cambridge, Harvard University Press, 1942.

[54] Teck, A., *Mutual Savings Banks and Savings and Loan Associations: Aspects of Growth*, New York, Columbia University Press. 1968.

[55] Tinic, S.M., "The Economics of Liquidity Services," *Quarterly Journal of Economics*, February 1972.

Comment: Towards a Theory of Financial Innovation

William C. Brainard

Many economists are preoccupied with the "real" side of the economy, and they sometimes forget that financial institutions, instruments, and markets are no less real than beer and bagels. I, and I am sure most of those who attended the conference preceding this book, believe, in contrast, that financial markets are as important to the functioning of a modern economy as the markets for physical goods and services. Financial innovations, the subject of this chapter, are of great theoretical and practical interest, since understanding the process of financial innovation is an essential part of understanding how efficiently financial markets fulfill their role in the allocation of resources and risk.

Explanation of the innovative process and the "real" sector has proven to be difficult, so it is not surprising, given its relative neglect, that we know little about the process of financial innovation. As in the case of the real sector, we would like to know how important financial innovation is, how much it contributes to increases in productivity, and how quickly it occurs in response to changes in environment. These questions would be primarily academic if financial markets were a bastion of laissez-faire, but in fact they are among the most heavily regulated in our economy, and therefore their answers have direct policy implications. How much do regulations interfere with the process of innovation, and to what extent are innovations a defensive response to regulations designed to improve "market performance" or the effectiveness of monetary control? As a macroeconomist, I would be grateful for any analysis that would decrease the frequency with which we have to resort to the use of dummy variables to "explain" breaks in the historical record reflecting innovation.

In the first portion of this chapter, William L. Silber takes a macro perspective in discussing the characteristics of financial markets and the factors that provide pressure for financial innovation. He correctly emphasizes the role of financial markets and instruments in matching deficit and surplus units, in the creation of liquidity, and in the efficient distribution of risk. Transactions and information costs, and related economies of scale are probably equally important in explaining what particular financial markets and instruments evolve. Although Silber mentions them, I would like to have seen more discussion of their importance and interaction with the other determinants. These costs are obviously important, for example, in determining what assets are liquid, and reversible. In the case of the

87

mortgage market these transactions and information costs seem central in understanding the difficulty in establishing standardized credit ratings and a secondary market. Although, as Silber says, the volume of mortgages outstanding exceeds the volume of corporate bonds, the dollar value per note issued is very low, and the resulting transaction costs quite high. Consequently, in the absence of government involvement, one would expect mortgage paper to change hands a minimum of times.

One of the desirable consequences of the macro perspective Silber takes in the first part of this chapter is that it does not take as a datum the existing financial structure. As he observes, there are important inter-dependencies between and among institutions and markets. For example, the development of financial intermediaries may considerably lessen market pressure for secondary markets by individual investors; on the other hand, such intermediaries may be of sufficient scale to create such a market themselves.

In contrast with his macro discussion, Silber looks primarily within the firm environment when he turns to his micro discussion. This quite naturally leads him to analyze product and process innovations by existing firms, rather than the emergence of new firms and industries. Understanding why existing firms create new products is, of course, important, but this emphasis means that Silber is not focusing on the factors that were responsible for the emergence and dramatic growth of new financial "industries." For example, in his empirical discussion of life insurance companies, Silber focuses on the innovation of "industrial" policies in the mid-1870s. Given the dramatic growth in the insurance industry (from 2 percent of the total assets of financial intermediaries in 1860 to 13 percent in 1912), it seems more likely that this particular event is related to the more fundamental determinants of innovation that Silber discusses in the first part of his chapter, than to the "adversity" that he emphasizes in his micro discussion.

Why do firms innovate? Silber discusses the general theory of financial firm behavior with a view to identifying the conditions that are likely to induce innovation. As he states, innovation will occur "when there is an exogenous change in the constrained optimization of the firm that stimulates a search for new policy tools" (p. 65). You don't have to be from Chicago to believe that profits have something to do with the process, and, of course, Silber's statement is consistent with the view that innovating firms are, indeed, seeking to maximize profits. Silber, however, places heavy emphasis on "adversity" as the stimulus rather than the attraction of profits of themselves. This proposition is surely debatable, since it is hard to identify the marginal profitability of new products, even ex post, and many of the causes of innovation Silber identifies in his list of examples are regulations that simultaneously decrease profits and increase the profitability of new activities. Similarly, Silber's case study of innovation in the insurance industry is far from conclusive. The firms that Silber identifies as examples of innovation under adversity (Metropolitan and John Hancock) in fact were emulating a new firm (Prudential). Similarly, as Silber indicates, of the two firms most adversely affected by the slowdown of growth between 1905 and 1910, one introduced group insurance and the other did not even follow the innovation. Although I found Silber's empirical discussion suggestive, it is apparent that distinguishing among the relatively subtle differences in the various behavioral hypotheses will require much more detailed statistical work than has yet been done.

Part II
Specific Studies of Financial
Innovation

Introduction to Part II

The chapters in part II provide a detailed analysis of selected financial sector developments. Dwight Jaffee examines the factors that have produced and impeded innovation in the mortgage market. The role of government intervention in the mortgage market is given substantial consideration. Specific proposals for recent innovations in the mortgage contract are described. Chapter 4 by Benjamin Klein seeks to explain the relationship between inflationary expectations and the maturity structure of corporate debt instruments. Klein develops measures of uncertainty in expected inflation and tests their empirical significance in explaining changes in corporate debt maturity between 1900 and 1972. These two chapters are examples of the type of detailed studies that must be undertaken to test hypotheses put forward to explain the evolution of financial market phenomena.

3

Innovations in the Mortgage Market

Dwight M. Jaffee

Introduction

For the 25-year period, from the end of the 1930s through 1965, the mortgage market remained in a remarkably stable and static state. The principal private sector lenders—savings and loan associations, commercial banks, mutual savings banks, and life insurance associations—were operating in much the same way in 1965 as they had been, say, in 1940. The 1965 mortgage contract—fixed rate, constant payment, long-term, fully amortized—was essentially identical to the 1940-vintage contract. And the policy instruments of the government, with their focus on the Federal Housing Authority (FHA) mortgage guarantees, Federal National Mortgage Association (FNMA) mortgage market support, and Federal Home Loan Bank (FHLB) system regulation of the savings and loan industry, also were basically unchanged.

This 25-year period of stability is bounded at both ends by periods of high innovative activity in the mortgage market. At the far end the proximate source of activity was, of course, the collapse of the mortgage market during the Great Depression into delinquency and foreclosure. The resulting innovation found the government in the lead, with the private market and institutions following, and for the most part quite willingly. This is not surprising since the major policy measures had the immediate objective of supporting near-bankrupt institutions and of purchasing delinquent mortgages at par value. Perhaps more surprising, however, is the speed with which the changes were introduced and how long they have lasted. Indeed, as already indicated, the 1965 mortgage market was, and for that matter the 1975 mortgage market is, fully a creation of the Depression legislation.

For the recent period of innovation since 1965, both the proximate cause and the innovative response are quite different. The source of the innovations are the sluggish flows of mortgage funds and housing investment, which in turn are the result of high and rising levels of both interest rates and inflation rates. The nature of the innovative response differs in two important ways: First, in terms of *actual* innovative achievements, relatively little has been accomplished compared to either the amount of concern that has been voiced or to the record of the 1930s. For example,

95

one major policy achievement was the Housing and Urban Development Act of 1968, with the intent of creating a major agency for the subsidization of housing. Interestingly, however, the major successes of this legislation have come in extending the FHA-FNMA nexus—ideas already suggested in the 1930s and predicted as growth areas—while the truly innovative policies have uniformly ended in administrative and fraudulent red tape. Second, in terms of *potential* innovations, there exist long lists of policy proposals for aiding the mortgage and housing markets that have not been acted upon. These innovations include, for example, the Hunt Commission proposals for restructuring the financial markets, and various policies for changing the mortgage contract. While strongly supported by the academic community, these proposals have been resisted by various factions in the financial markets and have only a clouded future in terms of supporting legislation.

The general topic of this chapter is an economic analysis of the innovations that have occurred in the mortgage market, and of the means by which future innovations might be anticipated. In particular, the chapter focuses on the question of why the seemingly sound proposals for current innovations have found such limited success in being implemented. The agenda is the following. In the next section, the history of innovative activity in the 1930s is reviewed. The stress here is on the innovative factors as they compare and contrast with the current situation, since complete histories of the period are available elsewhere.[1] In the third section the current innovations and proposals for innovation are developed and evaluated. The final section draws together the basic principles that appear to regulate innovations in the mortgage market.

Innovative Activity During the 1930s

The broad outline of the 1930s mortgage market experience is familiar terrain. The unprecedented wave of delinquencies and foreclosures on mortgaged properties stands parallel with bank failures and closings as financial hallmarks of the period. As a policy reaction, the government proceeded with an equally unprecedented set of legislation. Some of the key acts were:

The Federal Home Loan Bank Act of 1932, creating the FHLB Board with powers to borrow funds in the capital markets and provide advances to mortgage lenders against their mortgages.

The Federal Home Owners' Loan Act of 1933, creating the Home Owners' Loan Corporation (HOLC), which served as the primary vehi-

[1] See Miles L. Colean [5], Herman E. Krooss and M.R. Blyn [16], and Robert H. Skilton [25].

cle for the refinancing of delinquent and weak mortgages, and creating federal savings and loan association charters.

The National Housing Act of 1934, which created the Federal Housing Authority (FHA) and provided for federal insurance of savings and loan associations.

For the most part the legislation was motivated by the emergency conditions, and had the objective of refinancing the large volume of delinquent and near-delinquent mortgages, and then, later in the decade, of providing a thrust for new mortgage lending and housing investment. By most analyses the emergency aspects of the legislation were deemed a great success. The HOLC, for example, appears unique as a government agency that came into existence, did its job well, and then actually disbanded.

Contractual Innovations

Of more immediate interest, however, is the fact that the legislation created fundamental changes in the structure of the mortgage market. Changes in the technical features of the mortgage contract and changes in the institutional basis of the mortgage market are usefully distinguished, and we take up the mortgage contract first. Table 3-1 summarizes data on contract terms for the major lenders from the NBER Survey of Urban Mortgage Lending.[2] In all categories the terms are highly stable from 1920 through 1934, but then show abrupt shifts starting in 1935. The following are relevant institutional factors.

Contract Length. Commercial bank legislation significantly restricted the length of maturity, due to concern over the illiquidity of mortgage contracts. The increase in maturity in 1935 is the direct result of FHA loans, which were legal assets even with their maturity of 20 years, and which immediately comprised almost 50 percent of new lending. Life insurance companies show a similar pattern, although the pre-1935 maturities were somewhat longer. Mutual savings banks (not shown in table) also have a similar pattern, but were less affected by the FHA programs. Savings and loan associations started out with a significantly longer maturity, on the order of 11 years, which was due to the amortization plans in effect. Again, however, there is a noticeable shift in maturity after 1935. One note of caution should be interjected in the interpretation of these data. Except for savings and loan associations, the formal maturity of the contracts generally understated the effective maturity, since renewal of the loans was generally anticipated by both borrower and lender. Indeed, one of the

---

[2]See J.E. Morton [19] for a summary of the NBER project, and Leo Grebler, D.M. Blank, and L. Winnick [11] for a complete analysis of these and other data.

Table 3-1
Mortgage Contract Terms: 1920-46[a]

	Contract Length (Years)			Loan to Value Ratio			% Fully Amortized			Interest Rate (%)		
	CBs	LICs	SLAs	CBs	LICs	SLAs	CBs	LICs	SIAs	CBs	LICs	SLAs
1920-24	2.8	6.4	11.1	50.0	47.0	57.6	14.9	21.3	94.9[b]	6.2	6.0	7.1
1925-29	3.2	6.4	11.2	52.2	51.2	58.8	10.3	14.3		6.1	5.9	6.8
1930-34	2.9	7.5	11.1	53.6	50.6	59.8	13.6	26.4	93.3	6.1	5.9	6.7
1935-39	11.4	16.4	12.5	62.6	62.8	62.4	69.0	76.7	99.7[c]	5.3	5.2	6.1
1940-46	12.5	20.6	14.0	66.4	77.6	71.0	73.0[d]	95.4	99.8[e]	4.6	4.5	5.4

[a]Based on NBER sample of urban mortgages, one to four family houses. Source: Grebler, Blank, and Winnick [11], tables 64, 66, 67, and 0-6.
  CBs = commercial bonds.
  LICs = life insurance companies.
  SLAs = savings and loan associations.

[b]Data for 1920-29.
[c]Data for 1935-41.
[d]Data for 1940-44.
[e]Data for 1942-45.

major factors leading to foreclosures in the first years of the Depression was the unanticipated termination of contracts by lenders.[3]

Loan to Value Ratios. In the pre-1935 period there is limited differentiation between lenders in loan to value ratios, although savings and loan associations are somewhat higher. This reflected both legal restrictions and institutional rules of thumb, which placed prudent upper bounds on loans at somewhere between 50 percent and 60 percent of appraised value. Starting in 1935 there is again a distinct shift toward higher loan to value ratios, with savings and loan associations actually falling behind somewhat. This is the result of both the FHA programs (in which savings and loan associations rarely participated) and of other concurrent changes such as amortization. A note of caution must again be added. Increasingly in the 1920s standards of appraisal were relaxed, so that the data could significantly understate the ratio of loan to true market value. Also, junior mortgage financing was commonly used in the 1920s, thus raising the effective loan to value ratio for the borrower.

Amortization. In the pre-1935 period there is a wide divergence in amortization patterns.[4] Savings and loan associations clearly were amortizing almost all of their mortgages. One common plan, in particular, was the "share accumulation" arrangement. Under this scheme the borrower agreed to a contractual buildup of deposit shares in the savings and loan association, such that over some intended period, typically 10 to 11 years, the deposit shares with compounded interest would equal the amount due. While seemingly close to the "direct reduction" method of amortization used today, the plan had important flaws that arose during the Depression. In particular, as deposit rates fell, accrued interest fell short of expectations, and even worse, when institutions failed, the builtup equity in the deposit share was lost while the mortgage debt, of course, remained in effect. But, in any case, the lead of savings and loan associations in amortization was significantly reduced beginning in 1935.

Interest Rates. Savings and loan associations obtained considerably higher interest rates throughout the full period. In the pre-1935 period this can be attributed to the less stringent terms on savings and loan mortgages, while

---

[3]John Lintner [17] discusses the Depression experience of the mutual savings banks; see also Richard U. Ratcliff [22, p. 248].

[4]Table 3-1 presents data for the percentage of *fully* amortized loans. Data are also available for *partially* amortized loans and they indicate that commercial banks and life insurance companies did considerable amounts of their lending on this basis. Consequently, Grebler, Blank, and Winnick [11, p. 230] argue that the real change during the Depression was from partial to full amortization. On the other hand, there is also evidence (Lintner [17, p. 272]) that amortization was frequently waived in the early years of the Depression.

beginning in 1935 the ceilings on FHA loans also served to create a gap. As with the other terms, interest rates also showed a clear decline starting in 1935.

Taken at face value, the changes in the mortgage lending terms are very striking. Two types of explanations have been offered to explain the large and quick changes. First, it is argued that the necessity of these changes was generally acknowledged even prior to the Depression, and thus only a gentle governmental lead was necessary. Second, it is argued that the government lending programs, both FHA and HOLC, provided strong competitive pressure for the private lenders and they had no choice but to go along. Both views appear to have some validity.

The necessity of change was accepted at the time by private lenders with perhaps the exception of savings and loan associations. The high rate of delinquency and foreclosure was blamed during the Depression on the short-term, nonamortized nature of the contract; and analysis of cross section samples of mortgages differentiated by terms does indicate the expected pattern in terms of foreclosure rates.[5] Discussion of the legislation also indicated general acceptance of the need for long-term, fully amortized mortgages. Moreover, even the savings and loan associations, which strongly fought off the FHA, did so ostensibly on the basis of principles against government intrusion.

There is, however, somthing of a paradox with the "agreed upon necessity" argument. For one thing, foreclosure rates were significantly rising throughout the period starting with the peak of the housing boom in 1925-26. Yet, there is little indication of a willing change by lenders to long-term or amortized contracts; indeed, to the contrary, until 1935 some terms even show a reverse trend. As a second point, as discussed firmly by R.J. Saulnier [23], it is difficult to attribute any significant proportion of Depression foreclosures to particular contract terms. The major factor was clearly the general economic environment, and the marginal effects of differential contract terms seem minor in comparison. Thus, overall, while the desirability of some changes may have been agreed upon, the necessity was not strong enough actually to cause the changes without a significant push from government action.

This leads then to the second explanation for the change in contract terms, the competition created by government entry into the mortgage market with FHA and HOLC. For savings and loan associations the effects of competition seem to have been very strong. While the savings and loan associations fought the FHA legislation on the grounds of principle, it seems likely their motives were much more pecuniary. The lending advantage of the savings and loan associations was strongly in the direction of long-term, fully amortized contracts, and, as seen in Table 3-1, they were able to obtain higher interest rates on this account. The FHA contract,

[5]See Morton [19], chapter 5, and Lintner [17], chapters 13 and 14.

however, provided essentially all of the advantage of the savings and loan contract, but at a lower rate and in a form (with insurance) that quickly brought commercial banks and life insurance companies back into the market. It would thus seem that the changes in savings and loan terms after 1934 can reasonably be attributed to the FHA competition. On the other hand, it should also be noted that the mutual savings banks appear to have responded much less to this competition; even into the late 1930s mutual savings banks were not amortizing a large proportion of their loans. Indeed, interestingly, while mutual savings banks seem to have fared the best among major institutions in terms of deposit protection during the Depression, they also appear as the institutions most relunctant to reenter the mortgage market. This can be explained by the strong principle of depositor protection under which they operated, although ultimately their reluctance to maintain a mortgage portfolio resulted in significantly lower earnings for the same depositors. In any event, it was not until after World War II that the mutual savings banks responded with more equivalent terms.

Other Innovations in the Mortgage Market

Two other sets of innovations stemming from the Depression are worth considering. The first is the relatively straightforward increase in the proportion of mortgage lending by institutional sources. The second is the more complicated set of structural changes set off by the FHA programs.

Increased Institutional Lending. At the turn of the century (1900), at least 50 percent of nonfarm residential mortgage funds were originated in noninstitutional sources, which is to say by private lenders in the household sector. This proportion quickly dropped to slightly less than 40 percent noninstitutional lending by 1910, but then stabilized at this level into the Depression. Data starting in 1920 are shown in the last column of Table 3-2. Since 1934 a continuation of the downward trend in noninstitutional lending is evident, and recent numbers (1970-74) show less than 10 percent of mortgage lending from such sources.

This trend, which was noted and predicted to continue by L. Grebler, D.M. Blank and L. Winnick [11], has been explained as the result of a variety of factors. First, there has been an increasing tendency for private savings to take the form of time deposits at depository institutions. This is not, however, a fully independent development, since the rate of return paid on time deposits depends in large part on the net yield obtained from the mortgage portfolio. Second, the change during the Depression to a long-term, fully amortized contract may have placed large institutional lenders at a comparative advantage in terms both of the mechanics of originating and administering such loans, and in terms of the long-term

Table 3-2
Percentage Distribution of Nonfarm, Residential Mortgage Debt by Major Lendings

	Commercial Banks	Mutual Savings Banks	Savings and Loan Associations	Life Insurance Companies	Federal and Related Agencies	Noninstitutional Lenders[a]
1920-24	9.8	19.1	22.3	7.1	0	41.6
1925-29	11.1	16.3	23.0	9.3	0	40.2
1930-34	10.3	17.5	20.1	10.9	2.0	39.2
1935-39	11.0	17.5	15.6	10.2	11.3	34.5
1940-44	13.3	15.3	18.2	14.3	6.9	32.0
1945-52	18.3	12.9	24.1	18.7	2.5	23.5
1970-74	15.0%	13.4%	43.7%	9.8%	9.2%	9.0%

Source: 1920-52, Grebler, Blank and Winnick, [11], Table N-3; 1970-74, *Federal Reserve Bulletin*, February 1975, page A-44.

[a]Includes small amounts of unidentified institutional and governmental lending.

nature of the commitment. Third, the existence of FHA insurance allowed many of the regulations on bank and life insurance company lending to be relaxed, and in particular allowed these institutions to purchase mortgages on much more of a national basis. Thus, the private institutions were able to achieve the advantages of geographic diversification. Also, the noninstitution lender was simply ineligible under many of the FHA programs. Fourth, and finally, the tremendous growth in the magnitude of mortgage debt, and other technological changes in communication and transportation, worked to the advantage of large institutions that could take advantage of the economies of scale.

Other Innovative Aspects of the FHA Program. There are several other aspects of the FHA programs under the National Housing Act of 1934 that are worth stressing in view of later developments. Under Title I of the act there was authority for insurance on up to 20 percent of the amount of home loans for repair and modernization. This program generally did not succeed, and in particular there was fraud and misrepresentation during the short period it was in effect.[6] This, of course, is a forerunner of similar problems faced by the Department of Housing and Urban Development in recent years.

Title 2 of the National Housing Act provided the authority for the basic federal insurance of mortgages. Mortgage insurance was not itself an innovation. Particularly in New York State, a variety of private firms carried on a major business in mortgage insurance during the 1920s. Insured mortgages were then sold in the form of participations to individual investors (anticipating current government programs of this sort). The private insurance companies unfortunately, however, failed quickly and completely in the beginning years of the Depression. This raised the question, then, of why FHA insurance might be expected to fare better in a second depression. The main answer, of course, was the open-ended commitment of the federal government's fiscal and taxation powers. In addition, the FHA adopted unusually rigorous and objective criteria for the appraisal of values, for the standards of construction, and for the risk rating of the borrower. These standards tended to spill over into the conventional mortgage market as well, and thus did represent by themselves a major innovation. Finally, it should be noted that the success of the FHA program no doubt provided some basis for the revival of private mortgage insurance starting with the Mortgage Guaranty Insurance Corporation (MGIC) in 1957.[7]

Ceiling rates, originally set at 5 percent but soon lowered, were also an

[6]See Ratcliff [22, p. 263].

[7]See Chester Rapkin [21] for a history of mortgage insurance and an analysis of MGIC activities; also see R.J. Saulnier, Harold G. Halcrow, and Neil H. Jacoby [24].

important part of the FHA program and have continued to be so. Through-out the Depression the ceilings were significantly below market rates on conventional contracts. The rationale for the ceilings stemmed in large part from the view that relatively low rates were necessary for the safe function-ing of the mortgage market. In addition, the FHA was in a strong position in that FHA loans provided commercial banks and life insurance companies with insured and liquid investments in a period where comparable non-mortgage assets provided very low returns. Still another rationale for the ceilings was that they were an attempt to equalize interest rates across the geographic regions of the country. Of these reasons, the "quasi-monopolist" position of the FHA appears the most telling, at least as an explanation as to why the ceilings could be enforced. Over the years, of course, the Depression induced aversion to mortgage risk has subsided, and private lenders now tend to view either actuarially based self-insurance or private insurance (MGIC) as competitive alternatives. It is thus not surprising that today binding FHA ceilings drive lenders from this market, whereas when introduced, the FHA program was accepted even with strong ceiling restrictions.

Finally, Title 3 of the National Housing Act, together with later amendments, allowed for the establishemment of FNMA with the intention of both supporting the market for FHA loans and for providing a secondary trading facility. FNMA activity started off somewhat slowly, but acceler-ated significantly in 1948 with its support of the VA mortgage market. FNMA also experimented at this time with a commitment program that allowed lenders to originate a VA mortgage with assurance of a resale market; a system that has been again used in recent years. On the general level there have been continuing questions over the proper interpretation of the role of FNMA as a secondary market maker. FNMA has served basically as a primary investor to the extent it has accumulated a mortgage portfolio of its own. Also, FNMA has served clearly as a broker in expedit-ing the exchange of newly originated mortgages between the originator and the long-term investor. It is doubtful, however, that FNMA ever effec-tively provided a stable market for the purchase and sale of seasoned mortgages, the role normally associated with a secondary market.

Innovative Activity in the Mortgage Market: 1966-74

Following the stable years from the Depression through 1965, the mortgage market has again been the center of both actual and proposed innovation. The starting date for this innovation can be identified, with some simplifica-tion, as the money crunch of 1966. A key factor at that time, of course, was the sudden tightening of monetary policy with a particularly strong impact on the cost and availability of short-term funds. This led in turn to "disin-termediation" from thrift institutions, which is generally held responsible for the sudden downturn in mortgage and housing activity. Since 1966 there have been several cycles in monetary tightness and interest rates, but the general trend, spurred on by increasing inflation, has been for higher levels of interest rates. Similarly, mortgage and housing markets have cycled, with especially bad downturns in 1969-70 and 1974. At this writing the general outlook for mortgage and housing markets appears quite de-pressed, indeed exceptionally so for a recession period in which these markets usually recover quite quickly.

A main thrust for innovation in the mortgage market has thus come from the search for means by which the mortgage and housing markets can be stimulated. This source of innovation is thus shared by both the current situation and the Depression. The Depression problem with the mortgage and housing markets, however, was due to the foreclosures stemming from the depressed state of the economy and the aversion to mortgage lending that resulted, whereas the current dilemma appears to be the difficulty of the institutional structure to cope with high interest rates and inflation. In particular, although delinquency rates showed an upward trend during the 1960s, little concern has been voiced over the risk factors that were in the forefront of the Depression innovations.

We turn now to a brief survey of innovations actually carried out more recently, followed by a summary of the proposals for current innovation that remain outstanding.

Innovations Already Implemented

The dramatic increase in direct government support of the mortgage mar-ket through mortgage purchases by federal and related agencies is certainly the most impressive of the recent changes. For the first time since the Depression, government support of the mortgage market is approaching the 1935-39 level (see Table 3-2). The one to four family residential mortgage holdings of the agencies have increased from about $4.7 billion at year end 1965 to $47 billion at year end 1974, a ten-fold increase. Among the agencies with the greatest activity have been FNMA, GNMA, FHLB Board, and the recently created Federal Home Loan Mortgage Corpora-tion (FHLMC). In addition to the volume statistics, there have been a variety of changes in the methods by which the mortgages have been purchased.

FNMA has returned to the free market auction system for accepting mortgage commitments. At year-end 1974 FNMA had just under $8 billion in outstanding commitments (as against holdings of $29.5 billion). Similarly, FHLMC has greatly expanded its own commitments program such that about \$2.4 billion were outstanding at year-end 1974 (as against mortgage holdings of \$4.5 billion). The mechanism of these plans is that for a fee between 1/2 percent and 1 percent, the agency guarantees to purchase mortgages for some period and at a contractually set rate or formula.

Mortgage-backed and pass-through securities have been innovated in several ways. The principle of a mortgage-backed security is that a mortgage originator puts together a pool of insured mortgages and then finances them by selling a debt instrument backed by the pool. The timing of payments on the securities follows the standard bond formula, which will differ from the mortgage, and thus there is some residual cash-flow risk. The Federal Home Loan Bank Board, for example, has set regulations whereby savings and loan associations can issue such mortgage-backed bonds. Pass-through securities have a similar format, but the timing of payments on the bonds follows exactly the payments on the mortgages. Thus, any prepayments on the mortgages, for example, would be directly passed through to the bond holder. This creates uncertainty about the timing of the payment stream for the bond holder, but eliminates any risk due to the intermediation of the originator. In a similiar way, real estate investment trusts (REITs) are an innovative, although currently, some-what disastrous, way of generating new mortgage funds.

The Department of Housing and Urban Development has carried on a variety of mortgage and housing subsidy plans since 1968. Most recently in the mortgage market there have been "tandem plans" whereby GNMA purchases mortgages at subsidized rates, and obtains a commitment to sell them at market value to FNMA. The subsidies are thus located within HUD, while the investor owned FNMA holds the securities at market value.

The Federal Home Loan Bank Board has innovated its activities in two prime ways. Advances to member savings and loan associations were \$21.8 billion at year-end 1974, compared with \$5.0 billion at year-end 1965. During 1974, in particular, advances were provided to members at rates subsidized relative to the cost of funds to the Bank Board. On a different front, there has been a strong attempt at the Bank Board to liberalize and deregulate the mass of restrictions on member institutions. The major policy reforms, however, remain in the form of proposals (discussed below).

Two major aspects of these changes appear as the core of the innovative thrust: the raw quantity of government purchases, and the attempts to pool mortgages in forms more attractive to investors. The key to the success of these changes will rest on two questions: First, to what extent do the programs serve primarily to displace equal or nearly equal amounts of mortgages from private portfolios? Second, to what extent would success in increasing the net mortgage flow actually serve to stimulate housing investment?

With regard to both questions, quite negative appraisals for government mortgage activity have resulted from a variety of studies.[8] In the mortgage market itself, the displacement mechanism is the apparent high elasticity of marginal investors between mortgages and other debt instruments. Thus, as government agencies purchase mortgages and cause downward pressure on mortgage rates, while selling debt instruments and creating upward pressure on capital market rates, private investors have an incentive to swap bonds for mortgages in just the opposite direction. In the housing market the mechanism is similar in that the gearing ratio between mortgage debt increments and housing investment appears highly interest elastic. That is, as the spread between mortgage and other rates declines (as it has significantly since 1965), home owners substitute mortgage debt for equity in the financing of their investment. This increase in marginal mortgage-house ratios can result either from higher loan to value ratios on mortgaged homes, or because a larger proportion of homes are mortgage financed.

The theory and empirical evaluation of this "private market displace-ment" view of government mortgage purchases is most persuasive in the context of long-run equilibrium. The theory is less complete, and the evidence more ambiguous, when the setting is the short-run dynamics of a disequilibrium mortgage market. Then, in particular, it is possible that government mortgage purchases get directly to the fringe of would-be home investors that are otherwise rationed out of the market. Moreover, although sluggishness in the speed of adjustment of mortgage rates, and therefore short-run disequilibrium, characterized the mortgage market over a long period, the recent importance of state usury ceilings, in con-junction with inflation induced high nominal mortgage rates, has aggra-vated the problem significantly.

A summary appraisal of government intermediation in the mortgage market thus must rest more on forecasts of the disequilibrium status of the market than on the simple fact of government purchases. Were usury ceilings and other impediments to mortgage flows eliminated, then the evidence would suggest there is little value from government intermedia-tion. On the other hand, should the present policies of pegging interest rates well below their historic spreads against capital market rates continue as a permanent policy, then government intermediation would continue to be seen as necessary. The mortgage interest rate in such a system, it might be noted, is more an income distribution parameter than an allocational de-

[8]For recent discussion of the issue, see U.S. Senate [28, discussion of Dwight M. Jaffee, Allan H. Meltzer, and Shapiro], Francisco Arcelus and A.H. Meltzer [1] and [2], Barry Bosworth and J.S. Duesenberry [3], Dwight M. Jaffee [14, p. 170 ff], Allan H. Meltzer [18], and Bernard A. Gelb [10].

vice.[9] Indeed, such a policy would be very close to the housing finance systems long established in Western Europe, and would lead one to predict a significantly diminished role for private mortgage finance in the United States.

The actual innovations just described are attempts to compensate for the effects of high interest and inflation rates; they do not get at the basic causes of the problem. The basic causes of the problem, moreover, are less the high interest and inflation rates themselves, than the institutional and regulatory structure of the mortgage market. That is, in an idealized "perfect" mortgage market, contracts could be indexed so as to eliminate the negative effects of either anticipated or even unanticipated inflation. The proposals for innovation to be discussed now, in contrast, do try to go to the root of the problem. The proposals can be classified into two basic groups: recommendations for changing the nature of the mortgage contract; and recommendations for restructuring the financial markets. We take these up in turn.

Proposals for Innovating the Mortgage Contract

The current mortgage contract, with its Depression origin, was developed in order to minimize delinquency and foreclosure in a context of basically flat interest rate and price level trends. Although it is unclear whether the contract would actually forestall a breakdown of the mortgage market in an economic downturn of the magnitude of the Great Depression, it is true that it worked well in the 1950s and early 1960s, periods characterized by moderate trends in interest rates and inflation rates. In any case there has been concern that this conventional contract is not well suited to periods of high and changing rates of interest and inflation. In particular, a variety of possible mortgage instrument innovations have been studied recently in the MIT Mortgage project, and some of the results are noted here.[10]

Two aspects of the mortgage contract are the main concerns. First, due to the long-term nature of the mortgage contract, a portfolio of mortgages will suffer capital losses in periods of rising interest rates, and if the institution holding them is inadequately capitalized, then the capital losses may actually impair its ability to compete for funds with which to carry the assets or bid for new ones. One solution, of course, is to let such institutions die, and for new institutions to start fresh with higher yielding, newly issued mortgages. In practice this is not feasible. It would undermine confidence

---

[9] And from most viewpoints a perverse distributional parameter at that, since both the value of home purchases and the amount of mortgage debt correlate highly with income.

[10] The project is directed by Professors Franco Modigliani and Donald Lessard of MIT. A conference was held in January 1975, the proceedings of which are forthcoming from the Federal Reserve Bank of Boston.

in the capital markets; and the relevant institutions are where they are in part because of government regulation, and it would seem inequitable to ignore them now. So, instead, government policy has been directed to additional regulations in the capital markets (mainly Regulation Q) with the intent of keeping these institutions at least solvent; and then supporting the mortgage and housing markets in the ways already indicated. The alternative solution, proposed as a change in the contract, is essentially to shorten the effective maturity of mortgage contracts.

The second problem involves the borrowing household and its cash-flow constraint. On conventional contracts the nominal monthly payment is constant over time, and therefore the real monthly payment actually decreases when there is inflation. When inflation is not anticipated, moreover, the decline in real payments is simply a windfall gain for the borrower. When inflation is anticipated, both the price of houses and interest rates will rise, and therefore the nominal level of the fixed payment on new contracts will be *forced* to a level high enough to compensate for the anticipated decline in the real payment. This seems fair enough, and basically leaves the borrower (and lender) in the same real position independent of the anticipated inflation rate. The catch, however, is that anticipated inflation forces a higher nominal payment at the start, and thus requires that the household have the cash flow resources to make such a payment. In particular, households lacking these resources will have either to withdraw from the housing market or to settle for a smaller house with a proportionately smaller payment. One could argue, of course, that the household need only borrow the additional funds, since with decreasing real payments on the mortgage, it will surely generate a later surplus to pay back such a loan. The problem is that short-term consumer loan markets simply are not perfect enough to accomplish this. Instead, the proposals take the form that the mortgage contract itself should be restructured so as to allow, in one way or another, greater nominal borrowing during the early years of the contract (see W. Poole [20]).

Variable Rate Mortgages (VRMS). With this background, we can turn to some specific proposals, starting with VRMs. VRMs are fundamentally an attempt to shorten the effective maturity of the mortgage, and thereby provide lenders with a return that moves more closely with market rates, specifically with short-term market rates. Considerable interest in VRMs is being shown by lenders. Four California savings and loan associations have announced plans to issue VRMs. The Federal Home Loan Bank Board has a set of proposals for federally chartered association lending on a variable rate basis, and these are to be taken up shortly in congressional hearings. And a mutual savings bank in New York City has been offering five-year "roll-over" mortgages, that are particularly reminiscent of pre-Depression contracts. While the various plans differ in details, the principles are similar and involve the following parameters:

New Issue Rate: The interest rate set in the initial contract and that which forms the basis for subsequent variable rate changes. A key question with VRMs is how the new issue rate would compare with other rates in the capital markets, and particularly with conventional mortgages. The answer depends on the formula used for the "effective rate."

Effective Interest Rate: Over time, the effective rate on a VRM will deviate from the new issue rate by some formula or rule. The FHLB Board proposal involves pegging the effective rate to a base index such as the five-year government bond rate.[11] The effective rate in any year would thus be the new issue rate on that specific mortgage plus the cumulated changes (positive or negative) in the base index rate. Thus, given the formula, one should be able to determine the new issue rate on a VRM that is the equivalent of a conventional mortgage rate. In fact, however, this is complicated and the following two examples illustrate the issue involved:

Case 1: Descending Yield Curve. Consider a situation in which, after adjustment for risk and liquidity, the short-term interest rate is 10 percent, the long-term interest rate is 7 percent, and both rates are expected to converge over time to some lower value, say 5 percent. The question is how to set the new issue rate on a VRM that uses the long-term rate as the peg. First, the VRM rate must exceed the long-term rate (after adjustment for risk); otherwise, the VRM *lender* would start with a new issue rate of 7 percent, and then find the effective yield declining to 5 percent, and this would be inferior to investing initially in conventional long-term mortgages with the fixed return of 7 percent. Similarly, the VRM new issue rate must be less than the short-term rate; otherwise, the *borrower* would start at 10 percent and end up at 8 percent, which is clearly inferior to the conventional mortgage at the fixed (risk adjusted) rate of 7 percent. So, the VRM new issue rate is bounded between the long-term and short-term rates, with the actual value being a function of the exact form of interest rate expectations; let us say, for example, that 8.5 percent is determined. Now, if the new issue rate is 8.5 percent, then the effective yield will decline over time and converge to 6.5 percent. This raises a problem since the *new issue rate* on VRMs will itself converge to 5 percent over time as the long rate and the short rate both converge at this level. Borrowers on older vintage VRMs will thus have an incentive to change over to newly issued VRMs at some point. The FHLB Board solution is to maintain prepayment costs on VRMs such that it would be difficult for borrowers to carry out

---

[11]Four California savings and loan associations have recently announced VRMs where the rate is pegged to the average cost of funds for associations in the San Francisco FHLB region.

such arbitrage. Alternatively, the MIT Mortgage project has considered a VRM in which the pegging rate is the new issue rate itself, and thus all VRM mortgages are one year contracts with the rate effectively renegotiated each year. The five-year "roll-over" mortgage is a similar instrument but with the renegotiation every five years.

Case 2: Ascending Yield Curve. Consider a situation in which the short-term rate is 5 percent, the long-term rate is again 7 percent, and both rates are expected to converge over time to a 10 percent value. Now the incentives are just reversed, but the principle of a new issue rate between the short-term and long-term rate is still the same. For example, a new issue rate of 6 percent might obtain, and over time the effective rate on a newly issued mortgage would be expected to rise to 9 percent. This raises a problem in that the lender would have incentive at some point not to renew the mortgage, and to invest instead in conventional long-term mortgages as the risk adjusted rate approaches 10 percent. Thus, either the lender must be contractually locked into the contract, or the mortgage must be a short-term contract of the MIT project sort, with the new issue rate acting as the effective peg.

Prepayment Costs and Renewal Guarantee. It is thus clear that prepayment costs and renewal guarantees must be enforced if a VRM is to function with a long-term pegging rate. These would represent costs to both the borrower and lender in terms of locking them into contracts (where there is not a secondary market), and for this reason the MIT Mortgage project has been inclined to a short-term pegging for the VRM. On the other hand, it can be argued that a renewal guarantee by the lender, at least, should be adopted in any case, in order to avoid unexpected contract termination as occurred during the Depression.

Payment and Maturity. Another option for VRMs concerns the form in which payments are adjusted as the effective interest rate changes. A standard way is simply to reamortize the contract on a fixed payment basis over the remaining maturity using the new effective interest rate as the discount factor. In this way changes in the effective interest rate are fully reflected in the payment. Alternatively, within certain bounds, it is possible to change the maturity as the effective rate changes, keeping the nominal payment fixed. Still another technique, studied in the MIT Mortgage project, is to vary the payment with changes in the long-term rate, but crediting as amortization only that part of the payment not required to pay the actual effective interest rate. This could leave a "balloon" payment at the end if interest rates rise systematically over the life of the mortgage, although simulations indicate this is not a major problem. Finally, it is possible to use "graduated payment" techniques to dampen the cash flow effect of changing interest rates in a way to be described below.

Consumer Safeguards. Most formal proposals for VRMs stress explicit attention to consumer safeguards. These involve factors such as the number of changes in the effective rate allowed per year, the requirement of due notice before a change, truth in lending specifications, and similar factors.

Most current appraisals of the VRM indicate that the contract should benefit the lender in terms of providing him with a current yield, but may have a negative impact on borrowers due to the uncertainty of the future interest rate. There is also the view that consumers will not buy VRMs. From work carried out with the MIT Mortgage study, however, it seems that the common view overstates both the value of VRM to the lender and the cost of VRMs to the borrower. The overstatement of benefit to the lender is the result of calculating the benefit on the presumption that the rate of interest on VRMs will average over time the rate on fixed-rate conventional mortgages. But this is unlikely to be the case. Upward sloping yield curves have been the general feature of United States capital markets, except for unusual periods of monetary squeeze or panic, and one must presume that VRMs would generally have a lower yield than comparable long-term, fixed-rate mortgages. Thus, over time lenders will actually receive a lower average return on VRMs, although with the benefit of a more favorable timing. This also seems at least a partial answer to consumer reluctance: set the price low enough.

By the same score, the costs of VRMs to borrowers has been overstated. The traditional argument of an uncertain cost is based on a partial view of the borrower's portfolio, and in particular it ignores the house that is being financed. To the extent that variations in short-term rates reflect similar variations in realized inflation rates, the borrower will have offsetting gains and losses on his house and mortgage. For example, in periods of high inflation and high interest rates, the borrower gains on his house, but loses on his mortgage. Indeed, for a risk-averse individual, who calculates utility in real terms, this offset is a perfect hedge against inflation. There is a slight catch in that the cash flow implications of the offsetting again and loss could be different. For example, for the case just mentioned, the capital gain on the house would be realized only upon sale, while the additional interest on the mortgage might be due immediately. The simple solution, however, is to allow the individual to borrow against the increased value, and proposals discussed below do just this.

Low Start or Graduated Payment Mortgages (GPMs). A simple solution for the cash flow constraint associated with mortgage financing in periods of high inflation and high interest rates are innovations that change the payments stream of the mortgage, but keep the fixed rate feature of the conventional contract intact. The size of the monthly payment on a conventional contract is determined by calculating the constant payment that creates a present discounted value for the lender equal to the initial loan, using the agreed on mortgage rate as the discount rate. By the same procedure, however, one can introduce a second degree of freedom, and calculate an initial payment and a growth rate of payments that achieves the same discounted value. Of course, the initial payment on the GPM will be less than the fixed payment on the conventional contract, whereas toward the end of the contract the graduated payment will exceed the fixed conventional payment. In particular, if the payment is graduated at the expected rate of inflation, then the result is a fixed level of real payments on the graduated contract.

The acknowledged problem with GPMs is that they subject the lender to greater risk over the life of the contract, since less amortization takes place during the early years. Countering this, however, is the fact that the market value of the collateral will also be rising in a period of inflation. In other words, the ratio of loan outstanding to market value of house should be roughly the same for a GPM in an inflationary period and a conventional mortgage in a stable price period. Of course, a conventional mortgage in an inflationary period will generate a lower effective loan ratio, but that is the basis of the whole problem, not a drawback to the solution.

Simulations for the MIT Mortgage project have suggested another difficulty, and perhaps more important difficulty, with the GPM. Compare two growing worlds, one financed through conventional mortgages and one financed through GPMs. The average age of the mortgage stock will be greater for the graduated payment world since the repayment schedule lags behind. This effect vanishes in a static context, but it is present if there is any growth. The effect is particularly pertinent when interest rates are rising and the contracts have been made on a fixed rate basis. The older mortgage stock associated with the GPM will then accentuate the problem of a lagging return on mortgage portfolios that is associated in any case with fixed rate mortgages.

PLAMs, Tuckers, and Other Mixtures. One interpretation of the problem of implementing either VRMs or GPMs is that they have both benefits and costs, and although there may be a net gain, the gross cost acts as a factor inhibiting innovation. An appealing solution therefore is to devise a combination of the two plans such that the gross costs are reduced, while the net gains are retained. Several proposals have been made.

Price level adjusted mortgages (PLAMs), that is indexed mortgages, operate essentially on this principle. The basic interest rate on the contract is the market real rate of interest and this determines the initial payment. Thus, regardless of the expected rate of inflation the initial payment on a PLAM has the low-level characteristic of GPMs. If inflation does occur, then the principal remaining on the loan is escalated by the amount of inflation, and subsequent payments reflect this higher base for the principal. Thus, for the borrower, a PLAM is essentially a GPM, but with a graduation rate that is adjusted for the realized rate of inflation. For the lender, on the other hand, the contract achieves the benefits of a VRM at least to the extent that inflation rates and interest rates move together.

To be clear, some of the problems of both GPMs and VRMs are present with PLAMs. For the borrower, the payment will be rising with inflation, whereas the capital gain on the house will not be realized. For the lender, the average age of the PLAM will be greater than a comparable conventional mortgage, and this could cause a problem if real rates of interest rise. However, these problems appear limited, and the MIT Mortgage project has suggested other contractual arrangements than could reduce them even further.

Another route to the same solution has been suggested by D.P. Tucker [27]. Tucker's proposal starts with a VRM of the type discussed above. Each period, however, the payment schedule for the remaining principal is recalculated on a graduated basis where the graduation rate is increased by the change in the interest rate. Thus, for the borrower, although his interest rate may be rising, the increased graduation reduces the immediate cash flow impact. For the lender, the advantages of a VRM are achieved, although with the possible disadvantages of a GPM. On net, the Tucker mortgages will be very similar to PLAMs whenever market rates reflect inflation and real rates are relatively constant. Otherwise, some technical differences in the contracts do arise.

Finally, it is noteworthy that the innovation of "equity-kickers" in mortgage lending, especially by life insurance companies, can be interpreted as an attempt to achieve some degree of indexation.

Proposals for Changing the Structure of Mortgage Markets

A variety of proposals have been made in recent years for the restructuring of the financial markets in a way that would help both the thrift institutions and mortgage and housing markets. These include the study of the savings and loan industry directed by Irwin Friend [9] . The Report of the President's Commission on Financial Structure and Regulation—the Hunt Commission Report [13], the Financial Institutions Act of 1973, which remains before Congress, and a recent summary of proposals by the Federal Home Loan Bank Board [7]. The spirit of these proposals is very similar, and they have been widely discussed, so only a brief outline is presented here, using the Hunt Commission as guide.[12]

With respect to the structure of mortgage markets, the following are the main elements:

Statutory ceilings on FHA and VA mortgages should be eliminated, as well as usury ceilings set by states on mortgages.

Variable rate mortgages should be authorized and implemented by the FHA and VA, and a secondary market should be developed by FNMA.

States should simplify legal aspects of the mortgage contract, and eliminate barriers to interstate lending.

Statutory and regulatory restrictions on commercial bank real estate loans should be ended.

Credit unions should be allowed entry to mortgage lending to a greater extent.

Savings and loan associations should be allowed lending powers on all types of residential and nonresidential real estate.

With respect to the structure of thrift institutions, the following appear as the key elements:

Asset powers should include consumer loans.

Deposit and liability powers should allow full freedom for innovation in subordinated debentures, mortgage-backed assets, and variations by maturity.

Third-party transfers should be allowed.

Household service functions (mutual funds, income tax services, etc.) should be expanded.

Regulation Q should be eliminated.

While only an outline, the above gives the flavor of the proposals. The key element in these proposals is apparently the removal of Regulation Q ceilings as a protective device for the thrift institutions. To implement the proposals, the argument must be made that the net effect of the package will help thrift institutions, and housing and mortgage markets as well. Most studies indicate this is the case, and changes in the mortgage contract could help as well.[13] But at least the trade associations for the savings and loan industry and the housing industry remain unconvinced. Perhaps more importantly, there may, in fact, be a transition problem for the thrift institutions if Regulation Q is removed before the full advantages of the

---

[12]For summaries, see the Federal Reserve Bank of Boston [8], the November 1973 issue of the *Journal of Money, Credit and Banking*, and U.S. Senate [28].

[13]See Ray C. Fair and D.M. Jaffee [6] and Henry J. Cassidy and Donald G. Edwards [4] for empirical studies of the Hunt Commission proposals.

increased powers are achieved. A possible safeguard is then some sort of governmental guarantee to the thrift industry during the transition. For example, this could involve government purchase of low yielding mortgages at par, an idea reminiscent of HOLC purchases of high-risk mortgages at par.

In any case a large part of the recent actions on these proposals seem to reflect an attempt by the interested parties in obtaining better terms; and there does appear some room for compromise. Ultimately, however, the main issue seems to be the willingness of thrift institutions to accept a more competitive climate and to experiment with more innovative contracts in both asset and liability markets; or of the willingness of Congress to force such a situation on them.

Conclusions

The discussion so far has stressed the factual basis of innovation in two periods of activity in the mortgage market. To put this together we now consider what general propositions on the innovation process stand out from this experience, and, more specifically, what can be predicted as the likely course on the currently outstanding proposals.

General Propositions from Mortgage Market Innovation

Chapter 2 by William Silber in this book provides a useful theoretical framework, and it is interesting to see how the facts of the mortgage market fit in. The following examples illustrate various aspects of Silber's analysis.

Real Sector Changes as Source of Innovation. Silber stresses the importance of changes in the real sector of the economy as one source of financial innovation. This is amply illustrated in the mortgage market. The changes during the Depression had their fundamental source, particularly as argued by R.J. Saulnier [23], not in the financial sphere but in the real depression of income. Also, as a result, the increased aversion to the risk of mortgage lending forced the government to take a more positive position. More recently, perhaps all, and at least part, of the inflationary pressure should be counted as a real sector (as opposed to monetary) source, and thus stands as the origin of the need for innovation. Finally, technological improvements in computers and electronic transfer have been a partial source of the increased interest elasticity of small savers, which has been responsible for some of the new problems of thrift institutions.

Financial Sector Change as the Source of Innovation. The experience of the mortgage market equally well illustrates some ways in which conditions in the financial markets can be the proximate source of innovation. For one example, FHA rate ceilings had their origin in the disorganized mortgage market of the Depression, and thus could be enforced without a significant displacement of private funds from the market. The same type of ceilings in the current period, however, have themselves been a source of a variety of innovations. The most important reaction, of course, has been the growth of government intermediation in the mortgage market. But one also finds cases of private market innovation. For example, one interpretation of the shift by a mutual savings bank to five-year mortgages is that the term structure allowed such loans to be made at a lower interest rate, and thereby the ceilings were avoided. Another example, also involving ceilings, are the many innovations that have occurred to circumvent Regulation Q ceilings.

Private Initiative as a Source of Innovation. The mortgage market appears to be a case in which private initiative has played only a minor role in carrying out the major innovations. Both the Depression, where no effective action was taken until the government entered, and the current period, where the private institutions are reluctant if not strongly set against innovation, confirm this view.

Competitive Pressure as a Source of Innovation. Recent events in the mortgage market serve as an excellent example of how new competition in a market can have widespread ramifications in terms of innovations. An important element in the current situation is the increasingly competitive nature of the market for the savings of small household units. This factor, together with high interest rates, is clearly responsible for many of the current problems of the thrift institutions, and for the government actions to support the mortgage and housing markets. An immediate response of the thrift institutions has been to lengthen the maturity of their liabilities. Interestingly, in the long run this is likely to reduce the flow of funds through these institutions, since intermediation between long-term mortgages and long-term deposits is less valuable and has a smaller market as a service than intermediation between long-term mortgages and short-term deposits. Of course, something is better than nothing, and it seems to have been proven that, in the long-run, intermediation across a 20-year maturity spread is simply not feasible.

This example also illustrates how long the chain of innovation can be. Increased competition in savings markets could well lead to the entry, through regulatory change, of thrift institutions into consumer loan and third-party transfer markets. These markets have traditionally been much less than perfectly competitive, and thus the entry of thrift institutions could well set off a further stream of innovative change.

Regulation as a Source of Innovation. The interaction of regulation and innovation is a well-worn theme, and need not be extended here, although the mortgage market provides excellent examples. More interestingly, however, the mortgage market, and other financial markets as well, seem actually to exhibit something of a cyclical flow between innovation, regulation, innovation, and deregulation. Specifically, the pre-Depression mortgage market was generally not tightly regulated. The result of Depression innovation was, of course, a highly regulated market. This remained stable until set off by the shocks of the late 1960s, in which the initial reaction was to regulate even further. As this has proven not successful, however, a return to a more competitive environment seems suddenly in the offing.

The Timing of Innovative Change. Silber argues that what is termed "adversity" innovation frequently occurs well after the adversity itself has passed. The Depression innovations of the mortgage market certainly meet the condition of adversity, and the contractual changes did occur after the primary problem of refinancing had been solved. Silber attributes the time lag to the riskiness of such innovations and to the cyclical timing of "adversity." For the mortgage market, it is clear that the lag in innovation was due in part to the disorganization created by the adversity. Also, the adversity itself changed the ex ante risk appraisals for mortgage lending, and thus set off a secondary chain of innovations dealing with this problem.

The Innovation of Secondary Markets. The recent history of United States mortgage markets is replete with the basically unsuccessful attempts of the government and private markets to organize good secondary trading markets. In particular, it is worth repeating that the major role of agencies such as FNMA, GNMA, and FHLMC has been to expedite the transfer of newly originated mortgages, and to hold the mortgages themselves. In this way the agencies have functioned as underwriters and brokers, and when necessary as residual investors, but little has been achieved in the way of secondary trading. To some extent this illustrates Silber's principle that intermediation, in this case government intermediation, can serve as a substitute for secondary markets. In particular, the securities issued by the government agencies do trade in active secondary markets, so it is possible that the same final result is being achieved, and possibly even in the best way.

It is also possible that the need for secondary trading facilities in mortgages has been overestimated. The traditional argument for why secondary markets have not been developed points to the nonstandardized form of the mortgage contract. It could be, however, that there simply is insufficient demand. First, one entire side of the market—the borrower—has no current need for secondary markets: except for prepayment costs, borrowers already have the option of calling the bond. Second, on the lender's side, the primary need for a secondary market would appear in tight money periods when lenders would like to free funds for new originations. However, in such periods the market value of mortgages will be below book value, and thrift institutions appear to be the last domain of the locked-in effect. And perhaps for good reason. For example, were thrift institutions today to sell their mortgages at below par, the losses would reduce net worth, creating problems of meeting regulatory requirements, and in turn limiting the dividend rates they could legally pay.

How Should "We" Innovate the Mortgage Market?

Earlier we noted that many of the current proposals for mortgage market innovation have met strong resistance from either the affected institutions or from Congress, or in some cases from both. This situation stands in contrast to the Depression experience in which there was general agreement as to what should be done, and in which at least the "emergency" measures were carried out quite quickly. It is thus interesting to speculate, in conclusion, on some reasons for the current inertia.

With regard to the proposals for the restructuring of the financial markets, a variety of "political" explanations for inertia are not hard to find. First, the congressional politics appear such that any of the affected institutions has enough power to wield an effective veto. Consequently, one is led to a "package" of proposals such that *everyone* is better off, and this makes for a rather more restricted set of feasible policies than an ordinary Pareto criterion might indicate. It also lends itself to strategic behavior by the institutions to obtain the best possible deal. Second, the thrift institutions are predominantly mutual enterprises. This itself would suggest a conservative view toward innovation, particularly when the innovations are of a competitive sort. Also, it is probably felt by both the institutions and by Congress that, if the situation got sufficiently bad, Congress would bail them out anyway. Third, it may be that the current situation simply does not represent enough of an "adversity" or "emergency" to break the inertia that stands in the way of any innovation. Indeed, it does seem the case that congressional action on the Financial Institutions Act moves in a procyclical fashion with the level of interest rates.

The inertia in implementing proposals for innovating the mortgage contract also has more analytic elements, as well as the political considerations just noted. First, the experience of the Depression no doubt does linger on, especially so when the innovations have elements of "going back" to the pre-Depression form of the mortgage contract. This is unfortunate since the association of long-term, fixed-payment, fully-amortized contracts with mortgage market stability is surely much overdrawn. The usefulness of any financial contract must be evaluated in terms of the existing market situation. And in the current state of high interest rates and inflation, it seems that neither lenders nor borrowers find the current contract advantageous.

A second problem with mortgage contract innovation is related to a "chicken and the egg" problem between asset and liability innovation for the thrift institutions. The main message to these institutions from the current period has been the desirability of a better matching in the maturity structure of their assets and liabilities; but it has not been clear whether the equalization should be on the basis of all short-term or all long-term instruments. In particular, it is difficult to innovate one side of the balance sheet, say the maturity of mortgages, when the competitive forces on the range of maturities for deposits is still not fully clear. Similarly, the uncertainty over how Regulation Q deposit rate ceilings are likely to be regulated lends another related element of risk.

Third, we have noted above that many of the proposed mortgage market changes have both costs and benefits, albeit with a net benefit. Gross costs by themselves, however, may serve to deter innovative activity. And, finally, government intervention in the mortgage market, introduced as stop-gap measures, may act to forestall the basic and necessary innovation. For example, the disequilibrium created by usury ceilings would generally create pressure for change, but this pressure is reduced when the government attempts to support the market at the low usury ceiling rate levels.

So, in concluding, there does not appear any single factor that can be identified as *the* force behind mortgage market innovation, or, for that matter, as the force of inertia against innovation. It does seem the case that mortgages have achieved something of a "social good" status and thus a variety of political factors enter into decisions for change even when private institutions are to be the primary innovators. There are also, as indicated, certain problems of synchronization such that innovation in one market, say mortgages, is inhibited by uncertainty over likely developments in other related financial markets. And finally, for uplift, it is worthwhile recalling Keynes' concluding comments in the *General Theory*.

Madmen in authority, who hear voices in the air, are distilling their frenzy from some academic scribbler of a few years back. I am sure that the power of vested interests is vastly exaggerated compared with the gradual encroachment of ideas.

References

[1] Arcelus, Francisco, and A.H. Meltzer, "The Market for Housing and

Housing Services," *Journal of Money, Credit and Banking*, February 1973.

[2] Arcelus, Francisco, and A.H. Meltzer, "Reply," *Journal of Money, Credit and Banking*, November 1973.

[3] Bosworth, Barry, and J.S. Duesenberry, "A Flow of Funds Model and Its Implications," in *Issues in Federal Debt Management*, Conference Series No. 10, Federal Reserve Bank of Boston, 1973.

[4] Cassidy, Henry J., and Donald G. Edwards, "Technical Report on Simulated Results of Permitting S&Ls to Offer Consumer Credit and Checking Account Services," Working Paper #51, Federal Home Loan Bank Board.

[5] Colean, Miles L., *The Impact of Government on Real Estate Finance in the United States*, National Bureau of Economic Research, 1950.

[6] Fair, Ray C., and D.M. Jaffee, "An Empirical Study of the Hunt Commission Report Proposals for the Mortgage and Housing Markets," in *Federal Reserve Bank of Boston*, 1972.

[7] Federal Home Loan Bank Board, *A Financial Institution for the Future*, 1975.

[8] Federal Reserve Bank of Boston, *Policies for a More Competitive Financial System*, Conference Series No. 8, 1972.

[9] Friend, Irwin, *Study of the Savings and Loan Industry*, Washington July 1969.

[10] Gelb, Bernard A., *Mortgage Debt for Non-Real Estate Purposes*, The Conference Board, 1972.

[11] Grebler, Leo, D.M. Blank, and L. Winnick, *Capital Formation in Residential Real Estate*, Princeton, Princeton University Press for NBER, 1956.

[12] Gramlich, Edward, and D.M. Jaffee, *Savings Deposits, Mortgages, and Housing*, Lexington, Mass., Lexington Books, D.C. Heath and Co., 1972.

[13] Hunt, Reed O., *The Report of the The President's Commission on Financial Structure and Regulation*, Washington, D.C., U.S. Government Printing Office, December 1971.

[14] Jaffee, Dwight M., "An Econometric Model of the Mortgage Market," chapter 5 in Gramlich and Jaffee, *Savings Deposits* [12].

[15] Klaman, Saul B., *The Postwar Residential Mortgage Market*, Princeton, Princeton University Press for NBER, 1961.

[16] Krooss, Herman E., and M.R. Blyn, *A History of Financial Intermediaries*, New York, Random House, 1971.

[17] Lintner, John, *Mutual Savings Banks in the Savings and Mortgage Markets*, Division of Research, Harvard Business School, 1948.

[18] Meltzer, Allan H., "Credit Availability and Economic Decisions: Some Evidence from the Mortgage and Housing Markets," *Journal of Finance*, June 1974.

[19] Morton, J.E., *Urban Mortgage Lending*, Princeton, Princeton University Press for NBER, 1956.

[20] Poole, William, "Housing Finance Under Inflationary Conditions," in Board of Governors of the Federal Reserve System, *Ways to Moderate Fluctuations in Housing Construction* 1972.

[21] Rapkin, Chester, *The Private Insurance of Home Mortgages*, 1973.

[22] Ratcliff, Richard U., *Urban Land Economics*, New York, McGraw Hill, 1949.

[23] Saulnier, R.J., "Introduction," in Morton, *Urban Mortgage Lending* [19].

[24] Saulnier, R.J., Harold G. Halcrow, and Neil H. Jacoby, *Federal Lending and Loan Insurance*, Princeton, Princeton University Press for NBER, 1958.

[25] Skilton, Robert H., *Government and the Mortgage Debtor*, Dissertation, University of Pennsylvania, 1944.

[26] Swan, Craig, "The Markets for Housing and Housing Services," *Journal of Money Credit and Banking*, November 1973.

[27] Tucker, D.P., "The Variable-Rate Graduated-Payment Mortgage," *Real Estate Review*, Spring 1975.

[28] U.S. Senate, "Reform of Financial Institutions—1973," Hearings Before the Subcommittee on Financial Institutions of the Committee on Banking, Housing, and Urban Affairs, 93rd Congress.

Comment: Innovations in the Mortgage Market

Almarin Phillips

This is not the first occasion I have had to comment on work by Dwight Jaffee. Such opportunities must be received with mixed feelings. On the one hand, the task is easy since Jaffee's writings are of high quality and there is no need to fear that comments will produce acrimony. On the other hand, and for the same reason, there is little for the reviewer to say of a substantive nature. Thus, my remarks are brief and related primarily to minor questions of possible omissions.

There have been significant changes in the sources of institutional mortgage lending that are not emphasized in this chapter. The percentage distribution of mortgage debt shown in Table 3-2 is not incorrect, but neither does it show the importance of absolute changes in lending by major source. In particular, the move by insurance companies out of residential mortgages is hidden in the table and is not treated adequately in the text.

Whether one should characterize changes in institutional lending patterns as innovations is not clear. But it is clear that changes in the level and yield patterns of interest rates was an important factor in changes in private mortgage lending and, indirectly, in changes in government programs that clearly were innovations. Additional attention to these matters would improve the chapter.

Jaffee does not discuss the radical change in the mortgage banking industry in recent years. Again, this may not be an innovation but it surely represents the diffusion of new practices in mortgage commitments and mortgage holdings. The growth in mortgage banking both depended on and was instrumental in the development of a wider geographic market for mortgages.

Jaffee does discuss the innovation of mortgage-backed securities. Money and capital market changes could be discussed in this context also. More surprising, however, is the lack of explicit attention to Real Estate Investment Trusts—their early growth and sanguine prospects and the difficulties they have recently encountered.

But these are matters of emphasis. His chapter is a valuable contribution.

4

The Impact of Inflation on the Term Structure of Corporate Financial Instruments: 1900-1972

Benjamin Klein

Introduction

This chapter surveys the movement in the term structure of corporate debt that has occurred since the turn of the century and examines the influence inflation has had on this movement. In particular, I have attempted to test empirically the assertion that an increase in the rate of inflation produces a decrease in the term of new corporate debt. Although economic theory would lead one to expect that corporate financing decisions should be essentially invariant to alternative rates of price change, much common discussion attributes the recent shortening in the maturity of corporate debt and, for example, the growing importance of the commercial paper market to the rapid inflation we have been experiencing. In addition, the proximate cause of many of the recent financial innovations (e.g., the movement towards variable rate mortgages and other proposed changes essentially to shorten the effective maturity of the standard mortgage contract) is also often said to be the recent inflation.

A good example of this common argument that inflation has produced a movement towards shorter debt instruments can be found in the February 1975 issue of the Chase Manhattan Bank *Business in Brief* newsletter. The ratio of long-term to short-term corporate debt is charted, and the following description and explanation of the indicated fall in this ratio of about 40 percent since 1960 is then presented:

The increasing dependence of corporations on borrowed funds over the past decade has been accompanied by a persistent shift in the structure of their debt. A steadily rising proportion is short-term debt, mainly bank loans and commercial paper.

Here again, inflation is a factor. Inflation has kept interest rates higher than they would otherwise be—because lenders demand protection against loss of purchasing power—and the high credit costs make borrowers hesitant to commit themselves to long-term debt. The shift toward short-term debt has been most pronounced during tight money periods, when credit is scarce and costly. Most credit sources become difficult to tap, and long-term credits are very expensive if available at all.

I am especially indebted to Armen Alchian, Phillip Cagan, Milton Friedman, and Anna Schwartz for useful comments. I am also grateful to Noni Borisof, Stephen Ferris, Laura LaHaye, and Dicran Marcarian for research assistance above and beyond the call of duty. Scott Harris expertly drew the figures. I, of course, am solely responsible for any remaining errors.

As we shall see, from a theoretical point of view this argument makes no sense. But, unfortunately, although I have set up what seems to me to be a theoretical straw man, empirically I have not been able to knock this straw man down. The time series evidence generally indicates a slight downward secular trend in the term of new corporate debt offerings since the turn of the century, with the relationship of this phenomenon to the changes in the rate of inflation that have occurred over time remaining somewhat unclear. But even when I explicitly include measures of relative price *uncertainty* (a theoretically correct determinant of changes in the structure of financial instruments), a variable related to the rate of price change itself still seems to have a significant negative influence on the term of new corporate debt. This result, I think, is due to the imperfect measures of price uncertainty I use. Before these empirical results are more completely presented and analyzed, some theoretical considerations are outlined, and measures of price uncertainty are derived.

Theoretical Considerations

Current economic theory implies that there is no direct negative influence of changes in the rate of price change on the type and relative quantity of financial instruments used in the capital market. Abstracting from any possible changes in relative tax advantages of different instruments brought about by changing inflation rates and any wealth effects,[1] the only possible effect on corporate finance operates through regulatory constraints that may exist in the market. Increased inflation will raise nominal interest rates and if, for example, effective usury ceilings exist on particular types of debt instruments, this will produce a movement away from the use of this particular type of instrument. But if the capital market is unregulated, there is no reason to expect a change in the secular rate of price change to have any effect on the composition of financial instruments used in the market. If, for example, a lender and borrower both agreed upon the use of a particular type of financial instrument before any inflation, after an increase in the inflation rate and an upward adjustment in the nominal terms of the loan they will still use the instrument. If the terms of the debt are

---

[1] Since inflation increases effective tax rates on corporate profits by creating "illusory" inventory profits and distorting depreciation schedules for fixed capital, it is commonly asserted that corporations have been hurt by the increased inflation over the past decade. But this is only part of the story. Corporations are debtors and have also experienced a rather large capital gain from the unanticipated increase in inflation. A significant part of real corporate debt has probably been paid off by the rise in the price level over the last ten years. Although there have been estimates of the increased corporate tax cost I have not seen any estimates of this corporate capital gain. This is just one more example of the general public myopia when discussing how inflation has influenced them personally of ignoring any benefits while complaining about costs.

adjusted for the new higher inflation rate both lenders and borrowers should be indifferent between the zero and positive inflation situations. The higher inflation rate and the corresponding higher nominal interest rates should not, as the Chase newsletter claims, "Make borrowers hesitant to commit themselves to long-term debt." The demand for long-term credit should not decrease as long as the fully anticipated *real* rate of interest on this debt does not increase. And, similarly, there should also be no change on the supply of long-term relative to short-term credit side of the capital market.

What rational borrowers and lenders care about are expected *real* rates they will be paying and receiving over the term of the debt. An increase in *nominal* interest rates holding real rates constant, should produce an *increase* in the stated maturity of debt instruments to keep the duration constant, that is, to keep constant the length of time from the present at which the bond generates the average present value dollar. Full adjustment to a higher inflation rate therefore implies not only an increase in the nominal interest rate but a stretching out of the payment stream to keep the duration of the debt constant. Hence, we should expect issuers of debt to move to longer maturities and innovate in other ways to keep inflation from shortening the economic life of the financial security. But, instead, new debt issues and innovative pressure has been in the opposite direction towards a shortening of effective maturities.[2]

One possibility that may be lurking behind the Chase argument is that the increase in inflation that raises interest rates is temporary and therefore individuals do not wish to commit themselves to an abnormally high interest rate now when it is likely to fall in the future. But this belief cannot be generally held, or else long-term interest rates would not rise to abnormally high levels initially. If the demanders of funds expect long-term interest rates to fall substantially in the future the rates will adjust downward now. The efficient market hypothesis implies that the existence of "high" interest rates supplies us with no information regarding likely future changes in interest rates.[3]

---

[2]Poole's incisive comment (see p. 153) that an increase in the rate of inflation leads to a once and for all upward adjustment in the level of the interest rate by the full inflation rate increase while the price level adjusts upward continuously and gradually, and therefore will create a short-term gap between a firm's costs and income to be financed with increased short-term debt does not strike me as a reasonable explanation for the recent observations. Poole's point is, in fact, another force for corporations to lengthen the term of their debt. The necessary increase in short-term debt finance is only present under the assumption that some form of long-term price indexed security is not developed. But the market pressure appears clearly to be in the opposite direction—towards short-term variable rate (floating) securities. In addition, if Poole's explanation is correct, then the recent movement towards short-term debt is a transitory phenomenon that should soon be reversed. This is, of course, possible but seems highly unlikely, at least to me.

[3]Analogously, the Keynesian speculative demand for money argument is also inconsistent with the efficient market hypothesis.

The theoretical explanation for movements towards shorter term securities in the capital market must, I think, be based upon *price uncertainty*. Economic theory would suggest that it is not the *level* of the inflation rate but the price unpredictability associated with any particular level that crucially influences corporate financial decisions. It is *unanticipated* price change that decreases the usefulness of money as a store of value and unit for long-term contracts by redistributing income and wealth between individuals and by introducing a random element in all monetary agreements for future payment. The added uncertainty of an increase in the expected value of unanticipated price changes, that is, of an increase in the variance of the prior probability price change distribution, discourages the formation of long-term contracts (cf., for example, Fisher [12]).

If demanders of debt instruments are risk averse, an increase in the uncertainty associated with long-term relative to short-term price change will shift the demand for debt from longer to shorter maturities. In addition, *if* suppliers of debt instruments are risk neutral, the price of long-term bonds would, ceteris paribus, fall relative to short-term debt. In such a case there will be a shift leftward only of the demand schedule and not of the supply schedule of long-term debt and we would expect the difference between long and short interest rates ($r_L - r_S$) to rise. But this implication for the term structure of interest rates depends upon the risk preferences of suppliers relative to the demanders of debt instruments. If suppliers are also risk averse that will put downward pressure on ($r_L - r_S$). However, the quantity implication for the shift towards shorter maturities is unambiguous and this may explain the recent observations in the capital market. If long-term price uncertainty has increased recently and borrowers and lenders are risk averse this would produce a movement out of long-term securities. The recent increased inflation rate may merely be picking up the effect of increased long-term price uncertainty and therefore I try to separate out these two factors in the empirical analysis.

Before we go on to the empirical work it is important to recognize in this context that previous analyses that try partially to "explain" the shift towards shorter maturities (e.g., that has occurred in the postwar period) by an increase in the cost of long-term relative to short-term funds are quite misleading.[4] They are merely looking at two separate empirical effects (the change in price and in quantity) ultimately produced by a change in a third variable (e.g., a change in long-term price uncertainty). And since these two different effects on price and quantity are not related to one another in any necessary manner, it is understandable why the evidence on this

---

[4]See, for example, S. Kuznets [23], pp. 286-88, and A.W. Sametz [25], pp. 464-67.

mistaken (causation) hypothesis remains weak.[5] Long term changes that occur over time in the (r_L/r_S) price ratio must represent changes in equilibrium conditions (or else any change would be eliminated by arbitrage) and cannot be considered as exogenous movements. Any change is therefore determined by *shifts* in the supply *and* demand for short-term and long-term funds and not a movement along any given schedule. To explain both the change in the quantity and in the price of short-term relative to long-term funds requires an examination of what produced the shifts in the underlying demand and supply functions and the relative magnitudes of the shifts involved (for example, the relative degree of risk aversion on the supply and demand sides of the market.)[6]

The Measurement of Price Unpredictability

Table 4-1 below presents the annual rate of price change over the last century. To get some idea of the historical movement of the unpredictability of price change, we use this data in Table 4-1 to derive a measure of the variability of the annual rate of price change over the period 1880-1973. This is plotted in Figure 4-1, where variability is measured by the six-term moving standard deviation of the annual rate of change of prices.[7] If price anticipations are assumed not to be formed regarding the acceleration of price change (or of any higher derivatives), this series may be regarded as

[5]"In general, if the price of long-term external financing rises in relation to the price of short-term funds, we would expect the ratio of all long-term to all external financing to decline, *providing there were no offsetting movements on the demand side*. Yet, no such correlation is found." (Kuznets [23], pp. 286-87, italics mine). "Given little possibility of variation in financial risk, financial decision-makers can distinguish among sources of finance by selecting those with the least effective cost. . . . Comparisons of the differential movements of rates charged for the varieties of external funds seems to predict poorly the actual shifts in the use of particular types of external funds" (Sametz [25], pp. 464, 465-6).

[6]While we have not carefully examined the empirical implications for the term structure of interest rates, there is some evidence that during the gold standard period of 1880-1915, there was a relative shift in demand towards long-term securities and therefore a fall in $(r_L - r_S)$. The difference between the long-term (30-year) bond rate and the short-term (4-6 months) prime NYC commercial paper rate was -1.00 percentage points in 1880-1915, but $+0.94$ in 1916-55 and $+0.42$ in 1956-72. One possible explanation may be based on the possibility that short-term financial securities are closer substitutes for money than long-term securities. A lower, anticipated rate of inflation that increases the demand for money will lower the demand for short-term securities and lead to a fall in $(r_L - r_S)$.

[7]This is similar to the concept used by M. Friedman and A.J. Schwartz [13] as a measure of the variability of money and income. I first computed logarithmic first differences of a price index series centered in mid-year and then computed moving standard deviations from these year-to-year percentage rates of price change for six terms and dated the result as of the final year. The vertical scale on the chart is logarithmic to minimize the heteroscedasticity problem (cf. Friedman and Schwartz [13], p. 202).

Table 4-1
Annual Rate of Change of Implicit National Product Price Deflator, 1870-1973

Date	$(\dot{P}/P)$	Date	$(\dot{P}/P)$	Date	$(\dot{P}/P)$	Date	$(\dot{P}/P)$
1870	−5.66	1897	0.45	1924	−1.30	1951	6.49
1871	1.59	1898	2.87	1925	1.99	1952	2.20
1872	−5.14	1899	2.58	1926	0.49	1953	0.90
1873	−1.21	1900	5.17	1927	−2.68	1954	1.42
1874	−1.07	1901	−0.61	1928	0.70	1955	1.46
1875	−2.34	1902	3.39	1929	−0.10	1956	3.37
1876	−4.69	1903	0.98	1930	−4.60	1957	3.69
1877	−3.71	1904	1.54	1931	−12.83	1958	2.51
1878	−7.68	1905	2.08	1932	−12.27	1959	1.62
1879	−3.59	1906	2.04	1933	−1.36	1960	1.60
1880	9.88	1907	4.13	1934	6.34	1961	1.27
1881	−1.93	1908	−0.18	1935	−1.29	1962	1.05
1882	3.15	1909	3.47	1936	4.07	1963	1.29
1883	−1.21	1910	2.52	1937	0.87	1964	1.61
1884	−5.37	1911	−0.83	1938	−0.50	1965	1.87
1885	−6.85	1912	4.26	1939	−0.75	1966	2.72
1886	−1.39	1913	0.48	1940	1.12	1967	3.19
1887	0.99	1914	1.43	1941	7.61	1968	3.92
1888	1.76	1915	3.10	1942	12.27	1969	4.68
1889	0.58	1916	12.20	1943	12.37	1970	5.41
1890	−1.95	1917	21.12	1944	7.17	1971	4.53
1891	−0.99	1918	13.97	1945	4.32	1972	3.06
1892	−4.06	1919	1.51	1946	0.87	1973	5.42
1893	2.45	1920	13.15	1947	11.21		
1894	−6.47	1921	−16.01	1948	6.50		
1895	−1.52	1922	−5.04	1949	−0.66		
1896	−2.89	1923	2.31	1950	1.39		

Sources: 1870-1909—Gallman's annual NNP estimates; 1910-46—Kuznet's annual NNP estimates, adjusted in wartime; 1947-72—annual average of the Commerce Department's Quarterly GNP estimates.

an operational measure of the amount of unanticipated annual price change over the past six years and the amount of unanticipated price change (or price uncertainty) expected for the immediate future.[8]

---

[8]This is, of course, a crude measure of price unpredictability. A more complete analysis might contain an explicit model of the formation of price expectations based on the stochastic properties of the series and a measure of price change unpredictability based on the deviations of actual from expected price changes over time. But merely fitting a Box-Jenkins ARMA model (or an adaptive regression model) to past rates of price change to make price forecasts at every point in time will yield misleading results. As I have more completely discussed elsewhere (Klein [22]), the public considers other information when forming price expectations—such as the nature of the underlying monetary institutions. Variability is a good measure of unpredictability if the underlying stochastic structure is assumed to be one of a constant mean plus some random disturbance. Evidence presented in my earlier paper indicates that the assumption of a constant (zero) mean works reasonably well until 1955 and therefore substantiates our implicit model of the formation of expectations at least up to that point.

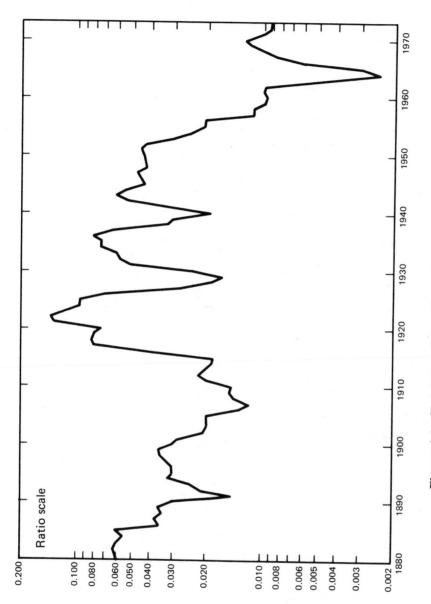

Figure 4-1. Short-term Price Unpredictability (σ_s), 1880-1973

We therefore consider this series to be a measure of short-term price unpredictability, σ_S. This measure clearly indicates that the unpredictability of short-term price change has been extremely low over the past 15 years. Although there is a positive relationship between the mean annual rate of price change and the variability of the annual rate of price change in some countries at some times, it seems *not* to be the case now for the United States. As we can see from Figure 4-2, which plots a six-term moving average of the annual rate of change of prices, the mean rate of price change over the last decade has been high by historical United States peacetime standards; while the variability in the annual rate of price change has been extremely low over this same period. We appear to now be experiencing, for the first time in our recorded history, a significant inflation that is relatively steady and therefore possibly highly predictable.

Although the moving standard deviation of price change is significantly lower during the last 15 years than in any other period on Figure 4-1 (reaching an historically unprecedented low level of 0.0024, i.e., 0.24 percentage points, in 1964), we cannot conclude from these figures that future price uncertainty is now relatively low. The series plotted on Figure 4-1 should be thought of for example, as an estimate of the standard error of the public's mean estimate of next year's expected rate of price change. But how great is the public's current uncertainty around estimates of the price change expected over a longer time period, for example, the 10-, 20-, or 30-year period over which price change estimates have to be made when buying or selling a long-term corporate bond?

To get some idea of the movement over time in long-term price uncertainty, I first divide our entire time period into three subperiods, what I have elsewhere [22] called: (a) the "gold standard" period from 1880 to 1915, (b) the "transitional" period from 1916 to 1955, and (c) the "new standard" period since 1956. The corresponding average level of the moving standard deviation variable over each of these subperiods is: (a) 0.0310, (b) 0.0569, (c) 0.0095. While the transitional period has the largest average standard deviation, this period contains the Great Depression, the two World Wars, and the Korean War, and comparisons with the other two periods are not entirely relevant. The comparison between the latest period and the gold standard period, however, is striking. The average standard deviation was more than three times as great during the gold standard period than during the recent period, indicating the historically unique character of the extremely low level of price unpredictability that now seems to exist.

But comparison of the recent period with the earlier "gold standard" period in terms of a moving standard deviation as a measure of the predictability of prices is misleading. The latest period contains only positive price changes while the earlier time period contains positive and negative

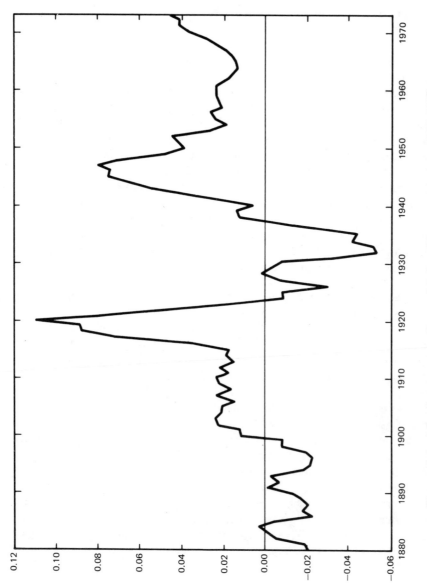

Figure 4-2. Moving Average Rate of Price Change $E_6(P/P)$, 1880-1973

price changes. And although annual price changes were previously unsteady, the long-term trend in prices was quite stable. The rate of price change over a period of, say, five years, was expected to be zero and any large price changes in one direction were expected to be reversed within that time horizon.

This gold standard phenomenon can perhaps be seen most clearly by examining the sample autocorrelations of the annual rates of price change presented in Table 4-2. Each of our first two subperiods has been divided into two equal periods, thus leaving us with five periods of similar length over which autocorrelations have been calculated. The first two gold standard periods are quite distinctly different from the final new standard period. The autocorrelations during the gold standard periods are generally negative or close to zero while the autocorrelations during the most recent period are positive, in fact quite strongly positive for the one- and two-year lag terms.[9] The gold standard can be considered to have been a period of *mean reversion* in the rate of price change while the current period is one of persistence or long-term *mean revision* in the rate of price change. Hence, the current rate of price change is now a good indication of what the rate of price change will be in the immediate future while under the gold standard the relationship between the current rate and future rates was negative and weaker.

Under a commodity standard, therefore, an average of past price changes has no direct *positive* relationship with long-term price anticipations, and so our standard deviation of the annual rate of price change variable cannot be regarded as a complete measure of the unpredictability of prices in such an economy. Although *annual* rates of price change may have been highly variable, the price level expected in five or ten years may have been more predictable during much of our early history than now.

If we assume stability in the underlying process generating the annual rates of price change in each of the five time periods isolated in Table 4-2 and consider these sample autocorrelations as the best point estimates of the true autocorrelations of the underlying statistical processes, we may conveniently define a measure of longer term price unpredictability than what is plotted in Figure 4-1. Our six-term moving standard deviation of the rate of price change variable, σ_S, is considered to be a measure of short-term price unpredictability or uncertainty in next year's rate of price change. If we wish to derive a measure of price uncertainty over a longer time period, consider the annual rate of price change expected for each

---

[9]Because our rate of price change data in the most recent period are annual averages of quarterly observations, there is an aggregation bias in the first-order serial correlation (cf. H. Working [33]). If the serial correlation of the quarterly data is zero, there is a positive bias of 0.227. Since we have positive serial correlation in our quarterly data, the bias is lower than 0.227. If, for example, we use the second quarter price level observation in each year to calculate the annual rate of price change, the sample autocorrelations for 1956-73 are essentially unchanged at 0.730, 0.535, 0.391, 0.176, 0.034.

Table 4-2

Sample Autocorrelations of Annual Rates of Price Change, 1880-1973 (Correlation of $(\dot{P}/P)_t$ and $(\dot{P}/P_{t-j})$

j	1880-97	1898-1915	1916-35	1936-55	1956-73
1	−0.132	−0.595[a]	0.418[b]	0.467[a]	0.751[a]
2	−.085	.058	.204	.013	.567[a]
3	−.363	−.009	.076	−.072	.419[b]
4	−.416[b]	.455[b]	−.153	.024	.240
5	−0.273	0.100	−0.088	0.078	0.087

Note: The asymptotic standard error of each sample autocorrelation is $1/\sqrt{n}$, where n is the number of observations in each time period under the null hypothesis that the true autocorrelations are zero; cf. Box and Jenkins [7, ch. 2]. The indicated dates refer to the $(\dot{P}/P)_t$ observation, implying that all autocorrelations within each time period have the same number of observations (although more data is used for the longer lags).
[a]Indicates autocorrelation significantly different from zero at the 0.95 confidence level.
[b]Same as note a, except at the 0.90 level.

future year as a random variable and merely use the formula for the variance of the sum of n random variables:

$$\text{Var}\left(\sum_{i=1}^{n} x_i\right) = \sum_{i=1}^{n} \text{Var}(x_i) + \sum_i \sum_j \text{Cov}(x_i, x_j) \qquad (4.1)$$

Uncertainty of the rate of price change over the next six years, for example, may be measured by the sum of our σ_S^2 variable over the current and previous five years plus a term to measure twice the expected covariance of the annual rate of price change over these six years, $\sum_i \sum_j \sigma_S(i)\sigma_S(j)r_{i,j}$, where the value of $r_{i,j}$ is taken from Table 4-2 for the year for which we are defining long-term price unpredictability. This variable is divided by six and the square root taken to get a measure of *uncertainty regarding the average annual rate of change of prices over the next six years*, denoted σ_L and plotted in Figure 4-3. This variable can then be compared with the σ_S of Figure 4-1.

The average level of this longer term price unpredictability variable over each of our three subperiods is (a) 0.0096, (b) 0.0801, (c) 0.0232. The transitional period, once again, has the highest average level. By far this period has the greatest degree of price uncertainty with both short-term and long-term price unpredictability, σ_S and σ_L, extremely high. But what has changed in comparison to the relative levels of our σ_S series is that the degree of price uncertainty experienced during the recent period is no longer only one-third what was experienced during the gold standard period but rather now nearly two and a half times as great. The current value of σ_L of slightly more than 2 percent, is a level we remained below for

136

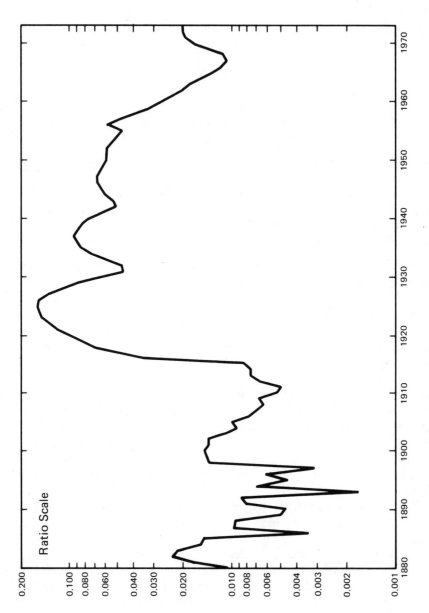

Figure 4-3. Long-term Price Unpredictability (σ_L), 1880-1973

the entire 1884-1915 period. Clearly, we cannot say, as we did with regard to σ_S, that over the last 15 years *long-term* price unpredictability has been at a historically unprecedented low level. What has occurred over time has been an upward shift in the amount of long-term relative to short-term price unpredictability. This secular movement can be seen by looking at the ratio of σ_L to σ_S over time, which is plotted in Figure 4-4. The average ratio of σ_L to σ_S over our three subperiods is: (a) 0.31, (b) 1.41, (c) 2.44. This phenomenon can be attributed to the general increase over time in the autocorrelations of the annual rate of change of prices. The σ_S variable indicates that it is less likely now than under the gold standard to experience next year a rate of price change that is more than, for example, two percentage points away from the mean estimate. But the high autocorrelations imply that if in fact we do experience such an unanticipated price change, it is more likely now to continue for a few years while under the gold standard it was likely to reverse or "correct" itself, that is, "average out" over time. And this fundamental change in the underlying monetary framework is what has produced the movement over time towards shorter debt instruments.

Empirical Analysis

Long-term Trends (1900-1972)

If there has, in fact, been an increase in the amount of long-term price unpredictability relative to short-term price unpredictability in the postwar period compared with the gold standard period, we should expect a change in the composition of debt towards shorter maturities in the recent period. An increase in (σ_L/σ_S) will decrease the demand for and therefore the quantity of long-term debt relative to short-term debt. On a cursory level, it seems to be obviously true that corporate bond issues have gotten shorter over time. One hundred year railroad bonds were, for example, issued around the turn of the century, while it is now quite uncommon to find a maturity of a new corporate issue that is greater than 30 years. But systematically demonstrating the existence of this secular downward trend has proven to be a much more difficult task than I originally expected. What I have done in attempting to verify this phenomenon is extend the W.B. Hickman NBER [16] estimates of the maturity distribution of United States corporate bond issues by using financial directories to compile and classify by term to maturity all listed new issues of single maturity United States corporate bond obligations, annually for the period 1944-72.[10] The yearly

---

[10] As a check, we also computed the average maturity using our techniques for 1943 and our figure of 22.2 is close enough to the NBER estimate of 22.0 to give us some confidence that we are extending Hickman's work in a consistent manner.

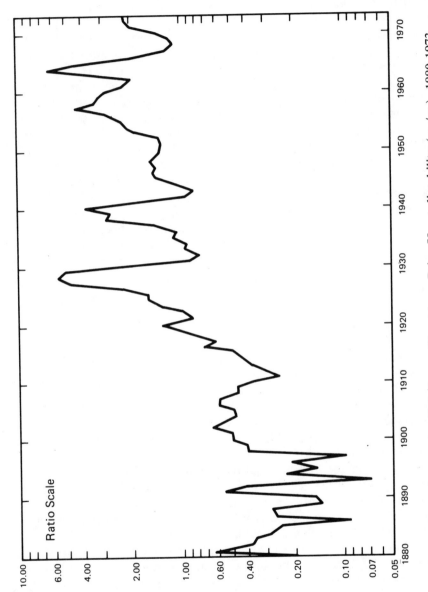

Figure 4-4. Long-term Relative to Short-term Price Unpredictability (σ_L/σ_S), 1880–1973

weighted average of this debt and for the earlier Hickman figures is presented in Table 4-3 as MAT_1.

Upon examining these figures a secular movement towards shorter term corporate debt issues can be seen on a very crude level. There is a lower average maturity of debt issued during 1956-72 (20.9 years) than that issued during 1900-1915 (29.2 years), or 1916-55 (21.7 years)—but this movement is quite erratic. In fact, the years in which the maturity of new corporate debt issues is lowest occurs before the most recent period; in particular in 1918-21 and in 1934.

Before these figures are examined more closely, we should first note that they are somewhat misleading. An improper amount of weight is given to long-term issues in calculating the figures in Table 4-3 because the length of time from the present at which the bond generates the average present value dollar (the duration of the bond) is certainly not, for example, ten times as great for a 100-year issue compared with a 10-year issue. That is, long-term bonds are not as long in an economic sense as they may first appear. This concept of the average life or duration of a bond (first defined by F.R. Macaulay [24], pp. 44-48) will also decrease, for a given maturity and coupon, as market rates increase. A given maturity is therefore economically of shorter term in the recent high interest rate period than previously. An increase in the inflation rate, which is adjusted to in the market solely by an increase in nominal coupon payments on debt instruments while leaving the final principal payment unchanged in nominal terms, implies an implicit shortening of the economic term of the debt. Nominal interest rates are adjusted upward for the new higher anticipated inflation rate to keep the real rate constant, but part of the real value of the principal is implicitly amortized over the term of the bond. The duration of the debt has fallen.

Since the upward inflationary adjustment of market interest rates shortens the debt, we should expect issuers of debt to move to longer maturities or innovate in other ways to offset this effect.[11] But instead, debt issues appear to have moved to somewhat shorter maturities and some recent financial innovations have taken the form of reducing the term to maturity of common financial instruments. For example, the recent introduction of much shorter than usual term (e.g., five-year) mortgages with a large "balloon" payment (to be refinanced) at maturity[12] is innovation in the direction of shortening the term of a major financial instrument. This cannot be explained by an increased inflation rate (which, by itself, shortens the economic term of standard mortgages) but is certainly consis-

---

[11] For example, an alternative way of adjusting or indexing the nominal terms of a security that would eliminate this shortening effect would be to multiply the coupon payment each year by the ratio of the price level in that year to the price level in the year the security was issued and to also multiply the final principal payment by the price ratio in the final year.

[12] See the *Wall Street Journal*, November 26, 1974, p. 30.

Table 4-3
Weighted Average Maturity of New Corporate Debt, 1900-72

Date	MAT$_1$	Date	MAT$_1$	Date	MAT$_1$	Date	MAT$_1$
1900	40.0	1919	11.3	1938	19.1	1957	22.8
1901	32.1	1920	10.4	1939	24.1	1958	21.6
1902	33.5	1921	15.5	1940	23.0	1959	22.0
1903	40.7	1922	25.7	1941	23.4	1960	22.2
1904	39.4	1923	23.1	1942	21.8	1961	20.7
1905	28.5	1924	25.0	1943	22.0	1962	22.1
1906	26.4	1925	21.4	1944	23.4	1963	21.0
1907	23.8	1926	22.8	1945	30.5	1964	19.9
1908	27.8	1927	25.1	1946	24.1	1965	19.5
1909	31.0	1928	25.6	1947	23.2	1966	21.1
1910	24.7	1929	21.0	1948	21.8	1967	20.4
1911	24.9	1930	26.6	1949	20.2	1968	19.3
1912	21.4	1931	29.1	1950	21.7	1969	21.2
1913	24.5	1932	22.2	1951	20.8	1970	19.6
1914	24.9	1933	20.6	1952	21.8	1971	20.9
1915	24.3	1934	14.1	1953	20.0	1972	19.1
1916	26.7	1935	21.7	1954	22.9		
1917	19.9	1936	23.5	1955	21.9		
1918	10.6	1937	19.0	1956	22.5		

Source: MAT$_1$—1900-43 from [16, Table 94], weighting the yearly dollar volume in each maturity classification by the median maturity of the class; 1944-72-NBER Table 94 was extended by categorizing the par values of all single maturity obligations offered yearly in the same maturity classifications and then obtaining a similar weighted average. The yearly debt offers were compiled from [10] (1943-49), [18] (1950-60), [19] (1961-63), and [20] (1964-73). Issues floated outside the United States and all issues of foreign corporations were excluded.

tent with an adjustment to an increase in long-term relative to short-term price uncertainty.

The average maturity figures in Table 4-3 are converted in Table 4-4 into average duration figures. The general secular movement towards a shortening of the term of new debt offerings seems to hold up. The average duration of debt issued during 1900-1915 is 15.7 years, during 1916-55 it is 13.9 years, while during 1956-72 it is 12.8 years. In addition, the average duration of debt has been generally declining during the most recent period (for 1968-72 it is only 10.3 years).

Equation (4.2) below reports OLS regression results of our ratio of long-term to short-term price unpredictability variable on the average maturity of new corporate debt figures of Table 4-3 for the period 1900-1972. (Absolute values of the t-statistics are reported under the estimated coefficients). As we can see, the relative price predictability term enters significantly in the theroretically expected negative direction, although there is a great deal of positive serial correlation in the residuals and the unexplained variance is very high. The regression is repeated in equation (4.3) using the duration figures of Table 4-4. And the results are statistically insignificant.

Table 4-4

Weighted Average Duration of New Corporate Debt, 1900-72

Date	DUR₁	Date	DUR₁	Date	DUR₁	Date	DUR₁
1900	21.3	1919	7.4	1938	14.1	1957	14.7
1901	19.4	1920	7.1	1939	16.2	1958	14.4
1902	19.2	1921	10.0	1940	16.0	1959	14.3
1903	21.9	1922	12.4	1941	16.3	1960	13.0
1904	17.0.	1923	12.4	1942	15.5	1961	13.8
1905	15.1	1924	12.7	1943	16.0	1962	14.2
1906	15.1	1925	11.6	1944	16.6	1963	13.9
1907	13.1	1926	13.6	1945	19.4	1964	13.5
1908	14.7	1927	14.8	1946	20.3	1965	13.4
1909	16.4	1928	14.7	1947	16.9	1966	12.7
1910	14.3	1929	12.2	1948	15.5	1967	12.4
1911	13.7	1930	14.4	1949	13.7	1968	10.9
1912	12.8	1931	15.4	1950	16.0	1969	10.7
1913	12.7	1932	11.2	1951	15.4	1970	9.2
1914	12.3	1933	11.7	1952	15.7	1971	10.6
1915	12.1	1934	9.3	1953	14.6	1972	9.9
1916	14.1	1935	15.3	1954	16.2		
1917	10.8	1936	16.2	1955	15.4		
1918	6.2	1937	14.1	1956	15.9		

Source: Same as Table 3. The underlying figures are converted into durations for each maturity classification by assuming that all securities were priced at par when issued. The annual term structure of interest rates is obtained from [11], Table 1 for 1900-42; [17], Table 52 for 1943-62; and [30] for 1963-72, with the one year bond rate for 1963-70 obtained from [29], series B74; and for 1971-72 supplied by Salomen Bros. If interest is assumed to be paid semiannually, the duration of a bond equals

$$\left[\frac{0.5(1 + r/2)}{(r/2)}\right]\left(1 - \frac{1}{(1 + r/2)^{2n}}\right)$$

where r is the annual yield and n the years to maturity of the bond.

$$MAT_1 = 23.751 - 2.384 \log(\sigma_L/\sigma_S) \tag{4.2}$$
$$(37.42) \quad (2.99)$$

$$R^2 = 0.11 \quad DW = 0.56 \quad SE = 5.149$$

$$DUR_1 = 14.083 - 0.173 \log(\sigma_L/\sigma_S) \tag{4.3}$$
$$(37.84) \quad (0.37)$$

$$R^2 = 0.00 \quad DW = 0.38 \quad SE = 3.019$$

We then entered the average rate of price change variable $E_6(\dot{P}/P)$, plotted in Figure 4-2 into our regressions with the following results:

$$MAT_1 = 24.819 - 2.541 \log(\sigma_L/\sigma_S) - 44.245 E_6(\dot{P}/P) \tag{4.4}$$
$$(32.69) \quad (3.27) \quad (2.40)$$

$$R^2 = 0.179 \quad DW = 0.59 \quad SE = 4.986$$

$$DUR_1 = 14.323 - 0.208 \log(\sigma_L/\sigma_S) - 9.952 E_6(\dot{P}/P) \quad (4.5)$$
$$(31.11) \quad (0.44) \quad\quad\quad (0.89)$$

$R^2 = 0.013 \quad DW = 0.37 \quad SE = 3.023$

The duration regression results remain insignificant, but the maturity results are improved with the rate of price change variable entering negatively and significantly.[13] The results indicate that a 1 percent increase in the ratio of our measure of long-term to short-term price uncertainty will decrease the average maturity of new corporate debt issues by about two and a half years and that an increase in the long-term level of the inflation rate of one percentage point will decrease the average maturity of new corporate debt issues by nearly a half a year. The regressions are then repeated with the modified maturity and duration variables and we obtain similar results.

The effect of relative price uncertainty on the maturity of corporate debt is understandable, but the existence of a negative effect of inflation on the maturity of corporate debt remains a mystery to me.[14] One possibility is that our measures of long-term and short-term price unpredictability are imprecise and that the moving average rate of price change variable is positively correlated with the unmeasured element of the true price uncertainty ratio. But then our task is to derive more precise measures of price unpredictability. As it now stands, the inflation rate (holding relative price uncertainty constant) must be considered to have a negative influence on the maturity of new corporate debt issues.

Examination of the Residuals and Previous Studies

The movement in the maturity and duration of new corporate debt figures of Tables 4-3 and 4-4 is generally consistent with what has been found in

---

[13]Merely entering the current rate of price change into the regression instead of $E_6(\dot{P}/P)$ yields poorer, statistically insignificant, results:

$$MAT_1 = 24.254 - 2.515 \log(\sigma_L/\sigma_S) - 19.381(\dot{P}/P) \quad (4.4)$$
$$(35.31) \quad (3.18) \quad\quad\quad (1.77)$$

$R^2 = 0.150 \quad DW = 0.60 \quad SE = 5.074$

$$DUR_1 = 14.203 - 0.204 \log(\sigma_L/\sigma_S) - 4.625(\dot{P}/P) \quad (4.5)$$
$$(34.63) \quad (0.43) \quad\quad\quad (0.71)$$

$R^2 = 0.009 \quad DW = 0.39 \quad SE = 3.029$

[14]This negative effect of inflation rates on the maturity of new debt issues is totally unrelated to the possible identification problem Poole notes (see p. 152) with regard to the duration figures. An increase in the rate of price change will raise interest rates and, given a maturity structure, will lower the duration of new debt. We should therefore expect to observe a positive relationship between inflation rates and average maturity.

previous studies. Earlier work, however, is not entirely comparable since it has merely classified corporate liabilities into either short-term or long-term components. Table 4-5, column 1, for example, presents the NBER estimates of the ratio of long-term to short-term debt of United States nonfinancial corporations for various time periods. (The 1930s and World War II periods are not reported because the NBER figures are negative for those time periods.) Table 4-5 also includes the average values of our maturity figures and the average values of (σ_L/σ_S) for the same time periods. Our average maturity figures (column 3) move in the same general direction as the NBER figures, first declining in 1913-22, then rising in 1923-29, and then falling again in the final postwar period. (Our figures do not seem to decline enough in the postwar period but this is probably due, as we shall see in the next section, to not including short-term bank loans in our figures.) The major inconsistency of the movement of the long-term to short-term debt figures when compared to the movement in our (σ_L/σ_S) variable appears to be the 1923-29 period when both ratios are at their highest levels. But this inconsistency and the severe fall and then sharp rise in the long-term to short-term debt ratio is eliminated if the entire 1913-29 period is considered as one observation rather than two. This clearly shows the entire 1901-58 period to have been one of a secular increase in long-term relative to short-term price uncertainty and a secular decrease in long-term relative to short-term debt.

By examining our annual average maturity figures we can gain some insight into this 1913-29 period. What we actually have is a very sharp decrease in term to maturity of new corporate debt in 1918-21 and then a small increase (from declining trend) in the following period. The 1922-28 period can be thought of as a slow adjustment of the stock of outstanding debt to the 1918-21 disturbance, but what produced the initial disturbance? This, I do not think, can be attributed directly to World War I. Although it has been asserted that short-term debt finance increases during wartime, I do not find it in my annual data. The decrease in average maturity occurs *after* World War I, largely in 1918-20. This movement, I think, can be explained by a large increase in long-term price uncertainty (not captured by our σ_L variable). The very rapid inflation during 1916-18 must have been somewhat expected by the public as the usual wartime increase in prices. But when prices did not start to decline after the war, and in fact continued to increase rapidly, especially during 1920, large doubts must have entered the public's mind concerning continued United States adherence to the gold standard or long-term price reversion. A large increase in long-term relative to short-term price uncertainty is very likely to have occurred at that point in time. Only after the very large deflation in 1921-22 were long-term gold standard price expectations restored and therefore did the maturity of new corporate debt issues increase.

144

Table 4-5
The Ratio of Long-term to Short-term Corporate Debt, 1901-58

Time Period	$\frac{LT\ debt}{ST\ debt}$	(σ_L/σ_S)	MAT_1
1901-12	2.81	0.47	29.5
1913-22	0.72	0.77	19.4
1923-29	5.02	3.18	23.4
1913-29	2.49	1.76	21.0
1946-58	0.87	2.05	21.9

Source: For (LT debt/ST debt) 1901-29 from Kuznets [23], Table 48 [p. 278], where LT debt equals column 2 plus column 3 and ST debt equals column 7; 1946-58 from Goldsmith [14], Table 37 (p. 142).

Another major fall in the maturity of new corporate debt occurs in 1934, while (σ_L/σ_S) remains unchanged. This discrepancy can also be explained by the use of an improper measure of long-term price uncertainty. Nineteen thirty-four was, of course, immediately after the failure of the Bank of United States and the banking panic of 1933, which certainly must have increased long-term uncertainty associated with survival of the financial system. This is not picked up in σ_L.[15] Rerunning regressions (4.4) and (4.5) with a dummy variable, D, for 1934 yields the following results:

$$MAT_1 = 25.326 - 2.678\log(\sigma_L/\sigma_S) - 56.556\,E_6(\dot{P}/P) - 13.659D \quad (4.6)$$
$$(33.83) \quad (3.60) \qquad\qquad (3.10) \qquad\qquad (2.76)$$

$$R^2 = 0.260 \quad DW = 0.65 \quad SE = 4.766$$

$$DUR_1 = 14.541 - 0.267\log(\sigma_L/\sigma_S) - 15.253\,E_6(\dot{P}/P) - 5.882D \quad (4.7)$$
$$(31.19) \quad (0.58) \qquad\qquad (1.34) \qquad\qquad (1.91)$$

$$R^2 = 0.062 \quad DW = 0.34 \quad SE = 2.968$$

Postwar Analysis

I have also attempted a somewhat more detailed examination of the movement towards shorter term corporate debt during the post-World War II period. The postwar period has seen a very rapid expansion in corporate commercial paper, short-term commercial bank loans and trade debt and

[15]Another major residual occurs in 1945 when (σ_L/σ_S) increases while the average maturity of new corporate debt rises dramatically. This movement I have not been able to rationalize.

Table 4-6
Weighted Average Maturity of Corporate Debt, 1946-72

Date	MAT$_1$	MAT$_2$	MAT$_3$	MAT$_4$
1946	24.1	23.1	9.3	3.9
1947	23.2	21.9	8.2	3.3
1948	21.8	20.6	7.7	3.2
1949	20.2	19.0	6.7	2.7
1950	21.7	20.0	5.9	2.2
1951	20.8	19.1	5.3	2.2
1952	21.8	19.9	6.9	2.7
1953	20.0	18.2	5.9	2.5
1954	22.9	19.8	6.6	2.6
1955	21.9	19.7	6.8	2.5
1956	22.5	21.5	6.7	2.5
1957	22.8	21.3	7.6	2.9
1958	21.6	19.3	7.4	2.7
1959	22.0	19.0	5.7	2.0
1960	22.2	19.0	6.1	2.2
1961	20.7	17.6	6.6	2.4
1962	22.1	18.2	7.0	2.5
1963	21.0	17.4	6.9	2.4
1964	19.9	16.5	6.3	2.2
1965	19.5	17.4	7.9	2.9
1966	21.1	18.4	7.6	2.7
1967	20.4	17.3	8.5	3.4
1968	19.3	15.4	6.4	2.8
1969	21.2	16.0	5.1	2.3
1970	19.6	14.9	6.4	2.9
1971	20.9	15.4	6.9	3.1
1972	19.1	13.6	5.5	2.6

Source:

MAT$_1$—Table 3

MAT$_2$ = MAT$_1$ plus commercial paper obtained from [5, Table 9] (1942-52) and Federal Reserve Bank of New York Financial Statistics Divison (1953-72). Annual averages of monthly data are used for all years.

MAT$_3$ = MAT$_2$ plus short-term commercial bank corporate loans obtained by multiplying total loans (from [3]) by one minus the ratio of term to total loans (from [15], Table IV C 9 and 9b for 1946-58, [1] and [8] adjusted for 1959-67, and [2] for 1968-72).

MAT$_4$ = MAT$_3$ plus corporate trade debt (from [3]).

Table 4-6 below adjusts our maturity figures by including these three financial liabilities.[16] We assume for simplicity that these instruments have

[16]We have not included term loans in our modifications because of the unavailability of a data series on the average term to maturity of these loans. In addition, over the postwar period there has been a substantial movement by corporations away from preferred stock issues (many of which are quite similar to long-term bonds). These issues were relatively much more important in the prewar period (cf. Sametz [25], Table 6). This movement is therefore consistent with the general trend towards shorter term debt finance.

Table 4-7

Weighted Average Maturity (TMAT) and Duration (TDUR) of Treasury Debt Held by the Public, 1946-72

Date	TMAT	TDUR	Date	TMAT	TDUR
1946	8.64	7.50	1960	3.38	2.79
1947	8.54	7.33	1961	3.78	3.12
1948	7.44	6.19	1962	4.40	3.50
1949	7.00	5.92	1963	4.66	3.72
1950	6.73	5.97	1964	4.82	3.81
1951	5.04	4.49	1965	5.21	4.10
1952	4.50	3.90	1966	5.12	3.77
1953	4.39	3.82	1967	4.82	3.60
1954	4.64	4.11	1968	4.60	3.36
1955	5.00	4.44	1969	4.44	3.14
1956	4.61	4.08	1970	3.67	2.59
1957	3.78	3.23	1971	3.72	2.79
1958	4.45	3.88	1972	3.70	2.79
1959	3.82	3.23			

Source: Maturity distribution by call classes of outstanding marketable interest-bearing total public debt, June 30, 1946-72, from [31], Table 25, where all debt of less than one year is assumed to be of six months maturity; the distribution of Federal Reserve holdings of treasury debt (obtained from [2]) is then subtracted from this total, where Fed holdings of treasury debt of five or more years maturity are assumed to be distributed by maturity classification in the same way as holdings by the general public.

a maturity of six months[17] and therefore making these modifications dramatically reduces the average level of term to maturity of all corporate debt. The general postwar secular decline in the maturity of corporate debt present in our earlier series is also present in these three new series. This shortening of corporate debt takes place in spite of the fact that during the postwar period the Treasury has also dramatically reduced the average maturity of its outstanding debt.[18] Table 4-7 presents this movement towards a shorter maturity of Treasury debt held by the public. But instead of corporate issuers partially substituting for the reduction in long-term government debt by increasing the relative quantity of their long-term issues, the movement appears to go in the opposite direction. This can be seen by

[17]Outstanding commercial paper, all of which has a maturity of 270 days or less but most of which has a maturity of 90 days or less, is assumed for simplicity to be of six months maturity. Since virtually all paper placed directly is issued by large finance companies and by affiliates and subsidiaries of commercial banks, it is excluded from our estimates. Most dealer paper is issued by nonfinancial corporations and is included in our estimates. I am indebted to Michael Hamburger and Fred Levin of the Federal Reserve Bank of New York for making this data available to me.

[18]Part of this movement towards shorter public debt can be explained by the constraint imposed by a statute that prohibited the federal government from paying yields greater than 4.25 percent on debt maturities over seven years and therefore since 1966 the Treasury has issued very little long-term debt (J.L. Jordon [21]).

Table 4-8
Average Maturity Regression Results, 1946-72

	$MAT = a_0 + a_1\log(\sigma_L/\sigma_S) - a_2 E_6(\dot{P}/P) + a_3(TMAT)$						
Dependent Variable	a_0	a_1	a_2	a_3	R^2	DW	SE
MAT_1	18.935 (17.14)	0.691 (1.13)	19.984 (0.91)	0.236 (0.93)	0.21	1.41	1.21
MAT_2	12.244 (7.19)	1.364 (1.46)	11.406 (0.34)	0.980 (2.51)	0.41	0.54	1.86
MAT_3	4.206 (5.36)	0.456 (1.06)	−7.844 (0.50)	0.502 (2.80)	0.35	1.46	0.86
MAT_4	1.953 (5.58)	−0.025 (0.13)	7.025 (1.01)	0.101 (1.26)	0.34	1.31	0.38

looking at the annual regressions on these variables, the results of which are presented in Table 4-8. Unfortunately, nothing much with regards to relative price predictability is picked up in these regressions (the coefficient is generally of the wrong sign and insignificant.)

These problems merely indicate the general difficulty of using regression analysis here, that is, of trying to explain year to year movements over a short time period rather than longer term trends. In addition, they also, once again, indicate the imprecise nature of our price uncertainty measures. Although somewhat crude, this work I have done in constructing historical series on the term of new corporate debt issues and on short-term and long-term price uncertainty since the turn of the century should, hopefully, be considered as a useful first step for further analysis.

References

[1] Arlt, C.T., Jr., "Term Lending by New York City Banks," Federal Reserve Bank of New York, *Monthly Review*, February 1961.
[2] Board of Governors of the Federal Reserve System, *Federal Reserve Bulletin*, various issues.
[3] _____, *Flow of Funds Accounts, 1945-72*, August 1973.
[4] _____, *Banking and Monetary Statistics*, Washington, D.C., 1943.
[5] _____, *Supplement to Banking and Monetary Statistics*, section 12, Money Rates and Securities Markets.
[6] Bosworth, B., "Patterns of Corporate External Financing," *Brookings Papers on Economic Activity*, 1971 (No. 2).
[7] Box, G.E.P., and G.M. Jenkins, *Time Series Analysis*, San Francisco, 1970.

[8] Budzeika, G., "Term Lending by New York City Banks in the 1960's," Federal Reserve Bank of New York, *Monthly Review*, October 1967.

[9] Chase Manhattan Bank, "Heavy Credit Demands Ahead," *Business in Brief*, February 1975 (No. 120).

[10] Counsel for Defendants in U.S. vs. Morgan Stanley and Co., *Issuer Summaries*, Security Issues in the U.S., July 26, 1933-December 31, 1949, U.S. District Court for Southern District of New York, January 1951 (Vols. I and II).

[11] Durand, D., "Basic Yields of Corporate Bonds, 1900-42," National Bureau of Economic Research Technical Paper 3, June 1942.

[12] Fisher, I., *The Purchasing Power of Money*, (New York: Macmillan, 1911).

[13] Friedman, M., and A.J. Schwartz, "Money and Business Cycles," 1963, in Friedman, *The Optimum Quantity of Money and Other Essays*, (Chicago: Aldine, 1969), pp. 189-236.

[14] Goldsmith, R.W., *The Flow of Capital Funds in the Postwar Economy*, (Columbia: National Bureau of Economic Research, 1965).

[15] _____, R.E. Lipsey, and M. Mendelson, *Studies in the National Balance Sheet of the United States, Volume II: Basic Data on Balance Sheets and Fund Flows*, (Princeton, N.J.: National Bureau of Economic Research, 1963).

[16] Hickman, W.B., *Statistical Measures of Corporate Bond Financing Since 1900*, Princeton, N.J.: National Bureau of Economic Research, 1960.

[17] Homer, S., *A History of Interest Rates*, (New Brunswick, N.J.: Rutgers University Press, 1963).

[18] Investment Dealers Digest, *Corporate Financing, 1950-60*, Dealers Digest Publishing Co., Inc., November 1961.

[19] _____, *Corporate Financing 1961-63*, Dealers Digest Publishing Co., Inc., 1964.

[20] _____, *Corporate Financing Directory*, Dealers Digest Publishing Co., Inc., Semiannual issues, 1964-73.

[21] Jordon, J.L., "Interest Rates and Monetary Growth," Federal Reserve Bank of St. Louis, *Review*, January 1973.

[22] Klein, B., "The Social Costs of the Recent Inflation and Our New Monetary Standard: The Mirage of Steady 'Anticipated' Inflation," forthcoming in the North-Holland-University of Rochester Conference series.

[23] Kuznets, S., *Capital in the American Economy: Its Formation and Financing* (Princeton, N.J.: National Bureau of Economic Research, 1961).

[24] Macaulay, F.R., *Some Theoretical Problems Suggested by the Movements of Interest Rates, Bond Yields and Stock Prices in the United States Since 1856* (New York: National Bureau of Economic Research, 1938).

[25] Sametz, A.W., "Trends in the Volume and Composition of Equity Finance," *Journal of Finance*, September 1964 (Vol. 19, No. 3), pp. 450-69.

[26] _____, "Patterns of Business Financing: Reply," *Journal of Finance*, December 1965 (Vol. 20, No. 4), pp. 608-18.

[27] Schadrock, F.C., and F.S. Breimyer, "Recent Developments in the Commercial Paper Market," Federal Reserve Bank of New York, *Monthly Review*, December 1970.

[28] Shapiro, E., and W.L. White, "Patterns of Business Financing: Some Comments," *Journal of Finance*, December 1975 (Vol. 20, No. 4), pp. 693-707.

[29] U.S. Bureau of Economic Analysis, *Long Term Economic Growth, 1860-1970*, Washington, D.C., 1973.

[30] U.S. Bureau of the Census, *Statistical Abstract of the United States*, various issues.

[31] U.S. Department of the Treasury, *Annual Report of the Secretary of Treasury, 1973*.

[32] *Wall Street Journal*, "Savings Bank Offers Five Year Mortgages, 'Balloon' Payments," November 26, 1974, p. 30.

[33] Working, H., "Note on the Correlation of First Differences of Averages in a Random Chain," *Econometrica*, October 1960.

Comment: The Impact of Inflation on the Term Structure of Corporate Financial Instruments: 1900-1972

William Poole

Benjamin Klein has presented an interesting and provocative chapter. And, I might add, he has presented us with an honest paper. The highest R^2 reported is 0.41, and he is quick to point out that he has uncovered no empirical propositions in which he has great confidence. Perhaps this honesty is part of the Watergate fallout; or perhaps it is the result of fear that California will be the first state to pass a truth-in-teaching law.

With respect to Klein's analysis of price level uncertainty I have only two brief comments: One is that once his time series is extended to include 1974 and 1975 I suspect that his statement that the variability of year-to-year price changes has been historically low in the last decade will have to be revised. Moreover, adding the 1974 and 1975 observations will probably lower the autocorrelations substantially.

My second comment on the inflation variability question concerns the data. As I understand it, the price data for the earlier years consist essentially of one price observation per year, centered on mid-year, while the data for later years consist of annual averages of quarterly data. Since the use of averages will tend to smooth the data and introduce positive serial dependence into the calculated inflation rates, it would have been better to construct the data for the later years on a basis comparable to that used in the earlier years.

In discussing the corporate debt maturity question, the best way to start is to define carefully the phenomenon we are trying to explain. The conjecture that apparently motivated Klein is that the average maturity of new corporate debt offerings has declined markedly in recent years. Klein has expended great effort to gather the data necessary to confirm this conjecture and finds that the conjecture is supported. He finds that the average maturity on new issues of long debt since World War II is definitely shorter than on debt issued between 1900 and 1915, and that this conclusion is reinforced if Macaulay's concept of duration is substituted for the more conventional concept of maturity.

I am not completely convinced, however, by the evidence for declining debt lengths. Klein has considered two dimensions of the measurement problem—maturity vs. duration and the long-term/short-term debt mix—but there are several others.

First, what should be done about call provisions? Klein reports that his series is obtained from single maturity issues, but his arguments for considering short-term debt issues would also seem to apply to callable and even convertable issues. I have not looked at the data, but nevertheless have the impression that investors have demanded and received increased call protection over the past ten years. The guaranteed minimum maturity may well have lengthened recently while the stated maximum maturity has declined.

Second, it has been not uncommon for bonds to contain sinking fund provisions that require that a bond issue be paid off gradually over its life rather than in one lump sum at maturity. From the point of view of the investor, the existence of call and sinking fund provisions converts a bond into an instrument with a probabilistic structure of payments from time of issue to maturity. My off-hand guess is that sinking fund provisions are less common now than formerly, and if so this factor has made for longer effective maturities. In short, the attention Klein pays to adding in commercial paper makes clear that he is seeking a measure of the average maturity, or duration, of all new corporate debt. There is, therefore, no reason to exclude callable and convertable issues, nor is there reason to exclude direct placements and bank term loans.

Changes in bond provisions other than coupon and maturity may affect our view as to what has actually happened to average duration. But there is another aspect of this problem that is, I believe, more important. Increases in the anticipated rate of inflation raise nominal interest rates and almost necessarily reduce duration. The duration measure of bond length picks up the effect of inflation because duration depends on the nominal rate of interest, which in turn reflects anticipated inflation. With a few quick calculations it can be shown that it is essentially impossible to maintain duration by adjusting the terms of conventional bonds in an inflationary environment. For example, if I have made the calculation properly, a 5 percent 30-year bond has a duration of 15.8 years. If the interest rate rises to 7 percent, even a perpetual bond will have a shorter duration, 14.9 years.

Klein points out in footnote 11 that a bond with a purchasing power clause would be one way of lengthening duration in an inflationary environment and in passing he implies that other types of innovations could also lengthen corporate debt. What he does not make clear, however, is that the only innovations that will do the job involve the abandonment of traditional debt instruments. Given recent rates of inflation there is simply not enough room to lengthen duration within the framework of traditional debt instruments. What is clearly needed is an instrument promising a rising nominal stream of debt service, perhaps in the form of interest coupons that rise steadily over time.

Klein's mystery, then, as to why duration has fallen with inflation is really the mystery of why the capital markets have not produced debt instruments with rising nominal streams. Before speculating on this question, however, I want to discuss another point. Given the lack of innovation, what would we expect to observe?

A conventional bond as noted earlier, is an instrument promising a stream of nominal debt repayments, constant except for principal repayments; sinking funds provisions, of course, enhance this constant repayment feature by requiring annual repayments of principal in the years before maturity. This instrument works well when inflation is low and nominal and real streams coincide reasonably closely. The real debt repayment can be met from the stream of real income realized from the capital project financed by the bond issue. During a period of inflation, even when the inflation is correctly anticipated, the real streams of debt service and income from capital projects diverge sharply.

Consider a firm financing in today's, or yesterday's, environment of vigorous demand pressures and significant inflationary expectations. The real debt service on these high-coupon bonds will tend to exceed the real income initially produced by the projects financed. An increase in the inflation *rate*, even if only partially anticipated, raises nominal rates of interest and, therefore, the debt service on new bond issues immediately, but does not immediately raise the price *level*. The price level does, of course, rise over time, and eventually the nominal income from a project will rise to match the debt service. Initially, however, there is a discrepancy between debt service and project income. In a 1972 paper on the residential mortgage market [1] where the same phenomenon occurs, I called this discrepancy the "financing gap." The firm must fill this gap by additional borrowing until inflation raises its nominal income stream, or, equivalently, reduces the real debt service on the outstanding bonds sufficiently for the income and debt service streams to match. This gap financing will obviously be of a shorter maturity than the long-term financing.

If the short- and long-term finance is combined into a single package, what the firm is doing in an inflationary period is borrowing in such a way that its *net* repayment stream will be rising over time in nominal terms. The firm is combining standard market instruments in a way that produces a result somewhat equivalent to that from a hypothetical bond with rising coupons. The risk features of the two alternatives are, however, very different.

The extra demands on the financial markets will be met with extra financial supplies if credit market investors realize that they must save all of the inflation premium part of interest income for their real capital to remain intact. The savings rate out of disposible income has risen recently, and a calculation I did a few years ago [2] suggested that the rise was about what was needed to reflect full saving of the inflation premium part of household interest income.

Now I want to return to the question of financial market innovation. Investment bankers, corporate financial officers, and institutional investors, are, as a class, a smart group of people. Why have we not seen extensive financial innovation to change the time shape of nominal repayment streams and reduce the uncertainty caused by variable inflation rates? As far as I know the only significant recent innovation along these lines was the introduction of equity-kickers into commercial mortgage contracts in the mid-1960s. This innovation not only puts an upward slope into the stream of nominal debt service but also makes the amount of nominal debt repayment depend in part on the realized rate of inflation as in a purchasing power instrument.

One possible answer is that expectations of a return to price stability are held with much more confidence than economists believe reasonable. After all, since 1965 long rates have frequently been well below short rates suggesting that investors expected a decline in short rates. Moreover, many long-term issues are callable well before maturity so that the existence of high yields on long-term bonds is not necessarily inconsistent with expectations of a falling inflation rate. Finally, the behavior of the stock market since 1965 is hardly consistent with the view that market expectations of long-term inflation are firmly entrenched.

In summary, it may well be that extra short-term borrowing can fill the financing gap caused by the inflation-induced decline in duration. Moreover, a corporate policy of simply rolling over short-term debt serves to turn the borrowing into the practical equivalent of long-term variable interest debt so long as credit-worthiness is retained and short debt rolled over without difficulty. Variable interest debt provides for a degree of price level indexing since short rates reflect actual inflation over a period of years more closely than a single long-rate set at the time a bond issue is sold. It is conceivable, then, that the greater use of short-term financing compared to long-term is the only "innovation" needed to cope with the level and variability of inflation in United States experience.

References

[1] William Poole, "Housing Finance Under Inflationary Conditions," in Board of Governors of the Federal Reserve System, *Ways to Moderate Fluctuation in Housing Construction*, Washington, 1972.

[2] _____, "The Role of Interest Rates and Inflation in the Consumption Function," in Arthur M. Okun and George L. Perry (eds), *Brookings Papers on Economic Activity*, 1:1972, pp. 211-19.

**Part III
Innovation and Monetary
Policy: The Past and the
Future**

Introduction to Part III

This part is devoted to an evaluation of the impact of recent innovations, and the possible effects of future innovation, on the conduct of monetary policy. Chapter 5 by Robert Holland suggests a number of innovations that are likely to take place in the not-too-distant future and describes the task facing the monetary authorities within such an environment. James Meigs tests the impact of recent innovations on the stability of the demand for money and concludes that there has been little, if any, noticeable effect. Much of the previous literature on financial innovation has been related to the conduct of monetary policy and part III extends that tradition.

5

Speculation on Future Innovation: Implications for Monetary Control

Robert C. Holland

Innovation in the financial system has a long history of important contributions to the growth of our nation's prosperity. Furthermore, there is every reason to believe that innovative efforts to improve our financial system will continue to play a key role in maintaining this country's economic well-being. Such innovation is needed in a vigorous society in order to insure continued progress in providing an adequate economic base for meeting national goals and aspirations. Its existence is actually a sine qua non for the nation's satisfactory economic progress.

Basic Types of Economic Innovation

When we look at innovative contributions to such economic progress, two types of innovation are readily distinguishable. The first has been a consequence of changes in scientific knowledge and its applications, changes that have produced the strong technological forces that have reshaped human life during the twentieth century. In the economy, these new technologies have given us the capacity to produce goods in volumes that were not conceivable before. Such alteration in our productive capacity can be termed *process innovation*. It has introduced a new era in history, typified by the capacity of industrialized societies to move away from the chronic goods scarcity that characterized all of prior history.

The second type of innovation has come about as a result of individuals' and corporations' desires for new and better goods. These desires both encourage, and are fostered by, technological changes and resulting process innovations, but are distinct from them. The innovations flowing from these changes in people's wants can be termed *product innovation*. This second type of innovation is abundantly displayed in the economic history of the more affluent industrialized societies during this century.

Many sectors of our society have generally relied with considerable success on market processes to stimulate both of those broad types of innovation. But this has not been entirely true in the case of the financial

Paul Metzger, the Federal Reserve Board's chief long-range planner, has assisted me in the preparation of this chapter. The views herein expressed are my personal responsibility, and should not be taken as official Federal Reserve positions.

159

sector, on which society has placed governmental controls of various types in order to achieve purposes that go beyond the progress achieved through innovation.

Limitations on Financial Innovation

To make an effective contribution to sustained economic progress, the financial system needs not only to be innovative but must also be reasonably strong and healthy. Innovations in other sectors of the economy cannot promote economic progress when the financial sector is unable to provide a flow of monetary resources adequate to nurture the growth of the economy.

My remarks focus primarily on recent developments and possible future innovations in the nation's banking system, since it lies at the heart of our financial system and insuring its continued safety and soundness is critical to the well-being of that financial system. We know that the banking system has recently been undergoing significant strains, due in significant part to the current adverse conditions in the economy generally. That our banking system is, by and large, weathering this period of difficulty well is a good measure of its resiliency and of the flexibility and competence of most bank managements.

The continued vitality of the banking system, especially during periods of stress, is dependent not only on its capacity for innovation, but also on the prudent conduct of bank managements and their continuing awareness of the need to promote public confidence in our banks. In times of economic uncertainty, concerned customers are particularly likely to scrutinize closely their banks' financial condition. Should signs of weakness multiply, uneasy money could decide to seek haven elsewhere, further increasing pressures on banks and on the entire financial system. If such pressures should exceed the limits of safety, the financing of economic activity in general could be disrupted.

The financial sector—and its keystone, banking, in particular—has therefore been subjected to monetary, regulatory, and supervisory limitations far more stringent than those typically applied to other sectors of the economy. In a sense, prudent banking conduct is deemed necessary to permit healthy innovation to flourish. There is thus a kind of dynamic tension between forces, on the one hand impelling the innovative activities of banks, and on the other hand compelling need for prudence and the avoidance of actions that would result in weakening the public's confidence in our banking system. While a measure of entrepreneurial aggressiveness by bank managements has helped make our banking system a progressive one, in the final analysis only a prudent management can assure that system's continued well-being. It is the overriding aspect of the public interest in banking, and in the financial sector in general, that establishes necessary limits on the scope of permissible innovations in this area.

Useful Distinctions Among Financial Innovations

The recognition that financial regulation constrains at least some financial innovation leads to a useful categorical distinction for the next stage of our analysis. While I apologize for introducing still another classification scheme for innovations, I believe the focus of decision of financial innovations can be sharpened by this division. Following the tradition that a label gains respect as it adds syllables, I shall term these two categories *circumventive innovation* and *transcendental innovation*.

Circumventive Innovation

The sort of innovation I call circumventive comes about when free market forces and institutions seek to bypass the monetary and regulatory controls imposed in the name of those public policy considerations to which I have referred. As a result, services and processes are invented that work around the rules, for example, those imposed for monetary policy purposes.

This process entails both benefits and dangers. The beneficial innovations tend to impel governmental decision makers to reassess their initial policies that have been partially circumvented. Through this process policies that are not in fact serving their original or justifiable purposes come to be reviewed more closely to see whether their elimination or modification might serve those same ends better. And, indeed, sometimes the underlying rationale for a policy itself needs to be reexamined in the light of changing circumstances to determine whether the policy and its objectives continue to be worthy.

Innovations have, for example, sprung up over the years seeking ways around Regulation Q concerning maximum rates payable on time deposits. In the course of examining these innovations in order to strengthen that Regulation, the policy on which it rests has come under close scrutiny. As a consequence of this review, over 20 percent of the dollar amount of all commercial bank time deposits has been exempted from interest rate ceilings. Furthermore, there now appears to exist a greater willingness among banks, bank customers, and banking regulators to consider the possibility of significantly altering or even removing the remaining limitations this Regulation imposes at the appropriate time.

Dangers can also arise, of course, whenever there are efforts to circumvent regulatory actions taken to promote the public interest. In several instances timely steps have needed to be taken to insure that desirable regulations are complied with substantially and that any loopholes in those regulations are plugged effectively.

Those who innovate circumventive processes thus have a significant responsibility to attempt to insure that those processes will not tend to weaken the financial system, either in the near future or over the longer run. They can do this best, I believe, if they examine carefully whether their actions are more likely than not to promote their own long-run interests. It seems to me that most institutions will find their long-run interests are best served when they are least likely to be seen by influential segments of the public as being antithetical to the best interest of society as a whole. Not to examine possible circumventive innovations from this longer viewpoint seems to me to invite substantial risks to future profitability.

Regulators, on their part, need to have the capacity to reassess the public interest objectively in the light of significant efforts to circumvent the policies they have initiated. In short, the public interest will be served best when financial innovators bear their own longer term interests more fully in mind, and regulators strive to retain the ability not to view actions that tend to thwart their policies as necessarily inimical to the public good.

Transcendental Innovation

Let me turn now to the second category of financial innovation, which I have called *transcendental innovation*. This occurs when changes are sought by customers and financial institutions of a kind essentially unrelated to regulatory control. To be sure, such changes might so alter banking performance as to call forth some new regulations to constrain their effects, but they are impelled basically by reasons that transcend the existence of regulatory handicaps.

Looking back over the past decade or so, a number of very significant such innovations come to mind. It has frequently been said that over the last 10 to 15 years a virtual "revolution" has been underway in the very nature of banking, as compared with Depression-era banking. I would agree with those observers who have noted that banking is taking on a strikingly new pattern, a pattern that is a key part of the evolution that the entire financial system is undergoing.

To appreciate this rather dramatic change more fully, we need only think about a few of the more salient developments that have been taking place in banking. These would include: widespread bank utilization of certificates of deposit and other money market instruments in order to raise funds; the growing reliance of banks on services for a fee to offset increasing customer economization on demand deposit balances; the spread of floating-interest-rate assets and liabilities among banks; the increasing integration and interdependence of financial systems throughout the world, particularly among the highly industrialized nations; and the growth and diversification of bank holding companies both in the United States and abroad.

These very significant changes have required most leading banks to develop a different style of management—more sophisticated, frequently internationally oriented, even to some extent entrepreneurial. It should be noted that all of these developments are by no means fully integrated as yet into banking or the broader financial system, but rather are gradually becoming assimilated, and so the full impact of these changes has perhaps still to be felt.

Aside from a few noteworthy innovations such as the floating-rate note, it seems to me that transcendental innovation has slowed both absolutely and relative to circumventive innovation during the current period of economic difficulty. As the economy recovers and business conditions stabilize, we can anticipate that changes will be promoted that are now being held in abeyance due to the uncertain economic climate.

Internal Financial Changes

With these classifications of innovation added to our tools of analysis, let us proceed to speculate about some current and prospective financial innovations and their implications.

No discussion of financial innovations can be complete, of course, without mention of the substantial internal changes that are underway in our financial and banking institutions. These changes have already exerted, and will continue to exert a significant impact on the capacity of these institutions to develop innovations under the two broad categories I have described.

I am referring here to the heavy reliance upon computer technology that has developed both within and between financial institutions. This shift to electronics has permitted not only the innovations in internal production processes that are most frequently noted. It has also, perhaps even more significantly, enabled decision makers to interact with computers in a manner that carries substantial implications for the future of the financial system.

The Information Revolution

Let me dwell a bit on this particular aspect of innovation in order to illustrate the breadth of the effects that can flow therefrom.

What has occurred constitutes what might be termed an "information revolution." Although it has had, and will continue to have, a major impact on all sectors of the economy, I will focus on its effect on the financial system. The computer has permitted us to assemble and retrieve raw data in tremendous volumes that could not previously have been handled. More important, it has enabled raw data to be manipulated and presented in a form that makes them usable as "information" that tells us what we previously did not, and perhaps otherwise could not, know. Thus, information that previously did not exist has been created, prepared in a manner that makes it useful to decision makers, and made available to them as it may be needed.

Corporate treasurers, as well as bankers innovating new services, have already taken advantage of the information capabilities of computers to keep a closer watch on their firms' cash positions than was previously possible. This new sophistication has, for example, in large part been responsible for the increased ability of corporate depositors to reduce their demand balances to minimal working cash requirements with significant consequences to the liquidity needs of the banking industry.

Just as bankers, treasurers, and many other decision makers in the private sector have benefited from the informational capabilities of the computer, so have policy makers in government. Through the use of computers, monetary policy makers have been able to prepare financial statistics that permit us to develop information essential to the formation of monetary policy. By employing econometric models that utilize computer-manipulated economic and financial data, monetary policy makers have been able to increase significantly the sophistication of the policy formation process. This is not to say, of course, that the information to which the Federal Reserve now has access is complete. On the contrary, much remains to be done to improve the scope, quality, and timeliness of the statistical series we employ; however, we believe that while substantial improvement in the information base of monetary policy is possible, we would obviously be in far worse straits without the information-generating capability the computer has given us.

What we and our banker friends may be most laggard in now is in conceiving the full scope of helpful questions that this new information technology can help answer. Our imaginations seem to me slow to grasp the full impact of what can be illumined by electronic information systems, and so we still depend basically on hunch and preconception in many areas where they represent an inferior substitute for obtainable knowledge.

There are, of course, caveats to be observed in developing and utilizing computer technology correctly. First, the effort to develop data for monetary, or indeed other public policy, purposes must be made consistent with the right of privacy of individuals and institutions. The preservation of this right is vital to the maintenance of a free society. Appropriate legal and technical safeguards must be designed to insure that the high value our society places on the right of privacy is not unwittingly undermined by the informational needs of public policy making.

A second caveat is that excessive reliance on computer-derived information for monetary policy can present certain dangers. The selection and development of significant data series and the construction of econometric models are processes that entail the exercise of sound judgment at many critical points. That same exercise of judgment must necessarily be applied in evaluation of the economic and financial projections that these computerized models produce. The use of the critical faculties cannot be supplanted because we employ computer technology. To rely wholly on computer output would be to elevate a helpful policy-making tool to the level of a deus ex machina. The consequences would be to distort the monetary policy-making process in the most serious fashion. Thus, while computer technology offers us considerable benefits in public policy formation, care must be taken that it is correctly employed and that its very real limitations are clearly understood.

The use of electronic technology has thus brought about in the financial system both an information revolution and a production process revolution. These two transformations, of course, tend to be mutually reinforcing. Together they expand considerably the capacity of financial institutions to develop new products in the form of services that better meet the needs of their corporate and individual customers. This capacity for innovation seems to me likely to continue to grow throughout the financial system at an accelerated pace.

Prospective External Innovations by Banks

Let me turn now to some possible changes we are likely to see in what the banking system offers its customers. To change the pace somewhat, let me set forth a number of changes that I foresee in brief and assertive fashion.

Banks with the wherewithal to do so will probably continue to press to expand the number and nature of the financially related services they can provide. They may also seek broader geographic scope for their expanded services, with some chance of success particularly through their near-bank corporate affiliates.

We can anticipate that additional efforts will be made to create instruments attractive to investors and rewarding to banks. As a consequence, variable-interest-rate instruments may be expected to proliferate, and the use of "equity kickers" may also grow.

Yet another consequence that may follow from the production process transformation I have described is the gradual emergence of an electronic payments system that would carry forward computer-linkages among financial institutions and between them and their customers. Such a means of transferring funds will offer many new opportunities for banks to develop innovative methods of meeting their customers' demands for more convenient and comprehensive services. Just as the banking industry will seek to utilize an electronic funds transfer system as a source of greater profitability, so too will other institutions that may also be afforded access to such a system. Thus, the electronic payments mechanism will no doubt become a source not only of heightened profits for those institutions that utilize it successfully, but also of heightened competition among them across a broad spectrum of both new and old services. It should also prove a source of benefits to customers, in the form of quicker, broader, and more integrated services.

In short, most banks (except those that, for reasons of size and market scope, are relatively insulated from the pressures I have examined) will have to be innovative and responsive to their customers' needs in order to perform adequately their basic function—gathering funds from saver-investors and disbursing them in an inventive manner and at a reasonable profit to the borrowers who seek them.

Both the information revolution and the emergence of an electronic funds transfer system seem likely to lead to still greater minimization of idle cash, not only by corporate treasurers, but also by a growing number of more sophisticated consumers. Corporate and individual customers will tend to expect and to demand an adequate return for money held for them by banks and other financial institutions. They will probably also come to rely more heavily on temporary extensions of credit to cover short-term variations in their own cash needs. Financial institutions, in their turn, can be expected to become even more reliant than today on fees derived from the performance of a wide array of diversified financial services. They will do this in order both to offset the decline of demand deposit balances and to insure enhanced profitability.

We can anticipate that as a broader array of allied financial services are offered by more financial institutions seeking to provide one-stop, multipurpose services, banks will experience increasing competition from a broader range of competitors. Thus, while the forces for change that I have outlined will enable banks to be more responsive to the demands of their customers, other institutions will increasingly provide services similar to those banks will offer.

This scenario of likely future developments in the financial system has significant implications for monetary controls. These are discussed below.

Impact of Innovations on Geographic Limits of Banking

As substantial innovations in production processes, products, and attendant information capabilities transform the services and procedures of our banking and financial system, they also expand the geographic limitations within which those systems function. Those limitations have become, and will continue to be, progressively less important in the changing environment I have described. Although the physical structure of our banking system in particular remains oriented to limits imposed by local and state boundaries, these are becoming less and less meaningful. Most larger banking organizations have already effectively expanded services to encompass regional and national markets. This expansion can, in part, be attributed to the dramatic changes in production process and information capability that we have witnessed over the past decade. These changes can be expected to gather momentum as we move towards implementation of an electronic payments mechanism. Such innovations should continue to exert powerful pressures on local and state restrictions on banking.

Moreover, the geographic limitations being circumvented or transcended by these financial innovations are not solely those within our own country. As I indicated earlier, we have witnessed a growing interdependence among the various national economies and financial systems. Barring unforeseeable social or political disruptions, I believe this trend will continue to gain strength, particularly among the industrialized nations.

This broad pattern of change has been transforming major corporations generally, and the banks that serve them have also been part of this trend. Banks and bank holding companies have expanded their international operations significantly, partly in response to the need to better serve the United States firms that have greatly enlarged their own overseas operations.

In the future, as more foreign corporations enter this country to operate from United States locations, American banks will no doubt have further reason for diversified foreign activities, since they will want to serve directly the overseas head offices of their foreign-owned clients here. Some major American banks and bank holding companies have already earned, and more will earn, a substantial portion of their profits from dealings with foreign customers both in the United States and abroad. In so doing they will need to be able to compete with foreign banks in the United States and overseas on an equitable basis. Competitive pressures among banks from various countries will undoubtedly push the different national limitations on banking services toward greater and greater harmonization over time.

Implications for International Monetary Control

The worldwide economic and financial integration that has been proceeding apace has significant implications not only for the structure of our financial and banking systems, of course, but also for worldwide monetary control. The vast amounts of investible funds that are now accruing to key oil-producing nations generate enormous problems of readjustment for the international financial system and for nations attempting to maintain adequate monetary control over their own economies. In a world in which chronic shortfalls can be expected to continue in the capital funds available to meet nations' wants, capital from such sources as the oil-producing nations should be welcomed. But the possible volatility and volume of such capital flows cannot help but increase the difficulties inherent in the conduct of national monetary policy.

For example, a policy of monetary restraint in the United States could become less effective if key borrowers had ready access to major overseas sources of credit to finance activities in the United States over which the Federal Reserve had little effective control. By the same token, a policy of monetary expansion here might have less predictable effects on expanding credit in the United States and might be rendered less effective if United States banks utilized available resources to expand their overseas activities rather than for loans that might expand business activity here in the United States.

Smaller countries than ours in which international trade and payments are a much larger relative share of their total activity have already experienced the above phenomena, sometimes to a painful extent. It seems reasonable to forecast a gradually increasing intrusion of that consideration in United States affairs as well. Furthermore, there is one respect in which such effects on the United States might be accelerated. I refer to the growing dimensions of the offshore Eurodollar market, which is free of reserve requirements and most other monetary controls. Funds borrowed in that market can pay for United States goods and services (or products in any other country in which the holder can transfer assets for dollars). It therefore seems important to me that central banking authorities consider the desirability of some extension and coordination of their reserve requirement and other monetary regulations so that this comparatively unregulated and reserve-free market in banking services does not evolve to such an extent that it threatens the ability of individual countries to pursue their domestic monetary policies.

This situation calls for renewed and persistent efforts, particularly by monetary authorities in the leading industrial and financial nations, to achieve an increased level of mutual understanding. If this can be done in a spirit of cooperation based on recognition of the interdependence of all nations in today's world, fears of the possible adverse consequences for individual nations of the continued free flow of international capital might be substantially allayed. This might do much to improve the climate in which needed sociopolitical agreements could be negotiated on a basis of mutual respect and amity.

We should remember, however, that the possibility of reaching under-standings with respect to capital flows is limited by the level of mutual confidence that can be attained. Such confidence can be much impaired or enhanced by the nature of each nation's legal institutions and the extent to which they assure that foreign capital receives, and is likely to continue to receive, nondiscriminatory treatment.

Implications for Domestic Monetary Controls

Let me elaborate further on the implications of these speculations about financial innovations for the future of domestic monetary controls in the United States. As I suggested above, the noninterest bearing deposits that have been the anchor of monetary policy are likely to dwindle relatively, to a significant extent as a consequence of the innovations that are taking place in the banking and financial systems.

As this process moves forward, the helpfulness of various measures of the money supply should decrease. This effect has already been noted with regard to the monetary aggregate, M_1, made up as it is of noninterest-bearing currency in circulation and demand deposits. In time, M_1 may come to play a role similar to that presently filled by currency, or even by subsidiary coin. That is, M_1 may eventually provide a satisfactory reflec-tion of small routine transactions taking place in the economy, but it will neither affect nor reflect dependably the extent of the discretionary spend-ing that is occurring. As this transformation of the role of M_1 takes place—possibly over several decades—it will become a less and less meaningful base upon which to predicate either monetary expansion or contraction. In contrast, the measure of liquidity most directly related to discretionary spending would probably come to be some amalgam of at least all deposit-type holdings, perhaps plus some fraction of the immediately convertible debt paper of others, with possibly even some allowance for the credit lines immediately available to borrower-spenders.

From the viewpoint of monetary policy makers, it seems likely that the magnitudes of such monetary or liquidity aggregates would continue to be important as ingredients of economic stimulus. In this environment central bank actions would need a broader base in order for monetary policy to maintain some effectiveness. Since a growing variety of interest-bearing deposits and credit instruments may come to satisfy the economy's liq-uidity needs, and affect its saving-spending decisions, it may become advisable to extend monetary reserve requirement to more of such instru-ments as well. In my view these reserve requirements could be effective monetarily even if set at a relatively low percentage level. While substan-tially broadening the base of monetary policy, such new reserve requirements would have the additional advantage of countering some of the pressures for circumventive innovations. As more nonbank institutions provide credit and deposit-type liabilities to corporations and consumers alike and come to approximate the functions of banks, it becomes increasingly inequitable, as well as decreasingly useful, to rest the full weight of monetary policy controls on the nation's commercial banks. A movement toward broader reserve requirements on such interest-bearing liquidity instruments might eventually be perceived as both a rational and equitable step to meet the growing need to strengthen the nation's capacity to execute better its monetary policy.

I am aware of a good deal of academic literature that argues that monetary reserve requirements are inefficient and unnecessary. But to me, such analysis too conveniently assumes that banks and other financial intermediaries will always want to hold some kind of central bank liability. I do not believe that necessarily follows in the kind of world toward which we are moving. I can even conceive of a system in which the payments mechanism has moved outside the central bank; and in that eventuality, without reserve requirements to provide it a fulcrum for its reserve-altering operations, the central bank's open market transactions might come to have a monetary effect not too different from those of the Social Security trust fund or the Mint. For assured monetary effectiveness at all times, the central bank needs to be able to control the available total of some asset which the financial system (or at least a key part of it) feels it has to have. Explicit monetary reserve requirements seem to be the most dependable means of providing that essential ingredient for monetary control.

There is one overriding evolutionary tendency in the financial system that should be underlined. In the future we can anticipate that more technically perfect markets will develop as the financial system evolves. These markets will be taking advantage of both process and product innovations to serve increasingly sophisticated saver-investors and borrowers better. In such markets the price of money reflected in the rates of interest will tend to have relatively even more influence than now on the discretionary spending decisions of consumers and corporations alike. To state the same point in reverse, nonprice rationing devices and similar market imperfections will fade, and a larger and larger share of the total implementation of monetary ease or restraint will have to be accomplished by means of interest rate changes. It also follows that the amplitude of interest rate changes that the financial system can stand will in effect set the outer limits for what monetary policy can contribute to economic stabilization.

It might be noted, incidentally, that reserve requirements fit well into such a financial system. One of their effects is a kind of internal interest cost to the affected parts of the financial system. Adjustments to the price effects of reserve requirement changes can be accomplished smoothly in the kind of financial system we are envisaging.

Concluding Observations

The forces shaping the broad categories of innovations I have delineated, are long-term ones that should prevail unless stemmed by the vulnerabilities of the financial system itself or excessively hampered by the public policy constraints under which our financial and banking institutions operate. The transformations that have been taking place have generally contributed to the national economic welfare. It therefore seems to be an important part of the responsibility of financial regulatory authorities to continue to provide a climate in which sound innovations that strengthen the financial system and improve its services to the public can flourish, while less well-considered efforts at change receive appropriate remedial attention.

Comment: Speculation on Future Innovation: Implications for Monetary Control

Stephen M. Goldfeld

Robert Holland has provided us with a stimulating and thoughtful piece on innovation in financial markets. The first part of this chapter sets forth in some detail a particular view of the process of innovation and it will help focus our discussion if we briefly summarize some of the salient features of Holland's framework.

Like most writers, Holland begins with the presumption that innovation, both historically and prospectively, is an important component of the advance in national economic welfare. Compared to innovation more generally, financial innovation is characterized as somewhat special because of the welter of regulations that restrict the behavior of financial institutions. It is perhaps noteworthy that this view is a bit reminiscent of the extended academic debate as to whether commercial banks are regulated because they are different or are different because they are regulated. In any event, Holland defends regulation on the grounds that the public interest demands that the financial system must be "strong and healthy." The net result is characterized as a "dynamic tension" between innovative forces and the "compelling need for prudence."

Holland goes on to distinguish between two types of innovation— circumventive and transcendental. As its name implies, *circumventive innovation* is the free market response of those who seek to escape or avoid the consequences of monetary and regulatory controls. Holland suggests that those who engage in circumventive innovation "have significant responsibility to attempt to insure that those processes will not weaken the financial system." On the other side of the coin, he indicates that regulators should learn from the appearance of circumventive innovation and in each instance reexamine the intention of the regulation in question.

There is absolutely no doubt that circumventive innovation is a very real and important phenomenon. Even the most casual reflection on recent financial history reveals many illustrations. On the other hand, I am somewhat bothered by the rather explicit test of social responsibility that Holland wants to apply to innovations. I am more inclined to the view that regulations which invite *and* permit substantial circumventive innovation are per se bad regulations. Put another way, I take the appearance of substantial innovation of this sort to indicate that either the regulators missed some fundamental truism about the way financial markets work or, that they knew what they were doing, but simply were not clever enough to close all the loopholes in the first place. Neither state of affairs seems to be particularly commendable.

Holland, of course, is fully aware of these points but nevertheless comes down on the side of prudence as a good first approximation and at a general level it is hard to argue with this. However, given our second-best world, if one believes that innovations increase economic well-being (as Holland does argue), then clearly one needs some sort of joint welfare analysis of both regulatory proposals and circumventive innovations. Needless to say, such analyses are rarely explicitly undertaken prior to the introduction of a regulation.

Given the definition of circumventive innovation, then by default *transcendental innovation* refers to all types of innovations unrelated to regulatory control. The widespread and growing application of computer technology to banking is a clear example of this phenomenon. On the other hand, many of the illustrations provided by Holland do not seem to be free of a regulatory stimulus. For example, Holland cites the use of CDs and other money market instruments to raise funds and the spread of floating-interest-rate liabilities. These illustrations, as well as several others provided by Holland, hardly seem unrelated to regulatory control. Indeed, from an outsider's (i.e., nonregulator's) viewpoint, it appears that an innovation is circumventive if the banks try to get around it quickly but transcendental if they meditate about it for a while before doing something about it. While this is undoubtedly an overly cynical view, at the very least, it suggests that the distinction between the two types of innovation may not be that clear-cut.

Semantic distinctions aside, there is a more important problem concerning the interplay between innovation and the need for prudence. Again from an outsider's perspective, this "dynamic tension" seems partly to translate into Federal Reserve schizophrenia between the needs of current monetary policy and the shaping of the evolution of the financial system. For example, in spite of its professed desire to foster competition for savings, the Fed's position on the Citicorp-Chase floating rate debentures questioned whether it was in the public interest "at this time." This seems to be a clear case of conflict between short-run stabilization objectives and more longer run considerations. I hasten to add that this problem is not unique to monetary policy in that tax legislation often gets bogged down in reconciling considerations of tax reform and current policy needs. Unfortunately, the text book distinction between the allocation, stabilization, and distribution branches tend to get rather blurred in the real world.

The second part of Holland's chapter considers a number of specific prospective innovations and examines the implications of these from a variety of points of view. I should say at the outset that, on the whole,

Holland's crystal-ball gazing makes eminently good sense and, except for some details, I have little to quarrel with it. Among the plausible developments Holland foresees is the increased reliance on computer technology in finance and the ultimate emergence of some sort of electronic funds transfer system (EFTS). An EFTS meshes well with a number of other prospective developments forecast by Holland such as the expansion of bank financial services, both in scope and geographically. Furthermore, assuming an EFTS will be available to nonbank intermediaries, this is also consistent with Holland's view that nonbanks will become more like banks, a development that should introduce a healthier competitive environment—especially for the small saver. Overall, then, technology and its consequences really are overriding themes of Holland's view of financial evolution.

The prospective developments forecast by Holland naturally carry with them several important implications for the future character of financial markets and for the nature of monetary policy. In addition, if these developments are to come to pass a number of existing regulatory impediments will need to be removed. The rest of my comments are devoted to this interrelated set of issues.

As to the character of financial markets, Holland speculates that market imperfections and nonprice rationing devices will gradually fade. This increased competitiveness will bring with it greater interest rate variability, which will become the major linkage between monetary policy and the real sector—thus moving the real world towards the textbook model (at least in some incarnations). This scenario is only consistent with the complete removal of interest ceilings of all types (usury, regulation Q, and the prohibition of interest pavements on demand deposits) and, although he does not say so explicitly, Holland clearly is assuming these will eventually disappear. He is more explicit on the likely relaxation of geographical restrictions on banking—restrictions that have probably already outlived their usefulness and that will become increasingly untenable as time goes on.

Another consequence that Holland suggests follows from his scenario is a decline in the significance of the narrowly defined money stock. Heretical as it may strike some, he conjectures that M_1 may go the way of subsidiary coin. Whatever one's personal views about the current significance of M_1, given Holland's scenario, I find it hard to see how one could argue with the qualitative nature of his conclusion (although even I think the subsidiary coin analogy may be a bit much).

The interesting question is, of course, what follows from this. Holland suggests that some composite liquidity measure would emerge to supplant M_1 in importance. From this he draws the policy punch line that we may well want to extend reserve requirements to a much broader array of instruments (and by implication, institutions). Holland's argument for this is two-fold. First, if banks and nonbanks become more similar, then it would be inequitable to treat them differently. Second, if the Fed wishes to control some aggregate liquidity measure, a necessary precondition for achieving this is an extended set of reserve requirements. The equity point seems well taken but the second argument is somewhat more problematical. Indeed, in view of the rather broad scope of his proposal, I wish Holland had been a bit more specific as to exactly how such an extended set of requirements might work. Such a discussion, it seems to me, would have to face up to a number of issues, especially if one is contemplating reserve requirements in a world with an EFTS.

Under EFTS the distinction between the various types of deposits might get blurred to the point that it would be difficult to sustain markedly different reserve requirements on alternative liabilities. It has been suggested that in such a situation we might want to consider flow (or turnover) rules that take the amount of activity in an account, rather than the stock of deposits, as the base for computing required reserves. Consideration of an EFTS aside, there are a number of other questions one could raise concerning Holland's expanded role for reserve requirements. For example, he does not spell out exactly what kinds of instruments might require reserves nor does he indicate how such requirements would mesh with the rather complicated regulatory structure that governs our various financial institutions. He is also silent on the political realities of such a change and whether one might have to (or should) pay interest on required reserves. While I have my own opinions on all these matters, they are hardly grounded in firm analysis and I suspect Holland and I would both agree that such an analysis is called for.

On the whole, while I have quibbled with a few details, I think Holland has provided us with a useful chapter that provides a quite plausible view of the future. Like all views of the future, however, the one thing I have trouble with is how we get "there" from "here" but that is really a subject for another paper.

6

Recent Innovations: Do They Require A New Framework for Monetary Analysis?

A. James Meigs

Introduction

Liabilities of financial institutions make up most of what we call money today. Financial institutions, furthermore, produce money-transfer services through which a large part of all monetary transactions are carried out. It is not surprising, therefore, that innovation and rapid technological change in financial institutions and markets raise doubts about the adequacy of conventional monetary analysis. The doubts arise from this question: Do changes in financial institutions alter the significance and characteristics of the money that the institutions produce and process?

J.G. Gurley and E.S. Shaw opened this line of questioning with their work on development of financial institutions in the 1950s [23]. They argued that monetary theory should take the growth of nonbank financial intermediaries into account, because nonbank intermediaries produced close substitutes for money that should be expected to influence the demand for money. As H.G. Johnson pointed out in his 1962 survey, "Monetary Theory and Policy," the mainstream of both classical and Keynesian monetary theory, before Gurley and Shaw, had treated the financial structure as of secondary importance [27].

Since the mid-1960s, G.W. Mitchell, vice chairman of the Board of Governors of the Federal Reserve System, has based somewhat similar criticisms of received monetary theory on technological changes in money-transfer services that have already occurred and some that he expects to come in the future [34, 35]. He argues, in particular, that the increasing efficiency of transfer services produced by the banking system and the Federal Reserve may sharply reduce the significance of narrowly defined money. In 1972, he said, for example:

The evidence from the recent past is clear—it takes less and less money to accommodate a given volume of transactions. As this trend becomes more and more pervasive monetary control may have increasingly to recognize another dimension than money supply, namely money efficiency. In the past, gradual changes in money's efficiency could safely be ignored for the short run. But for the electronic transfer future, this is a less comfortable assumption. At the very least there will be continuing attrition of demand deposit money and the substitution of near money. The probable result is that money holdings in the narrow sense will have to have little or nothing to do with decisions to spend or invest, or not to, but only with the scheduling or timing of payments previously agreed to or contracted for. Thus for monetary policy and liquidity purposes, everyone's horizon will have to be lifted beyond that narrowing magnitude [34].

In January 1975 Governor Mitchell continued the argument:

An end to the upward trend in the efficiency of money for transactions has been predicted for many years but the evidence—statistical, institutional and in money mores—has failed entirely thus far to support that expectation. To seek improved monetary control by reliance on a variable, M_1, whose characteristics are undergoing rapid change, involves unknown exposures. In my opinion, the concept of the narrowly defined money supply is becoming less and less appropriate even as a proxy for monetary action. Furthermore, optimal growth rates assigned to it based on past experience, by ignoring varying rates of change in its efficiency, additionally jeopardize users of M_1 as a guideline be they policy makers or the public [35].

In these two passages and in other writings Governor Mitchell states an intuitively plausible hypothesis: (1) Innovations in the payments mechanism reduce the influence of the money stock on the public's decisions to spend and invest; (2) innovations impair the predictability of relationships among money and other economic variables that may have been observed in the past; and (3) because of both of the preceding effects on the significance and characteristics of money, innovations in the payments mechanism make the money stock an unreliable instrument or indicator for public policy.

I cite Governor Mitchell here because he makes the most persuasive case I have yet seen for the proposition that financial innovations require a new framework for monetary analysis, or at least major changes in that framework. I shall argue, however, that the available evidence on effects of financial innovations does not indicate that either a new framework or major changes in conventional monetary analysis are needed. I shall argue further that the effects that might reasonably be expected to flow from financial innovations can readily be accomodated within conventional monetary theory.

The Framework for Monetary Analysis

The first proposition in what I take to be a widely accepted framework for monetary analysis is that changes in the money stock, however defined, have predictable effects on national income and prices, including interest rates. Although there is much disagreement over magnitudes of effects and channels of transmission, economists of virtually all schools probably agree today that the money stock is a significant variable in macroeconomic analysis. The second proposition is that there are predictable relationships between the nominal money stock and certain other variables, such as security holdings of the monetary authorities, that are under the direct control of government. Therefore, in spite of disagreement on relative importance and mechanics, most economists probably agree that governments have enough influence over the money stock to make it a major policy variable.

The key to the first proposition is the existence of a stable demand for money—demand in the sense of a functional relationship between the amount of money people want to hold and a few other variables, such as income, wealth, and interest rates. I take it as generally accepted that the demand for real money balances is positively related to real income or wealth and negatively related to the opportunity cost of holding money, which is usually measured by some interest rate. Financial innovations conceivably could make the demand for money less stable, which would reduce the ability of analysts and policy makers to predict the effects of changes in the quantity of money on income, employment, and prices. This is the gist of Governor Mitchell's criticism of the use of narrowly defined money, M_1, in theory and policy.

Financial innovations also conceivably could make the money-supply function—the relationship between the nominal quantity of money and variables that are under control of the monetary authorities—less stable. This would mean that even though effects of changes in the money stock on income and prices might be predictable, the monetary authorities could not influence the money stock with enough precision for it to be a reliable policy instrument. Some statesments by Federal Reserve spokesmen do seem to imply that such innovations as the use of Eurodollars by United States banks or the adoption of liabilities-management techniques by banks have impaired stability of the money-supply function.

In the body of this chapter, therefore, I review recent empirical evidence on the stability of both the demand for money and the supply of money in the United States. I also present some theoretical arguments for expecting these relationships to be stable in the face of continuing financial innovation.

Stability of the Demand for Money

Two recent studies by M.S. Khan [29] and S.M. Goldfeld [21], and a comment by M.J.Hamburger [24], bear specifically on the question of the stability over time of the demand for money. Their results do not support the thesis that innovations—or, for that matter, anything else—have either significantly changed the coefficients of the United States money-demand function or made the function less stable, since the acceleration of innovation in banks in the early 1960s.

Mohsin Khan fit money-demand functions with annual data for the United States covering the years 1901-65. He defined *stability* in the statistical sense of the estimated coefficients of the explanatory variables remaining constant over time. He also cited the Freidman framework prescription that "a demand-for-money function should be formulated such that it remains stable with respect to a given number of predetermined variables under differing institutional arrangements, changes in social and political environment, etc."

Khan wrote his demand-for-money function in the log-linear terms as

$$\log M_t = a_0 + a_1 \log R_t + a_2 \log Y_t + u_t \qquad (6.1)$$

in which M = real per capita money balances; R = rate of interest; Y = real per capita income; and u_t is an error term.

Because of the trends in both money balances and income, he specified the function in first differences of the variables:

$$\Delta \log M_t = b_0 + b_1 \Delta \log R_t + b_2 \Delta \log Y_t + w_t \qquad (6.1a)$$

Use of two definitions of the money stock (M_1 and M_2), and two definitions each of interest rates (short and long) and income (current and "permanent") yielded eight specifications for testing. Rather than splitting the sample period at points where changes in relationship might be suspected, Khan used a test developed by Brown and Durbin [29, p. 2] that is designed to detect shifts in a regression relationship.

Khan concluded that the demand-for-money function was stable over the entire period for both M_1 and M_2, except for an indication of a structural shift in 1948 when a short-term interest rate was used in the equation. The structural shift in 1948, however, did not appear when a long-term rate was used. The impressive aspect of the Khan evidence for our purposes is the extremely long time period covered, which included the two world wars and the great Depression. Furthermore, both the broad and narrow money equations were apparently stable. These results are consistent also with those of D. Laidler [30]. Laidler's evidence, however, ended at 1960, before the period of bank innovation that concerns us here.

Among the main questions examined by S.M. Goldfeld in his paper, "The Demand for Money Revisited," were the following:

Has the demand function for money remained stable over the postwar period? Put another way, is there any evidence of either systematic long-run shifts or marked short-run instabilities that make historically estimated relationships unsuitable for forecasting purposes? [22]

Goldfeld was especially interested in the question of the short-term stability of money demand in view of the experience of the early 1970s, when some observers thought there had been short-run shifts in the demand for money. On the question of the long-term stability of money demand he was concerned with whether quarterly data from the postwar period can be used homogeneously in the face of institutional developments such as certificates of deposit and Eurodollars. Thus, he was specifically concerned with the questions dealt with in this chapter. Although he covered a great many other issues in his paper, we can separate out the evidence bearing on the effects of innovation.

The Goldfeld demand-for-money equation is like Khan's in that the demand for real balances is a function of interest rates and real GNP. It differs from Khan's classical "store-of-value" explanation of money demand in being derived from a transactions view, in which the demand for money evolves from a lack of synchronization between receipts and payments and the cost of exchanging money for interest-bearing assets. This approach, incidentally, is similar to the implicit framework used by Governor Mitchell and other Federal Reserve spokesmen who emphasize transactions demand and transaction costs and short-term interest rates. His emphasis on transactions demand should make it natural for Goldfeld to expect innovations in payments practices to cause structural shifts in the demand for money.

Goldfeld tested for short-term instability by estimating his equation over 12 sample periods, each of which started in 1952:2 and differed in that the terminal point was systematically moved forward from the end of 1961 to the end of 1972 in steps of four quarters. With the coefficients estimated for each sample period, the next four out-of-sample quarters were forecast. As I interpret his results, he did not find the serious short-run instability in the demand for M_1 in a period of rapid change in the payments mechanism that was implied by Governor Mitchell's hypothesis. As Goldfeld views the results:

On the whole, the money demand function does not exhibit marked short-run instability. However, this is only one chapter of the short-term forecasting story. For one thing, the analysis has assumed both known interest rates and real GNP. In addition, it explains money demand in real terms so that to forecast nominal money demand would require a price forecast, which would introduce further error. Given those caveats, however, it is reassuring to find a reasonable degree of short-run stability [22, p. 590].

On the question of long-term stability, Goldfeld did find evidence of a possible structural shift in 1961. When the sample was broken at the end of 1961, the equations for the two subperiods differed somewhat. This result was consistent with the findings of a study by M.B. Slovin and M.E. Sushka who argue that the period 1955:1 to 1962:1 may be different from 1962:2 to 1968:4, possibly because of the introduction of certificates of deposit [39].

However, according to Goldfeld, the biggest difference between the two equations was in the coefficient on time-deposit rates (one of the two short-term rates in the equation) and this was largely attributable to the sizable jump in time-deposit rates that occurred precisely at the breaking point in the sample. Furthermore, a Chow test applied to the sample split did not allow rejection of the hypothesis of stability. Thus, the one bit of statistical evidence that might be related to an identifiable innovation is, at best, debatable.

M.J. Hamburger's comment was inspired by a view that was widely held in 1971 and for some time afterward that something strange had happened to the demand for money during that year [24]. The Council of Economic Advisers said, "In the first half of 1971, the public apparently wanted to hold more money balances at the prevailing level of interest rates and income than past relations among income, interest rates, and money balances suggested." The principal evidence for this view was that the growth of M_1 accelerated sharply in the second quarter in the face of rising interest rates and a deceleration of income growth. In the third and fourth quarters, growth of M_1 decelerated, while interest rates fell.

Although Hamburger did not discuss financial innovations in his comment, it was commonly believed at the time that financial practices were changing substantially during that year, partly because it was the second year in which the Federal Open Market Committee (FOMC) emphasized control of the monetary aggregates in its policy directives. Money market participants, such as banks, were believed to be adjusting their policies and practices to the new monetary environment. For example, in their report on open market operations during 1971 (prepared in 1972), A.H. Holmes, P. Meek, and R. Thunberg mentioned that an increasing number of banks had turned to aggressive portfolio management; that the 1969 revisions in tax laws had made securities trading by banks much less inhibited by tax considerations than previously; and that many banks had set up securities trading operations, which tried, like other professional underwriters of debt issues, to anticipate in short-term interest rates [26]. I would prefer to classify those observations under the heading of institutional developments that might possibly influence the money-supply function by altering the responses of banks to Federal Reserve actions. I cite them here, however, as evidence of a general climate of opinion in which money-market experts were prepared to discover significant changes in market behavior.[1]

---

[1] A.H. Holmes, Manager of the System Open Market Account, argued also in his 1974 Report that, "Important institutional and structural changes over the past 5 years have affected importantly the transmission mechanism set in motion by the System's operations" (p. 199). Evidence of such changes, he said, "has reduced the policymaker's confidence in the stability of the linkage between operational instructions and desired long-run economic goals" (p. 207). Among the changes he identified were: development of escalator clauses in loan contracts, the floating prime rate, bank emphasis on liability management, willingness of both banks and

Hamburger concluded that the announcement of shifts in the demand for money was a false alarm that had been based partly on an assumption that the quantity of money demanded in any particular quarter depends solely on events taking place during that period. Later tests with the Federal-Reserve-MIT-Penn (FMP) quarterly model, and with equations developed within the Federal Reserve System to explain month-to-month movements in M_1 [17], presented a different view. These equations, all of which included both current and lagged values of the variables, did not indicate that there had been an upward shift in the demand for money in the second quarter of 1971. Although the evidence for the second half of the year is not quite as clear, says Hamburger, he concluded that there appeared to be little evidence of substantial instability in the demand for money in that period.

Actually, it seems to me that the evidence for instability in the demand for money in 1971 is even weaker than Hamburger's tests indicated. I believe that at least some of the participants in the discussion were not clear as to whether they were explaining the demand for money or the quantity supplied. Hamburger alluded to the possibility of confusion on that point when he referred in a footnote to arguments for a simultaneous-equations approach that would include a demand-for-money equation [20, 21, 40].

The demand-for-money equations of Khan and Goldfeld that we discussed earlier had real money balances as the dependent variable. If they are to be interpreted as demand functions, income, prices, and interest rates must adjust so that the public will be willing to hold whatever nominal quantity of money is available. This is the familiar argument that, although the monetary authorities may control the nominal money stock, the quantity of real balances held is determined by the public.

The 1971 discussion concerned the demand for nominal balances. In the short-run analysis criticized by Hamburger, GNP (or some other proxy for transactions demand) was assumed to be predetermined. The observed change in quantity of M_1 held by the public each quarter, therefore, had to be explained by interest rates. Interest rates in 1971 moved in the opposite direction from the one required to produce the observed change in M_1. This suggests either one or the other of two possibilities: (1) the demand for money was unstable, as the demand-shift proponents argued, or (2) the equation on which their argument was based was not a properly specified money-demand function.

I believe a more plausible explanation for the behavior of M_1 in 1971 than shifts in the demand for money can be found in the way the Federal

---

businesses "to permit their liquidity to deteriorate," increased internationalization of credit markets, ability of multinational firms to shift cash balances and financing demands from market to market, and increasing integration of the Eurodollar market with domestic financial markets. [25]

Reserve and the banking system responded to changes in interest rates. In the second quarter interest rates rose, perhaps because the public expected recovery from recession or more inflation. The Federal Reserve and the banks bought assets at a faster rate, thereby increasing the growth rate of nominal M_1. In the second half, after announcement of the wage-price freeze, interest rates fell; the Federal Reserve and the banks then slowed down their purchases of assets, thereby slowing the growth of M_1. In short, I believe the observed changes in M_1 should have been interpreted as responses of the Federal Reserve and the banks to changes of interest rates, rather than as evidence of shifts in the demand for money function.

It is interesting that the Shadrack-Skinner equation, which is one of the equations Hamburger used in preparing his comment, is a reduced-form equation drawn from a structural model designed to explain the banks' demand for earning assets and reserves as well as the public's demand for bank liabilities (money) [17]. It is, therefore, not a pure demand-for-money equation but includes a money-supply function.[2]

If one concludes a supply response of the banking system and the Federal Reserve in the explanation of the way M_1 behaved in 1971, it is evident that there was either no shift in the demand-for-money function, or that the shift was smaller than was feared at the time. In their review of the 1971 experience, A.E. Burger and N.A. Stevens also rejected the hypothesis that there were shifts in the demand for money [9]. They attributed the changes in growth rates of M_1 to changes in the growth rate of the monetary base resulting from Federal Reserve attempts to counter changes in interest rates.

All of this argument about stability of the demand for money may seem like going the long way around the barn, but if financial innovations were to cause structural changes in behavior that were serious enough to justify abandoning conventional money analysis, evidence of these structural changes should have appeared in the demand-for-money function. Thus

[2]This can be seen by examining banks' responses to changes in the quantity of bank credit demanded. When the stock of bank reserves is increased by Federal Reserve open market operations, banks adjust actual reserves to desired reserves through buying earning assets, in effect supplying deposits in exchange. When banks respond to an increase in the quantity of bank credit demanded, through buying earning assets and supplying deposits, they adjust actual reserves to desired reserves by inducing the Manager of the Open Market Account to inject more reserves (under the lagged reserve requirement) or by borrowing from Reserve Banks. Thus, equations explaining the banks' demands for earning assets and reserves also explain the supply of deposits—given the public's demand for bank credit and the Federal Reserve's actions in increasing or decreasing the stock of reserves. This argument can also be made in terms of banks' reactions to changes of interest rates, if one admits short-run changes of interest rates resulting from changes in quantities of real assets and bank credit demanded by the public, rather than attributing short-run changes of rates mainly to shifts in the demand for money, or to Federal Reserve actions, as implied by the money-market-condition mystique.

far, it has not done so, in spite of the supposed instability in some versions of the money-demand function in such years as 1971.

Other evidence of structural changes resulting from financial innovation could be sought in the behavior of income velocity, although I have not made a thorough search there. One implication of Governor Mitchell's analysis of technological changes in the payments mechanism would be a rise in velocity, perhaps at an accelerating rate. M_1 velocity has been on a rising trend since World War II and the slope increased slightly to an average increase of 2.6 percent per year after 1960. However, deviations around the trend have been smaller since 1960 than they were before. M_2 velocity has been virtually constant since 1960 (average annual rate of change 0.2 percent, 1960 through 1974). The existence of a trend in velocity, or deviations around the trend, of course, are not sufficient grounds for jettisoning the monetary analysis framework. What we would need for that would be a showing that velocity had become so variable (and unpredictable) that we could no longer make useful predictions of income from changes in the money stock. Innovations in the payments mechanism do not appear to have had any such effect. The truly interesting question is why velocity has been so stable in recent years, in spite of the facts that many of the variables that would be expected to influence velocity have moved over extremely wide ranges and that there have been many changes in financial institutions and in the conduct of monetary and fiscal policies.

It also should be useful to survey the performance of M_1 and M_2 in forecasting models, such as the St. Louis model and others, to see if the stability of their estimated relationships between money and income has deteriorated. Again, it would not be necessary to compare the predictive ability of these models with that of others but merely to compare their performance with performance of the same models in earlier periods. I am not aware that the ability of these models to forecast nominal income has deteriorated significantly. I would concede, however, that the monetary models have had some trouble recently with short-term changes in the inflation rate and in real income, as have the nonmonetary forecasting models. Nevertheless, a monetary analysis can explain the current inflation, both for the United States and for the world at large, as demonstrated in recent studies by M.W. Keran and D. Meiselman [28, 33].

The recent unveiling of eight versions of monetary aggregates by the Board of Governors does raise the old question of how money should be defined. The fact that the Board suggested six in addition to the two we have been accustomed to use, suggests a degree of dissatisfaction with the suitability of M_1 or M_2 as analytical concepts or policy tools. The Board's reason for wanting to use a broader aggregate presumably is based on arguments like those of Govenor Mitchell quoted at the beginning. Because of innovations or secular changes, some members of the Board apparently believe that narrowly defined money is becoming less significant as an influence on the public's decisions to spend or invest; money substitutes and other liquid assets, they argue, are becoming correspondingly more significant.

The Chairman, A.F. Burns, presented this argument before the Committee on Banking, Currency and Housing, U.S. House of Representatives, on February 6, 1975:

> ...the Board and the Open Market Committee pay close attention to monetary aggregates. We do not, however, confine ourselves to the particular monetary aggregate on which H.R. 212 focuses—namely demand deposits plus currency outside of banks. The reason is that this concept of the money supply, however significant it may have been 10 or 20 years ago, no longer captures adequately the forms in which liquid balances—or even just transactions balances—are currently held. *Financial technology in our country has been changing rapidly.* Corporate treasurers have learned how to get along with a minimum of demand deposits, and to achieve the liquidity they need by acquiring interest-earning assets. For the public at large, savings deposits at commercial banks, shares in savings and loan associations, certificates of deposit, Treasury bills, and other liquid instruments have become very close substitutes for demand deposits [Italics added] [11, p. 63].

From an a priori definition of money as a source of liquidity and his observation that financial technology is changing, Dr. Burns argues that functions formerly served by M_1 have been taken over by other instruments. This implies that a broader definition of money should be used.

The choice of a definition cannot be settled by a priori considerations; we need empirical evidence. I have not tested the eight definitions to determine which of them are most closely related to income, or to find which ones may have become more significant or less so over the 10 or 20 years mentioned by the chairman. I would be much surprised, however, if any of the broader versions proved to be markedly superior to M_1 or M_2, either with respect to their current relationships with income or the stability of the relationships over time.

The various aggregates on the Board's list of candidates are so highly correlated with one another that there is not likely to be much difference among the income predictions that could be made with them. Since the Board, furthermore, must be more than a detached observer of these relationships, the selection of an aggregate, or aggregates, for policy use also will require considering the relative degrees of precision with which the authorities can control each aggregate. Adoption of, say, M_6 or M_7 as a policy variable would achieve little, if any, gain in predictability of income at the cost of much greater control problems. It would be quite a test of the innovative talents of the Federal Reserve to design ways of controlling an aggregate consisting of currency + demand deposits + time deposits at commercial banks other than large negotiable CDs + large negotiable CDs + savings and loan shares and mutual savings bank deposits (nonbank thrift) + savings bonds and credit union shares + short-term marketable United States government securities + commercial paper.[3]

Stability of the Supply of Money

As William Silber said in chapter 2 above, some financial innovations have been made in order to get around a constraint imposed by government regulation [38]. I do not doubt that some Federal Reserve objectives tend to be thwarted by financial innovations, such as the use of Eurodollars. These, however, are primarily in the area of policies designed to influence the amounts of credit of particular sorts that banks can extend and are not part of my assigned topic. The relevant question here is whether innovations in banks and other financial institutions make the relationship between variables that are under the control of the Federal Reserve and the nominal quantity of money more or less predictable. I believe it can be argued that the direction of innovation in banks actually is toward improving Federal Reserve control of the money stock rather than impairing it, by shortening the time lags in responses of the banking system to Federal Reserve actions and by making these responses more nearly uniform.

It is difficult to find much evidence on this question because the period since the Federal Reserve began trying to control the money stock in 1970 is so short. And the System itself has been the most influential innovator in the market. Furthermore, the reactions of financial institutions to changes in Federal Reserve behavior will be influenced by the methods the authorities choose in trying to influence the money stock and other aggregates. I believe that the current method—trying to control growth of the aggregates through setting a federal funds rate target—exacerbates the difficulties of the task and fosters an illusion of Federal Reserve impotence, if not incompetence.

[3]In a paper that came to my attention after the Conference on Financial Innovation, Leonall C. Anderson reported on tests he had made of seven monetary aggregates, including the monetary base. On the basis of variability of income velocity, his broadest definition, M_6, which was the same as the one used here, could be expected to yield the smallest errors in forecasting nominal GNP over intervals of time relevant for economic stabilization. However, there was little superiority of M_6 over the monetary base, or M_1, or M_2. In simulation tests with a monetary model of nominal income determination, he found that the monetary base forecast the level of nominal GNP with the smallest error, on average, and the smallest maximum error. As the monetary base is the aggregate that is most directly under Federal Reserve control, Anderson's tests indicate that the monetary base should be the preferred aggregate for policy use, on the basis both of predictability of effects on income and of controllability [1]. In earlier tests of six monetary aggregates, reported in 1971, Andersen concluded that M_1 would be the best to include in the FOMC directive [2].

There is some evidence of market innovation or adaptation in response to the use of the federal funds rate target in the last two years. Banks and securities dealers now try to predict movements in short-term interest rates by deducing which way the Federal Reserve will move its federal funds rate target in order to keep growth of the money stock on track. Short-term rates consequently lurch up or down in big steps when market observers conclude that the Federal Reserve intends to shift the funds rate target. Although one of the Federal Reserve's reasons for using the interest-rate target is to minimize fluctuations of short-term rates, the new response pattern of the banks and securities dealers appears to have made fluctuations in rates wider rather than smaller. This in turn, I believe, has made the Open Market Committee more cautious in shifting the funds rate target and thus has widened deviations between the desired and actual growth rates of the money stock (desired as stated in the FOMC's policy directives).

At this point I would like to make some predictions about future innovations in efforts to control the money stock and how financial institutions will respond to them. The research that is now going on inside the Federal Reserve and outside eventually should make the money-supply process more clearly understood and thus should lead to improvement in the monetary authorities' performance, that is if they decide to give preeminence to the money stock. At the moment, the official conception of the process is that the Federal Reserve sets the federal funds rate at a level that is expected to induce the banking system and the public to bring about a desired change in money stock.[4] But unforeseen responses of the public or the banks at times make actual money-stock growth exceed or fall short of the rate desired by the FOMC. Thus, as we saw in the discussion of 1971 upward shift in the public's demand for money balances was said to make the money stock grow more than desired. More recently, weakness in demand for credit has been said to account for a short-fall in money growth. Chairman Burns told the Joint Economic Committee in February 1975:

Growth of the monetary aggregates has reflected . . . cautious behavior on the part of the banks. Despite a series of expansive monetary actions, the narrowly defined money stock (M_1) grew at an annual rate of only 1½ percent in the third quarter of 1974 and 4¼ percent in the fourth quarter. In January of this year, moreover, a decline occurred in M_1, probably because demands for bank credit were unusually weak during the month [10, p. 71].

It seems evident to me that episodes such as the fall in the money stock in early 1975 will motivate the Board to find ways to offset the influence of such changes in demand for credit on the money stock. Not many economists any more would agree that a fall in the money stock at a time when unemployment is rising rapidly is either desirable or immaterial. This

---

[4] See [25] for a recent official description of the procedure.

particular episode, furthermore, is eerily reminiscent of the fall in money stock in early 1960, when Dr. Burns and others tried, without success, to get the Eisenhower Administration and the Federal Reserve to do something about the recession they saw coming.[5]

Within the framework of the Federal Reserve's current method of influencing the monetary aggregates, Dr. Burn's statement could be interpreted to mean that the quantity of bank credit demanded in early 1975 was not great enough to push the Federal funds rate up to a level that would have induced the banks to borrow more reserves from the Federal Reserve Banks—in order to hold more assets—or that would have induced the Manager of the Open Market Account at the Federal Reserve Bank of New York to buy more securities—in order to keep the federal funds rate from rising above the target range specified by the Open Market Committee. If the problem, instead, had merely been the banks' unwillingness to use all of the reserves available to them, excess reserves would have risen enough to account for a significant part of the difference between actual growth in demand deposits and the growth implied by the FOMC's aggregates target. Excess reserves did not grow. In short, there must have been a lower federal funds rate at which the quantity of credit demanded would have been sufficient to induce banks to borrow more reserves or to induce the Manager of the Open Market Account to conduct open market operations that would have produced a larger money stock. If the FOMC was unwilling to let the federal funds rate go that low, the problem was one of a conflict in objectives rather than evidence of the Federal Reserve's inability to induce the banks and the public to produce a larger money stock.

Unless new evidence convinces the President, the Congress, the financial community, the press, the general public, and economists that changes in the money stock no longer influence income, employment and prices, I expect the Federal Reserve to continue to seek improvements in its ability to influence the money stock.[6] If the efforts to improve control of the money stock is one of reinforcing the current approach, we should expect to see more rapid adjustment of federal funds rate targets to changes in economic conditions and to discrepancies between desired and actual rates of money-stock growth. Perhaps some evidence of this will appear later in 1975 and 1976, when the problem will be one of offsetting growth in the

---

[5]See [32, pp. 27-31, 176-78] for an account of that monetary accident.

[6]The Proxmire Resolution of March 24, 1974 (H.R. Con. Res. 133), and Chairman Arthur Burns's reply in a statement to the Committee on Banking, Housing and Urban Affairs on May 1 should increase the Federal Reserve's incentive to improve money-stock-control procedure. By specifying an increase of 5 percent to 7½ percent in M_1 for the 12 months from March 1975 to March 1976, the chairman focused attention clearly on the money stock, in spite of his caveats about the possible necessity of changing the objective later. Any deviation in actual money-stock growth from that objective, therefore, will have to be explained either as an accident or as a specific change in objective.

190

quantity of credit demanded by the Treasury and by those businessmen and consumers who believe recovery from the recession is on the way.

More vigorous use of federal funds rate targets probably would induce banks and other financial institutions to increase the resources they devote to analyzing Federal Reserve actions and statements. Whether or not the volatility of interest rates would increase, however, is not clear. I suspect that banks and securities dealers have found some of the results of acting on their predictions of Federal Reserve interest-rate policies to be painfully instructive. Consequently, we may find that interest rates and other money-market variables adjust more smoothly to Federal Reserve actions, as people at the money desks of banks and in board rooms of the dealers learn to avoid overreacting to changes in the federal funds rate.

The System conceivably might shift to an entirely different strategy—one of regulating the monetary base and adjusting for changes in the multiplier as they occur. Under this approach, a desired growth rate for M_1, or some other monetary aggregate selected by the FOMC, would be translated into a program of net securities purchases to be made through open market operations. I do not propose to review the voluminous literature on this alternative approach here but just to comment on a few issues relating to financial innovation.[7]

The first of these is the interest elasticity of the money supply. It has long been argued that an increase in interest rates would increase the money stock by increasing the incentive for banks to borrow from Reserve Banks and to reduce their ratio of reserves to deposits. The greater the interest elasticity of the money supply, the greater would be the Federal Reserve's problems of producing some desired money stock through changes in nonborrowed reserves. In a 1972 paper R.H. Rasche looked into the possibility that financial innovations of the 1960s might have increased the interest elasticity of the money supply. Although he said it was difficult to get empirical evidence on some of these innovations, he was able to draw some conclusions from studies by R.L. Teigen, S.M. Goldfeld, K. Brunner and A.H. Meltzer, and others. "A broad, but valuable conclusion," he said, "is that the interest elasticity of the money supply during the sample period of these studies appears to be extremely low." He went on to say:

The available evidence suggests quite conclusively that the short-run feedbacks through interest rate changes, which would be generated by policy changes in reserve aggregates, are very weak and should cause little, if any, difficulty for the implementation of policy actions aimed at controlling the money stock through the control of a reserve [37, p. 19].

There did not appear to have been an increase after 1965 in what was in any case a smaller interest elasticity than some analysts would have expected.

---

[7]See, for example, [6, 7, 8, 16, 21].

The second issue is a mirror image of the first. Federal Reserve spokesmen argue that relying on nonborrowed reserves or other reserve aggregates as operating targets, without attempting to stabilize interest rates, would generate intolerably large fluctuations in short-term rates. Unless the Federal Reserve conducts an experiment, however, there is no way of knowing if this is actually true. In a Federal Reserve Staff Study published in 1971, R.G. Davis cited the System view that a shift to a nonborrowed-reserve operating target might result in erratic and large movements in the federal funds rate and related rates, if there were sharp week-to-week fluctuations in demand for bank credits and deposits. He went on to argue, as I would, that, "After banks and other financial institutions began to acquire some experience with the new environment, however, they might well discover ways of adapting to it that would themselves tend to dampen rate instability in the market" [16, p. 58]. Although he said that the precise nature of the institutional adaptations could not be predicted, it seemed clear to Davis that adaptations would occur, "tending to dampen random and seasonal fluctuations in money market rates."[8]

It is understandable that the Federal Open Market Committee might hesitate to experiment with an aggregate quantity target, for day-by-day fluctuations in the federal funds rate would probably increase, at least initially. Some, or many, money-market practitioners also would oppose a shift to a pure quantity-control system, because the change in Federal Reserve operating procedures would force them to develop new reflexes. Their skill in anticipating the Federal Reserve's reactions, under the current regime, to various shocks and events in the money markets—such as Treasury financings—is part of their capital. Nevertheless, they could and would learn to live with the new Federal Reserve procedures, as they have learned to live with other changes in the regulatory environment. I believe, moreover, that the monetary authorities could expedite the adaptation process by clearly announcing their money-stock in advance.

Market incentives for institutional adaptation or innovation should work in the direction of improving Federal Reserve control of the money stock, by reducing deviations from the desired money-growth path that now result from operations intended to suppress fluctuations of interest rates. Or, perhaps this should be put another way; institutional adaptations or innovations that dampen fluctuations of interest rates would reduce

[8]Simulation tests run by Davis, although open to numerous questions, indicated that the potential money-market instability under a nonborrowed-reserves operating strategy would be surprisingly mild. The estimated weekly changes in the federal funds rate were larger than the average changes that actually occurred in his sample period but, in his words, "not more than the market would seem able to handle without undue stress" [16, pp. 56-62]. The Davis work suggests that the Federal Reserve will be able to improve money-stock control considerably more than is now generally implied by the statements of Members of the Board of Governors of the System.

deviations from the desired money-growth path by reducing the frequency and amounts of Federal Reserve open market purchases or sales designed to keep rate fluctuations within ranges considered tolerable by the Open Market Committee. As I argued earlier, I expect institutional adaptation to be in this direction even if the Federal Reserve continues to use federal funds rate targets instead of shifting to an aggregate quantity approach.

The final issue is the influence of the development of the federal funds market on the responses of commercial banks to Federal Reserve actions. L. Currie argued long ago that interregional shifts of funds could impair Federal Reserve control of the money-supply process by altering the aggregate reserve-deposit ratio [15]. If reserves were transferred from city banks with low desired reserve-deposit ratios to country banks with high desired reserve-deposit ratios, for example, the aggregate ratio would rise and the money stock would go down, for any given stock of total reserves. Development of the federal funds market, whether it be classed as an innovation or a secular change, I believe, has reduced variation in that part of the aggregate reserve-deposit ratio over which the banks have some discretion—the ratio of excess reserves to deposits. Country bankers, in Currie's time, were slow to convert excess reserves into other assets when funds flowed their way. Thus, they tended to have higher actual and desired reserve ratios than city banks. Development of the federal funds market has provided them with a convenient means for adjusting reserve positions quickly through selling excess reserves to other banks. It, therefore, probably has narrowed regional differences in excess-reserve ratios. G.J. Benston found that differences in excess-reserve ratios among classes of banks narrowed between 1951 and 1967 [3]. He attributed the narrowing to the rise of interest rates over the same period, which is not inconsistent with my argument on development of the federal funds market.[9]

Finally, development of the federal funds market surely has shortened time lags in the responses of the banking system to Federal Reserve open market operations. The influence of an open market operation (or one of the market factors affecting reserves) spreads through the federal funds market within minutes and, I believe, can produce its full effect on the stock of bank deposits within two reserve accounting periods.[10]

The Federal Reserve argument that the money stock responds to changes in monetary policy with a lag of two months or more applies only to the method of attempting to control the money stock through manipulating

---

[9]Federal Reserve innovations in reserve requirements have made control of the money stock more difficult by worsening the impact of shifts of funds on the aggregate required-reserve ratio. Many critics have recommended returning to a simpler, perhaps uniform, set of reserve requirements. See, for example, [36].

[10]See Culbertson [13, 14] for an interesting treatment of this argument.

interest rates.[11] If and when the monetary authorities abandon the interest-rate approach for a reserve-aggregate approach they will find that the money stock responds to their actions much more rapidly than they now believe.[12]

Conclusion

Many empirical questions have necessarily been left unanswered in this chapter. Nevertheless, the evidence that is available on the demand for money and on the supply of money suggests that the conventional framework of monetary analysis is a durable construct. It is in little or no danger of being rendered obsolete either by recent financial innovations or by those on the horizon. We should not be surprised by this.

The services of money are so crucial in an exchange economy that, as Brunner and Meltzer point out, people persist in holding and using money even in hyper-inflations [5]. A.E. Gandolfi's evidence indicates that the demand for money remained stable even in the Great Depression [19]. If the monetary framework of analysis can remain useful in the extreme circumstances of hyperinflation and depression, therefore, innovations in financial institutions should hardly be expected to present problems it cannot overcome. Indeed, the long historical studies by C. Warburton, M. Friedman and A.J. Schwartz, K. Brunner and A.H. Meltzer, P. Cagan, and others, and the studies of money in many countries, demonstrate that changes in the money stock influence incomes and prices in predictable ways whatever the institutional setting is. The framework of monetary analysis may occasionally require minor adjustment to changes in financial institutions, but it need not be abandoned.

[11] A.H. Holmes, Manager of the System Open Market Account, recently stated a System view on response lags in this way: "Evidence illustrated the long and variable lag between System action and the behavior of the aggregates. Several econometric models showed that changes in short-term interest rates exerted most of their influence on money demand only after a number of months [25, p. 199]." The key to this view is the assumption that System actions control monetary aggregates through manipulating interest rates.

[12] The monetary authorities could shorten the response lag further by abandoning the lagged reserve requirement also. See [14, 15].

References

[1] Anderson, L.C., Paper prepared for presentation before the Committee on Financial Analysis, Federal Reserve Bank of Chicago, April 23-24, 1975. Federal Reserve Bank of St. Louis, processed.

[2] _____, "Selection of a Monetary Aggregate for Use in the FOMC Directive," in *Open Market Policies and Operating Procedures—Staff Studies*. Washington: Board of Governors of the Federal Reserve System, 1971.

[3] Benston, G.J., "An Analysis and Evaluation of Alternative Reserve Requirement Plans." *Journal of Finance*, December 1969.

[4] Brunner, K., "Monetary Policy and the Economic Decline." Position Paper Prepared for the 4th Meeting of the Shadow Open Market Committee. University of Rochester, March 7, 1975.

[5] _____, and Meltzer, A.H., "The Uses of Money: Money in the Theory of an Exchange Economy." *American Economic Review*, December 1971.

[6] Burger, A.E., "Money Stock Control." Federal Reserve Bank of St. Louis, *Review*, October 1972.

[7] _____, "Money Stock Control." in *Controlling Monetary Aggregates II: The Implementation*. Federal Reserve Bank of Boston, 1972.

[8] _____, *The Money Supply Process*. Belmont, Calif.: Wadsworth Publishing Company, Inc., 1971.

[9] _____, and Stevens, N.E., "Monetary Expansion and Federal Open Market Committee Operating Strategy in 1971." Federal Reserve Bank of St. Louis, *Review*, March 1972.

[10] Burns, A.F., Statement before Joint Economic Committee, February 7, 1975. *Federal Reserve Bulletin*, February 1975.

[11] _____, Statement before the Subcommittee on Domestic Policy of the Committee on Banking, Currency and Housing, U.S. House of Representatives, February 6, 1975. *Federal Reserve Bulletin*, February 1975.

[12] Cagan, P., *Determinants and Effects of Changes in the Stock of Money, 1875-1960*. National Bureau of Economic Research, 1965.

[13] Culbertson, J.M., "The Destructive Effects on Monetary Control of the 1968 Amendments to Federal Reserve Regulation D." Unpublished draft paper, University of Wisconsin.

[14] _____, "The Expansion Process of Demand Deposits and Bank Credit." Unpublished draft paper, University of Wisconsin.

[15] Currie, L., *The Supply and Control of Money in the United States*, 2nd ed., rev. Cambridge: Harvard University Press, 1935.

[16] Davis, R.G., "Short-Run Targets for Open Market Operations." *Open Market Policies and Operating Procedures—Staff Studies*. Board of Governors of the Federal Reserve System, 1971.

[17] _____, and Schadrack, F.C., "Forecasting the Monetary Aggre-

gates with Reduced-Form Equations." *Monetary Aggregates and Monetary Policy*. Federal Reserve Bank of New York, 1974.

[18] Friedman, M., and Schwartz, A.J., *Monetary Statistics of the United States: Estimates, Sources, Methods*. National Bureau of Economic Research, 1970.

[19] Gandolfi, A.E., "Stability of the Demand for Money during the Great Contraction—1929-1933." *Journal of Political Economy*, September/October 1974.

[20] Gibson, W.E., "Demand and Supply Functions for Money in the United States: Theory and Measurement." *Econometrica*, March 1972.

[21] Goldfeld, S.M., *Commercial Bank Behavior and Economic Activity*. Amsterdam: North-Holland Publishing Company, 1966.

[22] ———, "The Demand for Money Revisited." *Brookings Papers on Economic Activity*, 3, 1973.

[23] Gurley, J.G., and Shaw, E.S., *Money in a Theory of Finance*. Washington: The Brookings Institution, 1960.

[24] Hamburger, M.J., "The Demand for Money in 1971: Was There a Shift?" *Journal of Money, Credit and Banking*, May 1973.

[25] Holmes, A.H., "Monetary Policy in a Changing Financial Environment: Open Market Operations in 1974." *Federal Reserve Bulletin*, April 1975.

[26] ———, Meek, P., and Thunberg, R., "Open Market Operations and Credit Aggregates—1971, Excerpts from the Report Prepared in 1972." *Monetary Aggregates and Monetary Policy*. Federal Reserve Bank of New York, 1974.

[27] Johnson, H.G., "Monetary Theory and Policy." *American Economic Review*, June 1962.

[28] Keran, M.W., "World Inflation and Its Implications for the U.S. Economy." Federal Reserve Bank of San Francisco, processed, 1975.

[29] Khan, M.S., "The Stability of the Demand-for-Money Function in the U.S., 1901-1965" *Journal of Political Economy*, November/December 1974.

[30] Laidler, D.E.W., *The Demand for Money: Theories and Evidence*. Scranton, Pa.: International Textbook, 1969.

[31] Levin, F.J., "Examination of the Money Stock Control Approach of Burger, Kalish, and Babb." *Journal of Money, Credit, and Banking*, November 1973. Also in *Monetary Aggregates and Monetary Policy*. Federal Reserve Bank of New York, 1974.

196

[32] Meigs, A.J., *Money Matters: Economics, Markets, Politics*. New York: Harper & Row, 1972.

[33] Meiselman, D., "Worldwide Inflation: A Monetarist View," in *The Phenomenon of Worldwide Inflation*, ed. by D. Meiselman and A. Laffer. Proceedings of a Conference sponsored by the Hoover Institution, Stanford University, and the American Enterprise Institute for Public Policy Research. Washington: American Enterprise Institute, 1975.

[34] Mitchell, G.W., "Banking and the Payments Mechanism." Remarks at the Annual Meeting of the Association of Reserve City Bankers, April 11, 1972.

[35] _____, "Inflation and the Federal Reserve." Remarks at a conference on "The State of the Economy," sponsored by College of Business Administration, The University of Iowa, January 15, 1975.

[36] Poole, W., and Lieberman, C., "Improving Monetary Control." *Brookings Papers on Economic Activity*, 2, 1972.

[37] Rasche, R.H., "A Review of Empirical Studies of the Money Supply Mechanism." Federal Reserve Bank of St. Louis, *Review*, July 1972.

[38] Silber, W.L., "Towards a Theory of Financial Innovation" chap. 2, this volume.

[39] Slovin, M.B., and Sushka, M.E., "A Financial Market Approach to the Demand for Money and the Implications for Monetary Policy." Board of Governors of the Federal Reserve System 1972, processed.

[40] Teigen, R.L., "Demand and Supply Functions for Money in the United States: Some Structural Estimates." *Econometrica*, October 1964.

Comment: Recent Innovations: Do They Require a New Framework for Monetary Analysis?

Michael J. Hamburger

James Meigs takes issue in this chapter with a thesis put forward originally by J.G. Gurley and E.S. Shaw and developed in recent years by George W. Mitchell, vice chairman of the Board of Governors of the Federal Reserve System. A restatement of this view by Governor Holland is contained in chapter 5. As summarized by Meigs, the Mitchell-Holland position is that changes in the financial structure of the economy are likely to: (1) reduce the influence of the narrowly defined money stock on the publics' decisions to spend and invest, (2) impair the predictability of the relationships among money and other economic variables, and, as a result, (3) make the narrowly defined money stock an unreliable instrument or indicator for public policy.

Meigs' argument is that if financial innovations are to require a new framework for monetary analysis, it must be because either the demand or the supply function for money will be less stable in the future than in the past. Only under these circumstances is there likely to be a significant deterioration in the usefulness of the money stock as a guide for macroeconomic policy. I find myself in substantial agreement with this point of view. It is far more persuasive than Governor Holland's contention that innovation will cause money to grow more slowly than other assets and that this is sufficient to reduce its usefulness as a policy indicator. Clearly it is the stability of the relationships between money and other variables that matters and not the relative size of the money stock.

The bulk of Meigs' analysis is devoted to a review of the empirical evidence on the demand for and supply of money in the United States during the first seven decades of the twentieth century. The conclusions drawn from this analysis are that the Federal Reserve continues to have ample control over the nominal money stock and that there is no evidence to support the hypothesis that innovations—or, for that matter, anything else—have either significantly changed the coefficients of the United States money-demand function or made the function less stable, since the acceleration of innovation by banks in the early 1960s. I have no serious quarrel with Meigs' interpretation of this evidence. On the contrary, like him, I am impressed by the stability of the demand and supply functions for money considering the substantial changes that the financial system of the United States economy has undergone during this century. Among these are the establishment of a central bank in 1913 and its reformation in the

1930s; the experimentation with various systems for organizing international payments and the continuing evolution of private financial institutions. Not the least of the latter have been: the development of markets for Eurodollars and negotiable certificates of deposit; the rapid growth in the use of credit cards and the movement that has occurred towards an electronic funds transfer system.

In addition to the work on the stability of the United States relationships there is other evidence that also provides important support for the proposition that the conventional framework for monetary analysis is a durable construct that is unlikely to require major alteration in the near future. I refer here to the similarities in the money-demand functions for different countries. The institutional settings in Germany and the United Kingdom are very different from those in the United States. In the United Kingdom the bulk of retail banking is conducted by less than 20 banks, not the thousands that exist in the United States, and the use of overdrafts is a common and well established practice. Nevertheless, the money-demand functions that have been estimated for the two countries are extremely alike. [1, 2]. The same is true for Germany even though it is a much more open economy than the United States and perhaps the United Kingdom as well. Not only are the demand functions very similar, but it appears that the same narrow definition of money is appropriate for all three countries.

To be sure, there are differences in the results. For example, in Germany, where the market for corporate equities is relatively small and underdeveloped, such claims appear to be much poorer substitutes for money than they are in Britain and the United States. Moreover, in the United Kingdom, where the authorities have made some effort to control domestic interest rates, the results suggest that foreign rates (e.g., the yield on three-month Eurodollar deposits) provide a better measure of the opportunity cost of holding money than published domestic rates. Such variation hardly seems important and, in my judgement, is thoroughly consistent with the view that institutional changes may warrant adjustments in the framework for monetary analysis but not an entirely new approach.

There are certain respects in which Meigs' analysis is incomplete. He does not provide a detailed discussion of the nature of recent innovations or give his forecast of the future. In addition, he devotes little attention to the ways in which innovations may alter the effects of monetary policy on particular sectors of the economy. However, I believe that his general approach to the problem is correct and as indicated above I agree with his conclusion.

References

[1] M. Friedman and A.J. Schwartz, "Velocity and the Interrelations

Between the United States and the United Kingdom," National Bureau of Economic Research, mimeo, 1973.

[2] M.J. Hamburger, "The Demand for Money in an Open Economy: Germany and the United Kingdom," Federal Reserve Bank of New York, Research Paper No. 7405.

Index

Index

Accumulation process, 11
Adaptations, institutional, 191, 192
  market, 188
Adversity, cyclical timing of, 118
Agencies, federal credit, 35
  role of, 118
Agents, 30
Agriculture, finance intensive, 12
  western development of, 24
Akerlof, G.A., 61
Amortization, 99
Armstrong Investigation, 76
Arrow, K.J., 55
Ascending yield curve, 111
Automated quotation system, for over-the-
  counter securities (NASDAQ), 61

Banking, Currency and Housing, Committee
  on, 186
Banking, depression-era, 162
  investment, 36-40, 46
  limits of, 166-167
  national branch, 18, 50
  strains on, 160
  transfer services of, 177
Banking industry, liquidity needs of, 164
  mortgage, 32, 123
Banks, international operations of, 67
  liabilities-management techniques of, 179
  long-term credit, 13
  from New York City, 36
  in northeastern U.S., 14
  prospective external innovations by, 165-
  166. *See also specific banks*
Becker, S.W., 62, 63, 64
Behavioral scientists, 62
Benston, G.J., 192
Blank, D.M., 101
Board of Governors, of Federal Reserve
  system, 185, 197
Bonds, conventional, 153
  interest rates on, 81
  railroad, 137
  sinking fund provisions for, 152
Borrowers, 54
  and inflation, 127
Brokers, 54
Brown, 180
Brunner, K., 54, 190, 193
Buchanan, J., 9
Burger, A.E., 184

Burnes, A.F., 186, 188, 189
Business in Brief, 125

Cagan, P., 193
Call provisions, 152
Canada, nationwide branch banking in, 16
Capital, mobilization of, 10-14, 27-32
  transfer of, 15, 46. (*see also* Transfer
    systems)
Capital flows, interregional, 24
Capital markets, innovations in, 24
  interregional variance in, 17n
  localization of, 14-16
  long-term, 33
Carnegie, Andrew, 15, 39
Ceilings, FHA rate, 117
  Regulation Q, 115, 117, 120, 161, 173
Census, Eleventh, 21, 22, 47
Certificates of Deposit (CDs), 174
  introduction of, 181
  negotiable, 53, 60, 63, 64
Change, 1
  timing of, 118. *See also* Innovation
Chase Manhattan Bank, 125
Chow test, 182
Citicorp-Chase floating rate debentures, 174
City banks, nonreserve, 17
Clough, S.B., 77
Collective action, 60
Commercial banks, portfolios of, 67
Commercial paper houses, 19, 39, 50
Communication, technological changes in,
  103. *See also* Information
Competition, imperfect, 65
  and innovation, 117
  and interest rate variability, 175
  monopolistic, 62
  perfect, 68
Comptroller of Currency, 17, 21, 35, 50
Computers, 116
  privacy and, 164
  reliance on, 163, 165
Connecticut, land mortgage companies in, 26
Constraints, public policy, 171
Consumers, preference of, 33
  safeguards for, 112
Consumption, per capita, 1
Contract, mortgage, 108-109
Cooke, Jay, 37, 38
Corporate bond issues, 137
Corporate debt, 144

About the Contributors

William C. Brainard received the Ph.D. from Yale University where he is currently professor of economics. His publications have focused on monetary theory, stabilization policy, and financial markets.

Lance E. Davis received the Ph.D. from Johns Hopkins University and is currently professor of economics at California Institute of Technology. He has written a number of books and articles on economic history.

Stephen M. Goldfeld received the Ph.D. from Massachusetts Institute of Technology, and is currently professor of economics at Princeton University. His publications include studies of financial institutions, econometric models, and econometric methods.

Michael J. Hamburger received the Ph.D. from Carnegie-Mellon University and is currently an advisor at the Federal Reserve Bank of New York. He has written articles on various aspects of monetary economics.

Robert C. Holland holds the Ph.D. degree in economics from the University of Pennsylvania and is currently a member of the Board of Governors of the Federal Reserve System. His research and publications have focused on monetary policy.

Dwight M. Jaffee received the Ph.D. from Massachusetts Institute of Technology and is professor of economics at Princeton University. His publications include studies of financial institutions and markets and monetary policy.

Benjamin Klein received the Ph.D. from the University of Chicago and is currently associate professor of economics at the University of California—Los Angeles. He has written articles on monetary theory and history, and inflation.

A. James Meigs received the Ph.D. from the University of Chicago and is professor of economics at Claremont Men's College. He was formerly with Argus Research, Inc. and the First National City Bank. His publications have focused on bank behavior and monetary policy.

Almarin Phillips holds the Ph.D. from the University of Pennsylvania where he is currently dean of the School of Public and Urban Policy. His publications have ranged from industrial organization to financial structure and regulation.

William Poole received the Ph.D. from the University of Chicago and is professor of economics at Brown University. He was formerly with the Federal Reserve Board. His publications have focused on monetary theory and policy.

Anna J. Schwartz holds the Ph.D. in economics from Columbia University and is currently a member of the senior research staff of the National Bureau of Economic Research. Her research and publications have focused on monetary theory and history.

About the Editor

William L. Silber is a graduate of Yeshiva College (1963) and received the M.A. (1965) and the Ph.D. (1966) from Princeton University. He is currently professor of economics and finance at the Graduate School of Business Administration, New York University, and an associate editor of the *Review of Economics and Statistics* and the *Journal of Finance*. In the past Dr. Silber has been a Senior Staff Economist with the President's Council of Economic Advisors and has served as a consultant to the Federal Home Loan Bank Board, the Board of Governors of the Federal Reserve System, the U.S. Senate Committee on the Budget, the President's Commission on Financial Structure and Regulation, and the House Committee on Banking, Currency and Housing. In addition to his contributions to professional journals, Dr. Silber is the author of the following books: *Money* (with Lawrence S. Ritter); *Portfolio Behavior of Financial Institutions*; and *Principles of Money, Banking and Financial Markets* (with Lawrence S. Ritter).